In My
Dark Dreams

By J. F. Freedman

Against the Wind

The Obstacle Course

House of Smoke

Key Witness

The Disappearance

Above the Law

Bird's-Eye View

Fallen Idols

A Killing in the Valley

In My Dark Dreams

In My Dark Dreams

A Novel by

J. F. FREEDMAN

MADISON
PARK
PRESS™

NEW YORK

Published by Madison Park Press, One Penn Plaza, New York, NY 10119. Madison Park Press is a trademark of Bertelsmann Direct North America, Inc.

Book design by Christos Peterson

ISBN: 978-1-58288-294-9

Printed in the United States of America

For Georgia, Matthew, and Susannah

PART ONE

PART
ONE

ONE

IT IS ALMOST MIDNIGHT, and I am running through the dark arboreal streets that are south of Montana Avenue, which starts at the ocean in Santa Monica and continues on into Brentwood, two of Los Angeles's most expensive neighborhoods. In three months I am going to run my first marathon, so I have to pile up the miles wherever and whenever I can. My targets are to complete the race and break four hours. I have no doubt that I can pull them off. When I set a goal in my mind, I almost always achieve it. It takes full focus, full determination. I have an abundance of both. Some people say I'm obsessive-compulsive. But always behind my back, never to my face.

I run in the streets because they are paved with asphalt, which is easier on the legs and back than the concrete of the sidewalks. Now, as I lift my eyes, scanning the block ahead of me for potholes or other obstacles, I see a man on the sidewalk. He is in shadow, and is as still as the tree he's leaning up against.

I've been running on the same side of the street as the shadowed man. Now I veer my path so that I cross to the other side. The street is four lanes wide: two traffic lanes and two parking lanes. When I run past this solitary sentry, there will be almost thirty feet between him and me. I have no reason to fear this man, but I'm a woman running alone, late at night. I'm not stupid.

As I draw abreast of the stranger, I can't help but glance over at him, and it's as if he's telepathic, because at that precise mo-

ment he turns and looks at me. His face is visible in the moon-
light, which means mine must be, too.

He smiles at me and takes a step forward. I smile back as I
slow down, turning in his direction and stopping in front of him,
sucking in large gasps of air as I brace myself, leaning forward
with my palms on my thighs for balance.

"Hey," I gasp out a greeting.

"I thought that was you, Counselor," the man says to me in
surprise. "What are you doing at this time of night out here by
yourself?"

"Running. What does it look like?"

His smile is faint to the point of near invisibility. "That I can
see." The smile disappears, replaced by a skeptical frown. "Do
you live around here?" he asks, trying not to come across as nosy,
but failing.

"No." Not that where I live is any of his business. I wave my
hand in a general southerly direction. "I live down by Rose Avenue, near Ocean Park. There's no way I could afford to live
around here."

"You could have a trust fund," he says, with no inflection of
sarcasm.

I almost laugh in his face, but it might piss him off. "Yeah,
right."

He looks up and down the block for a moment, then back at
me with concern. "You're pretty far from home. How come
you're out so late?"

" 'Cause I was busy earlier." I don't have to explain, but I do.
"I'm running a marathon in a couple months. Gotta get in my fifty
miles a week, rain or shine, whenever I can fit it into my schedule."

His eyes shine in surprised appreciation for my resolve. "No
shit. How many have you run?"

"None, so far."

He smiles again. It's apparent this time. "Well, I'm impressed.
Another gold star on your already notable résumé."

That's a flattering remark, but it's also a bit unnerving. "What do you know about me?" I ask him.

My directness seems to take him aback. "Nothing," he answers. "Just Temple Street." The city within a city where we both work.

I relax, and straighten my posture. I'm tall, but he's on the sidewalk while I'm in the street, so I have to look up at him. I lob the ball back into his court. "What are *you* doing out here at this time of night? Do you live around here?"

He shakes his head. "North Hollywood. Laurel Canyon, near Chandler."

"You're even farther from home," I state the obvious.

He looks skyward. "Don't you get it?"

I follow his stare, which brings my eyes to the moon. It's at the beginning of its fullness, a fat, pale-yellow obelisk hanging from a sparsely clouded sky. Since we're not far from the ocean, the fog and haze blanket any starlight.

"Oh," I blurt out. "Because . . . ?" There's a sudden clutching in my stomach.

He gives me a tight nod of understanding.

"So you guys are out, in case? Is there a special task force?" I haven't heard of one, but it makes sense.

He frowns. "I wish. But, no. I'm here on my own."

That brings me up short. "Why? You can't actually believe one man on his own is going to catch him."

I pause. Does he know something? My heart rate, which had dropped from the aerobic stress of running, starts to spike again. I can feel it. I can also feel the cold breeze on my sweaty back and legs.

"Do you?" I press him. "Have a reason to expect to?"

His look of sorrowful resignation cuts through me. Such personal anguish is almost never shown by his tribe. It's way too dangerous, emotionally.

"No," he answers. "But I didn't want to just sit home and do nothing. So . . ." He spreads his hands as if in supplication. "I figured, better here than anywhere else in the city tonight."

God, talk about Don Quixote. There's a tinge of sadness here, a loneliness. "The boy with his finger in the dike?" I gently chide him. I've known this man, only through work, for more than five years. This is by far the longest conversation we've ever had. For the first time, I realize with a guilty pang, I'm seeing him as a human being, rather than as an abstraction, one with whom I'm usually in conflict.

"I guess." He shrugs. "Although he didn't stop the flood, as I recall. The dam still burst."

The breeze, this late at night, is building to a chilly wind. My muscles are tightening up. I need to move on. "Maybe he isn't on the prowl tonight," I offer in thin solace.

"Maybe," my accidental companion agrees, reluctantly. "There are two more days of full moon."

There's nothing more either of us can say at this moment in time. I give each calf a quick stretch. "Got to go," I say in parting, offering what I hope is a friendly smile.

"Right." His return smile doesn't work, either.

As I start running again, I call back over my shoulder. "See you on the reservation, Lieutenant."

His answering voice is faint as he recedes behind me. "Be careful. There's danger lurking out there."

TWO

"ABANDON HOPE ALL YE *who enter here.*"
That pitiless phrase isn't actually carved into the façade of this massive, intimidating building, but it ought to be. The Men's Central Jail in downtown Los Angeles, a few blocks from my office, is the largest jail in the free world. Every time I see a client in here, usually several times a week, I feel the need to shower vigorously afterward, send my jackets, slacks, blouses and skirts to the cleaners, and boil my underwear. If I could afford it, I'd burn the garments. If I could afford to do that, of course, I wouldn't be meeting my clients here. I would be a private defense attorney with a tricked-out suite of offices in Century City or Beverly Hills. But I am a Los Angeles County Public Defender, and I share my cubbyhole office (eight feet by sixteen, the same size as a regulation California prison cell, which I think is a rather Kafkaesque coincidence) with Sam Marx, who is retiring next year after thirty-seven years of stalwart duty, bless his old leftie soul. Sam has not handled an active case for over a year, and never will again. He's a fast-moving target who always knows how to duck when assignments are passed out. Our tiny office does have a window, thanks to Sam's seniority, with a lovely view of the parking lot that is located between our building and City Hall, made famous by *Dragnet*.

It's nine o'clock in the morning. I'm waiting to see one of my clients, a young black man named Reginald Morton, who is going to trial in a couple of days (he tried to sell some Mexican heroin

to an undercover cop, a truly boneheaded move) unless I can persuade him to take the D.A.'s plea bargain, which is more than
fair—two years, time already served to be counted—and if he
keeps his nose clean on the inside, they'll drop one of his strikes.
This will be his second, so this is a big concession from them. So
far, the moron has refused the deal. It's not that he's innocent, or
can claim to be. He did it; they've got him boxed, all four corners.
But he has convinced himself that because of my *fantastic lawyer-
ing skills* (his phrase, not mine), he can beat the system. How he
knows how good or bad a lawyer I am escapes me, since we had
never met before I was randomly assigned to him, but he believes
that I'm the cream of the crop, as good as a six-hundred-dollar-
an-hour private lawyer. I am, in fact, very good at what I do, but
the reality is that Clarence Darrow and Johnnie Cochran rolled
into one couldn't win this case for Reggie. But he doesn't want to
hear that. He doesn't want to do any prison time at all; he did it
before and it fucked him up, badly. He got the shit stomped out
of him by some Latino gangbangers, and although he's been
promised he'll be segregated, he doesn't want to take the chance
that the state will keep its word. On that issue, I can't blame him.

My problem is that Reggie *has* beaten the system, through a
fluke so unbelievable that people who know about the case are
still in hysterics about it. Last year he was caught robbing a liquor
store in Koreatown, your standard brain-dead stick-'em-up. Somehow, the store's security video tape, one of the D.A.'s choice pieces
of evidence, got mixed up with a different tape while in police
storage, but no one knew that until the day it was shown at Reggie's trial. Instead of the tape showing our man coming into the
store and pulling a gun on the female owner, a Korean woman
who barely spoke English, forcing her to the floor while he cleaned
out the cash register, then compounding the idiocy by copping a
feel before he vamoosed (for her, testifying on the witness stand,
that was the ultimate insult), those in attendance in the courtroom, including the judge, jury, members of the woman's family
and the Korean activist community, and a few reporters, were en-

tertained by a segment of *Cathouse,* the HBO late-night adult show featuring hookers from Nevada. In this episode, the whores were playing dominatrix cops, dressed in glittery thongs, lace-up high-heeled boots, Sam Browne belts with fake guns, patrolmen's hats, and absolutely nothing else. They were leading some pathetic-looking naked men on leashes that were attached to studded leather dog collars, the kind the brothers in the 'hood favor to adorn the necks of their pit bulls and Rottweilers. One of the ladies, apparently confused about the difference between a police motif and that of a circus, also had a bullwhip, which she cracked in the air like a lion tamer.

Upon seeing this travesty, half the jurors were mortified beyond belief, while the other half were laughing like hyenas. The judge, the Honorable Wilson Slocombe, a man who holds a very short leash himself, didn't get the joke, not one bit. He was so pissed off he threw the whole shebang out then and there, even before Ronnie Shwarz, my colleague in our office who was handling the case, could move for dismissal because he was laughing his own head off.

I have tried to make Reggie understand that he didn't win that case on the merits; he skated because of a once-in-a-lifetime screwup the police definitely will not let happen again. He inadvertently made them look like fools, which is why they set him up on the dope bust. They want him behind bars—payback for humiliation.

So far, Reggie hasn't budged. His trial is in two days. This will be our last session before we meet again in court.

The wait to see him is interminable. It's a little head game the jail sheriffs play. You grin and bear it because there's no alternative. Finally, Reggie is brought in and seated in the chair across from mine. We're meeting in a large room that is divided in half, wall to wall, by a thick Plexiglas window. The room is lit up like a football stadium with bright fluorescents to ensure that there are no shadows to hide behind. There is a strong odor of disinfectant to cover the BO from the hundreds of sweaty visitors who come here daily to visit the prisoners, who smell even worse. Reggie is wearing a standard-issue county-jail jumpsuit and is manacled head and foot. His hair is unkempt, and he looks as if he hasn't shaved or showered for a couple of days.

Prisoners and visitors, including lawyers like me, talk through phone receivers. In the old days, pre-9/11, you could meet with your clients in a private room (which was only bugged some of the time). Now heightened security mandates that you talk to them over the phone through the Plexiglas window, like the civilians do. You are separated from the regular visitors to maintain the fiction of attorney-client privilege, but it's a crummy way to communicate. If this were a really big crime, a life-without-parole or capital case, I could badger them into giving us our own space; but for a garden-variety charge like this, we're just part of the deep-flowing river.

"How are they treating you?" I start out. I like to know. Sometimes it's an issue.

"Okay," he answers, waltzing past my tepid concern. We're in the homestretch now, only a few more days (in his mind) before he walks out of the courtroom a free man. His mind is not a steel trap. "You got your shit wired, Miss Thompson?" he asks me, his voice chipper and upbeat. It's the same question he always asks me.

"As ready as I can be." My stock reply, but it's true. I just wish I had more ammunition. If something doesn't come up at the eleventh hour it's going to be David versus Goliath in the courtroom, and I don't have a slingshot.

"That cop that set me up. You gonna crush his lyin' ass?" he asks now. Reggie is convinced the only reason they nailed him was because he was entrapped, that the police violated his civil rights. And it's true—that's exactly what happened. But that will not matter one bit. This is a dog-and-pony trial in Los Angeles County Superior Court, not a Harvard Law School evidence class.

"I'll try my best." I have to warn him: "They're going to have their act together, Reggie. They're not going to get caught with their pants down again."

"They're punks," he says dismissively.

He needs an attitude adjustment, and part of my job is to give it to him. "You bring that vibe into the courtroom, you're going to get whacked," I tell him, fiercely. "These cops are on a mission, and the mission is to put you in the hole for a long time. A lot longer than the two years the D.A. is offering," I yet again remind him. Jesus, what do I have to do to get this doofus to take the best offer he's ever going to get in his life? He could pull five hard years if he's found guilty, which is about as certain as death and taxes. More, if he really comes across as an arrogant asshole, which is more than likely. "That deal is still on the table, but once the trial starts, they'll pull it."

He shrugs off my plea with a dismissive wave of the hand, like a king giving his subjects the bird. "You the woman," he says, as if he knows what he's talking about. He picks at a piece of gristle wedged in his crooked teeth. "They gonna be some brothers on the jury?" he asks me, squinting his eyes in deep thought.

"I'm going to try as hard as I can. It'll depend on the jury pool," I answer honestly. "I don't have a lot of control over that."

Ten or fifteen years ago, a substantial number of jurors in the downtown courts would have been black—witness the makeup of O.J.'s jury. But the demographics have changed. Los Angeles is more and more Latino. A little over a decade ago, Tom Bradley, a black ex-cop, was the mayor, and he ruled with an iron fist. Now our mayor is Mexican American, and the power has shifted from black to brown. There are more Latinos in the state prisons and jails than blacks, and the wars between the black and brown gangs, both in and out of jail, get worse every year.

"Gotta get some brothers on the jury," Reggie instructs me. He actually raises a finger to make his point, as if I don't know what he means. "Not sisters. They be church women, too likely. A jury of my peers. Is that too much to ask for?" he asks rhetorically.

"I'll do my best," I tell him again. Which will be to persuade him to take the plea before the trial starts. I don't have much time left to change his mind.

I'm ready to leave—I have a ton of other cases to deal with to-day. "Think about that offer," I throw at him as my parting shot. "You could do a lot worse."

"I'll think about it," he says by rote. "You gonna dress up nice?"

"What?"

"What you gonna be wearing in the courtroom," he says pa-tiently, as if he has to explain the basic facts of life to me. "Nice skirt and blouse. Stockings, quality shoes. Not this bag-lady shit you see some of them lesbian female lawyers wearing." He tosses his head as if he has lice, which he might. I'll remind him to take a shower and shampoo the night before we go to court. Whether his keepers will let him is anyone's guess, it's always chaotic in this place, and screwing prisoners over is considered great sport.

"I might not have no money," he says defensively, "but I want the jury to see that my lawyer has class. So they know I have class," he declares, sitting up straight in his plastic chair.

If we weren't separated by the thick Plexiglas wall, I'd slap this moron upside his head. The last thing a lawyer wants, espe-cially a woman lawyer, is to present a less-than-dignified image to a jury.

"I won't embarrass you," I tell him coolly. I jam his file into my bag—this session is over, mercifully. "Think about that offer," I warn him again. "Pride goeth before a fall."

Reggie stares at me, slack-jawed and uncomprehending, as I stand up. The deputy who escorted him down here immediately hoists him out of his chair and begins shuffling him back to his cell before I've taken two steps toward the door on my side. I don't look back, but I can feel Reggie staring at me as I retreat.

The rest of my morning is spent jumping from one courtroom, lobby, and cubicle to another: conferences with prosecutors and judges, setting future trial dates, pretrial hearings with other clients (unlike Reggie, they can read the writing on the wall and will plead out), general court-calendar stuff. There are dozens of courthouses scattered all over Los Angeles County. I work in the

Clara Shortridge Foltz Criminal Justice Center, on Temple Street in downtown L.A., which was named after the first woman admitted to the bar in California and a founder of the modern public defender system, back in the nineteenth century; she is a role model for all those women, like me, who have followed in her footsteps. It is the central office, and the largest. The courtrooms, officially known as departments, are spread out among several floors of the twenty-one-story building, which is also where our main offices—those of the public defenders as well as the main offices of the district attorneys—are located. Just as the central jail houses more prisoners than any other in the country, this building has one of the largest collections of courthouses. We're Los Angeles—everything we do is supersized.

The Los Angeles County Public Defender's office is the oldest and largest public defender's office in the world. We have over 1,000 employees: 650 lawyers, 80 investigators, 50 paralegals, 20 psychiatric social workers, a handful of Spanish interpreters, other support staff. We also hire additional interpreters, as needed, for other foreign-language defendants. Last year, sixty-eight different languages were spoken in one or another of the Los Angeles County courtrooms.

We handle an incredible number of cases. In a normal year we'll defend about 350,000 misdemeanors and 90,000 felonies. It makes for a heavy caseload—the average is twelve to fifteen new cases a month, with twenty to thirty cases outstanding at any given time. All of our work is criminal law; we don't do civil cases. It's a lot of work, and we're always hopping.

It's twelve-thirty; I break for lunch. I usually eat lunch at my desk. It's the only free time I have during the day. Most of my colleagues can't wait to flee the building at lunchtime, and occasionally I'll join a group, but I need my solitary time. I function perfectly well in most social situations, but at heart I'm most comfortable when I'm by myself. My jagged and ultimately violent relationship with my mother reinforced that part of my personality, but I'm convinced I was hardwired from birth to be a loner. I understand that nurture has an important place in one's personal history, but I'm from the school that believes nature trumps everything.

Today I'm feasting on chicken salad with real mayonnaise, macaroni salad, and buffalo mozzarella with fresh tomatoes swimming in olive oil. I prepare my meals at night before I go to bed, pack the food in individual plastic containers, and store them in the community refrigerator down the hall from my office. There are a lot of groceries stacked up here on my desk, and I don't stint on the portions. If I have a break in the afternoon, I'll often grab a milkshake from the coffee bar on the eighth floor. People who see me put all this food away marvel at how I can eat so much and not gain weight.

It's a piece of cake, I tell them: when you're running fifty miles a week you burn more calories than your body can possibly consume. Upon hearing my explanation, they nod sagely, then change the subject—everyone wants to lose weight, but that's too rigorous for most folks.

"Damn, that smells good," Joe Blevins exclaims as his head pops into my doorway. Joe is my boss, one of the senior deputies in the office in charge of assigning cases. "How much garlic do you use in that dressing?" he asks, sniffing the air.

The reek he's inhaling comes from the olive oil on the tomatoes and cheese. I douse it liberally with garlic, for health reasons and to keep the werewolves and vampires and malodorous clients at bay. It's an old family tradition, which I initiated last year.

"Forty cloves," I tell him.

He laughs. "Seriously?" People aren't always sure if I'm joking.

"Actually, three," I confess. "But I do have a pea soup recipe that calls for forty cloves. From a restaurant in Guerneville, up in Sonoma."

"With their crappy weather, they need forty cloves," he remarks. Joe's a dyed-in-the-wool Southern Californian, for whom everything north of Santa Barbara is enemy territory. You should hear him curse out Barry Bonds when Vin Scully is broadcasting a Giants-Dodgers game on the radio. The entire building shakes.

He sniffs again. "Does all that garlic help you run faster?" He knows I'm in serious training.

"No," I answer, "but it keeps my pursuers at a safe distance."

"You don't have any courtroom appearances the rest of the day, I take it."

"Actually, I do have one, but there will be nary a scent on my breath," I promise him. I always gargle after eating garlicky food, as a courtesy to my coworkers. I wish the smokers, some of whom have really foul halitosis, would reciprocate, but few of them do.

"Now you have two," Joe says, handing me a thin manila folder. "An arraignment, this afternoon." He explains: "One of Lorrie Patuni's kids got sick at school and she had to pick him up. Since you have a window, you can pinch-hit for her, if you don't mind."

Lorrie is one of the younger lawyers in the department; she handles arraignments. Arraignment presentation, the first appearance a defendant makes before a judge after being arrested, is one of the ways we break in new lawyers. The only time an experienced member of the staff does one is in unexpected circumstances like this. After defendants plead out, almost always not guilty, they are assigned the lawyer who will be with them for the remainder of their case. Selection is random—new case files, comprising a police report, rap sheet (if there is one), and the charges, show up in your mailbox, or they'll be left on your desk, sometimes half a dozen at once. New assignments can be aggravating, because everyone feels like they're overworked, and everyone is always complaining about the heavy caseload. The average number of active files for a senior PD is about thirty cases. The exception is murder cases. No one has more than two or three murder cases pending, because if one does go to trial, that's all you work on; others on the staff have to pick up the rest of your work, so the system tries not to overburden any particular member. Sometimes, however, the distribution isn't always equitable.

"No problem," I tell him about pinch-hitting for Lorrie, who's a sweetheart when she isn't stressed by juggling being a mother to three young children and a full-time professional. We're a collegial group—we try to help out each other. When you work for the government, your salary is set by number of years in service and department rank, not by how many cases you handle or win. It makes for a less ego-driven environment than the private sector, which is one reason I'm still here. "Where is it?"

"Department 83, Judge Rosen," Joe tells me.

Judge Rosen's first name is Judith. You call her Judge Judy at your peril. Other than that, she's okay—competent, fair, and not too impatient.

"What's the charge?" I ask, tossing the folder onto my cluttered desktop. I'll look at it later; I don't mix lunch with work.

"Grand theft. Sony hi-def televisions. Plasma, top of the line. It's in the arrest report, which I trust you'll read before your initial meet and greet."

"I could use a new TV," I banter back. Joe's an easy boss to work for; he isn't full of himself. "Think there's any spares?"

"You mean after the boys in blue took their piece off the top?" he replies. "Chat up the arresting officers; maybe you can cut a deal. Eyes wide shut."

"I'm on the wrong side of the aisle, Chief. As you always remind us."

"All cats are gray in the dark," he tells me with no wit at all. Meaning, we're all part of the same system, even though we like to pretend we aren't. Joe has been a public defender for decades. His cynicism is deeply ingrained.

"It's bright daylight out," I reply, cocking a thumb at my window, where the half-drawn venetian blinds are dissecting the piercing sunlight into long shadowy strips across the room. You can count on me to take the other side of almost any argument and mount a stout defense.

"For you, it is." Joe raps a knuckle on the thin file. "For this chump and the rest of his tribe, it's always lights out."

I'm ahead of schedule, so I duck into the eighth-floor coffee bar to get a milkshake. I normally go with chocolate, but today I decide to be daring and try strawberry. The strawberry is sweeter, and I want an extra dose of sugar to knock down the garlic residue that's still percolating in my stomach. I need to cut my salad dressing recipe back to two cloves.

"Did you hear the news?" a man asks from behind me.

I turn. It's my nocturnal friend, LAPD detective Luis Cordova. Last night, when I saw him on his lonely vigil, he was wearing jeans, a black pocket T-shirt, scruffy New Balance running shoes, the same brand as mine, which is why I noticed them. Today, on the job, he's dressed in a charcoal-gray blazer, white dress shirt fresh out of the dry cleaner's box, the collar and cuffs stiff with starch, dark slacks with a sharp crease. His cordovan dress shoes are spit-shined. I'd lay odds he was in the military when he was younger; a lot of Latino men go that route out of high school, then segue into police work. Probably the marines, he gives off that "the few, the proud," vibe. To me, it's macho bullshit. But I'm a woman, and Anglo. He and I breathe the same air, but we live in different worlds. This building, and what it represents, is our lone common denominator.

"What news?" I ask him, not tuned in. I take a sip of my milkshake. Yummy! It's wonderful what you can get away with when you're running eight to ten miles a day, six days a week.

"We found another victim."

A cold tremor runs down my back. I put the milkshake cup on a nearby table so I won't spill any of it, because my hands are shaking. "Same MO as the others?"

He gives me a tight nod. "Close enough."

"Where?" I ask. I'm both repulsed and wired, the way you feel when you're driving on the freeway and pass a bad car wreck. You don't want to look, but you can't help yourself. Human tragedy can be both ugly and compelling. "When?"

"A mile from where I saw you last night." His voice is a deep, rumbling baritone. Big and strong, like the rest of him. "Off Gretna Green. The medical examiners don't know when yet. Last night, sometime. The body was only found a few hours ago."

"Who knows?"

"Almost no one, yet. I'm telling you because . . ."

Because I was there. Inwardly, I shudder.

"We're keeping it under wraps until we can notify the family," he continues. "We haven't been able to get in touch with her husband yet; he's on the road and we don't want to tell him over the phone, especially if he's driving. After that, there will be a news conference." He grunts. "White women murdered by a serial killer. This is going to be a disaster."

Less than a mile from where I was running through the streets, alone. Jesus.

A good cop can read minds, and bend them. Luis Cordova is a very good cop. "It could have been you."

My reply is firm. "But it wasn't."

I'm not a victim. I haven't been a victim for more than twenty years, and I have vowed never to be one again. Besides, this man doesn't know me. I'm one of thousands of faces who have passed in front of him over the years; ditto him for me. Until last night, we had never had a real conversation. He's a cop, I'm a defense lawyer. We work the opposite sides of the street.

"There's one thing you won't have to worry about for the rest of the month," Cordova tells me.

I don't want to rise to the bait, but I can't help myself. "What's that?"

"Assuming it's the same psychotic bastard who killed all three, and that the pattern stays the same, he has his victim for this month. You're safe for the next thirty days." He gives me a sad-eyed look, as if we're friends and he really cares.

"After that, you had better run in the daytime," he cautions me. "Or carry protection when you go out at night."

THREE

T HE NEW PRISONER'S NAME is Roberto Salazar. Like over 90 percent of people arrested each year in Los Angeles, he can't afford a private lawyer, so we were assigned to defend him.

Salazar is in his mid-thirties, handsome in an androgynous way, like Mick Jagger back in the day, or Johnny Depp. His eyes are fawnlike, Bambi as a young stag. He looks as if he could be part Anglo—his eyes are hazel-green, not brown, and his nose and lips are northern European thin. This is not uncommon in Los Angeles, where the different races have been intermingling for generations, going back to the Spanish land-grant families.

Salazar is dressed in a forest-green, short-sleeved khaki shirt, matching pants with shiny knees, well-scuffed work boots. It's the uniform you see on thousands of gardeners all over the Southland. His ingratiating smile doesn't convince either of us—this man is scared shitless.

I'm interviewing him in the small room off Judge Rosen's courtroom that's set up for client-lawyer meetings. In fifteen minutes, Salazar goes up before the judge. A formal copy of the complaint will be entered, he'll plead not guilty, and a date will be set for his bail hearing. It's all boilerplate; we'll be in and out of court in less than five minutes.

"Breaking and entering, grand theft, transporting stolen property," I read, flipping through the pages in his folder, which I did get to skim, barely. "Those are serious charges and, I'm sorry to say, it looks as if they caught you red-handed, Mr. Salazar. These televisions match the serial numbers of a load that was stolen out of a Best Buy shipping container down in San Pedro, the day before yesterday." San Pedro is the hub of the Port of Los Angeles, the largest shipping depot in the United States. The incidence of robbery is astronomical, in the billions of dollars.

I put the folder aside. "You don't happen to have any paperwork for these televisions, do you?" I ask Salazar.

He stares at the floor. "No." His voice is soft, barely audible. It doesn't matter that I can hardly hear him; I knew the answer already.

He's shaking his head from side to side as I'm reciting the damning bill of particulars. "I didn't steal them," he declares. His English is almost without accent, just a touch of Latino inflection. We won't need to converse through an interpreter, which is always an impediment. "I swear it," he tells me. "Get me a Bible. I'll swear on it."

In a situation like this, where the evidence against the accused is strong, you assume he is lying, but you have to hear him out. "So what happened?" I ask. "They just jumped into your truck all by themselves?"

He stares at me balefully. He isn't in the mood for humor. "No, they did not jump into my truck. I loaded them in. Me and Armando." He looks at me again with a combination of fear, anger, and, yes, contempt. For how I'm disrespecting him.

I take a mental step back. You're patronizing him, I chastise myself. It's easy to slide into cynicism—witness Joe, my boss, and lots of other lawyers in this building, probably the majority. Most of them are good men and women who don't think of themselves as cynics at all, but realists. I'm not that tough skinned yet. Will I ever be? Maybe, if I stay the course and put in my thirty years, like old-man Sam, my office mate. Right now, my uncynical inner voice is reminding me that I am this man's advocate, his only voice in a system that has been designed to crush him. You have to give him your best effort, even if the outcome, like most, is preordained.

"Who is Armando?" I ask. I pick up the file and leaf through the few pages. "I don't see any Armando in here. Was he arrested along with you?"

He shakes his head. "He wasn't there."

Of course not. "Okay. Tell me what happened. Try not to leave anything out." I glance at my watch. It's a TAG Heuer, an expensive athlete's timepiece. My boyfriend gave it to me last Christmas, when he realized I was serious about running a marathon. It's too heavy to actually run with, but it's a lovely piece of wrist candy. "You have ten minutes before we see the judge," I notify my client, "so make it crisp."

My first surprise: Salazar has never been arrested, not even for stealing a pack of bubble gum from the neighborhood candy store as a kid. That's shocking, given where he comes from: the area east of the L.A. River, where Boyle Heights meets East Los Angeles, one of the toughest neighborhoods in L.A. County; his ethnicity, Latino; and the basic life for minority men on the gang-infested streets of our wonderful city. I didn't see anything incriminating in his file, but I'd only had time to give it a cursory look-over.

The more Salazar tells me about his history, the weirder this stolen-television episode feels. It's totally out of character with everything else in his life. Besides never having been arrested for any crime, not even a minor misdemeanor, he is married and is the father of two small children; he is a self-employed gardener with a full client list, including customers who live in Beverly Hills and the Westside; and he is a lay preacher in a storefront church. To top off his pristine résumé, he's also a youth counselor for his local Boys and Girls Club. That someone with these credentials would be involved in stolen goods, or any criminal activity, doesn't make sense. His entire life has been about staying out of trouble, not courting it.

I check the time on my expensive watch. "This is all good and helpful, Mr. Salazar," I nudge him, "but I need the facts of what happened last night. You can fill in the rest of your life story later. We've got five minutes, so cut to the chase."

All this woe has befallen him, he tells me mournfully, because he was trying to do the right thing: help a friend in need. The aforementioned Armando, last name Gonzalez. Gonzalez is a wholesaler who buys goods in Mexico and then resells them for a higher price in the states. Sometimes, if he needs help transporting a shipment, he hires Salazar to help him. There has never been a problem. As far as he knows, everything Gonzalez did was legal and aboveboard.

"I wouldn't do anything against the law," Salazar tells me. He sounds honest. They all do, at first.

"I'm glad to hear it. Go on," I prompt him.

He continues with his story. Gonzalez had bought a load of Sony televisions in Tijuana, which he planned to sell in Los Angeles. Late last night, he had called Salazar in a panic. He was en route to Panorama City, an industrial location in the San Fernando Valley, where he was supposed to deliver the televisions, but his truck had broken down in Wilmington, which is the next city up the 110 freeway from San Pedro. He had managed to pull off the 110 onto a surface street, but he couldn't go any farther—his generator was shot. The televisions had to be in the delivery warehouse by six in the morning, when the retailer's truck would show up. If he, Gonzalez, didn't get them to the Panorama City location, he wouldn't be paid; and worse, he would lose his contact with the man who had contracted with him to buy the televisions. He was in a real bind, and he didn't know who else he could call. Would Roberto drive down to Wilmington, load the TVs into his truck, and take them to Panorama City?

Normally, this proposed delivery would be a nightmare commute, because the L.A. freeways, particularly the 110 and the 405, are the most congested freeways in the country. But in the middle of the night, the traffic is manageable. Salazar could jump onto the 60 on-ramp near his house, connect to the I-10, then the 110, and be in Wilmington in half an hour. He and Armando would load the crates into his cube truck, he could take the 405 over the pass, deliver the shipment to Panorama City, off-load them, and be home in time to wake his children before heading back out for his day's work. There wouldn't be any problems, Gonzalez assured him, and he would be doing a friend in need a huge favor.

"You use a cube truck for gardening?" I interrupt.

"No," Salazar answers doggedly. "I have a pickup for gardening. The cube truck is for deliveries and local moving." He allows himself a small smile. "It's a sideline business. I'm cheaper than the big companies, and the people in my neighborhood know me." His smile fades. "And trust me."

A second business? Plus raising a family, running a rump church, and doing youth work? This guy's practically a poster boy for upward mobility in the barrio.

"Armando must think you're an awfully good friend to get out of bed in the middle of the night and do this for him," I say.

He shrugs. "What could I do?" he says. "He needed help." He hesitates a moment. "And he was going to pay me for helping him."

So it wasn't all about the milk of human kindness. I feel better, learning this. It makes the episode seem more believable. "How much?" I ask.

"Two hundred and fifty dollars." He ducks his head, as if pronouncing the figure embarrasses him. "More than my usual hourly rate, but it was a big favor to ask."

Considering the circumstances, $250 doesn't seem like an overcharge to me, but I'd guess his pay scale is pretty low. There are thousands of gardeners in L.A.; you can get a good one for under $20 an hour. "You named the price, I assume."

He nods.

"If you feel guilty that you overcharged Mr. Gonzalez, you shouldn't," I tell him. "Asking a man to get out of bed in the middle of the night and drive sixty miles is a big favor." I pause. "Especially if the cargo you're being asked to deliver is stolen goods." I look at him critically. "Did Armando know those television sets were stolen?"

He stares at me, shaking his head from side to side. "He said he bought them legally, in Mexico." He pauses for a moment. "But . . ." He trails off into mortified silence.

You're a nice guy, Roberto, I think, staring at his crestfallen face. And if you're telling the truth, a dupe.

Another glance at my watch. We only have a couple of minutes left. "You drove down to Wilmington," I prompt him again. "Then what happened?"

"Armando was parked where he told me he would be. The crates were in his truck. Armando was real jumpy. He kept looking around, real nervously."

"And that didn't arouse your suspicions?" I ask.

He shakes his head. "I thought it was because he was afraid I wouldn't show up, and the load wouldn't be delivered."

"Okay," I concede. "Go on with the story."

"We loaded them out of his truck and into mine," he says. "Armando gave me the directions how to get to the Panorama City warehouse. I got in my truck and left."

"Without him?"

"Yes."

"Why didn't he come with you? It was his delivery, not yours."

"He wanted to stay with his truck. He was going to call a tow company."

Another plausible answer. "Go on."

"I took off. It was easy going; there wasn't hardly no traffic. Then, as I was passing through Westwood, I had to go to the bathroom." He blushes; he's embarrassed telling that to a woman he doesn't know, particularly a woman who is an authority figure.

"So you pulled off?"

"On the Sunset Boulevard exit. There is a twenty-four-hour ARCO station near there, where I could use the bathroom."

That piece of information gives me pause. "How did you know that?"

"Because I have clients in that area," he explains. "It's where

I fill up my truck if I need to, since it is cheaper than the other gasoline stations."

Yet another reasonable explanation. So far, his story is holding up. We only have a minute or two left. "Keep going," I say.

"I came out of the station and drove up Sepulveda Boulevard to get to the freeway entrance. And then, all of a sudden, there was a police car behind me. He flashed his lights and made me pull over."

"Were you speeding, driving without your lights on, what?"

He shakes his head in resolute denial. "He said I ran a stop sign."

"Did you?"

"No. I'm a very careful driver. Especially in that part of town."

"When he stopped you, could he see inside the back of your truck?"

"No. It's closed off from the cab."

"So why did you open the door to the cube?" I ask. "What reason did he give to make you open it? You didn't open it voluntarily, did you?"

Salazar is twisting in his chair, reliving the ordeal. "He said he had to look inside to make sure there wasn't an electrical short. Because besides running the stop sign, one of my tail-lights was flickering."

That's a load of bullshit, which I've encountered a hundred times, as has every defense lawyer in the county. This man wasn't pulled over because he ran a stop sign or had a flickering tail-light. He was pulled over because he was a Mexican driving a beat-up truck through the streets of a rich, white neighborhood at two o'clock in the morning.

"And there were the televisions, and you didn't have the paperwork for them, and . . ." I don't have to finish.

The judge's deputy sheriff, a roly-poly Bakersfield cowboy named Ike, with bright red hair and freckles like a grown-up Howdy Doody, sticks his head in the door. "You're up," he informs us.

"Here we go," I say, nodding to Salazar. The deputy stands aside so we can enter the courtroom, which is of no particular distinction. Windowless, no pictures or friezes on the walls. Except for the Los Angeles County and California state flags, it could be in any state in the union.

"How do I get in touch with Gonzalez?" I ask, as I guide Salazar to the defendant's table. "Do you have a phone number?"

He seems to be in shock. From his look it's obvious that he's never been in a courtroom before, certainly not from this perspective. "On a piece of paper in my wallet," he answers. "Which the police took from me, along with everything else," he adds, his voice forlornly bitter.

"I can get the wallet," I assure him. "And the rest of your stuff." I need to talk to this Gonzalez character as soon as I can. Although I shouldn't buck up my client's hopes, I add, "We're going to work this out."

He turns to me with a look of pure anguish. "We have to, Miss Thompson. Because I am not a criminal."

"All rise."

I prompt Salazar to stand up as the Honorable Judith Rosen, a petite woman in her fifties whose hair is dyed jet-black and cut in the severe style of a silent movie star, enters the room. The only other people in the chamber are Wayne Dixant, the young assistant D.A. with ambitions who is running this case, the court clerk and the stenographer, deputy sheriff Ike Plowman, and a few other lawyers who have cases before the judge after ours is dealt with.

"Be seated," the deputy intones.

The clerk reads the complaint and hands me a copy. Judge Rosen peers at us from over her bench. I know for a fact that her chair is padded to give her extra height. "Do you understand the charges that have been brought against you?" she asks my client.

"He does, Your Honor," I answer for him. I've instructed Salazar to keep his mouth shut except when she asks him how he wants to plead, which will be two words: *not guilty.* She asks him that now, and he answers. His voice is low and shaky.

The judge looks at the papers in front of her. "What are you requesting bail to be set at?" she queries Dixant.

"Fifty thousand dollars."

The judge lifts an inquisitive eyebrow. "Explain."

"The property in the accused's truck was stolen from a bonded warehouse in San Pedro that was forcefully broken into," Dixant tells her. "That's one felony in itself. The retail value of the stolen goods is over fifty thousand dollars. We think setting bail at fifty thousand dollars is more than reasonable."

"It's utterly unreasonable, Judge," I break in. "This man has never been arrested for anything in his life, and there are extenuating circumstances that I believe will prove his innocence, certainly of the charge of breaking into the warehouse. I ask that the court release him on his own recognizance."

"Absolutely not," Dixant cries out. "That would be irresponsible, Judge."

Rosen glances at the paperwork in front of her. "How about ten thousand?" she asks me. "Is that doable?"

I shake my head. "No, Your Honor. Maybe . . ." I take a stab. "Twenty-five hundred." Salazar would have to come up with two hundred and fifty dollars to cover the 10 percent payment on a five-thousand dollar-bond, plus post a bond for the rest. I hope he owns his house, so that he has equity to support that.

"Judge, come on," Dixant whines. "This isn't Sunday school."

Rosen nods. She's left of center on the scale of judges in the county, but she isn't a bleeding heart. There are no bleeding hearts in the Los Angeles County judicial system.

"Set formal bail hearing for . . ." she glances at her clerk for a date.

"Tomorrow, please, Judge," I implore. "This man needs to know where he stands as soon as possible."

The clerk nods to the judge that the timetable is okay. Dixant also nods in agreement, reluctantly.

"Tomorrow afternoon, three o'clock," Judge Rosen agrees, making a note on her calendar. "It's on you to set up the probation interview and arrange for references in that period of time, Counselor," she cautions me.

"I understand, Your Honor," I reply. The probation interview I can handle; I'll set it up for tomorrow morning as soon as I get back to my office. References, I don't know. I'll ask Salazar if he knows anyone solid who will help us.

The judge bangs her gavel. "See you tomorrow."

Deputy Ike escorts us back into the interview room. I have a few minutes with Salazar before he's taken back to the jail.

I grab a notepad and pen from my purse. "I'll try to reach your friend Gonzalez," I tell him. "In the meantime, who do you know who can come in here tomorrow and say good stuff about you, besides your wife?"

He names several of his parishioners. His wife will know how to contact them. I can see from both his facial expressions and body language that the world is spinning way too fast for him.

"Can I go home now?" he asks me, looking at the door. It's as if he didn't hear anything that was said in court, or wasn't able to process it. Either way, he isn't thinking clearly.

"Not yet," I have to tell him. "Hopefully, tomorrow."

He turns ashen. "I have to go back to the jail?" he whimpers.

"For tonight." Poor bastard. He's never done time. It's a scary prospect for anyone, but for a first-timer it's unfathomably frightening. "Just for tonight."

I shouldn't have made that promise, because I don't know if I can back it up, but I can't leave him hopeless. He's too fragile. "You can handle one night," I say, trying to buck up his spirits. "We'll be in better shape tomorrow. I know it's inconvenient, but you can do it."

Inconvenient. Christ, what a lame platitude. But it's the best one I have.

"What I'm going to tell you now is very important," I caution him. "The walls have ears. Don't talk to anyone, especially about what you were arrested for. No one in there—another prisoner, a guard, nobody—is your friend. Keep it zipped, okay?"

He nods. He can't believe this is happening to him.

"One more thing," I remember to ask him. "Did your friend Gonzalez pay you? Was there money in your wallet when the police brought you in?"

He shakes his head dolefully. "No. He was going to pay me when he got paid."

All this trouble and he didn't even get paid for it. Talk about being a fall guy. In a way, though, that's good. If he had the money, that could be incriminating evidence against him. In this case, being broke is a blessing.

I nod to Ike through the window. He comes in and takes Salazar by the arm. They exit through one door. I go out the other.

FOUR

<u></u>

As I GET OFF the elevator at my floor and head for my office I see my roomie Sam and several other lawyers milling around in the large conference room, watching the television set, a fifteen-year-old curved-screen Panasonic. The D.A.'s office recently installed a big flat-panel high-definition TV, courtesy of an anonymous donor, but that generosity wasn't extended to us. We're the poor cousins; we rarely get a bone thrown our way.

The city brass is holding a press conference in front of City Hall, across the street. It's one of the most recognizable buildings in the city. Everyone uses it for photo ops, even those who don't work there. Since the set is tuned to Channel 9, I assume whatever they're watching is a red-meat story; our local channels love blood and guts, we lead the world in televised high-speed chases shot from helicopters.

Mayor Villaraigosa, Chief of Police Bratton, County Sheriff Baca, along with several other high-ranking officers from both departments and sundry politicians from the city and county, crowd the frame. In the background, a stoic statue, I spot my new friend, police lieutenant Luis Cordova. The mayor, the alpha dog among alpha dogs, is hogging the microphone. As usual, he is impeccably dressed. The man could be a model for *GQ*.

"Earlier today, the body of a thirty-two-year-old woman was found in West Los Angeles, where she resided," the mayor speaks into the cameras. "The circumstances of this killing are similar to two previous murders that have taken place over the past few months in this same area." He rises up on his toes. He's a short, slim man, but he has a large aura. "After consulting with Chief Bratton, Sheriff Baca, and members of their departments who specialize in crimes such as these," he continues, "we have concluded that these killings were all done by the same person."

"Ya think?" one of our tribe catcalls to the television screen, as the video headline flashes on and off across the screen, superimposed over the dignitaries: FULL MOON KILLER STRIKES AGAIN.

"Full Moon Killer?" another member of my crowd voices. "That's lame. Can't they do any better than that?"

What's really lame is dignifying these murders with a title. If this killer is a publicity hound, as most of them are, this will only make things worse.

"Detectives from both the city police force and the county sheriff's department will be working together to find this vicious killer," the mayor continues, staring intently into the lens, as if to make direct contact with the thousands of viewers (voters) who are watching his slick yet earnest performance. "If any one of you has any knowledge of who he is, or any information at all that might lead to his capture and arrest, contact us immediately. A special hotline has been established to handle these calls."

On the screen, a telephone number flashes in bold type. That the victims, now three, were young, attractive Anglo women who lived on the wealthy Westside, has already produced a predictable barrage of vitriol on television, in the newspapers, and particularly on talk radio. The fear (and secret blood-sport excitement) is that we could be facing another Hillside Strangler/Night Stalker saga that will yet again tear open the city's fragile, delicately stitched coalition.

The men and women standing behind the mayor have on their professional grim faces. My mind drifts as they talk, because it's all so predictable. Yes, they want to do the right thing, but more important, they want to advance their careers, which is why the mayor himself is up there in front of the cameras. Everyone knows that the public outcry about these murders, already shrill, is going to ratchet up, and they're all going to feel the heat. Everyone also knows that hundreds of blacks and Latinos are killed in Los Angeles every year, and that no one, except members of their own communities, raises a voice. But someone knocks off a few white girls and it's red meat for the television and radio talk-show Neanderthals who love to wallow in the gore. If you're a politician, you have to pay attention to the mob.

I snap to as I hear the mayor announce that "a reward of fifty thousand dollars will be paid for information that directly leads to the arrest of this killer, hopefully before he can strike again."

My fellow barristers, cynics that they are, mutter snarky comments at the size of the reward. Fifty thousand dollars is serious money. That much temptation will definitely bring the loony tunes out from under their rocks.

His Honor wraps it up. "If anyone out there can help solve these vicious murders," he says, looking into the camera, "this reward will be yours. Don't hesitate to call."

The images from City Hall fade from the screen. As the local talking heads start to masticate the story like dogs fighting over a chicken bone, someone mercifully clicks off the set. Jill Lewis, a middle-aged woman lawyer in the office who's seen it all, shakes her head in resigned revulsion. "I hope to God this isn't racial," she says.

I agree with her, although I keep my opinion to myself. The tension among the racial and ethnic groups that make up our alphabet soup of communities has risen during the past decade, which is saying a lot, because it was awful ten years ago. We're still paying the emotional and psychological price for Rodney King, the Rampart scandal, and the ongoing harassment of the minority communities by the police, especially the LAPD, who are their own worst enemies—witness the fiasco last year when the police assaulted the May Day protesters in MacArthur Park. They're the modern-day gang who can't shoot straight, but unfortunately, their stray bullets kill people.

"Five dollars says this makes Larry King tonight," someone calls out.

"Wrong," Sam contradicts the prognosticator from his self-appointed perch of éminence grise. "*Nancy Grace* tonight; she's the lead dog on the sled—that woman is rabid. Probably O'Reilly tomorrow. Then Larry." He grins, showing his desiccated gums. "That *alter kocker* never sticks his neck out until he knows which way the wind is blowing."

Takes one to know one, I laugh to myself; but I sober up fast. I'm not going to tell anyone here about where I was last night, because my life is none of their business; but I have a hollow feeling inside. I don't know what time last night this latest victim was murdered, but it could have been when I was out running. Less than a mile away.

Back in my office, I call the jail's property room and notify them that I'll be stopping by shortly to get some information from my client's wallet. I don't want to have to wait forever to get it, which would happen if I showed up without an appointment. They won't let me take the wallet, but I can copy what I need. Before I leave, I call Salazar's house.

"Hola?" A woman's voice, worried and suspicious, picks up on the third ring.

"Habla Inglés?" I ask.

"Yes," comes the soft reply.

I identify myself as her husband's lawyer, quickly explain what happened today and what will transpire tomorrow, then ask for the names and telephone numbers of anyone who might be willing to come to court tomorrow and speak on his behalf. She puts me on hold for a few minutes, then comes back on and rattles off a series of names and numbers. All Spanish surnames—neighbors, friends, and members of his church.

"You'll be there, won't you?" I ask her. "It's important to show family solidarity."

There is a moment's hesitation. "I will do my best," she tells me. "I have to find someone to watch my kids. Maybe my sister, if she can get off work."

"Please try," I beseech her. "It's really important."

This is a small example of how having enough money to afford a private lawyer is of immeasurable value to someone who has been arrested. A private lawyer would hire a babysitter to go to her house to watch her kids while she came to court to stand by her husband. We don't have those resources, unfortunately.

"If you can't find someone to stay with your children," I tell her, "I'll pay for a sitter. I really want you there."

Okay, so on the rare occasion I can be a soft touch. What will it cost me, twenty or thirty bucks? I know public school teachers who spend hundreds of dollars out of their pockets to buy supplies for their classrooms that the school district can't afford. I'll pass on the Starbucks Caffè Latte Venti for a week. I should stay away from dairy anyway; it builds up lactic acid, a bane for runners.

"Thank you," she tells me. I can feel the gratitude flowing through the line. "I will try very hard to get someone for free."

"Let me know," I tell her. "You need to be there."

For once, the property room attendants are cooperative. Salazar's wallet is waiting for me at the counter when I arrive. The duty sergeant hands me a form to fill out, then passes it over. I copy down Gonzalez's phone number and some other names written on scraps of paper that are stuck in the frayed leather case along with a few dollars and a debit card. I give the wallet back, walk outside, and dial Gonzalez on my cell phone.

Surprise, surprise. The number I have dialed is no longer in service. Please make sure I have dialed correctly.

It's almost five o'clock. Outside my office window I observe the evening shadows lengthening across the sidewalks, the sunlight softening from lollipop yellow to a muted orange-magenta twilight glow. In a few minutes I'll be in my car, watching the sun dropping into the horizon through my windshield, because my work day will be over.

If I were in private practice, I could be making two or three times what the county pays me. My student loans of $130,000, which I took out to go to college and law school, would be paid off instead of looming in front of me for most of the rest of my life. I wouldn't be driving a ten-year-old Volvo; I would buy my clothes at Neiman's and Nordstrom's, not Banana Republic and the Gap (and Ross Dress for Less, which I keep a tightly guarded secret); and I definitely wouldn't be living in my dead mother's house, which is full of bad memories.

But there are important compensations for my relatively meager pay. I work a forty-hour week, eight-thirty to five, Monday through Friday. No weekends, no evenings, no holidays (eleven paid). My clients meet me in my office, the jail, and the courts. Never in my home—or anywhere else—unless I choose to do so, which I don't. They do not have my personal phone numbers, so they can't call me whenever they feel like it. I don't have to ass-kiss self-important clients and dun deadbeat ones for overdue payments.

I'm here by myself because Sam is long gone, the phantom of the twentieth floor. I was surprised to see him hanging around the water cooler this afternoon; he usually takes off after lunch, and he's too much of a short-termer for our bosses to care. I stuff some paperwork into my briefcase and lock up my desk.

My phone rings.

I instinctively reach for it, then hesitate. Whoever it is can wait until tomorrow. But what if it's personal, like Jeremy, my boyfriend? Although if it is him, or another friend, they will call me in a few minutes, on my cell.

It's five o'clock. Time to turn off the lights and shut the door behind me.

The phone keeps ringing. Twice more, and the service will answer it.

I pick it up. "Hello?"

"Jessica Thompson, please," the voice on the other end requests. It's a woman's voice, soft and cultured, but forthright—not a supplicant's voice.

"This is she." I put my briefcase on the floor and sit in my chair. Something tells me this call is going to take more than five or ten seconds.

"Miss . . . is it Miss?"

"Yes," I reply.

"Miss Thompson, my name is Amanda Burgess. I'm sorry to be intruding on your time, but this is an urgent matter." The words are apologetic, but the tone isn't.

Amanda Burgess? "What can I do for you, Mrs. Burgess?"

"It's Ms.," she corrects me. "I'm divorced. Which is irrelevant for the purpose of this call. I've connected with you; that's what counts."

Connected with me? What in God's name for? "What can I do for you, Ms. Burgess?" I ask again.

"I understand you are representing Roberto Salazar on a criminal charge, is that correct?"

"I handled his preliminary arraignment this afternoon," I tell her. "How did you find out?"

"His wife called me. She's very upset, as you can imagine."

Roberto Salazar's wife called one of the wealthiest and most influential women in Los Angeles and talked to her about Roberto's arrest? What the hell is that about?

"I know," I say. "I spoke to her myself, a short time ago."

"Yes, she told me you had called, and that you were very decent, for which I thank you, as does she," Ms. Burgess replies. There is a moment's pause, then: "Whatever crime Roberto is being charged with, he did not do it. I give you my word on that."

"And you know this because?" While it's true that I've started to think Salazar might be an innocent rube, where is this society lady coming from?

"Because I know Roberto," she answers in a voice that does

not brook disagreement. "He is completely honest. Trust me on that, Ms. Thompson. I've employed enough men like Roberto to know the honest ones from the criminals and con artists."

I'm too nonplussed to rebut her, and she continues: "Roberto does some gardening for me. I have a landscaping staff, of course, but Roberto has a special touch, which is unique." There is a brief pause. "But to the point of my call: there have been instances where Roberto, were he of a criminal mind, could have made the wrong choice. But he never has, which I know from experience is unusual in a person of his background."

Listening to this patrician woman extolling her gardener's virtues, I can't help but think, another limousine liberal. Condescending without even realizing it. Still, that a person of her position would inconvenience herself enough to call and plead the case for a man who is being represented by the office of the county Public Defender is something I've never encountered before.

A sudden thought comes into my head. If Salazar works for a very rich woman, has a roster of other clients, and owns two trucks, why is my office defending him rather than a private lawyer? When he was arrested and Mirandized, he was advised that if he couldn't afford a lawyer, one would be provided for him. He chose us. Does that mean that he really can't afford a private lawyer, or that he just panicked and agreed to take whatever the system gave him? An experienced public defender is better than the average private defense lawyer, but that doesn't mean anybody can use one. *If you can't afford a lawyer*—that's vital. We're supposed to be the safety net for people who really are broke. Our office would be paralyzed from overload if anyone could use us.

From what this woman is telling me, Salazar can afford a lawyer, unless she doesn't pay him very well, which is possible. Rich people can be cheapskates, especially toward those lower down the social ladder.

"I'm coming around to agreeing with you about Roberto," I tell Ms. Burgess, putting Salazar's financial status out of my mind for the moment, "but the evidence against him is pretty solid. I do think I have a decent shot at getting him off, though," I add impulsively; immediately, I wish I had bitten my tongue. I shouldn't express optimism over this case, particularly since I probably won't be defending him. After tomorrow, any of the several hundred qualified lawyers in the office could be assigned his case.

There is a hesitation on the line, which I feel like a sudden fog of uncomfortable humidity. I swivel in my chair and watch the sun slide toward the horizon, waiting for her to fill the void.

Which she does. "Are you a competent lawyer?"

I sit up. "Am I what?"

"I mean no disrespect," Amanda Burgess says, with nary a hint of embarrassment. "But I know nothing about you, and I want to make sure Roberto is properly represented."

The impulse to hang up on her comes and goes quickly. You don't hang up on the Amanda Burgesses of this world.

"I am a good attorney," I respond in a calm, even voice. She just forced a decision, and she doesn't even know it. Tomorrow morning, I'm going to make sure that if Salazar does qualify for public assistance, Joe assigns this case to me, because now it's personal. "Roberto has first-class representation," I tell her, calmly and coolly.

"I'm pleased to know that," she says, relieved that I'm qualified to represent her gardener.

I'll bet she's pleased that I'm free of charge, too. She may believe Salazar is the salt of the earth, but she isn't going to hire a private lawyer for him, because if she was, she already would have. Her concern for his welfare isn't unlimited, obviously.

"If there is anything I can do . . ." she continues.

I interrupt her. "Show up tomorrow."

"Excuse me?" she says, as if I had suddenly begun speaking in a foreign language.

"Come to Roberto's hearing tomorrow afternoon. A woman of your stature in the community, speaking on his behalf, could really help."

Silence from the other end. Then, "I'm not available tomorrow afternoon."

Of course you aren't. Pardon me for even asking.

"But I'll see if I can change my plans. Where should I come, and when?"

FIVE

JEREMY GILBERT, MY BOYFRIEND, is the assistant principal bassoonist for the Los Angeles Philharmonic. For a classical musician, that is a fantastic job. He plays music he loves with some of the best musicians and conductors in the world; his base salary is six figures; plus there's record company money, travel to great locations, off-orchestra work, studio jobs, and ensembles. Besides being in the Philharmonic, he is also in a chamber group; a woodwind group; and as a baritone sax player, his second instrument, he plays jazz clubs and theaters, and records for a jazz-specialty label that sells over the Internet.

To someone who isn't an aficionado, the bassoon can be a comical instrument, the musical voice of the wily wolf with slouch top hat and chewed-up cigar who is trying to sneak into the henhouse; but if you actually sit down and listen to the deep, gorgeous tones it produces, it can be as soulful as a cello. Sometimes I'll snuggle up in an armchair and listen to Jeremy practice, and it's almost as good as sex.

Jeremy is thirty-two, three years younger than me (which he never lets me forget), so he is set for the rest of his professional life—thirty years or more, if he wants to stay active that long. The symphony is always looking for fresh blood to invigorate the institution, but there's no mandatory retirement age. Talent is talent, regardless of how old or young you are. All that matters is that you're better than the competition. Jeremy works his tail off to maintain his edge.

He has a concert tonight at Disney Hall, which I'm attending. Bartok's Second Piano Concerto, with a hot young Russian pianist, and Beethoven's Fourth Symphony—a meaty program. Salonen is conducting, which makes it extra special; he spins gold from his orchestra. I didn't know squat about classical music before I met Jeremy, but now I'm pretty knowledgeable for a newcomer, enough so that I can hang out with him and his friends and not embarrass either of us. I go to about half a dozen concerts a season, when Jeremy can get me a good ticket.

The Music Center is two blocks from my office, so I could walk there; but since I have three hours to kill, I'm going to work out at the gym in Jeremy's loft-apartment building on Figueroa, near Sixth Street. He'll be gone already, having an early snack and warming up for the performance, but I can shower and change at his loft after I exercise. I'll run on the treadmill, and lift weights. You have to be aerobically fit to run a marathon, but it helps if you're strong as well, because all that pounding wears your body down.

I park in a public lot across the street from Jeremy's building and stand on the corner, waiting for the light to change. My purse is slung over one shoulder, my gym bag across the other. Already, at five-thirty in the afternoon, downtown Los Angeles is emptying out. The loft scene has exploded over the past decade, but that is only relative to the black hole that was here before. Although a few thousand yuppie professionals now make downtown their home, it is still pretty much a wasteland after dark. People do come here, from Beverly Hills, Studio City, Cheviot Hills, hundreds of outlying neighborhoods. They go to the Water Grill, Ruth's Chris, Staples Center and the Music Center and the Mark Taper and the Pacific Dining Car and Philippe's French Dip and the Original Pantry and Chinatown and all the other attractions. They park as close to their destination as they can (valet park, if possible), go inside, eat, drink, watch a game or a concert or a play, get back into their cars, and go home. Once the workday is over, downtown Los Angeles, despite all the hype, is still a place for tourists who don't know any better, adventuresome young hipsters, and the downtrodden—especially the dregs. L.A. has the largest skid row in the country, a statistic the city doesn't include in its promotional brochures.

"Got any spare change?"

I tighten my grip on my bags as I turn and look at a woman who is standing a few steps away, not so far that I can ignore her presence, nor too close to break through my personal space, which she has learned the hard way to respect; that's how you get your teeth knocked in, if you have any left. My beseecher is of indeterminate age; she looks as if she's sixty, but she could be forty, or as young as twenty-five. Living on the street is comparable to dog years—you age seven years for every actual one. What a sad, poor creature she is, her hair a beehive of snarls, her face caked with street grime. She looks as if she hasn't washed or changed her clothes in days, if not weeks. They're all poor creatures worthy of our compassion, even if they smell like piss, shit, and puke, and they include psychotics, alcoholics, junkies, and combinations of those diseases and others. Her tribe, thousands of them, a much larger population than the new loft and chic apartment dwellers, lives right around the corner from here, centered on Fifth Street, between Alameda and Main.

Most of my clients are petty criminals with no money, no prospects, no hope. My world, like that of the cops and prosecutors and other members of the criminal justice system, revolves around and is dependent on them. If there weren't any crooks, a lot of people would be out of work.

All day long I'm surrounded by sad creatures like this woman. Maybe not as down and out as she is, but they're all in a level of hell that regular people can't conceive of. In that world, I have no fear of them, because I'm in control. I don't even think about it.

Out here, though, in the real world, I am not in control. If some of her friends suddenly materialized and wanted to mug me, or worse, they could easily do it and I would be powerless to stop them. Although that rarely happens; most fights around here are among themselves. People kill each other over a six-foot-square area of sidewalk, a pint of cheap wine, or an imagined insult.

Jeremy loves it down here—the newness, the rawness, the urban vibe—and he's tried to get me to move in with him, but I could never live here. I can run through the streets where I live at midnight and feel safe, despite these recent murders. I could never do that around here. I would no sooner take a walk by myself on these streets after dark than try to swim to Catalina Island.

Despite myself, I can't help but look at this woman again. Where does she sleep, I wonder, how many blow jobs will she have to perform to buy a cheap pint of booze or a few rocks of crack? That's if she can wangle any customers. It's terrible how far a person can fall, right here in one of the richest cities in the world.

Tomorrow, she could be a client, and if she is, I will treat her with dignity and respect. But now, I turn away from her. If you let them engage you, you're a fly in their spider's web.

The light changes from red to green and I quick-step across the street, looking both ways to make sure no one else can ambush me.

The concert is wonderful, one of the best of the year. Afterward, Jeremy and I go to Pete's Café on South Main, a few blocks away, for drinks and a late meal. Heads turn as we make our way through the room. I'm five-ten barefoot, and tonight I'm wearing three-inch heels. Jeremy is six-five, and his mop of hair, which he wears semi-long, is so blond it's almost white. We're dressed formally, he still in his orchestra attire, I in a black spaghetti-strap dress that stops just below my knees. We're a striking couple.

I hadn't eaten after my workout, so I polish off a plate of lamb Bolognese and a Caesar salad, with a glass of the house red to wash it down. Jeremy, who is not in training, has the house cheeseburger, shoestring fries, and a couple drafts of Sam Adams. The fries are tempting, hot and sizzling, but fried foods are a no-no until I run my race.

I tell him about my day. When I get to the telephone call from Amanda Burgess, the hand holding the french fry he was about to pop into his mouth pauses in midair.

"No shit." His brow furrows; in surprise? I don't know. "She was probably at the concert tonight," he informs me. "Eighth row, orchestra. She's had her seats since the hall opened."

The french fry disappears into his mouth. "She's a member of one of the circles, probably Founders'. I've spoken with her at a few fund-raisers. She's quite impressive."

"I'm sure she is. I'm interested in meeting her," I say. "And a little nervous," I admit. I amend that. "Curious, not nervous."

"Yeah," Jeremy agrees. "Rich lady coming down from the clouds to mingle with the plebeians, gotta be on your best behavior." He pokes me in the ribs and I jerk away, almost spilling my wine. "Make sure you brush and floss."

"I'm a professional," I remind him. I twirl strands of spaghetti onto my fork and bite in. It's delicious, the perfect midnight meal. I drink more wine.

It's too late to drive home, and I had a second glass of wine, so I'll spend the night at Jeremy's. I sleep over about once a week, and he spends one or two nights at my place, depending on our schedules. We strip off our clothes, wash up, climb into bed, and make love. There aren't fireworks, we're both too tired, but it's good, comforting. I cuddle against him for a few minutes before rolling over to my side of the bed.

In less than five minutes, he's asleep. I'm not.

We have been a couple for almost two years now. We have an easy relationship, which is part of the problem: it's too easy. The difference in our ages has been affecting our relationship recently, but the anxieties are one-sided—I have them; he doesn't. It's not the fact that he's younger than I am—two and a half years is not a big enough gap to matter—but I'm beginning to hear the ticking of my biological clock.

We've talked about getting married and starting a family. Jeremy isn't sure he's ready for fatherhood yet, whether he can handle the restrictions or responsibilities. As far as he's concerned, he still has time before he has to settle down. I do too, but a lot less.

Because of my own history, the idea of bringing a child into the world is a complex issue for me. I'm still not sure that given the liberty to do so, I would. But I would like to be able to have that choice, and I don't, at least not now. And when Jeremy decides he wants to be a daddy, will it be too late for me to conceive? Women in my family go into menopause early. I may not be able to get pregnant much past forty, and there's always the worry about birth defects. If I'm going to get pregnant, it should be sooner, not later.

There is another element to this problem I try not to think about, but I have to. I may not be able to get pregnant. I never have been, even when I, or my partner, didn't use birth control. I don't know whether that is because of my body chemistry, a consequence of having been shot in the gut as a kid, or just random chance. But when I think that I might not have the option, I feel incomplete.

I have to be up early, and I have to be sharp; I can't lie awake all night, my mind thrashing about with negative thoughts. I creep out of bed, being careful not to wake Jeremy, and get a 10-mg Ambien out of my purse, which I wash down with a glass of water. I set my cell-phone alarm to six-thirty and get back into bed, sliding my body lightly against his, for emotional security.

I love him. I really want us to make it. I fall asleep to the rhythm of his deep, unworried breathing.

As an officer of the court I am sworn to uphold the law (which I do, except for smoking pot, which shouldn't be against the law), but I can break the rules. One of the rules is that I get to work at eight-thirty. But it's barely seven-thirty, and I'm already on the job.

On the way to my first stop, I drop a couple of quarters into a sidewalk vending machine and take out the *Los Angeles Times*. A page-one headline below the fold screams FULL MOON KILLER CLAIMS THIRD VICTIM. I read the opening paragraphs, then toss the paper into a trash container. The *Times* used to be a good paper. Now it's down in the gutter with the rest of the rags.

Roberto Salazar's cube truck is being held at the sheriff department's impound lot located in the industrial section of downtown L.A., near the train yards. The truck is part of the evidence against him, so it's being kept under lock and key until his case is settled.

The lot is huge, a maze of vehicles of all shapes, sizes, descriptions. Even with the help of a friendly deputy, it takes me half an hour to find the truck, which is parked in a crowded row of other confiscated vehicles alongside a chain-link fence that borders the L.A. River.

Looking at this truck, I'm beginning to figure out why Salazar didn't hire a private lawyer. It's a piece of junk. The tires are threadbare, there are dents and rust spots all over it, and it's sagging on its shocks. Even if you threw a cheap Earl Scheib paint job on it, it wouldn't fetch three hundred dollars at auction. If the rest of Salazar's equipment is this ratty, he isn't worth spit.

One thing is working properly, though: the tail-lights. The deputy pumps them several times, and they respond the way they are supposed to. Which means the arresting officer's reason to check inside the truck was an improper search and seizure.

I thank the impound officer for his help, and leave. On the short drive to my office, I think about the search. Under a by-the-book application of the law that search should not have been made, which means the stolen televisions would not have been found, and Salazar would not have been arrested. Fifteen years ago, if I had been practicing law back then, I could have made that argument and the case might have been dismissed. But the rules governing the Fourth Amendment aren't black and white anymore. There's a lot of gray area, all to the benefit of the police. That officer's decision to look inside the truck could be upheld, or it could be kicked out. Judge Rosen is a good judge, but like every other judge in the system, she knows which way the wind's blowing.

There is something else I have to acknowledge, even though I don't want to. People whose lives are wrapped up in law enforcement, including me, see the dark side of humanity every day. Upstanding citizens don't get arrested; criminals do. No matter how you sugarcoat the justice system, those are the facts. You wind up categorizing people—us and them—and you judge them accordingly. And harshly.

Yesterday afternoon, I was repulsed and frightened by a homeless woman who was timidly begging for a quarter or fifty cents. What was I afraid of, for God's sake? She was a bag of bones, a strong wind would have blown her away. And what would it have cost me to donate my so-called spare change to her? Nothing. Yes, I might have been besieged by a horde of her fellow travelers, the way well-meaning tourists are mobbed in Africa or India, but that's conjecture. That woman, and what she represents, yanked me out of my comfort zone, which freaked me. So I turned my back on her.

My cowardly act, because that's what it was, took place in broad daylight, on a populated city street. Now, in my mind, I step into another person's shoes.

I'm a cop who is cruising the late-night streets, protecting and serving. A beat-to-shit truck comes lurching into view. A quick look-see tells me the truck is in violation of a dozen vehicle codes. The driver, who is Mexican, is not from this area. I'm a professional law enforcement officer. My instincts, honed over years of life on the streets, real life, not some fairy-tale bullshit, tell me this doesn't add up. So I pull him over.

Do I have reasonable cause? What's reasonable cause—not in some law book but in the world which is imperfect and mean? The tread on his tires is too low; that's probable cause. His muffler sounds loud to me, which means it may be emitting too much exhaust; again, probable cause.

He hands over his license and registration, and I can see he's nervous. Maybe it's because he's Mexican and I pulled him over. I can understand that. Cops make everyone nervous. But there could be another reason.

I call in his documents. In a minute, the results come back—he's clean. I could write him up for the tires, and the exhaust, and the stop sign which he did run, although at two in the morning, on a deserted street, I'm not going to do that, it's too petty.

But he seems awfully nervous. He keeps looking back at the closed part of his truck. Is he hiding something in there? Christ, what if there are a dozen illegal aliens in there that he's smuggled into the country? They could be dying.

I need to see inside that truck. So I tell him I think he has a problem with his tail-lights. I've decided I'm not going to give him a ticket, although I could. I just want to make sure there's nothing in there, and I'll send him on his way.

He resists, which further fuels my suspicions. He gives me some song and dance about the lock being hard to open, he's already late, yada yada yada. But finally, he reluctantly obeys. I'm a cop—you don't say no to a cop, not under these circumstances.

And what do you know? Jackpot. Once again, my instincts have been proved right.

I pull into the parking lot adjacent to my office building. It's eight-thirty. My official workday is about to begin.

SIX

IT'S MIDAFTERNOON. EARLIER, SALAZAR met with a probation officer, who certified that he met the requirements to be granted bail via self-recognizance. One obstacle removed. Now, as I enter Judge Rosen's courtroom, I see a young Latina sitting by herself, in the back. She looks at me with hopeful eyes as I walk over to her.

"Mrs. Salazar?"

Her nodded *yes* is guarded. She is obviously frightened out of her wits.

"I'm Jessica Thompson, your husband's lawyer. We spoke on the phone." I put out my hand. Her hand is rough; it's a hand that does manual labor. "I'm glad you could come," I say. "So you were able to find someone to stay with your children?"

"Yes." Her voice has an anxious trill. "My sister."

That's good to hear. Not that I was worried whether I'd have to shell out twenty dollars, but whether her family was supporting her. Family support in these circumstances is important.

I look around. Except for the regular court personnel, no one else is here. "Is anyone else coming? Any friends, or members of his church?"

She shakes her head. "No. Work."

That's understandable. For people in the Salazar's financial bracket, missing a day's pay would be a hardship. "Well, you're here, and that's going to make a difference," I assure her. She needs all the assurance she can get.

I lead her to the front row and show her where to sit. Then I cross to the other side of the partition. Deputy Ike escorts me to the holding room where Salazar is waiting for me. He looks the worse for wear.

"How are you?" I greet him.

"Will I be able to leave today?" he replies, question to my question.

"I don't know," I answer truthfully. "I hope so."

He groans. "Why can't I?"

You were arrested with stolen goods, pal. This isn't parochial school, where Sister Mary Martha raps you across the knuckles with her ruler and keeps you in at recess. "It's up to the judge," I explain. No matter how many times you tell them the facts of life, it doesn't penetrate. Like that dumb ass Reggie Morton, whose trial starts tomorrow. "If she gives you bail on your own recognizance, you'll be out. That means free," I explain; he's not going to understand legal terminology. Against my better judgment, I add, "I think she will. She seemed sympathetic yesterday."

I have to stop doing that—giving clients hope when I shouldn't. But I need him to be in a positive frame of mind during this hearing. If he comes in with a hangdog attitude, the game will be over before the opening whistle.

"Did you talk to Armando?" he asks.

"No. His cell phone is out of order. Not in service."

He jerks, an involuntary spasm. "Really?"

Christ, he sounds like a kid. "Really."

"But I just talked to him, two night ago," he says.

"And one night ago, when I tried to talk to him, his phone was no longer connected."

He's completely bewildered at hearing that. "Do you think he knows?" he asks. He sounds like a little lamb who's lost his mother.

"That you were arrested with his televisions?"

"Yes."

"I'm sure he does," I answer. Only a man grasping at straws, or a dupe, would ask such a question. Of course Gonzalez found out—either because whoever he was supposed to deliver them to called and asked where they were, or because he (Gonzalez) heard about Salazar's arrest through the grapevine. Whichever reason it was, he's nowhere to be found. If I were a private lawyer, and my client had money, I'd hire a detective and track Gonzalez down. But I'm not, and he doesn't.

Deputy Ike sticks his head in the door. "Ready?" he asks rhetorically.

I take Salazar's arm and pull him to his feet. "You're humble, but not meek," I prep him, like a trainer giving a boxer last-minute instructions before the opening bell. "If the judge asks you a question, answer precisely and look her in the eye, but don't stare. And only answer questions; don't give opinions. The judge doesn't care about your ideas on life, liberty, or anything. Leave the driving to me, okay?"

"Okay," he parrots. "I trust you."

Great.

We follow Ike into the courtroom. As we walk to the defense table, my counterpart representing the state gives me a perfunctory nod and turns away. He's going to hang tough. He knows he's holding the cards and that I don't have a strong enough hand to bluff him.

As I guide Salazar to his seat next to mine, I look behind me to make sure his wife is where I left her. She is, but now she isn't alone. Another woman is sitting with her, holding her hand for support.

I walk to the railing. The second woman stands to meet me. She is dressed modestly and her makeup is minimally understated, but nonetheless, she is very attractive, in a highbred, almost old-fashioned Katharine Hepburn way. From what I know about this woman, she is in her mid-to-late sixties, but she looks a decade younger. Money may not be able to buy happiness (which I personally think is debatable), but it can buy a lot of other things, including retarding of the aging process.

"How do you do?" she says. Her cultured voice is warm, generous. "I am Amanda Burgess."

"Jessica Thompson. Thank you for coming." I turn to Salazar. "Look who's here, Roberto," I say, in the sappy tone of a mother talking to a six-year-old in the presence of special company.

He jumps up. "Mrs. Burgess," he says, with genuine surprise. It's obvious he didn't know anything about this.

"Roberto," she says warmly, but she keeps her distance; she doesn't try to hug him or make any physical gesture. "I'm sorry you're in this mess. But everything will be fine." She smiles at me. "You're in good hands. Miss Thompson will take good care of you."

Thank you for that, I think. I've known the woman for five seconds, and she's already setting me up to fail?

"All rise."

We turn as Judge Rosen comes in from her chambers and takes her seat at the bench. "People versus Salazar, bail hearing," the bailiff calls out. "Be seated."

Dixant, the deputy D.A., has grudgingly lowered yesterday's bail request. "Twenty-thousand dollars, Your Honor," he says, when the judge asks him again for his bail recommendation. "Which is generous. The people have no reason to further lower that amount; it's already a big concession." He sounds bored, as if this is all a waste of time.

He sits down. Judge Rosen glances at the probation statement, then nods at me. "Your turn."

"Bail in any amount is unnecessary and unwarranted, Your Honor, I announce as I stand up. "This man should be released on his own recognizance, today. Let me explain why."

I tick off my reasons: "Mr. Salazar's record is clean. Not only has he never been convicted of a crime, he has never even been charged with one. When was the last time a defendant standing in front of you could say that, Your Honor? He is married, with two children. He has his own gardening business, and he also has a delivery business. He is a minister of a church in East Los Angeles. A minister," I repeat. It never hurts to play the God card. "There is no possibility that this man is a flight risk. Zero. He will show up for his trial." I place a hand on Salazar's shoulder. "Let him go home, do his jobs, take care of his wife and small children, administer to his flock." That's laying it on a little thick, maybe, but subtlety doesn't work. I want to help the judge support my position, so I have to give her as much ammunition to defend doing it as I can. "He's going to show up, Your Honor. You know it, I know it, everybody in this room knows it, including my distinguished colleague sitting across the aisle."

Dixant waves a hand in the air. "Don't speak for me," he says cheerlessly. "I don't know it, and neither does anyone else. This guy was caught red-handed with stolen goods, at three in the morning, forty miles from his house. He's not an angel." He gets to his feet and points a finger at my client. "In fact, I think the fact that the accused does not have a record is a negative in this case, not a positive."

"Because?" the judge asks.

"Because the accused has too much to lose." That's a standard prosecutor's ploy, to always call a defendant "the accused." It taints them right from the start. "His jobs, his ministry, his family. Even for a first offense, the guidelines for a case like this are four years, minimum. It's *precisely* because he isn't some bum off the street that he's a prime flight risk, Your Honor. This man could run in the blink of an eye without taking any consequences into consideration, out of sheer panic." He shakes his head sternly. "Giving him a get-out-of-jail-free card is not in the people's interest. Make him pay for it. Better still, keep him where we know he'll show up. Across the street, in lockup."

I look at Rosen. To my dismay, she seems to be taking this dipshit's arguments seriously. I raise my hand.

"Yes, Ms. Thompson?" Rosen says.

"May I have a minute, Your Honor?"

"All right."

I stand and go over to the railing where Amanda Burgess is sitting with Salazar's wife. I make eye contact with the older woman. She pats Mrs. Salazar's hand supportively, and gets up. I lean into her, my mouth almost touching her ear. "Are you willing to speak up for Roberto, Ms. Burgess?" I whisper. "Publicly, now?"

"Yes," she says. "I am." She touches my hand lightly. "And please—call me Amanda."

I turn back to the judge. "I have a character witness who would like to speak in my client's behalf. May she?" I ask.

"Any objections?" Judge Rosen asks Dixant.

"No, Your Honor." He's made his case, and some do-gooder civilian isn't going to change the judge's mind. He did what he needed to do: he gave the judge a reason to keep the bail requirement out of Salazar's reach, which is the same thing as denying it outright. Ninety-nine out of a hundred times, when the prosecutor requests a specific cash bail, the judge agrees—better safe than sorry. So he's cool.

"Come forward, please," the judge instructs Ms. Burgess.

Deputy Ike pushes the swinging gate open, and Amanda walks through, taking her place in front of the bench. This is an informal situation, so she won't be sworn in.

"Please state your name, and your relationship to the defendant," the bailiff instructs her.

"Amanda Burgess. Mr. Salazar is my gardener."

Dixant doesn't know who Amanda Burgess is, so nothing registers; but Judge Rosen sure does. Her mouth flops opens like a lipsticked clamshell. Finding her tongue, she says, "Welcome to my courtroom, Mrs. Burgess. I'm honored to have you here."

"Thank you for having me," Amanda replies. "Although I'm sorry I'm here under these circumstances."

"Of course." The judge practically bats her eyelashes. "You wish to speak on the defendant's behalf?" she coos.

"I do, Your Honor," Amanda says, and turning, smiles at Roberto, whose own smile back at her is a combination of embarrassment and gratitude.

I steal a look at Dixant. He doesn't know what's going on, but he knows it isn't good for him. He sits up, paying attention now.

"Whenever you're ready," the judge says to Ms. Burgess. I've been coming up before this judge for more than five years, and I've never seen her this deferential.

Amanda's bearing is erect and commanding, as if this were her chamber, not Rosen's. "Thank you, Your Honor. I have known Mr. Salazar for a number of years," she states. "He has worked for me, and for several friends of mine."

She turns to face Dixant. "All of whom live in the vicinity of where Mr. Salazar was arrested." Her point being that Salazar is no stranger to that area, and could have been there legitimately. She holds his look until he turns away, then she addresses the judge again.

"Mr. Salazar's work is exemplary. But more important is who he is as a human being. He is one hundred percent trustworthy. He has never taken advantage of anyone, and has never cheated or fudged or done anything underhanded. Mr. Salazar is an honest and good man. And a good, honest man is hard to find," she says with conviction, as if she were Mrs. Diogenes.

"I would certainly agree with that," Judge Rosen replies.

Almost gleefully, I watch this lovefest. It's as if we're not in a courtroom, but on the set of a woman's television talk show.

"That Mr. Salazar would abandon his family, his parishioners, and his obligations is absurd," Amanda continues. "The idea is not only preposterous, it's insulting."

She turns and looks at Salazar again sympathetically, then locks eyes with the judge. "Mr. Salazar deserves his day in court, which he will have in due time, I assume."

Judge Rosen, listening carefully, nods assent.

"I know that if he is found guilty, he will pay his penalty," Amanda goes on, "although I cannot imagine that he is. But that's what trials are for, so I've been taught. Until then, however, it would be cruel and wrong to keep him in jail."

She takes a step toward Rosen. "Mr. Salazar will show up for his trial, and every other hearing at which he is required," she says. "I give you my word on that."

Dixant, whose expression has become more and more a study in irritation, scrambles to his feet. "Excuse me, Your Honor," he calls out. "Some woman off the street waltzes in here and vouches for the accused's character, and that's supposed to influence your decision? What is her legal standing? Does she have any?"

Rosen's look to him is withering; you could cut glass with that stare. You just shot yourself in a place that's really going to hurt, pal, I think with delicious pleasure, as I look at him, back to Rosen, then to Amanda, who stands in place, calm and composed.

Rosen leans over the front of her podium—she must have gotten up on her tiptoes. Her cheeks are flushed, as if she had put her rouge on in a closet. "Amanda Burgess is not some woman off the street, as you have blithely and carelessly characterized her," she tells the hapless deputy D.A. "If Steve Cooley came in here and testified on someone's behalf, would you think he knew what he was talking about?"

Steve Cooley is the Los Angeles District Attorney, Dixant's boss.

"Well, yeah, of course," Dixant mumbles. He's in deepwater and he knows it, although he still doesn't understand how his boat capsized.

"What about Mayor Villaraigosa?" the judge asks. "Governor Schwarzenegger? President Bush?"

Sigh of annoyance: "Yes."

"Well, maybe not Bush," the judge says, deadpan.

The sparsely occupied room bursts into laughter, Dixant and the Salazars excepted.

"Only kidding," Rosen says. "Don't anybody tell on me to

the Justice Department. So, Mr. Dixant. The well-established concept of a credible person, a person who carries weight in our community, is one that you accept and understand. That there are people whose word speaks truth to power, which the community pays attention to."

I stuff my papers into my briefcase. This hearing is over.

"Yes," Dixant answers. He can barely keep his head up now.

"I'm glad you feel that way," Judge Rosen says to him. "So do I. Which means we are on the same page." She preens a moment for her special guest. "Defendant is released on his own recognizance, pending the outcome of his preliminary hearing, which we will schedule for . . ." She looks to her clerk, who is scrolling through the court's schedule on her computer. But before she can announce a date, I make a snap decision. Quickly, I raise my hand.

"What is it, Ms. Thompson?" the judge asks.

"We'll waive prelim, Your Honor, and go straight to trial."

Rosen mulls over my request. "Have you discussed this with your client?"

I glance back at Salazar, who doesn't understand what's happening, which is good. "Yes," I answer. "We have."

That's a lie, but only technically. Salazar wants out; not just for a week, but until he goes to trial. Although I won't get a preview of the state's case against him, I already know the basic parameters. I also know that Dixant will again request that bail be revoked, and his office might come up with a better reason to do it, one that will change the judge's mind, regardless of how starstruck she is at the moment over Amanda Burgess.

Rosen looks to Dixant. "Any objections from the people?"

My worthy opponent shakes his head. He wants out of here so he can lick his wounds and return to fight another day. "No, Your Honor," he acquiesces.

The judge is brisk. "Set trial for sixty days from today," she instructs her clerk. "Good for both of you?" she asks Dixant and me.

The marathon is in eighty-two days; I know the date to the

hour. This trial will be all wrapped up long before then. If I run into a problem, I'll ask for a continuance.

"I'm good," I announce.

"Also me," Dixant tells her.

"The defendant will sign the required documents, then will be free to go," Rosen pronounces. She reminds me: "Make sure your client knows all of his obligations and responsibilities, Counselor."

"Absolutely, Your Honor," I assure her.

Rosen makes a note in her calendar, then smiles at Amanda, who has come over to stand next to Salazar. "Thank you for your participation, Mrs. Burgess," she says. "It was a privilege to have you in my courtroom."

"The privilege was mine, Your Honor," Amanda responds with a generous smile. "And it's Ms., not Mrs."

SEVEN

"W"HY AREN'T YOU WEARING a skirt?" Reggie Morton confronts me.

Idiot. As if my attire in any way matters. "It's at the cleaners," I answer tartly.

But to him, obviously, apparel is critical. He's like the student who writes a crummy term paper but presents it in a fancy binder from Kinko's. In his mind, that warrants a passing grade—sizzle without steak. "Can't you get nothing right?" he mutters under his breath.

"Excuse me?" I bark. I'm not in a forgiving mood this morning. Knowing that I'm going to get my butt kicked always puts me in a sour frame of mind.

"Nothing," he says, taken aback by my abruptness.

We're in the prisoner's holding room adjacent to the courtroom. In a few minutes, Reggie's trial will begin. He spurned my last attempt at pleading out, so now we are going into the pit.

For the record, I am dressed in a navy-blue blazer and slacks, one of my sharpest outfits. I will probably be the best-dressed person in the courtroom. But all Reggie cares about is what is covering my lower body. He has never gotten his priorities straight, and never will. Which is why he will go down.

"See you inside," I tell him as I stand up. Usually, at this juncture, I throw the client a bromide, like "It's going to be fine" or "We'll get through this," but with him I can't fake it.

He nods, but doesn't speak; he's freezing up from tension. I leave him and enter the courtroom.

Lorraine Tong, my District Attorney counterpart, an old hand about a decade my senior, is sitting at the prosecution's desk going over some last-minute notes. She gives me a professional smile of greeting as I place my briefcase on the defense table and take out a sheaf of papers, which I thumb through to make sure they are in the proper order.

"How's the running going?" Lorraine asks me.

"Fine," I answer. It seems as if everyone in the building knows about my quest.

"Good luck. With your training," she adds. She turns away and speaks to another D.A., a young lawyer on their staff who is sitting second chair for the experience. Lorraine has this case wired, and she knows it. And she knows I know it. The wheels of justice are going to grind to the only conclusion they can. Part of being a good lawyer is doing your best for your client. The best I could have done for Reggie was to get him to take the D.A.'s plea bargain. But he wouldn't, so for the next couple of days we're going to be stuck in a leaking boat that's heading straight over a waterfall.

This is your basic off-the-rack trial, so there are almost no spectators. Judge Hodgkins, who is finishing his last term on the bench, will run a brisk trial, which is fine by me. I want to take my medicine as quickly and cleanly as possible. By lunchtime, the jury has been selected. It's a Los Angeles mosaic—some young, some older, various ethnic groups, including blacks, Latinos, Asians (Taiwanese, Thai, Filipina), whites.

After the lunch break, Lorraine delivers her opening statement, and I follow with mine. I don't pull any rabbits out of the hat; there aren't any in there. Reggie, who had psyched himself up to expect a miracle, shows his dismay with obnoxious bodily language, which is noticed by everyone in the courtroom, including the judge, who is displeased, and the jury, who will be, once the prosecutor finishes presenting the damning evidence against Reggie. I've never bailed on a client, but if I could today, I would.

The state's principal witness is the cop who arrested Reggie. A veteran narcotics detective who ran the operation from start to finish, he looks like he could have been sent over from central casting—Samuel L. Jackson or Richard Roundtree (without the retro Afro). Lorraine walks him through the whole enterprise, step by step, from the initial encounter to the actual arrest. We've been through all this during discovery, so there won't be any last-minute surprises. He is well rehearsed—he would be a tough nut on cross-examination even if I had a hammer to crack open his shell, which I don't.

The motel room where Reggie's drugs and the state's money changed hands, after which he was promptly and forcefully arrested, had been rigged for video, and now it's showtime. Lorraine cues the operator to run the tape. The courtroom lights are darkened and we all turn our attention to the monitor, which has been placed so everyone can see it: judge, jury, Reggie and me, and the prosecutors.

Unfortunately for Reggie, lightning doesn't strike twice. The bust unfolds on the screen exactly as it has been described. I watch the jurors watching the screen. They are riveted. I swivel in my chair to see how my client is reacting.

Reggie, too, is staring at the television set, but there is no acknowledgment that he's seeing his life wash away like water going down a drain. It is as if he is disassociating from reality, and has found a portal into another world.

Maybe that's good. Because this video has ruined him in this one.

The tape is over, the lights come on. "I have nothing further from this witness, Your Honor," Lorraine tells the judge. She steps down, and I replace her at the podium.

"Who initiated this transaction?" I ask the detective.

Calmly, he answers, "I did." He knows what I'm trying to in-
fer: entrapment. And he's not going to get caught up in my snare.
"It was all done by the book. No shortcuts." He looks away from
me, at Reggie. His eyes remain fixed on my hapless client as he
adds, "There was no need to. He made it easy for us."

"Just answer the questions, please," I tell him, barely conceal-
ing my irritation.

"Yes, ma'am," he says back to me.

He's solid granite. I don't budge him, not an inch. I don't spend
much more time with him; if your questioning is going badly,
don't compound the misery and make things worse by hanging
around.

"No further questions, Your Honor."

I walk back to the defense table. Reggie looks at me, hollow-
eyed. "You let him off too easy," he hisses in a harsh whisper.
"Fucker suckered me."

I tune him out and turn away to watch the next witness, a lab
tech who will certify the heroin as real, being sworn in.

I hear a whoosh, like air escaping from a tire. "Shit," Reggie
murmurs.

My thought exactly.

By the end of the day, Lorraine has finished presenting her case.
She did a tight, clean job. I wasn't able to lay a glove on any of
her witnesses. I hadn't expected I could, but still, it's a numbing
feeling. Judge Hodgkins thanks the jury, gives them the usual ad-
monitions about not discussing the case or watching anything
about it on television or in the press, and reminds them to be back
at ten tomorrow morning, when it will be my turn.

Reggie and I huddle for a moment before he's taken back to
lockup. "What happens tomorrow?" he asks.

"It's our turn," I say.

"What are we going to do?" His voice is heavy with doom.

The question is good. The answers aren't. I don't have any
witnesses to counter the cops, the lab work wasn't compromised,

there wasn't an egregious violation of the law. I only have one decision to make: do I put Reggie on the stand? I know he is his own worst enemy, but at this point, I don't see what we have to lose. Maybe he'll be able to charm (make that con) one juror into believing he was improperly seduced, or maybe there is a hidden sob sister who will feel sorry for him. Or maybe there is a mole in this jury, a radical who will vote against authority just because all authority is corrupt, the system screws the individual, the LAPD is racist, or one of dozens of other biases, all of which have a foundation in the truth. That kind of defense does work—again, witness O.J.—but it's rare. The officers who set up Reggie and arrested him were brothers, so the claim of white or Latino racism against a black man won't wash.

So, do I have Reggie testify? If I do, the odds are he'll finish the prosecutor's job for her. But if I don't, the presumption of his guilt will be strengthened even more than it already is. Juries want to hear the accused's side of the story from his own mouth. To deny that opportunity to them, even if the witness sucks, usually hurts your case.

I don't have anything else. It's either him telling his story, or betting all my chips on my summation. Either hand is a loser. I have to decide which one gives me slightly better odds: a thousand to one or a million to one.

"Can you handle taking the stand?" I ask him. "Without freaking out, or pissing off the judge and jury?"

We have batted this option back and forth, at length. Initially, he was all for it, but lately he's been reluctant. He's scared that he'll be eviscerated on cross-examination. I don't blame him. It's a legitimate fear.

"Do I have to?" he asks.

"No."

"Will it hurt if I don't?"

"I don't know," I answer. "I don't have a crystal ball. Every jury is different." I hesitate to go on, but I have to. "At this point, I don't see that we have anything to lose."

"You mean anything else to lose," he corrects me. " 'Cause from what I heard in there today, I already have lost."

He's finally being truthful to himself. It's awfully late in the game, but better late than never.

"It isn't over till it's over," I tell him.

His reply is flat, emotionless, candid. "It's over. So I'll do it, 'cause what can it hurt?"

There it is. He's decided to be the master of his fate. I have to applaud his bravery. "All right," I tell him, trying to sound optimistic, but knowing I don't. "We'll meet tomorrow morning, before court opens, to go through your story."

As I get up to leave, he grabs my wrist to stop me. Quickly, as if he's afraid the guard waiting outside will rush in and restrain him, he lets go.

"Sorry," he apologizes.

"It's okay. Is there something else?"

He stares down at the floor. "That offer the D.A. made? Do you think . . . ?"

Now he's ready to make a deal? "Reggie, I warned you: once we started the trial, it was off the table."

"Yeah," he mumbles. "You did. Should've listened to you."

God, he's so miserable. "But I'll ask her."

I call Lorraine Tong from my office. The answer, as I knew it would be, is an emphatic *No.* So tomorrow, Reggie Morton will take the stand in his defense.

Jeremy and I aren't seeing each other tonight. Except on weekends, we usually don't when I'm in trial. I need to be completely focused, and I can't be if I'm with him; that's particularly important tonight, because I have to prepare for Reggie's testimony tomorrow, and the stakes are high. Reggie's going down, that's not in question. The unknown is how stiff his sentence will be. The difference could be almost a decade. He wasn't entrapped, so I can't play that card. But there are mitigating factors; there always are. I need for him to convince the jury that he isn't hard-core, that he understands he did wrong and is going to turn his life around. Tomorrow morning I'll come in early and spend an hour with him to make sure we're on the same page. I'll bring a Bible, in case we decide to try a Hail Mary *I-found-Jesus* ploy. There are lots of passages in the Good Book about forgiveness and salvation. Maybe Reggie can come up with an appropriate quote (spontaneously, of course). There may be one or two Christians on the jury who would be sympathetic to a jailhouse conversion, however belated. It's a shameless ploy, but we aren't playing touch football. Lorraine will have a cow, and the judge will probably put the kibosh on it and warn me not to grandstand; but when all you have are lemons . . .

My house is quiet when I enter. Dark, even though sundown is an hour away. I keep the shades drawn to keep it cool, and to keep it private. I have no pets. The street is small, and it isn't a through street, so there isn't much traffic, or noise. The house is a compact structure, one of the old clapboard Cape Cod–style bungalows that were built in the thirties and forties, when Santa Monica was still a small town. This block and a few others between Pico Boulevard and Rose Avenue have managed to withstand the upscale development that has transformed this community during the past twenty-five years, and especially the last decade, into one of the most expensive places to buy a house in the country.

If I ever sell, I'll be set for life. But I'm not ready to do that yet. This house has too many of my old memories absorbed in its walls, its floors, its ceilings, like tobacco smoke and mildew stains. Some of those memories are bad, horrifying. But they are an essential part of me. I'm not ready to let go yet. If I get married and have a family, I'll move, because I won't allow my children to grow up exposed to my old ghosts. But until then, I'll stay here. I've earned my claim, a hundred times over.

EIGHT

IN 1987, WHEN I was fourteen, my mother almost killed me. It was my own dumb fault. I should have known better than to try to sneak back into the house at three in the morning, given that my mother, Claire Thompson, was a paranoid lush who kept a loaded gun within close reach. It was just a peashooter .22 Ruger, a target pistol, not a gun with much stopping power, but she didn't know that. All she knew was that it was a gun, it fired bullets, and it didn't cost much. She had bought it at a swap meet under the table, no registration, no background check. The asshole who sold it to her out of the trunk of his car threw in a box of bullets and loaded it for her, on the spot.

We lived alone, she and I, in a perpetual state of undeclared warfare. My father had left us when I was barely out of my diapers, and I was an only child. I couldn't blame my old man for bailing out—you can only live with a crazy person for so long, or you'll go nuts yourself. My only regret was that he didn't take me with him.

My mother had decided she needed a gun out of an irrational fear that we were going to be assaulted by some nameless, faceless crazo roaming the mean streets of Santa Monica. The reality was that the possibility of our house being broken into was slim to none; where we lived was statistically one of the safest neighborhoods in Los Angeles, but my nutty mother was convinced danger was lurking everywhere. Watching the local news channels night after night—all those lurid freeway chases shot from helicopters—can really mess with your head. She had never fired the gun, nor had she ever taken a lesson in how to properly shoot it. It was available, close by, a security blanket.

So there the gun was, in the top drawer of my mother's bedside table, half hidden under a pile of worthless Lotto tickets—unfired, untested, mostly forgotten. She had shown it to me when she brought it home, and I had hefted it in my hand out of morbid curiosity. We had a gun in the house! Cool! I wanted to take it to a deserted stretch of the L.A. River and shoot off a few rounds, but she nixed that—guns weren't toys; you don't fire them for fun. They are serious business, to be used only for life and death emergencies, she recited solemnly.

Even back then, at my relatively tender age, I was more practical than she was, so I pointed out that if we had the damn thing we ought to test it out, to make sure it worked right. And also to feel what firing it felt like. But she didn't buy that sensible argument. I was to keep my hands off the goddamned gun, she warned me sternly, unless I was alone in the house and a doped-up sicko had burst in and was going to kill me. After he committed unspeakable crimes against my person, such as rape and other horrendous tortures. I don't know where she came up with that bullshit spiel; she'd probably heard it on television.

Anyway, I never got to fire the gun.

So now it was three in the morning and I was sneaking back into my house through the kitchen window, the same window I had snuck out of earlier, after she had gone to sleep. At that specific moment in time my mind wasn't working right, because a few hours earlier I had lost my virginity to James Cleveland, on the foldout sofa bed in the basement of his parents' house. James was seventeen, a junior in our high school, two grades above me. He wasn't the sharpest knife in the drawer, but he was sexy, played halfback on the football team, and all my friends were hot for him, so I was confident I had picked a winner.

All the lights in my house were out. I wriggled through the

kitchen window, trying to keep as quiet as an Indian scout. James and I had celebrated my deflowering (there really was blood, which freaked out both of us a little) by drinking a couple shots from his father's stash of designer bourbon, so I had a bit of a buzz. I could walk a straight line and talk without slurring, but my senses were a tad off, just enough so that as I was maneuvering my way through the dining room on my way to the stairs leading up to the second floor, I bumped into one of the dining-table chairs and knocked it over. Fortunately, the floor was carpeted, but the impact still made a dull sound, like a phone book dropping onto a counter.

I froze in my tracks. Had my mother heard the crash? Usually, by the time she called it a night, she was pickled enough that she would sleep through a thunderstorm. But I was scared shitless that this time would be the exception—that she would wake up, discover my deceit, and rag on me for being out at three in the morning in my street clothes, with whiskey on my breath, when earlier that night I'd concocted this big song and dance about how I was *exhausted,* and was going to bed *immediately.*

The sounds of the nighttime house—the hum of the refrigerator, the deep throbbing of our old gas heater, the slight creaks of the windows as the wind rattled the cracks—were humdrum in their normality. I carefully picked the chair up, set it back in place, and stood there, rigid, listening for my mother's clomping footsteps; when she was in her cups, she had the finesse of a Clydesdale.

But nothing happened; she hadn't awakened. I was free to sneak up to the safety of my bedroom. I knew how to avoid all the squeaks in the stairs, so I figured, smug little wiseass that I was, that I had pulled it off.

Halfway through my tiptoe journey up the staircase there was a sudden flash of light, like the flare of a match being struck, and at the same time I heard a *pop*. It wasn't the eardrum-bursting explosion you hear in the movies when a gun goes off. It was more of a snapping sound, about as loud as when you step on a dry seaweed pod at the beach. And for an instant, the sting from the bullet was not awful. It felt like someone had punched me in the stomach.

But then the pain slammed through me, searing my gut like it was on fire.

I screamed. My knees buckled; my legs turned to water. I lost my balance and fell backward down the stairs, all the way to the bottom, where I lay in a writhing heap.

The hall light popped on. My mother appeared on the landing above me. Her face was Kabuki white with bedtime facial cream. She was wearing a short nightgown; in the shadowy light, her mottled legs looked like cottage cheese. The gun was in her hand. I was losing consciousness, but I thought I saw smoke drifting out of the barrel, like in an old cowboy movie. Or maybe I was already hallucinating.

My mother was staring down at me. "Jessica?" she whispered. Then she screamed my name: "*Jessica!*"

"Mom," I croaked. "Mother . . ."

She stood in place, as if her toes had grown roots into the floor. Her mouth was moving, but for a moment, no sound came out. Then she gasped, "I thought you were an intruder, I swear it!" She started crying, big globs of tears running down her cheeks. Her smudged makeup against the marble whiteness on her face made her look like Gene Simmons. "I thought . . ."

Suddenly, the crying stopped as abruptly as if she had turned off a faucet. She bared her teeth at me, like a wolf closing in on a wounded deer. "*What are you doing up at this time of night?*" she shrieked. "*Did you sneak out again, goddamn you!*"

The pain in my stomach was excruciating. I was sure I was dying, and all she could do was scream at me like a harpy.

My voice in my ears sounded as if it was coming from a ghost. With all the strength I could muster, I yelled back at her. "*Call nine-one-one, you crazy fucking bitch!*"

After I got out of the hospital I moved in with my aunt Jill, who lived in Bronson Canyon, an old section of Hollywood up in the hills below and slightly east of the HOLLYWOOD sign. Jill wasn't really my aunt; she was a friend of my mother's, from when they were girls growing up in the Valley after World War II, at a time when there were still more orange groves along Victory Boulevard than houses. Like my mother, she was divorced, but she had her act together. She was a dental technician, made good money, paid her mortgage down monthly, and was a member of a travel group of single women who took two trips a year. Her house was full of knickknacks from her journeys. She loved my mother, but she understood that her childhood friend Claire was unstable and that I couldn't live with her anymore. So she made room in her life for a sullen and withdrawn teenage girl, an act of kindness and generosity for which I will always be grateful.

For the remainder of my high school years, I went into a shell. I was enrolled in a new school in the middle of the year. I didn't know anyone. All the cliques had been formed, all the clubs had their memberships, all the cool guys were taken. My old school had been a United Nations of races and ethnicities, but here, being white put me in a very small minority. The school population was mostly Latino, and there were a lot of blacks and Asians of dozens of stripes as well, but only a handful of Anglos. The races didn't mix much, which was further isolating. Because I'm tall, the basketball and volleyball coaches tried to recruit me, but I shined them on. I had played sports at my old school—volleyball and track—but I didn't want to join any of the teams at this new place. I kept my head down, did my work, and tried to be as invisible as possible.

Jill was a sweet woman, and she tried her best to provide me with a semblance of regular life, but my time living with her was strained. A week after I graduated, I moved out. I got a job waitressing at Ben Frank's on the Strip, and found a room in the heart of Hollywood, near Fountain and Orange. The other tenants were kids, dropouts and discards like me. Except for me, they were all stoners. Most of them lived on handouts from their parents and by panhandling on Hollywood Boulevard. They supplemented their incomes with menial jobs, small-time drug dealing, occasionally selling their bodies. I stayed away from that stuff, but we got along all right. I did smoke their weed and drink their alcohol.

Even though I didn't know where I was going, or if I was going anywhere at all, for the first time in my life I was free. Sometimes I was lonely—I wasn't as nihilistic as the people I lived with—but I got by, and slowly, little by little, I found a sense of confidence I hadn't had since the night I felt my life bleeding out of me. I was still basically a kid who didn't have a vision of the future beyond her next paycheck.

I had become friendly with another waitress named Maude, an actress wannabe from Arkansas with a Southern accent so thick you could pour it on pancakes. She was in her mid-twenties, sweet and cheery, and she didn't take life too seriously. We would go out together occasionally, to a movie or a club (she was the one who scored me my phony ID card). Two single girls having fun and looking for adventure.

One day, as we were leaving work, she asked me, "Ever done any modeling, Jessica?"

That threw me. "Modeling?" I'd seen the models in the Victoria's Secret catalog and *Vogue*. I was pretty enough, but I didn't look like them, not remotely. "No."

"Want to make some extra money?" Maude asked. "Nothing illegal or sexual," she added, to reassure me.

"I guess." I was getting by, but barely. Any added income would really help.

"Are you free now?"

I was going to catch the bus back to my place and do some laundry, but that wasn't urgent. "I guess."

"Come with me."

Maude's Volvo, so ancient it had the old black-and-yellow California license plates, was festooned with dozens of bumper stickers dating back to the anti-Vietnam War period. It was parked illegally on Kings Road. Maude plucked the ticket from under the windshield wiper and tossed it onto a batch of other unpaid tickets in the glove box. The old sedan fired up with a belch of exhaust and we headed east, down Sunset Boulevard.

It was a prime L.A. day, warm, only a whisper of smog. We cruised along with the windows rolled down, the radio tuned to K-EARTH 101, an oldies station. The Supremes were singing "Baby Love." I sang along with them.

We took Sunset all the way to downtown. Back then, the downtown arts scene was just starting to happen. A few abandoned factories had recently (mostly illegally) been converted into lofts. Real lofts, with exposed plumbing and brick walls, radiators that sputtered and clanged, and grimy industrial windows covered with decades of soot—not the new apartment-style lofts full of amenities that exist now, like my boyfriend's. The rent was cheap and the spaces were huge, which was perfect for artists.

I had never been down there. Looking out my window, I could see the train yard, filled with freight cars. When Maude parked behind one of the old buildings, near the L.A. River off First Street, I didn't know what to expect, but I was nervous.

"This is the easiest money you'll ever make," she promised me, giving me a reassuring wink. "And you don't have to lift a finger. Come on."

She locked the car and walked across the cracked asphalt and gravel parking lot to the building's entrance. I followed, close on her heels. A large sign over the entrance to the building read DOWNTOWN COLLEGE OF THE ARTS.

"Art school?" I said, reading the sign. "You're an artist?" I asked Maude, without thinking I might be slighting her.

"Hardly," she laughed, not offended by my gaffe. "I can't draw a straight line with a ruler." She gave me one of her conspiratorial winks again. It was part of her Southern charm. "We're not here to draw."

"Then why are we?" I asked.

"You'll see. Come with Mama."

Maude pushed the heavy industrial door open and led me inside. A few shrouded lightbulbs hanging from the high ceiling cast puddles of light on the concrete floor. Gang-related graffiti were spray-painted on the walls.

A freight elevator at the far end of the long corridor carried us up three floors, slowly grinding to a stop with a gnashing of gears. Maude pulled the wooden-slat door open, and we stepped out.

We were in a huge room that took up the entire floor. The plywood subfloors were covered with cracked linoleum that was torn and peeling. The place looked as if it had once housed heavy machinery, like lathes or printing presses. One entire wall, facing north, was floor-to-ceiling windows, the old factory style that would tilt open, rather than rise vertically. Light streamed in across the floor, bathing the room in a wash that was more bright than warm.

Scattered throughout the room, more than a dozen artists were sitting at easels. Most of them were my age or a few years older, but there was a smattering of people in their thirties and forties as well. All but two of them were men. Some were drawing in charcoal, others in watercolor, the rest with oils. The instructor, a middle-aged effeminate man, moved from one artist to another, looking at their work and commenting on it in quiet whispers.

Everyone was drawing the same thing: one of two women who were seated on stools that were set on raised platforms at either end of the room. The women looked bored. One of them was reading a paperback novel.

None of that registered with me at first. All I could see were their bodies. They were completely naked, not a stitch of clothes on, not even a pair of socks. They were both mature women, in their late thirties. One was average looking all around, breasts, hips, face, behind. The other model was shorter and plumper. Her breasts were large and sagging, with long dark nipples. Her behind was heavy, with a roll of flab. Her thighs and arms were heavy, too. Neither woman seemed embarrassed about how they looked, or that a bunch of men were staring at them.

The instructor spotted us. He waved his arm, called out "Hi," glanced at his watch, and said, "Fifteen minutes."

Maude led me over to him. "Roy, this is Jessica," she said, making introductions. "She wants to work. Do you have anything for her?"

"As a matter of fact, yes," he said, looking me up and down quickly. There was nothing lascivious in his appraisal; it was more that he was checking to see that I had the right number of arms, legs, hands, feet, and the rest. "Celia called in sick," he explained. He had a pronounced lisp. He gave me another quick evaluation. "Have you modeled before?"

My blush was enough of an answer, but I managed to say, "No."

"It's easy," he told me. "The main requirement is to be still. The artists can't draw you if you're moving around. You pose for half an hour, five-minute break, another half hour, same thing. Can you do that?"

"Of course she can," Maude answered for me. "She's a natural." She gave me another wink, this one of reassurance, I assumed.

"Good," the man said. "Fifteen dollars an hour. We pay in cash at the end of each session. You'll work two hours today. All right?"

"Perfect," Maude chimed in again on my behalf. "Come on," she said to me. "We'll change in the bathroom."

Thus began my so-called career as an artist's model. Initially, posing in the nude was a real challenge for me. Because I hadn't played sports since the tenth grade, I wasn't used to being around naked bodies. While I knew I had some good features—long legs, a firm butt, an athletic figure—I was uncomfortable about my breasts, which are small. Also, to my critical eye, my hips were too wide. The idea of stripping down and standing in front of a dozen strangers, most of them men, was flat-out frightening.

There was another reason I was squeamish about standing naked in front of the world. I had not had sex since that one encounter with James Cleveland, four years earlier. I had immediately moved to a new school and never made any real friends there, never had a boyfriend. I was living with kids now who were so sexually profligate that loose sex turned me off. And most important, no one ever had asked me. Customers at the coffee shop would flirt with me, and I'd flirt back with them, but none of them hit me up for a date. Same at the clubs, where it's hard not to get picked up, if that's what you want. I know I threw off a vibe that said "Keep away." It wasn't the attitude I wanted to present, but I couldn't help it. Self-protection, self-preservation.

No one knew that I wasn't getting it on. Among the people I worked and hung with, not having sex would have been analogous to belonging to some weird religious sect. I would have been an object of pity and ridicule, like a sideshow freak. I bantered and flirted as much as anyone else, and I was able to keep my secret well hidden.

With all that psychological baggage hanging over me, being naked and having sex were intertwined and inseparable. By that reasoning, going out there naked would be like inviting those men to violate me.

"I can't do this," I pleaded with Maude, as soon as we were in the safe confines of the ladies' room. I felt a panic attack coming on.

Maude was already disrobing. Looking over in surprise, she asked, "Why not?"

"Because . . . I never have."

"So what? There's a first time for everything."

I stood there like a mule that wouldn't budge. "You can pose stark naked in front of a bunch of strangers and not be freaked out?" I said.

Maude put her hands on her hips and gave me a stern look. "This isn't *Playboy*, Jessica," she lectured me. "It's serious work. Artists have been drawing naked women from the dawn of time. Go to any museum in the world, you'll see hundreds of naked women. Men, too." She was down to her bra and panties now, removing clothing as she lectured me. "Nobody cares what you look like, how big your tatas are, or how fat your ass is. Christ, look at those women out there. You think any of these guys go home and jack off thinking about them? If anything, it desensitizes you."

She glanced at her watch. "Come on. Take 'em off."

I was trapped. I couldn't leave because we had come here in her car, and I didn't want her to think of me as the prude I secretly was.

"We'll compromise," Maude said. "After this session, if it still bothers you, you don't have to come back, and no one's the wiser."

She was buck naked now. She had a great body, if a bit oversized. Those men out there probably wouldn't go home thinking about sleeping with the models they were drawing, but I couldn't believe some of them wouldn't be turned on by Maude.

Slowly, excruciatingly, I got undressed. My sandals were easy, and my blouse and skirt weren't too painful. I still had my bra and underpants on—more cloth on my body than when I went to the beach.

"Man, do I wish I had your legs," Maude remarked as she looked at them. "I always wanted long legs. Not short, stubby ones like these." She extended a leg and pointed her foot in a classic cheesecake pose. "I'd give anything to have those legs."

"Yours are very nice," I told her. Truthfully, they were a bit on the short side compared to her torso, but they were nicely shaped, with large, firm calf muscles. I figured she was either a dancer or exercised a lot.

"Fine, whatever," she conceded. "Come on. Time's a-wasting."

I closed my eyes, took a deep breath, and shed my remaining garments. Maude grabbed a couple of well-worn hospital-style robes that were hanging from hooks on the wall. We put them on, and like a child following her mother into the pool, I let her lead me out.

After all the mental torture I had put myself through, the actual posing was a letdown. I could have been wearing a long winter coat and earmuffs for all the prurient looks directed at me. Roy, the teacher Maude had introduced me to, showed me how to pose in a way that was good for the artists to draw. He also showed me how to find a comfortable position that I could maintain without cramping or tightening up.

The process, once I got over my shyness, was boring, but the two hours passed quickly. The next pair of models (one a man in his sixties) relieved us, we changed into our street clothes, and Roy handed me thirty dollars in tens.

"We can use you three times a week, if that works for you," he told me.

"Sure," I agreed immediately. Ninety dollars a week, tax-free, for sitting on my butt? Of course I was going to do it.

Maude drove me home. On the way, we stopped at the Dresden Room on Vermont for a celebratory drink, two mai tais apiece. They packed a real wallop. I wanted to treat her, but she wouldn't let me, she insisted on going Dutch.

"Save as much as you can," she advised me. "You never know when you're going to need it."

That turned out to be some of the best advice I've ever gotten.

For the next year, I waitressed and modeled. I was making enough money that I could move out of the stoner boarding house and get a room of my own, an illegal studio over a garage in Miracle Mile, near the Los Angeles County Museum of Art. I also bought my first car, a five-year-old Honda Accord sedan, which I accessorized with love beads and other hanging doodads. I was feeling very grown up and self-sufficient.

I turned twenty on a Tuesday. I wasn't working that day, either at the coffee shop or the Art School. I had no special plans for celebration. As far as I was concerned, it was just another day. I took a leisurely shower, shaved my legs and underarms, washed my hair, touched up my pedicure, and put on shorts, a tank top, beach flops.

I had just finished getting dressed when the phone rang. It was

Aunt Jill calling to wish her special niece a happy birthday. We weren't in contact very much anymore, and it felt good to hear from her, to know she was still thinking about me. She asked how I was doing and I told her great, and asked about her, and she said she was doing well, too. It was awkward talking to Jill, because we didn't have much to say to each other, but the feeling of being loved was there, and that's what counted.

Before we hung up she encouraged me to have a wonderful day and do something special for myself, and I promised her I would, although I didn't know what that would be. I still didn't have a boyfriend, and I didn't want to be with Maude or any of the other women I worked with. None of them knew it was my birthday, which was deliberate. I still kept to myself. It was safer that way.

My mother didn't call. I didn't expect her to. I hadn't heard from her in more than four years.

I walked to The Egg and The Eye on Wilshire and had a caviar omelet, which I washed down with two cups of coffee sweetened with real cream. I felt decadent and pleasurably guilty.

It was a beautiful day, much too nice to be inside, so I decided to go to Venice Beach. Not to swim—the water would be too cold that early in the season. I'd sit on the sand, read a book, work on my tan, check out the hard-body weight lifters. It was my birthday. If I wanted to indulge myself by doing nothing, I was allowed.

I threw my beach paraphernalia into my jazzy little Honda and headed west on Pico Boulevard. The morning rush hour was over, so the traffic was light, by L.A. standards. I cruised through West Hollywood, Beverly Hills, past Fox Studios, Westwood. KRTH was playing the Beach Boys' "Surfin' USA." Everything about my life, except for sex and drugs, was Southern California to the max.

The low-slung campus of Santa Monica City College came into view as I got to Twentieth Street. Groups of kids were wandering around. I stared at them as I waited for the light to change.

What would it be like to go to college, I wondered? I was by now a seasoned working woman, with no thought in my head of furthering my education, but something about how these students looked, on their way to class or the bookstore or wherever college kids went, gave me pause. They looked like they knew where they were going.

As the light turned from red to green a car half a block ahead of me pulled out of a parking space. Why I took that spot, instead of continuing on my way, was one of those random decisions that changes your life forever. Seeing those kids triggered something inside me. I didn't know then what that was, but I went with my spur-of-the-moment impulse. I maneuvered my car into the opening, dropped a quarter in the meter, and wandered onto the campus.

The first thing I noticed was that almost everyone looked like me. Not physically, of course, but age-wise. The people I rubbed elbows with in my daily life were all older than I was, so that without realizing it, I thought of myself as older than my actual age; I was biologically twenty (barely), but I was living and acting as if I were twenty-five.

My teen years had been terrible. Basically, they hadn't existed. Now it struck me that I was giving up my young adulthood as well. All of a sudden I felt sorry for myself, for the young girl who never was.

It was my birthday. I was supposed to have a happy, carefree day. I spun on my heel and headed back to my car. I didn't belong here.

"Jessica? Jessica Thompson?"

A girl's voice, tentative, uncertain. I turned around to see who was calling my name.

The girl was my age. Shorter—most women are—and cute rather than pretty. Red hair, face full of freckles, dressed casually. She was staring into my face as if she were seeing a ghost.

"My God!" she exclaimed. She looked shocked. "It is you." There was a pause. "Isn't it?"

I stared back at her. She looked vaguely familiar, but I couldn't place her face. "Yes, I'm Jessica," I said, feeling weirded out by her behavior. "Who are you?"

"Cassie Middleton," she told me. She kept staring at me like I wasn't real somehow. "We were in the same grade at SaMo."

Santa Monica High School. Where I had been a student until I was shot and moved out of my mother's house.

"English, tenth grade," she further reminded me. "Mr. Cohen."

I still didn't remember her, but I faked that I did, because I didn't want to hurt her feelings. "Oh, right. It's good to see you again, Cassie. How are you?"

"I'm fine. But . . ." She shook her head as if she didn't believe what she was looking at.

"But what?"

"I thought you were dead. We all did."

I almost choked. *"What?"*

"We heard you were shot, and you never came back to school . . . maybe a teacher said something . . ." She trailed off again.

Oh, my God! I thought to myself. Oh, my God!

"I *was* shot," I confirmed, "but . . ." I spread my arms high and wide, like Moses parting the Red Sea. "I'm definitely not dead." I dropped my arms. "I transferred to another school. It seemed like a good move at the time."

I didn't tell her about the Sturm und Drang with my mother. I didn't like to talk or think about that, and it was none of her business, anyway. "I'm alive and well," I said. "As you can see with your own eyes."

She looked as if she was going to cry. "That is so fantastic!" she enthused. "Everyone is going to be freaked when I tell them."

I didn't know who everyone was, but the idea that there were kids who had been sorry about my demise gave me a good feeling.

"So, are you a student here?" she asked me. "I haven't noticed you before."

"No," I said.

And then the lies started. Why, I don't know. Wanting to belong, trying to recapture some of my lost years. Maybe some day, if I can ever afford it, I'll go into analysis and figure it out. "But I'm going to enroll." The lies rolled off my tongue like water flowing downstream. "For the next session. That's why I'm here."

Part of me was saying, Shut up, you fool, and another part was saying, *Yes!*

"Great!" Cassie gushed. "Where are you transferring from?"

Once you start that snowball tumbling, you can't stop it. "Nowhere. I've been traveling," I improvised. "Getting life experience." That part was true. The rest, of course, wasn't.

"Wow!" She exclaimed. Obviously, she was one of those people who gets excited about everything. Cutting her toenails would be a rapturous experience. "Like where?"

"Here and there. Europe. Australia. You know."

"God, that's so great!" she enthused. "I've never been out of California, except to Mexico. And Oregon. Well, Arizona," she kept amending. "But, Europe! That is so cool."

Me, neither, I didn't say. I had been to Mexico, if you count Rosarito Beach, which is basically an extension of Southern California. But that was it.

"So, like, are you going to sign up for classes?"

"Yeah, I am. Can you tell me where you do that?"

"I'll walk you over," she volunteered. "I have time."

We walked across the quad. "Jessica Thompson," Cassie said again. She kept glancing over at me, as if to make sure I was actual flesh and blood. "Unbelievable."

My feeling exactly, I thought.

The summer quarter was starting in two weeks. I signed up for three classes: Introduction to Biology, Spanish I, and Twentieth-century American Fiction. I wanted to take more, but three classes was the limit for first-time enrollees. I whipped my checkbook out of my purse and paid my fees, on the spot. I was now an official college student, community college division.

To this day, I don't know the specific reason that prompted my detour. Destiny, fate, karma, all or none of the above. But whatever it was, that decision changed my life. Within two weeks, I had quit my waitressing job and plunged into college life. It was a tough transition—I hadn't been in school for two years, so I had forgotten how to study, and losing my main source of income forced me to scramble to fill the financial void. During the next six years, which is how long it took me to amass the necessary credits at Santa Monica Community College to transfer to UCLA, then finish my bachelor's degree there, I was a model (which I could keep doing because the hours were flexible), a file clerk, janitor, temp secretary, dog walker and groomer, babysitter for faculty members, and any other odd job I could fit into my schedule.

Between working, going to school, and studying, I had almost no social life, but I didn't mind. I had a future. What it was going to be, exactly, I didn't know, but I wasn't going to be a waitress or some other dead-end worker for the rest of my life.

Despite having almost no free time, I did manage to get laid. The first time, with an instructor from an ethics class, wasn't anything special, but I felt like I was shedding a giant albatross. After that, I slept with whomever I found attractive. I wasn't promiscuous—I was never with more than one man at a time—but none of my encounters were serious love affairs. I took the proper precautions, rode the particular relationship until it ran its course, and moved on, like the other young women I befriended along the way.

In that critical respect, I was no different from other young people my age. I wasn't an outcast anymore.

My decision to apply to law school came as a fluke as well. I was going to college around the clock, including in the summer. My hectic, irregular schedule forced me to work nights, weekends, whenever I could squeeze in a few hours. One of my jobs, which I had the summer before I graduated, was at a Century City law firm. I worked Saturdays, Sundays, even holidays on occasion, filing, running errands, whatever they asked me to do, including mundane stuff like picking up dry cleaning. The work was boring and numbing, but they paid well, thirty dollars an hour. They had to, to get drones like me to give up their weekends. They were awash in money, so they could well afford it.

This particular Sunday night I worked until almost nine o'clock, organizing files for a lawyer who was about to start a major class-action case. He was in his thirties, attractive, self-assured. A rising star, he had recently made partner. When we were finally finished, he asked if he could buy me dinner, as compensation for keeping me so late.

He was single; I knew that much about him. I didn't think he was putting the make on me. My assumption was that he didn't want to eat alone, and I was presentable and handy. I was twenty-five years old. I could take care of myself. I said yes, that was thoughtful of him.

He took me to Michael's, a famous restaurant on Third Street in Santa Monica, in his BMW M5, a rocket ship on wheels. We sat on the terrace under the tent and ate and drank like potentates. Warren Beatty and Annette Bening were at the table next to ours. I managed not to gawk. I don't remember most of the specifics of the meal, but I clearly remember that we drank Château Latour with our entrées. The bill, with tip, came to over a thousand dollars. He dropped his credit card on the check without batting an eye.

A nightcap at his place? Why not? I wasn't drunk, but I was comfortably mellow, and pliant. He lived nearby, in a penthouse apartment on Ocean Avenue that was perfectly decorated and included some killer works of art. After five years of modeling, I had learned enough about art to know what was good. And the views were fantastic. Even though it was dark out, I could see the lights of Catalina Island, twenty-six miles across the sea.

We drank some cognac, started necking, got all hot and bothered, and fumbled our way into his bedroom. He was a good lover. For the first time in my life, I had an orgasm that I didn't induce myself.

We got dressed, made out some more, and then it was time for me to leave. My car was in the garage at his office. He offered to drive me back, but I declined. I didn't want to drive, I was too out of it. I would cab it to my house, then take another taxi in the morning to retrieve my Honda.

Since I was half in my cups, my normal discretion was out of order, so as I looked around his impressive pad one last time, I couldn't help asking him how much the rent for a place like this was. He laughed at my audacity, and told me he owned it. Then he told me how much it had cost.

I was dizzy, and that put me over the edge. I had to sit down. He got me a glass of water and held my hand while I drank it, so it wouldn't spill. Looking up at him, I asked, "How much money do you make, Mark?" His name was Mark Levinson.

"A million a year."

It was as if I were back in third grade. "Really?"

"Yes." He smiled. "That sounds like a lot of money, doesn't it."

"Well, yeah," I said. With all my different crummy jobs, I was making less than twenty thousand dollars a year, before taxes. "From being a lawyer?" I asked. I couldn't believe it.

"Some of my partners make more."

I shook my head in disbelief. "Jesus. I should become a lawyer," I said.

He sat down next to me. "That's a very good idea, Jessica," he said. He wasn't jerking me around; he was serious. "You're smart. You'd make a good one."

"You think?"

"I'm sure of it."

And that is why I went to law school: to get rich. I stayed at UCLA. I got into Stanford and USC, but UCLA, being a public university, was less expensive, and being a poor girl, I was going to have to max out on student loans.

I knew early on that I didn't want to practice Mark's kind of law. Too boring. I liked the drama of the courtroom. I could still live large—defense lawyers make a lot of money, too. After graduating and taking the bar exam, I would work in the Public Defender's office or the District Attorney's office for a couple of years to get trial experience, then I would join a big firm that did criminal law, or find a couple of like-minded partners and set up our own shop.

Two days before I was scheduled to take my law exams, I got a call from Jill. I hadn't heard from her in almost a year, and as soon as I heard her voice, I felt guilty. But before I could apologize for being a shitty, inattentive niece, she threw her thunderbolt.

"Your mother is at Cedars," she informed me. "Cancer. It's terminal. She's not going to last more than a few more days. It could be sooner."

I was almost twenty-nine years old. I hadn't had any contact with my mother for more than fourteen years.

"Why didn't anyone tell me?" I upbraided her unpleasantly.

Jill charitably ignored my rudeness. "I wanted to," she answered, "but your mother insisted that I shouldn't bother you. She's been carrying that guilt inside for all these years. She knew that if you did come, it would be out of obligation, not love."

Jill was right. But I was still in shock. "Then why are you calling me now?"

"Because she is your mother, your only living blood relative, and she is dying."

"I'm going to see her," I said without thinking.

"Good." From the tone of Jill's voice I knew that was the only answer she would accept from me. "Although she probably won't know you're there. She's heavily sedated. I'm at the hospital now. How soon can you get here?"

My mother had shriveled up like a doll's face carved from an apple. She was tiny in her hospital bed, with tubes like malignant snakes from the head of Medusa coming out of every orifice. She was out cold. The machines at her bedside graphed barely rippling slow lines.

Jill greeted me with a suffocating hug. She had the dry-eyed look of someone who was all cried out. "I'm glad you came." She took my hand. "As much for you as her." She gave me a kiss on the cheek. "I'll leave you alone with her."

The door closed behind her as I sat in the chair at my mother's bedside. "I'm here," I whispered. I didn't want to wake her. I didn't want to have to look into her eyes.

I had gotten to the hospital at four in the afternoon. Jill was with me when my mother died at one-thirty-six the following morning. We were the only visitors Claire Thompson had the entire time she was there.

A day later, I took the law exams. They were a piece of cake, I knew I had aced them before I turned in my book. I guess I did well because I was still numb, so I didn't give a damn. My attitude going in was that if I passed, great. If not, I'd take them again.

The following day my mother was cremated, and a month later I went to her lawyer's office in Santa Monica for the formal reading of her will. As had been the case at the hospital, Jill and I were the only ones present, because we were the only people my mother had named as beneficiaries. Claire Thompson's life hadn't merely been narrow, she had lived her final years in an emotional straitjacket.

My mother had $7,500 in her bank account. No stocks or bonds. Everything else she owned—her clothes, cheap jewelry, books, records, furniture, the debris of a small life—was in the house. Which she owned outright, she had paid the mortgage off three years earlier.

Jill and I split the cash. Jill got the clothing, most of which she would donate to Goodwill, the cheap trinkets, the movable things. I got the other half of the $7,500 and the house.

I very much did not want to move back into that house. Too many ghosts. I compromised with myself: I would move back in for just the length of time it took to get a job and get settled. Then I would leave. I could have used my share of the money my mother had left me to take a better apartment, but I wanted a nest egg. That was my only reason, or so I thought at the time.

When I started working for the Public Defender's office, I set myself a timetable: two years maximum, then out. I remembered Mark Levinson's apartment, and all the goodies in it. I wanted that for myself. But as I had learned a long time before, the hard way, life is messy and unpredictable. To my surprise, I love my job. Unlike a traditional practice, it is action all the time, and I make a difference. The people I represent really need me. So here I am, six years later, and I haven't left. I still might. But for the foreseeable future, this is where I am. Where I want to be.

That decision, to stay in the public sector, is why I'm still living in my mother's house. My monthly nut, which is the property taxes prorated and the utilities, comes to less than twelve hundred dollars a month. People living on welfare spend more than that.

The ghosts are still with me. They always will be. I've learned to manage them. I've also learned that it isn't this physical house they live in. They live inside of me; so wherever I move to, I'll still have them.

I own a house, I have a job I care about, I'm in a good relationship. Things could be worse. For most of my life, they have been.

NINE

I HAVE A LOT OF prep work to do for tomorrow and I want to get a good night's sleep, so I cut my run short, but I increase my speed, really pushing myself. When I get back to the house, I'm panting for breath and my legs are tight. I stretch, take a shower, pop a Lean Cuisine into the microwave, and lay out on the kitchen table my material for Reggie's examination.

The telephone rings. It isn't Jeremy; he knows not to call tonight. I'm tempted to let the service get it, but it might be Lorraine Tong calling to offer Reggie a last-minute reprieve.

"This is Jessica," I say into the receiver.

"I'm glad I reached you," Amanda Burgess announces. She sounds a bit, I don't know, impatient? My number's unlisted, and I don't recall giving it to her, but for a woman with her connections, getting an unlisted number wouldn't be hard.

"I phoned earlier, but I didn't want to leave a message, in case you don't always check them," she informs me.

"I do. So in the future, you can." I look at the pile of papers on my table, which seems to be growing like mushrooms around a rock. "What can I do for you, Ms . . ." I catch myself. "Amanda."

"I want to talk to you about Roberto Salazar."

Shit. Not now. "What about?" I ask, trying not to sound curt.

"His case, of course." She sounds surprised that I haven't read her mind. "That man who gave him the televisions is still missing. The police procedures that led to his arrest. Shouldn't you . . ."

I need to stop her before she builds up a head of steam. "We'll deal with all of that in due course," I say, cutting her off in mid-sentence. "But I can't discuss it with you now. I'm in the middle of a trial and I'm putting my main witness on the stand tomorrow morning. I still have hours of preparation to do tonight. I'll call you in a few days, when this trial is over, and we can discuss everything in detail."

Can you feel a chill wind over a telephone line? "I hope you are taking Roberto's situation seriously," she says, after too long a silence from her end.

"Of course I am," I reply, trying not to reveal my annoyance. "I take all my clients' cases seriously."

Another uncomfortable silence. Is she playing games with my head? "I'm sure you do. Good night, then. I'm sorry to have bothered you."

Her hanging up on me sounds like a church bell ringing in *Day of the Dead.* "You're welcome," I say to the air, as I drop my phone back into its cradle.

TEN

REGGIE MORTON IS AN unmitigated disaster on the stand. All the prep, all the coaching, goes right out the window. He can't give a simple yes or no answer, he has to explain everything, at length. And not only explain, but complain. And preach. And rail. And admonish. And most damaging, everything that comes out of his mouth is a lie, which everyone—judge, jury, and prosecutor—sees through. He's like a boxer who, knowing he's hopelessly behind on points, tries to knock his opponent out in the last round with one wild haymaker. But all he's connecting with is air.

I steal a glance at Lorraine, who's laughing in my face, not even doing me the courtesy of covering her mouth. The jurors are slack-jawed at this freak show I'm so not orchestrating.

I don't mind losing a case; most of my clients go to jail. But I hate being humiliated. "I would like a five-minute recess," I ask the judge abruptly, cutting Reggie off in middeclaration.

"Granted." Judge Hodgkins's gavel resounds like a rifle shot in the high-ceilinged courtroom. "Attorneys in my chambers."

He storms out of the room. As I'm following Lorraine out, Reggie rises up in the witness chair. "What's going on?" he asks me, his face a rictus of panic.

I point a threatening finger at him like a schoolmarm facing down the class bully. "Sit," I hiss at him. "Don't move. Not one muscle."

"Exactly what are you doing, Ms. Thompson?" Hodgkins asks me in an angry rasp as he drops into his desk chair, which bounces under his weight. "Your client's destroying himself, not that he has much left to destroy. Can't you control him?"

I just want this to be over. "Apparently not." I remain standing; sitting would be presumptuous. "This is not what I expected, believe me."

"I hope you're not angling for a mistrial," Hodgkins warns me. "Don't think you can play me for a sucker."

"I'm not, Your Honor," I promise him in alarm. That's all I need: to be on the wrong side of a judge whose courtroom I'm in every week. "I have no intention of doing that."

"I can't allow this man to continue to sabotage himself like this. It's inhumane, and mocks the system." He cracks his gnarled knuckles in frustration. "What are we going to do about this, Counselor?" he queries impatiently. He is really pissed off at Reggie, and he's taking his anger out on me. I'm Reggie's lawyer; I deserve it.

I'm totally abashed. Not for Reggie—that cretin can hang from the gallows as far as I'm concerned. My embarrassment is for me, for my pride as a professional. "I'll wrap it up fast, Your Honor," I promise.

"That's the first intelligent statement I've heard this morning." He hoists his considerable bulk out of his chair. "Let's get this over with."

As we walk back into the courtroom, Lorraine pipes up. "The people will waive cross-examination," she offers, as if she's compromising for the sake of justice. She knows she won't need to. The fat lady has sung, loud and clear.

Reggie Morton is crazy, but he isn't stupid. He knows he's down the tubes. But he still doesn't realize it's his fault. He broke the law, he turned down a generous offer from the District Attorney's office, and finally, despite all our preparation, he made a fool of himself on the stand. He was going to be found guilty—that was never in question—but by being such a public buffoon, he lost any chance of sympathy from the jury.

After we resume, I wrap up my questioning in less than ten minutes. True to her word, Lorraine doesn't question him. I have no other witnesses, so by lunchtime, closing statements have been given, Judge Hodgkins has charged the jury, and after lunch they go into deliberation.

At four-fifteen in the afternoon, while I'm at my desk trying to make a dent on my backlog, the phone call comes that the jury has arrived at a verdict. Now I'm back in the courtroom. My client is sitting next to me. He's a bundle of twitches: knees dancing, shoulders rolling, fingers tapping.

"This is good, ain't it?" he whispers as we wait for the jurors to be brought in. "Quick verdict usually means not guilty, don't it?" He's still hoping against hope.

"Sometimes," I whisper back. Actually, the reverse is true, but I'm not going to tell him that now. He's too fragile. "No matter what, keep your feelings to yourself. This judge doesn't like shows of emotion." I should tell him it could affect the length of his sentence, but I don't have the heart.

"That's the problem with this damn system," he wails. "They don't want you to be human."

Those are the first rational words I've heard from him in all the time we've been together. Too bad they came so late.

Judge Hodgkins emerges from his chambers and nods to the bailiff to bring the jury in. They enter single file, like circus elephants entering the ring trunk to tail. None of them make eye contact with Reggie. Hodgkins asks them if they've reached a verdict.

"We have, Your Honor," the foreman, a black retired postal worker, calls out as he stands up. He hands the slip of paper to the clerk, who passes it to the judge. Hodgkins glances at it, hands it back. There's no surprise on his face.

"The defendant will rise."

Reggie and I stand. He's shaking. "No matter what, stay cool," I remind him again.

"Read your verdict, please," Hodgkins instructs the foreman, who says the seven words no defense lawyer wants to hear: "We find the defendant guilty as charged."

Everything moves fast now, herky-jerky, like a speeded-up film projector. Hodgkins thanks the jury for their service and dismisses them. He announces he'll formally sentence Reggie the day after tomorrow. He makes a note on his calendar and brings his gavel down. "Court is adjourned," he states, as he gets up and disappears through the back door.

I turn to offer Reggie some hollow words of encouragement. He's slumped over, crying. I keep my mouth shut.

The court deputy takes Reggie by the elbow and pulls him to his feet. As the poor sap is being led out, he turns to me.

"Would it have killed you to wear a skirt?"

ELEVEN

A S PREDICTED, THE POLICE were flooded with phone calls from hundreds of nutcases, along with as many from earnest but misguided do-gooders, each of whom claimed to have information that would lead to the arrest of the Full Moon Killer, or a theory that would bring about the same result. The scam artists threw in their ante, too. The money was there, someone is going to get it, why not me? As is always the case in this kind of overheated and frantic situation, all the so-called leads turned out to be bogus, but they all had to be checked out. Luis Cordova, who was running the operation, personally read the transcripts of every conversation between his detectives and the callers, no matter how preposterous. If there was a needle buried in that haystack, he didn't want to miss it.

A week went by. Nothing tangible emerged.

This latest caller seems saner than most; he is elderly, a retired accountant. Accountants don't believe in fairy tales, and they're pretty good about knowing what's real and what's bullshit, because their clients try to blur the line; it's human nature. So when this man tells one of Cordova's detectives that he had seen something the night of the latest killing that might be a clue, he isn't dismissed out of hand. He is picked up at his home and driven down to Parker Center, where he is escorted into Cordova's office so the task force leader can hear the story firsthand.

Cordova's small office is strictly functional. Desk, chairs, filing cabinets, shelves overflowing with files and directives. Nothing on the walls, no family photos on the desk, no plants, no personal momentos. There is a window to the outside world, but the blinds are kept closed. The window looking out to the bullpen also has blinds, but they are open so Cordova can maintain visual contact with his troops, and they with him. Except when he is having a private interview, the door is open as well; there are no secrets in Cordova's squad, no hidden agendas. Cordova hates secrets. That's how cops get into trouble, by not being transparent. Secrecy leads to temptation, which leads to crossing the line. A rogue cop is worse than a civilian criminal, because upholding and enforcing the law is his job, what he is paid to do. Cordova is outspoken in his contempt and hatred for cops who go over to the dark side. They violate a sacred trust.

Which is not the same thing as using your instincts, even if that means technically violating a statute, like going into a house where someone's life might be in danger without waiting for a proper warrant, or searching a suspicious car for drugs or weapons. A cop without good instincts is worthless; worse, he's dangerous, not only to himself and his brothers and sisters on the force, but to all of society.

Luis Cordova has great instincts. Steve Lopez of the *L.A. Times,* a crusading columnist who doesn't lob softballs, once wrote a glowing story about Cordova's gift for the instinctive. Those instincts, honed and nurtured over two decades as carefully as a botanist grows and nurtures a rare orchid, were the reason he was chosen to run this task force. Those same instincts tell him, within a minute after meeting this possible witness, that this nice old man might be for real.

"Can I get you anything?" he asks solicitously. "Water, coffee, a soda? Please, sit down."

The witness, whose name is Aaron Lazarus, lowers himself into one of the battered wooden chairs that face Cordova's desk. Although he is retired, he is dressed smartly, including a tie, as if for work. "No, thank you," he answers. "I'm not thirsty."

Cordova sits opposite him. He shows his digital recorder to Lazarus. "Do you mind?" he asks.

"Not at all. Accuracy is important."

Cordova smiles to himself as he turns on the recorder. Accountants, unless they're crooks, deal with facts. This man isn't a crook, and he's too old to be looking for his fifteen minutes of fame. He's simply a good citizen trying to do his civic duty. The odds are slim to none that, like all the other leads they've been chasing, nothing will come of this, but nice Mr. Lazarus isn't a bullshitter. Cordova's instincts tell him so.

Cordova recites his name, the time, date, and location of the interview into the recorder. "Please state your name for the record, please," he instructs Lazarus, which Lazarus does, slowly and clearly, spelling out his last name letter by letter.

The formalities out of the way, Cordova asks, "What do you think you know that can help us, Mr. Lazarus? Try to be as complete and precise as possible." He hopes this witness's statement will flow easily, without much prompting. When you have to keep suggesting, you're on a dead-end road.

The elderly accountant tells his story straightforwardly, without embellishment. On the night the latest victim was murdered, he had been out walking his dog. After she did her business, and they were heading back to his house, a truck came around the corner and drove down the street, in the opposite direction from where he was headed. The motion of the truck had caught his eye, and for a second he instinctively turned and watched it. That's when he saw the woman. She was walking on the sidewalk, in the same direction the truck was heading.

Cordova listens carefully. The other detective in the room, the one who brought Lazarus down here, stands in the corner, also listening. Cordova has a pad and pen in front of him, but he hasn't made any notes yet.

Lazarus continues. "The truck pulled over to the curb."

Cordova perks up. "Where?" he asks. "Which side of the street?"

"At the far end of the block," Lazarus replies. "On the same side of the street the woman was walking on."

Cordova and the other detective exchange a look. Maybe this won't go anywhere, but it's better than nothing. "Go ahead," he tells Lazarus. "I didn't mean to interrupt you," he adds deferentially. "Just go on as you were. So then . . . ?

Lazarus nods pleasantly. He appreciates Cordova's politeness. Most people are afraid of the police, but they do their best.

"A man got out of the truck," he continues.

Cordova can't help but interject. "Was he looking at the woman?"

"I don't think so," Lazarus answers. "At least, not at first." He hesitates momentarily. "You have to understand," he says, sounding a bit sheepish. "I was at the other end of the block, so I can't say for sure, but it appeared that he was looking at his truck. Like he thought he had a flat tire."

"Okay," Cordova says, meaning, go on.

"The woman drew abreast of him, and stopped."

That catches Cordova by surprise. He looks to the other detective, whose own brow is furrowed. "Stopped?" Cordova asks. "When she reached this man?"

"Yes."

"Was there any force involved? That you could see?"

Lazarus shakes his head. "Not at all. Again, I was on the other end of the block, but it appeared to me that she knew him."

An involuntarily outburst: "She knew him?"

The old accountant withdraws his declaration, partially. "Perhaps she didn't know him," he amends. "Perhaps she was asking him a question, or replying to one of his." He smiles as a thought suddenly occurs. "Maybe he was saying something about his truck, or asking her a question about it. Does this tire seem flat to you? That sort of thing."

"But you don't know."

"Oh, no. I was all the way at the other end of the block." There is another slight hesitation. "I don't think either of them saw me," he says. "There's only one streetlight on the block, and it's at the other end from where I was."

"Near where they were?" Cordova asks, for certainty. He starts writing notes on his pad.

"Yes." Lazarus watches Cordova's penmanship. "Do you want me to wait while you . . ."

Cordova shakes his head. "Keep going." He looks up and gives Lazarus a reassuring smile. "I can write and listen at the same time."

"That's handy in your line of work, I'm sure," Lazarus says admiringly. "Well, there wasn't much after that."

"What did the driver do then?"

"I don't know. I was right outside my house. I stood there for perhaps a second or two more, and then I went inside."

"And the driver and woman were still there?"

"They were when I went inside, yes," Lazarus replies.

"And you don't think they saw you," Cordova asks again.

"I don't think so. Like I said, my end of the block was in darkness, and my dog was quiet." With a touch of embarrassment, he adds, "I was standing behind a tree, a bit."

So they couldn't see you watching them, Cordova thinks. This nice man didn't want to admit he was peeping at them. The detective's thought is not judgmental. He knows from long experience that everyone's a voyeur, even the local pastor. It's the getting caught that's mortifying.

But does this mean anything? A driver out at night, a woman out at night. There would have been dozens of both. "How late was this, do you recall?"

This answer is firm. "After eleven-thirty. Mollie and I—Mollie's my dog—we took our constitutional after the eleven o'clock news was over."

That narrows down the field. There wouldn't be that many people out that late at night, certainly not a woman alone on foot. Cordova makes a note to canvass the area to see if anyone else might have seen the victim that night, after eleven. They've already done that, but they'll do it again, this time more thoroughly.

He puts his pencil aside and retrieves the murder book that is sitting in his top desk drawer and opens it to the relevant page. "Did you by any chance notice what the woman was wearing?" he asks. "Was there enough light to see that?"

Lazarus's head bobs up and down, a cork on a pipe cleaner. "Oh, yes." He squints in recollection. "A sweatshirt and sweatpants. Light blue." He smiles that he still has excellent memory at his age. "And she had these funny clog-type thingies on, like my wife wears for gardening. Crocs, they're called."

Cordova drops his pen on his desk and leans back. This old man has the attire pegged, even down to her shoes. This wasn't public knowledge; the department had kept that a secret, to smoke out impostors. This guy is the real deal—the first one.

"All right," he says, keeping his emotions in check. He has a good poker face, which comes in handy at times like this. "What about the man? The driver?"

"His clothes were dark," Lazarus says, not as certain. "They didn't stand out like hers."

Meaning you were watching her more than you were watching him. An attractive young woman—that's what catches a man's eye, all the way to the grave, apparently.

"Work clothes," Lazarus continues. "You know, like maybe a mechanic?"

Dark work clothes. Another line of notes. The other detective is doing the same with his notepad. "Did you get a good look at him as well?" Cordova prompts.

"No," Lazarus admits. "He was wearing a hat, which covered most of his face. A baseball hat," he offers meagerly.

"Any insignia you could identify?"

"A Dodgers hat?" the man ventures. "I'm not sure."

Half the male population in Los Angeles wears Dodgers caps. Not much help there. "Did you see his face at all?"

The old accountant shakes his head sadly. "I couldn't identify him, if that's what you mean," he says. "He was dark skinned,"
he offers.

"Black? I mean African American?" Cordova asks, quickly
correcting himself. The walls have ears. Political correctness and
civilian commissions have been ruining the department for more
than a decade.

Lazarus shakes his head. "Not that dark. Like you."

"Latino."

This time, a nod. "Spanish, yes. Maybe Middle Eastern. But
in Los Angeles, you're probably right."

A Latino in work clothes in Santa Monica near midnight.
Something else to check on.

One more thing to find out. Cordova mentally crossed his fingers. "This man's truck. Did you get a license plate?"

"No."

That was too much to hope for. Lazarus hadn't been suspicious. His attention was based on curiosity, with a little checking
out of tits and ass. He must be a liberal, Cordova thinks. A con-
servative seeing a Latino man around there at that time of night
would have called the police. "Make?" he asks. "Model? Color?
Style?"

"I don't know the make," Lazarus answers. He's fumbling now,
on shaky ground. This cop isn't as much of a friend as he initially
thought. "Japanese, I think. It was a pickup truck—that I do know.
Small. Dark color."

Not as much as Cordova would like, but better than nothing—
a Mexican in work clothes driving a small, dark-colored pickup
truck. There's probably no more than half a million men in L.A.
who fit that description. Still, it's more information to throw into
the neighborhood canvass, which he will initiate first thing tomorrow.

"Anything else, Mr. Lazarus?" he asks, wrapping it up as he
stands. The older man gets up more slowly; it's an effort to get
out of the chair. Cordova hands Lazarus his card. "My office and

my cell," he explains, pointing out the numbers. "If you can think of anything else, call me, twenty-four/seven, late or early, I'll be there." He extends his hand, and adds a smile to it. "We appreciate your help, sir. I wish there were more people out there like you," he says, meaning it.

Lazarus smiles back, almost shyly, from the praise. This man is okay, really, he has a hard job to do. "I wish I could tell you more," he tells Cordova, looking from him to the other detective. "I wish I had paid more attention."

"You've done fine," Cordova says. "And again, if you do remember anything, even if you think it isn't important, don't hesitate to call." He nods to the other detective. "You'll see that Mr. Lazarus gets a ride home?"

"Right away."

Lazarus leaves with his escort. Cordova watches until they're in the elevator. Then he picks up the phone.

TWELVE

MY MOTHER DIDN'T KNOW squat about guns, but I do. I own one, and it's not some pissant little peashooter like the one she shot me with. My weapon is a SIG Sauer P239 semiautomatic, the .40 S&W model. It's small for a powerful gun, which is why it's a popular weapon for women, because our hands are generally smaller than guys'. Even so, it really packs a wallop—it could stop a bull elephant in its tracks. Not that I'm ever going elephant hunting, or any kind of game hunting. I'm not a hunter; I don't believe in killing animals that have done me no harm.

What I do believe in, and care about deeply, is my safety. I'm a woman who lives alone in a modern city, which means there's a potential for danger in my life. The three women who have been murdered lately, along with the thousands of other victims of violent crime every year in L.A. County, are powerful testament to that.

I have never fired my gun in a real-life situation. I hope I never have to. But if I do, I want to be ready, which is why I go to a firing range out in the West Valley four or five times a year and shoot off a few magazines' worth of rounds. That's where I am now: Annie Oakley in Lucky Brand Jeans, wraparound Ray-Bans, Banana Boat SPF 50 sunblock, and shooter's earmuffs. I am woman, hear my gun roar.

It's hot out here, and bone-dry. The temperature is over a hundred degrees, but the humidity is under 10 percent. When you live

near the ocean and work downtown, it's easy to forget that Southern California is basically a desert. The only reason we're not as
arid as Joshua Tree or Palm Desert is that we have a good water
supply, which we stole from Northern California decades ago. If
you've seen *Chinatown,* you know that story. When every house
in the county, from Long Beach down south to Palmdale in the
north, has a lawn, and many of them, even in tracts, have swimming pools, you live under the delusion that we have an abundance of water. But when you're standing out in the midday sun
and your mouth is as dry as a cotton ball, the fragile reality of our
ecosystem is right there in your face.

My companions on the range today are the usual variety of
men and women you see on any street. They aren't gangbangers,
outlaw bikers, or disenfranchised loners. They are people who
like to shoot guns. They love the power of explosion, the feeling
of lethal heat in their hands. They want to be able to protect themselves, because they know the established forces of law and order
can't do a very good job of it. Some of them, from time to time,
try to right the wrongs that beset modern society, like rude driv-
ers on the freeway, rude civil servants, rude bosses. You worry
about those people, and hope they won't have their hands on their
guns when their minds are clouded with temporary rage.

I finish firing and check my targets. Not bad for someone who
doesn't practice enough. I don't score any bull's-eyes, but with a
weapon that has the stopping power my gun has, you don't have
to hit your target between the eyes. You take a 40-mm hollow
point almost anywhere in your body and you are going down—I
don't care if you're the size of King Kong.

I police my area for the empty shell casings, fold up my targets, put my gun in its case, and lock everything in the trunk of
my car. I wish I lived in a society where I didn't feel I had to have
a gun. But I do. My mind-set is an occupational hazard. At home,
I keep my weapon handy, but I don't think much about it. I hope
I never have to.

Jeremy doesn't know I have a gun. He's against personal

firearms; he's never fired a gun in his life, not even a shotgun at a clay pigeon. He would never stay over in my house if he knew I kept my gun stashed under my mattress springs. He might even break up with me—he's that much against them. If we ever live together, I'll get rid of it, because a relationship has to be a two-way street, particularly about trust. But for now, I am a woman living alone, whose job puts evil in her face every day. So I keep it handy.

The shipping warehouse in San Pedro that had the television sets Roberto Salazar is accused of stealing was broken into between nine and eleven o'clock, the night before he was arrested. The prosecution and I have both stipulated that this information is indisputable. So today is a good day for me, because I have just found out that Roberto has an alibi that will knock out the charge of breaking into the warehouse, which is the most serious one against him. He was holding a youth-group meeting at his church. The meeting didn't end until ten. He could not have left the East Side, driven all the way to San Pedro, and stolen the television sets.

It's an axiom that rules are made to be broken. Usually, I only meet with clients and others involved in their defense in the jail, the courtroom, or my office. But now I am in a coffee shop a few blocks from my office building with two of the parents, both women, who have kids in the program. They are stepping forward to swear that Salazar was with their children that night.

Both women are about Salazar's wife's age. They are friends of hers—they watch one another's kids, cook in one another's kitchens. Neither of them speaks English, and they are intimidated by the surroundings. Every time a sheriff's deputy or city patrolman saunters in from off the street to grab a cup of coffee or snack, they cringe. Even though I have assured them that no one is paying attention to them, they are two Latinas in a sea of brown faces. Fear of *la Migra* is basic in the Latin community, especially for recent arrivals; where they come from, cops are never your friend.

I didn't want to meet with them in my office because I want

to keep this encounter off the record. I don't know if these women are legal in this country or not. I could care less; I don't work for ICE. All I care about is that they tell me the truth. Fortunately (and humanely), the D.A.'s office doesn't care about their status, either. They don't hassle people about that. But these women don't know that, so it took real guts for them to come down here. Guts and love for their minister, who has been wrongly accused of a crime.

Salazar, who brought them to me, hovers nervously as my translator reads their statements back to them in Spanish. Both witnesses agree that everything they said is true, that their testimony was given freely and voluntarily, and they sign the documents. I put them in a manila envelope, seal it, and stuff the envelope in my briefcase. My opponent, Assistant D.A. Dixant, that arrogant asshole, will eventually learn about this, but not yet. For now, the less he knows about my case and my witnesses, the better. I'm not going to show my hand until I absolutely have to.

I can hold back information for a certain amount of time because the rules concerning discovery, particularly witness identification, allow me to. The prosecution has to give me the names and other relevant information about all the witnesses they are going to call at trial. I have to do the same once I decide a witness will be called. That's where I have wiggle room: *once I decide*. Will I use these witnesses? Probably. But until I'm absolutely committed to them, I can withhold their information. There's no reason to show your cards early. Often, once the prosecution gets your witness list, they will send an investigator to interview your witnesses, interview being a politically correct term for hassling them. Sometimes it works; they scare off a witness. So that's another reason to play it slow. The statute requires me to come clean thirty days before the trial starts. But I can also make the argument that I don't know if I'll call a witness until I've heard the prosecution's case at trial. That's kind of slippery, and the judge can rap your knuckles if they think you're bullshitting them, so it's not a ploy to overuse.

I thank Salazar's witnesses for their help and cooperation, and try to reassure them that they are not in danger. I ask them to wait for a moment, and walk Salazar over to an empty table so we can talk without anyone hearing us. It's vital that I preserve attorney-client confidentiality.

"This is going to help," I compliment him. "You did good, bringing them down here. I know they were worried about coming."

"They were pretty worried," he admits, "but I promised them they would be safe."

That's not a promise you should make, I think, but I don't tell him so. "They are safe, at least for now," I say. "But let me ask you this, Roberto. Will they testify for you at your trial?"

He blinks nervously. He hasn't thought that far ahead. "Do they have to?" he asks with anxiety. "Isn't this enough?"

I hate giving bad news, but pussyfooting around doesn't do anyone any good. "No, it isn't." I explain: "If they're not willing to take the witness stand and swear that these statements are true, we can't use them."

His eyes crinkle shut with worry. He sighs, a deep worried breath, opens his eyes, looks at me. "They will testify."

"For sure?"

"Yes."

He's saying that because he has to, but he can't know with certainty that they will. Even if they say they will do it, they may chicken out on the day of reckoning. I've had that happen to me, many times.

"It's on you to make sure of that," I caution him.

We both turn and look at the women. They are huddled together, talking quietly, looking like old photographs of refugees coming off the boat at Ellis Island a century ago. Scared, bewildered, but in some unfathomable way, hopeful.

"They will come," he promises me. "For their children."

I feel a pang of envy. I wish I had friends who have my back the way his friends have his. Except for Jeremy, I can't think of one.

"Is there anything else?" he asks. "I have to bring them back. They are missing work from their jobs."

The women work at motels, as maids. If they don't show up, they don't get paid. They have not only stuck their necks out on the line for him, they've also given up money. They must really believe in this man. Knowing that strengthens my resolve to get him off.

"There is one thing," I say. "Armando. We need to find him."

He shakes his head in anger. "I have been trying. Everyone is looking for him. He has vanished." He stares at me, his face a stone mask. "But he will be found. Unless he is no longer alive."

I react viscerally: that worries me, it sounds so confrontational. "Why do you say that?" I ask him. "Have you heard something about him being dead? Are there other people out there he's screwed over, people who would kill him?"

Salazar puts up a hand like a cop stopping traffic. "No, no," he says quickly. "It is a figure of speech."

I hope that's all it is. "We need to find him," I admonish him. "If you hear anything, be sure to let me know."

He nods. His eyes are hooded. "Of course I will."

As we get up to rejoin his friends, I warn him again: "If you find this Armando dude, call me. Don't take matters into your own hands."

"Don't worry, I won't," he promises me, sounding annoyed that I'm distrustful of him. "I am nonviolent."

A regular Martin Luther King Jr., my client. I need to cut him more slack. He really is a good guy.

I walk him and his friends to the door, but before they leave, I pull him aside again. "One thing I forgot to say," I tell him, lowering my voice so the others don't hear me.

He's anxious to leave. "What?" he asks impatiently.

I stage-whisper: "I don't want to say this, but I have to." I feel as if I'm condescending to him, but this is important. "I know you have to be on the Westside to take care of your clients' lawns and gardens. But I don't want you in that part of town at night."

He gives me a queer look.

"We're going to kick their behinds, and they're not going to like that," I try to explain. "The cops don't like being made to look bad. You getting out on bail like you did is a thumb in their eye. They're going to be looking for an excuse to mess with you, Roberto."

He gives me an understanding look; he knows exactly what I'm talking about. He might be part saint, but his head isn't in the clouds. "Like frame me for something?"

"I'm not saying that. But it will be better if you aren't there to give them any reason to hassle you."

He nods. "I hear you. Stay where I belong."

"Roberto . . ."

"I'm not mad at you, Ms. Thompson," he says. "I'm not mad at anyone. I just wish things were different." He gives me a sad smile. "I'll stay away from there, don't worry. I don't like being on that side of town at night anyway. There's no place to get menudo with your scrambled eggs."

"Good." Thank God he still has a sense of humor.

"You think they'd bust the mayor if they caught him on Barrington Avenue after midnight?" he asks, more serious than playful.

A good question. "If they didn't know who he was, they might."

Dixant calls me, wanting to talk. He's a jerk, but he's no dummy. "I've been authorized to make you a deal," he says. "It's sweet. Better than your boy deserves."

Now we're sitting in the back row of one of the courtrooms on the eleventh floor. It's slow at the moment; there's a lull while the next prisoner is brought up from the jail for a prelim hearing. Not my client, or Dixant's case either, so we have time to palaver.

I can guess where this is going. I sit back, crossing one leg over the other. I'm wearing a skirt today, so he gets a flash of thigh. He pretends he isn't looking, but he can't help himself. "I'm listening," I tell him.

The aging frat boy forces himself to look me in the face. "There's a new syndicate operating down at the harbor. It isn't the usual Mexicans and Colombians, something new. Maybe Chinese, Russian, Arabs." He grimaces. "Homeland Security's a sieve, a joke. Us, the FBI, DEA, ATF, the other alphabet agencies—we're all digging at this. We've come close to breaking through a few times, but so far, no cigar."

"Sounds like exciting work," I say. "Better than beating up on deadbeat dads and flashers."

"For the cops, maybe. I'm a paper pusher. All the exciting stuff happens out in the field."

"And I'm a grade-three public defender, even lower down the totem pole than you. I only know about that stuff from what I see on the news."

"Well, here's a chance to get a taste of the major leagues." He leans in toward me, gives me a friendly smile. For a moment I'm afraid he's going to put a hand on my leg, strictly as a friendly gesture, of course. I manage not to flinch, and he refrains from making actual physical contact. Even a chauvinist like Dixant knows that the most innocent touch could put him in boiling water on sexual harassment charges.

"Your client, Salazar," he says. "We've got him dead to rights; I know that and you know that."

"I don't know that."

"Not the actual theft," he concedes, "but the transport. Come on, Jessica, smell the French roast. He's gonna get convicted."

He called me. Let him do the talking. Now he says, "He's a minnow. We're trolling for whales."

The picture is beginning to come into focus. "What are you offering?" I ask. "What does my client get out of this?"

Dixant smiles. He thinks he's hooked me. Now he begins to

reel me in. "Clean and simple. He gives us some names. Players higher up the food chain. In exchange, we knock everything down to one count of receiving stolen goods. No jail time, minimum probation." He sits back, smiling like the cat that ate the canary. "Win-win, baby. It's a sweet deal."

I shake my head in disagreement. "For you, maybe. Not for us. This man has no record. He'd be tarnished for life. That's not a win for us."

The smile turns. "Jessica . . ."

"And he's already given you a name," I remind him. "Armando Gonzalez. It's in the filing, you've seen it."

"That's not a name that means anything to us."

We are at an impasse. "Sorry. It's the only one we have."

At the front of the courtroom, a fresh prisoner has been brought in and seated at the defense table. He's a young black man, big and mean-looking, shackled hand and foot, a bona fide menace to society. This prisoner has a private lawyer, Glen Adkins. Glen is a sharp attorney; he bills out at four hundred dollars an hour, which means that this defendant has money, from drugs or something else that isn't legal, unless he's an entertainer, in which case he wouldn't be in jailhouse clothes. Whoever he is, he'll be able to make his bail, even if it's set for a million dollars. There's something intrinsically wrong in a world when a small-time minister can't make the most meager bail payment, but a thug like this one can buy and sell anything, even justice.

"Not necessarily," Dixant says, jerking me back into my own world. He takes an eight-by-ten folder out of his briefcase and hands it to me. "Open it. See what's inside." He glances around the room. "For your eyes only, please."

I open the envelope and pull out a handful of photographs: mug shots of Middle Eastern men. They look brutish, cousins of the 9/11 suicide bombers, or Iraqi insurgents.

After staring with incomprehension at each picture for a few seconds, I slide them back into the folder and hand it to Dixant. "Who are they?"

"Subjects of interest."

This feels smarmy. "Whose interest?"

"Yours."

"You're talking over my head." I tap the folder, which is lying on the bench between us. "What in the world could these men have to do with my client?"

"They're whales."

"So?"

"So I want to harpoon them. At least one of them."

I can be slow on the uptake, but I'm not comatose. My stomach starts to knot up. "In plain English," I say, putting more space between us by sliding away from him along the smooth bench.

If Dixant is offended by my show of repulsion, he doesn't let on. "Your man identifies one of these mutts as his contact. I'd like two, but I'll settle for one." He taps his fingers on the folder. His nails are polished; he must get manicures. Vain twerp. He must actually think women find him attractive.

"Someone he doesn't know, has never met."

His look at me doesn't waver. "The sum is greater than the parts, Jessica. You know that, you're realistic—that's one of the things I admire about you." He drums the folder more quickly, a nervous tick. "Tell you what. He gives me two of them, any two, and I'll drop all the charges. He flies home free." He sits back, looking as satisfied as if he had just polished off the twenty-four-ounce porterhouse at the Pacific Dining Car.

I find the idea that this toad admires anything about me repulsive. "Just like that," I say.

"Just like that."

I pretend that I'm considering his offer. "Does he have to testify in open court, or will an affidavit be good enough?"

Dixant hesitates before answering, which tells me he's going to lie. "An affidavit might be good enough. I'll have to check with my higher-ups. But I have to know, now, that we have a deal, Jessica. Do we?"

My head is spinning, so I stall. "What about protection?"

"That can be arranged."

"For how long?"

He hesitates. "That would depend . . ."

"Because for however long, it wouldn't be long enough," I spit at him, stopping whatever lame excuse he's going to concoct. I have to be careful to keep my voice down—we're in a courtroom. I wish we weren't, because I feel like screaming. "You are setting my client up to be murdered, you bastard!" I hiss at him. "He's not some gangbanger, he's a stand-up citizen who doesn't have a blemish on his record! You think men like those . . ." I jab a finger at the folder, which to my incensed eye looks as if it's shimmering with radioactivity, ". . . would let that go? They would pursue him to the ends of the earth." I can't get away from this slime fast enough. "I'm going to tell my boss about this. You can't pull this kind of crap."

Dixant throws up his hands in appeasement. "Back down, girl. Don't shoot the messenger. I'm only following orders here."

I'm shaking. I've never encountered anything like this before. "Whose orders?"

"Can't tell you." He stuffs the folder back into his briefcase. "I'm trying to help you, Jessica, but okay. Forget we had this conversation. I'll see you at trial."

Before he goes, he zings me one last time. "Your man is going to prison. We're going to make sure that happens."

THIRTEEN

JOE BLEVINS, MY BOSS, goes ballistic when I tell him about the ugly threats Wayne Dixant made against Roberto Salazar and, by proxy, me. "You're positive he wasn't screwing with your head?" he grills me.

"He was dead serious."

Joe is incredulous. "That's not only criminal, it's idiotic." He immediately picks up the phone and calls his counterpart in the D.A.'s office, demanding that they meet, right away.

Less than an hour later, Joe summons me back to his office. He has a big shit-eating grin on his face. "I guarantee you Mr. Wayne Dixant is getting the chewing out of the century, even as we speak," he tells me with relish. "He was way out of bounds. Ted Archibald was so angry I was afraid he was going to rupture an artery."

Ted Archibald is a senior assistant D.A., the equivalent for their side as Joe is for ours. He can be an uptight martinet, but he plays by the rules.

"He had it coming," I say. I'm still enraged. "I've never been threatened like that in my entire life."

"Well, you won't have to worry about that anymore," Joe assures me. "He'll be as docile as a little lamb."

"What was all that about, anyway, that big cartel knocking off warehouses down at the port?"

"That's real," Joe says. "The county's working with the state and the feds. Dixant's a tiny cog in the machine. He was trying to make brownie points with the big boys. Instead, he's gonna have a reprimand in his file."

"So has he been taken off this case?"

"Archibald offered. I told him it wouldn't be necessary. We'll go as planned."

"Why?" That disturbs me, that Joe made the decision without consulting me. He is my boss, but we work as a team, and everyone's opinion should be considered. Usually, it is.

"You want this over, don't you? You want your client to be done with this as soon as possible, I thought."

"Yes, I do," I agree.

"If a new D.A. gets assigned, they'll want a continuance, at least a couple of months. The sword will be hanging over your fellow's head all that time. Get in fast, clean it up, get out," he advises me. He smiles again. "Besides, you're going to own Wayne Dixant. He'll be your little lap dog. You'll practically be able to put a collar around his neck and make him beg for treats."

I see the twisted logic to that, but I don't like it. Dixant is being publicly humiliated. He's wounded, and wounded animals are the most dangerous.

"They're going to drop the grand theft charges," Joe says. "They know they won't be able to make those stick. It's just going to be accessory to transporting. You can cut a sweet deal on that."

"No, I can't," I say.

"Why not?" He's surprised. We plea-bargain almost everything.

"Because he didn't do it," I answer. "He doesn't have a record. No matter how good a deal we could cut, he'd be marked for life. I can't be party to that, it's not fair." My hackles are up about this case because of Dixant's vile threats. "I'm going to get him off, Joe."

Doubtfully: "You sure?"

"I feel very confident."

Joe's a pessimist. Given the District Attorney's high conviction rate, he has to be. "The client is good with that? He knows the downside? You've had that conversation with him?" He gives me a stern look. "Confident and dead certain are not the same thing, Jessica. Don't make this a personal vendetta between you and Dixant. He isn't worth it, and that's not the right way to conduct a case, which you know."

"Salazar didn't do it," I repeat. "He was sandbagged by a friend. I can convince the jury of that. He's good people, Joe, the jury's going to see that."

Joe gives in. "Okay. It's your case. Do right by it." He picks up his phone, signaling me our meeting is over.

"Oh, one more thing," he says, as I'm halfway out the door.

"What?"

"Don't just win. Kick that moron's ass."

I smile. We have people's lives in our hands, but we play a high-stakes game too.

"Whatever you say, boss."

FOURTEEN

TONIGHT IS THE BEGINNING of the full moon. In the past month, gun sales in Los Angeles County have quadrupled, especially west of the 405. Most of the new buyers have been women. For their own safety and those close to them, I hope they learn how to use their weapons properly.

To err on the side of caution, I have changed my running schedule. I still run after work, but I do it earlier. Now that daylight saving time is here I can get home, change into my running clothes, and get in my ten to twelve miles before it's dark. It's not as easy running at seven at night, because the streets are clogged with traffic, and I've had to alter some of my routes to avoid constantly stopping and starting, but safety trumps inconvenience. Now, instead of running through the quiet residential streets, I run down to the bike path that parallels the ocean and take it north, where I pick up Palisades Park until I get to San Vicente Boulevard.

My route is a pedestrian freeway in the early evening hours. There are thousands of runners, walkers, bikers, and skaters cruising up and down, most of them in their own little cocoons. They are oblivious to everything—they could run down a granny creeping along with her walker and never know it. It's like running an obstacle course; I can't let my mind wander as I do when I run late at night, I could get wiped out if I'm not alert.

There is a benefit to training in all this congestion. When I run my marathon, I'll be bunched in a tight pack for at least the first half of the race, so this is good practice for learning how to navigate in a mob. Occasionally I'll strap on my iPod and zone out, but usually not, because I like to be aware of my surroundings, and I need to monitor my pulse, speed, stride. As an extra precaution now, I run with a fanny pack. I keep it light, only three items: my cell phone, driver's license, and a pepper-spray canister. I don't expect to be attacked—I'm a moving target, and I will not stop to talk to anyone I don't know—but I'm more vigilant now than I was before these killings began.

I don't carry my gun. Not only is it too heavy, I don't want to bring that vibe into my running. Running is a physical activity, but there is also a Zen aspect to it. You want to mesh your spirit with your body, to be in the moment. That's what my running coach told me when I started training. He is very much into the spiritual side of running. He is also a vegetarian, a practicing Buddhist, and has almost zero body fat. I am an omnivore who has no strong religious or spiritual beliefs, and I have more padding than I would like, but I understand where he's coming from. Taking life as he does is the antithesis of the kind of lifestyle most of us practice, and it can be summed up as "Get over yourself." For me, that is an important axiom to think about, because I take myself too seriously. I consider it a major character flaw. I want to change that part of my personality, and running helps, even if only a little bit.

I cross Ocean Avenue where it meets the San Vicente median, and as I run along the grassy strip I see the first one. He's near the corner of San Vicente and Sixth Avenue. He is outfitted as a cable repairman, but to my practiced eye, *cop* radiates off him like blue light off a neon sign over a country-western bar. He's futzing around, trying to look inconspicuous, but even from forty yards away I can see that his eyes are in constant motion.

He sees me looking at him, and the faintest smile of recognition plays across his face for a moment, then vanishes. I can't imagine he knows who I am or what I do, but we made some kind of connection. Maybe he's subliminally trying to say *I'm out here to protect you*; or maybe he just likes my legs. Whatever the reason, he's out here tonight. Which means dozens of his brother and sister officers are too.

As I run, I look at my fellow runners more closely, particularly the women. If they can dress up female cops as hookers and send them out cruising Hollywood Boulevard, they can outfit them as joggers and deploy them here as decoys. Not only as runners, but anyone. I don't know if any of the women who have been murdered were runners, but that doesn't matter. They were alone, presumably, vulnerable prey.

All the killings happened late at night, so these officers are going to be putting in long hours, because it isn't even dark yet and they are already here. That's how serious this is to L.A. law enforcement. The heat from above must be intense. If the killer strikes again this month and doesn't get caught, the fear factor will go through the roof, and careers will be in ruins.

The first night of the full moon comes and goes, and no one is killed. The second night, the same. Tonight will end the official full-moon cycle. The previous three murders took place during this specific three-day period, so theoretically, tonight is the last time the killer will strike, if he is going to.

All day long, at work, I can feel the tension building; everyone can. It's like when a pitcher takes a no-hitter into the ninth inning—no one says anything about it, but the air is electric with anticipation.

I go for my evening run, and I see them everywhere, I'd bet there are twice as many undercover cops out tonight as on the previous two. In their minds, the killer has to strike. He's done it three months in a row, the pattern has been set. I wonder where Cordova is. Cruising all around, I assume, checking with his troops, his cell phone glued to his ear. This is his show—if there is another murder tonight, his ass will be in a sling. If there is another murder and the killer isn't caught, that sling could be a coffin.

As I run, I scan the passing faces for a clue, a telltale giveaway.

Every man I see looks suspicious to me. But my time on the streets is without incident—I finish where I began, at the front door of my house. Nothing is different tonight from any other night. I hope that's true for every other woman in this city.

It's four in the morning. I went to bed early. Now I'm awake, and can't get back to sleep. I'm as wired as if I had drunk six cups of coffee and eaten a box of doughnuts. Standing barefoot in my pajamas, I look out my living-room window. We don't have street lights on our block, but because it is the full moon and there is no fog rolling in, it is bright outside. I can see all the way down the block, almost to the end of the next. If I walked outside and went to the edge of my street, I could turn the corner and see the ocean, six blocks away.

This would be a great time to go running. I've done it before when the streets were deserted and I could be alone with nothing but my thoughts. I'm not going to do that now, of course. I ran less than twelve hours ago, and somewhere out there, a killer is at large.

But I'm too antsy to go back to bed. There is an all-night coffee shop on Broadway, across from the pier, where the night owls— the late shift and the insomniacs—hang out. I can drive there, park right in front, have a coffee or hot chocolate. I won't be alone—there is safety in numbers.

And I'll bring an extra ounce of protection. I take my gun from its safe place, check the magazine to make sure it's full, and stick it in the day pack I sometimes use as a purse. I throw on a pair of jeans, a lightweight sweatshirt, and I'm out the door.

The coffee shop is almost empty—only a few diehards sit as solitary sentries the length of the counter. I'm the only woman, but these men are too much into their private worlds to do more than register my arrival with a quick look, then turn away. There is no waitress service at this wee hour; I wave to the cook behind the counter, tell him I want a cocoa with a shot of coffee, and sit down in one of the booths.

"And a short stack," I call to him. I burn calories like a match burns kindling; I need all the carbohydrates I can get.

As I eat my pancakes, drink my coffee, and glance at the other customers, I feel as if I am a character in an Edward Hopper painting. A sad mixture of lonely people with nowhere to go. That isn't me, but it could be. There is nothing more pathetic than an old woman alone.

The pancakes are rubbery and the coffee is greasy, but I wipe my plate clean. Pushing away from the table, I fish some bills out of my wallet to cover my tab, and leave a generous tip on the counter. I remember back to my waitressing days, how crummy I'd feel if a customer stiffed me. That extra dollar won't break anyone's bank, and the server has been acknowledged as an equal human being, not a servant.

By my TAG Heuer, it's five-fifteen. The faintest line of pale light is starting to show, night fading away, morning creeping in. Did the Full Moon Killer strike? I wonder. If not by now, then the time has passed. That would throw the city for a loop.

A block away, where the Third Street Mall ends at Broadway, there is a cluster of newspaper vending machines. I didn't get the scores last night, and I want to know how the Dodgers are doing. It's great to have a winning team—it boosts the entire city's morale, especially since the Lakers tanked again this year. I walk down the street, drop a couple of quarters into one of the machines, pull out a *Times,* and turn to the sports section.

A car screeches to a stop behind me. As I turn, startled, two men jump out and approach me. They are robust, tough looking. One of them has shaved his head. He sports a dangling cross in his left earlobe. The other man, who is older, is Marine Corps square.

Immediately, they hold up their hands to reveal their badges. "Police. Don't panic."

"Jesus, you scared me," I say. My heart is fluttering.

"Sorry, miss," the taller one says. "We just want to make sure you're all right."

They certainly are on the job. How many other women have had this level of observation tonight? "I'm fine," I say. "Thank you for your concern." I start to walk away.

"You're not on foot, are you?" the cop persists.

"No." I point. "My car is right there. The blue Toyota."

"We'll walk you."

"That's not necessary, really. It's only a block."

"We'll feel better."

To protect and serve, for real. "Okay. Fine."

We walk toward my car, and before we reach it, two other cars careen around the corner from Ocean Avenue and slam up to the curb. A lone man gets out of each one. Like my escorts, they are dressed for action in jeans, running shoes, short-sleeved shirts. Their holsters are clipped to their belts.

"You?" One of them exclaims, staring at me. He looks surprised, and angry.

He's not someone I want to see. "Hello, Lieutenant Cordova," I answer, feeling sheepish.

Cordova turns to the others. "Thanks, fellows. I've got this."

The other detectives look askance at me. "Okay," one of them answers. They walk back to their vehicles and drive off, staring at us again as they go.

Cordova shakes his head at me, like a schoolteacher admonishing a truant. Technically, we are in the Santa Monica Police Department's jurisdiction, but since he's in charge of the task force, he can cross boundaries.

"For God's sake, Jessica, what are you doing out here at night?" he asks. "You know better."

He's right, and I'm grateful for the concern, but I don't like being scolded. "I couldn't sleep, so I came down here for coffee. Besides, it's morning now." I look east, in the direction of the first blush of pink that's peeking through the dark gray sky.

"Technically, it's still night," he refutes me. "You should not be outside. Definitely not alone."

"I'm not alone," I tell him.

He looks around. There is no one else on the street. "Who are you with?" he asks suspiciously.

I open my pack and show him my gun. "Mr. Equalizer."

He stares at it, at me. "You're licensed, I presume."

"Of course. Do you want to see it?" As I reach in to take the automatic out of my purse, I can't, despite the tense circumstances, resist tweaking him. "I'll show you mine if you'll show me yours."

He puts his hand on top of mine, restraining me. His hand is huge—it dwarfs mine. I feel the muscles in his fingers; this man is powerful. "Don't be brandishing that, for God's sake," he admonishes me. "You don't joke around with guns." He pulls his hand away, a bit self-consciously. "You know how to shoot it, I hope."

"Sorry about that," I apologize. If anyone should know that guns aren't playthings, it's me. "Yes, I know how to shoot," I say. "Anytime you want to come out to the range and watch me, let me know," I offer. I smile impishly. I don't know why I'm flirting with him—must be nervous energy. "We can have a contest."

"You'll lose."

"Don't be so sure of yourself."

He smiles. The tension between us has dissipated, smoke drifting away.

"Has anything happened with . . . ?" I can't finish my question, the subject is too fraught.

He knows what I mean. "Not that we know about—so far."

"So maybe he hasn't killed anyone this month?" I ask with rising excitement.

Cordova won't buy into that supposition—it's too optimistic, a luxury he can't afford. "We won't know until later today, or maybe tomorrow."

There is another question I've been wondering about since I spotted that undercover detective the first night. "Do you think he might have picked up on your surveillance?" I ask him. "I knew you guys were there, I picked up on your people right away. If I could spot you, maybe he did, too. He must be extra careful now, with all the publicity."

He gives me a grudging nod of agreement. "I don't know. But if he did, and that stopped him, all to the good."

"Or maybe he's finished. Like the Zodiac."

From his expression I can tell he has considered that possibility. "Or he might have moved somewhere else, where he can start fresh." His lips curl, showing his teeth. They are large, white, straight. Right now, they're clenched. "It would be healing for this city if you're right, although there would still be a cloud, for a long time."

He takes my arm and walks me the few steps to my car. "But my gut tells me we're not done with him." He looks up into the predawn sky, as if looking for a sign from above. "Or him with us."

FIFTEEN

"THE DEFENSE WILL TRY to convince you the accused was an innocent victim of his so-called criminal friend," Wayne Dixant tells the jury as he delivers his opening statement. "Do not believe it. He was caught red-handed. They'll also insinuate that his truck was illegally searched. That's a bunch of baloney, too. The police did everything by the book. In fact, they bent over backward to insure all of the defendant's rights. They'll also trot out a sob story about his being a good father, good husband, breadwinner. That's all fine and good, *but it does not matter*. What matters—the only thing that matters in this case—is that this man is an accomplice to the break-in of a federally bonded container, that he was transporting stolen goods for financial gain, and that he was caught. The fact that he doesn't have a prior record is irrelevant. At some point in life, everyone's record is clean. Some criminals take the wrong path early in life. Others don't succumb to temptation until later on. But whatever their age, if they break the law, they have to pay the price."

He's better than I thought he would be. After his meltdown, I had wondered if he would be able to get through this with real energy and zest, or would go through the motions, take his licking, and slink off to lick his wounds. Obviously, that isn't going to happen. He's here to win. I have to concede that he's off to a good start.

He steamrolls on. "Armando Gonzalez, the so-called mastermind of this enterprise, does not exist, at least not in Los Angeles County or anywhere else in Southern California. There is no record of him on the tax rolls, the DMV, any of the utilities, property rolls, welfare, nothing. He's a phantom, a ghost, a figment of the accused's imagination." His eyes sparkle, as if he and the jury are in on the fix. "That's very convenient, isn't it? You create a fictitious character and make him the bad guy. Then you create a set of circumstances that make it plausible why he can't be found to substantiate your defense—he's in hiding because he's the real criminal. That's a nice enclosed circle." He pauses to catch his breath and to let the jury catch up with him. "A nice *vicious* circle," he continues. "You can't prove a negative, so you set it up so that it can't be *disproved*. They know that," he continues, pointing at me and Salazar, sitting at the defense table. "They know that the burden of proof is on the state, so they create this phony world of disappearing criminals and altruistic motives and an innocent dupe . . ."

I tune him out for a moment, because I know where he is going. I'm concerned about my client. Sitting next to Salazar, I feel his tension. He is vibrating like a tuning fork. He is extremely distressed as he sits here and hears himself being described as both a thief and a moron.

I pat my client on the knee, under the table. "Tune him out," I counsel. "It's all hot air. By tomorrow, the jury won't remember a word he says."

Salazar nods, but I know he can't help listening and letting Dixant's accusations get to him.

Dupe was Dixant's second use of the word, which I have privately thought myself about Salazar. When I thought it, it made me think he could be innocent, even back at the beginning when I didn't know any of the background of his life, his devotion, and good works. Coming out of Dixant's mouth, though, the portrayal makes him seem like a jerk who fell into Gonzalez's world and went along with the program, maybe not as an enterprising instigator, but as a willing, if naive, accomplice. Unfortunately for us, should the jury agree with Dixant, naïveté is not a legal defense.

I am also worried about the Armando Gonzalez quandary, which Dixant has now telegraphed he is going to hammer home. The man has not turned up, not a trace. It is the one element of Salazar's story that has given me pause. The best answer I have been able to figure is that Armando Gonzalez is a fictitious name, and Salazar didn't know it. That's not uncommon among people who have criminal records. They create new identities with phony documents to stay ahead of the law. The way I did as an underage kid, with my fake ID card.

That is going to be a thorn in our side. Hopefully, I'll diffuse it with a barrage of character witnesses.

Dixant winds it up. "This is a simple case, ladies and gentlemen. The accused was caught with stolen goods. That is indisputable, the defense is not going to contest that. How he got them, what the circumstances were, doesn't matter. He had them. That is a crime. And it will be your duty, your civic responsibility, to find him guilty."

He leans into the podium to deliver his finishing argument: "Almost always in a case like this, there are smoke screens the defense will throw at you, to try to confuse you about the facts. You had to buy medicine for your sick mother, you were trying to help a neighbor who was down and out, the dog ate your homework." He waits for the requisite chuckles, and plunges on. "These stories can bring a tear to your eye, a lump to your throat. If you were watching him on Oprah, your heart would go out to this poor victim. But this is not television, ladies and gentlemen. It is real life. Do not be influenced by what the accused has done in other parts of his life. Lots of killers, thieves, even rapists are good fathers and husbands. But they are also criminals, and when they break the law, they are sent to prison."

He turns again, faces Salazar and me, and points the accusing finger. "He broke the law. He has to pay the price for doing that.

When all the evidence is in, you will be convinced that he broke the law, and you will find him guilty as charged."

My workload has been heavy, and as the marathon date looms closer, I've intensified my training. The weekend after next I'll go for my final long run of twenty miles, then I'll taper off. Last week I bought a new pair of running shoes, New Balance 1223s for women. They are comfortable on my feet, which, being long and narrow (11AA), can be hard to fit. They were expensive, but I don't skimp on shoes. I'm expecting a grueling experience, and I don't want to worry about my equipment.

I don't want to worry about running at all. My sole concern for now is winning this trial. I think we have a decent chance, but I never allow myself to be too optimistic. The defense, whether a public defender or a six-hundred-dollar-an-hour private lawyer, loses most of the time, so optimism is an unaffordable luxury. It would actually be better if my client did have some skeletons in his closet. I could have worked out a deal for him, probably kept him out of prison. But that's not an option.

I have to win this case. I don't want this man to go to jail.

Neither does Amanda Burgess. She's been indefatigable in her support, which is a thorn in my side at times, because she's relentless. Phone calls at all hours of the day and night, endless questions. Can she hire a private detective on her own? The answer to that is no, we have our own. What about an assistant to help me? Again, not possible. After fielding these repeated questions, I asked an obvious one of my own. "Why don't you hire a private lawyer for him if you're not happy with the job I'm doing?"

She immediately goes on the defensive. "I'm completely confident in you, Jessica," she assures me. "More than most of the lawyers I know. I just don't want to leave any stones unturned."

"Well, there always are some." I look at the clock. It's eleven-thirty. I should be asleep; I'm in serious training. "That's human nature."

"I know that," she answers, in a tone of voice that says she doesn't.

"Do you mind if I ask you a personal question?" I say. I am pushing in a direction I'm not comfortable in, because of our relative statuses, but she has been hounding me so hard I can't help myself.

"What is it?" she asks suspiciously.

"Why are you so concerned about your gardener?"

The moment the words are out of my mouth, I regret them. Not the question, but the implication: that he is a Latino gardener rather than a white person of so-called importance. Backpedaling furiously, I stammer, "I don't mean that in a racist way. Economic. Whatever . . ." Which makes the situation worse, particularly since we are talking on the phone, which is more impersonal than face-to-face. I can really step in it sometimes.

She takes a moment before answering. "I know you are not a racist, Jessica, so I am not going to take offense at your question, although I could," she replies coolly, a put-down masquerading as a compliment. "The answer is, precisely because of that. His ethnicity, his economic status, or lack of it. As you know, I have come to know him as a good man, a good father—all that. I know he is not a thief, he couldn't be. It's not in his DNA, it simply isn't."

I could cite cases where good people do bad things, but I keep my big mouth shut.

"I'm fighting against the system as much as I can for Roberto," she says. "All these black and Latino men locked up in jail, so disproportionate to their percentage of the population. It's institutionalized racism. Why did I and millions of others march in all those civil rights marches back in the sixties and seventies to allow the system to fall into such perversion?"

Even over the telephone line I can feel the passion in her voice. I've never felt that strongly about an abstraction. One of the major differences between our generations.

"I appreciate your confidence in me, Amanda," I say, "but if you feel that strongly about this, you should hire a private lawyer for him, someone with more resources than I have, who can turn over every rock. My office can't do that. Our resources are very limited. That's why we only defend people who can't afford private lawyers. With your help, he could."

Her answer to that question is immediate. "I can't do that."

"Why not?"

"Think of how that would look. A wealthy white woman hiring an expensive lawyer to defend the Mexican man who trims her trees. The press would have a field day, especially those despicable right-wing radio talk shows. At best I would be ridiculed as a lightweight do-gooder, and at worst as a meddlesome manipulator trying to throw my weight around, which, let's face it, I already have, to some small extent."

Finally, the truth about Amanda Burgess's reluctance to really jump in: the fear of public ridicule. And as I hear her articulate what she thinks (and fears) is a shameful weakness, I realize I knew that all along. For the first time since we met, I feel for her. Her heart is in the right place, even if she can be exasperatingly high-handed.

"I hear you," I commiserate. "We all do our best," I say, sounding like some inane television psychologist dispensing trivial solipsisms. "That's all anyone can ask of us."

"It is," she agrees eagerly, as if grateful that I'm not putting her down for her reticence to fully engage. "We can only do what we can do. We are only human." Then she laughs. There is no merriment in her laugh. "Especially me."

My cross-examinations of the cop who arrested Salazar, and the other two officers who responded to his call for backup, is perfunctory. There is no denying there were stolen goods in Salazar's truck, and I don't want to belabor the issue of illegal search and seizure. It would be a tenuous argument, and could alienate the jury against him. My defense is going to be based on building good will for Roberto, so anything that could muck that up would be foolish, even dangerous.

By the end of the first day, Dixant has finished putting on his case. Besides his star witnesses, the first officer who arrested my client and the two cops who backed him up, Dixant trots out the inspector who discovered the break-in down at the port and the customs official who verified the contents. Since the D.A.'s office has already dropped the theft charges, these witnesses were merely presented to establish that the televisions really were stolen. My quick questioning of them clears up any possible residue that Salazar himself broke into the container, or was even there. So now I have to convince the jury that he wasn't part of an organized criminal ring, but was an unlucky victim of circumstances.

Court is adjourned at quarter to five. I'll begin my defense in the morning. Salazar and I have a brief meeting before we part company. He is going to be my first witness, and the impression he makes will be crucial. He is nervous, of course, but I have convinced him that if he tells the truth, we will be all right.

"Why would I lie?" he asks. "What would I lie about?"

Nothing that I can think of, so we're in synch. The only fly still in the ointment is Armando Gonzalez, the phantom thief. Why has this man not shown up? I don't mean in the physical sense—he has good reason to lie low. But the fact that there is no paper trail, that his very existence is in question, is vexing. I can't avoid bringing up his name, because he is a critical element in our defense. I know Dixant will home in on that when he cross-examines Salazar. All I can do is mitigate his absence, as best I can.

"See you tomorrow," I tell Salazar, giving him a reassuring pat on the arm. "Make sure all of your witnesses show up," I remind him. "That's real important."

"They will be there," he promises me. "They are my friends."

That is reassuring. With friends like his, I think we can overcome the absence of Gonzalez. I wish I had such good friends.

It's seven-fifteen; the sun is slowly dropping down toward the horizon. I stand at the edge of the bike path, stretching before I start my evening run.

Tonight is the beginning of the last full moon of this cycle. So far, there has not been a murder this month that fits the pattern. If the next twenty-four hours pass without one, it will be two months since the Full Moon Killer last struck. Maybe I was right, back when I had my early morning encounter with Lieutenant Cordova outside that coffee shop, about my theory that he had either quit or moved on. I wouldn't wish this scourge on another city, but if he is finished here, the women who live on the Westside of Los Angeles will breathe a lot easier. I know I will.

Roberto Salazar is sworn in and takes his seat in the witness chair. He is dressed in a navy blazer, tan slacks, pressed, white Oxford shirt, dark dress shoes, shined but not glossy. No tie, that's too slick for his image. We went shopping for his wardrobe last week at a Men's Wearhouse in Glendale, since he didn't have any suitable clothes for court. Amanda Burgess paid for the new clothes. They agreed it was a loan that he will pay back with sweat equity.

He looks good. Appealing, but not threatening. A couple of the woman jurors, middle-aged Latinas, eyeball him appreciatively. If he weren't already married and a potential felon, he would be desirable son-in-law material. I file their gut-empathetic response toward him in my memory bank, to be cashed in at the end of the trial, when I will tug at their heartstrings.

As promised, all the character witnesses I'm going to call have shown up. They sit behind us, on our side of the aisle. Amanda Burgess is among them, but I'm hoping I don't have to use her. She asked me to leave her out unless I think her appearance could tilt the scales. If we were conducting this trial without a jury, I would definitely use her, because Judge Rosen is clearly starstruck with her. But I doubt that any of the jurors know who she is, of her importance in the rarified world they are not part of. The participation of this high-bred Anglo could boomerang on us, causing resentment that would negate the good feelings I want them to have about Roberto.

Salazar recounts the events that led to his arrest. He talks freely about how he had helped deliver stuff for Gonzalez before, with never a problem. I bring out this information because I know Dixant will seize upon it on cross, so I want to blunt the disclosure, my point being that this was nothing unusual, and Salazar had no reason to believe that he was part of an illegal enterprise. He was helping a friend, and making a little extra money. He answers all of my questions calmly and clearly, without any glitches or fumbling. When I'm finished, I feel the jury can justify believing his story, thus providing them the necessary cover to find him not guilty.

Dixant immediately rips into my client. "Didn't you think it strange that this so-called Mr. Gonzalez was making his delivery at three o'clock in the morning?" he rants. Before Salazar can answer, he adds pugnaciously, "What warehouse have you ever heard of that is open at that time of night?"

I smile—I've been waiting for this. Salazar does his job, answering the question precisely as we rehearsed it. "I did not know the televisions were stolen," he says. "Armando told me he had bought them in Mexico. Legally. So his being in Los Angeles at that time of night seemed reasonable to me."

Dixant scowls. He was hoping to trip up Salazar, to confuse him into admitting that he knew the televisions came from a warehouse in San Pedro, rather than from Mexico. He's still smarting from getting his ears pinned back two months ago, and is swinging wildly, trying for a knockout, instead of staying cool and piling up points. Now he will have to do damage control, which is never a situation you want to be in. A lawyer needs to be aggressive, not defensive—not only for real, but also in appearance, which is often the more important of the two. Jurors, like sharks, can smell blood, and a lawyer who is wounded is vulnerable. So is his case.

Dixant regains some traction when he switches his questioning to "the so-called mastermind Armando Gonzalez," as he derisively terms Salazar's Achilles' heel. I think about objecting to the derogatory expression "so-called mastermind," but I let it ride.

The less attention brought to this, the better. Let the jury think I'm not concerned, a speck of dandruff to be easily brushed off.

"Have you spoken to him since you were arrested?" Dixant asks.

"No," Salazar answers.

"Have you tried to get in touch with him?"

Salazar glances over at me. Technically, he hasn't, as far as I know. Since Gonzalez's cell phone was out of service, he would have no other way to contact him, because he didn't know where Gonzalez lived, or whether he had e-mail or any other normal way of communication. But I nod *yes* anyway. I tried, and since I'm his lawyer, it's as if he did. I want the jury to think he tried as hard as he could to make contact, that he didn't let that slide.

"Yes," he says, picking up on my signal. "Me and my lawyer."

The right answer. He hasn't impeached himself. He's smart, he understands subtleties.

"But you couldn't," Dixant says.

"No."

"Because he doesn't exist."

So much for hoping to ride this out. I'm on my feet in a jiffy. "Objection!" I call out in the loudest voice I've used in this trial. "That's conjecture on the D.A.'s part. The fact that Mr. Gonzalez has not been located yet does not mean he doesn't exist. It stands to reason he would take pains to hide from us."

"Sustained," Judge Rosen agrees with me. She's giving me the benefit of the doubt, because she is playing up to Amanda Burgess, subconsciously. I make a mental note to make sure Amanda is present every moment until the jury returns their verdict.

Still, Dixant has succeeded in weaving the issue of Gonzalez's disappearance into the fabric of this trial: Why haven't we found him? Why hasn't anyone found him? As he did in his opening statement, I know Dixant will hammer at that in his summation. And he'll be smart to do it. Even though Gonzalez would have been a hostile witness for us, his mere presence would have been a big asset for our case. Without him, we're vulnerable. Those stolen television sets were in Salazar's truck, after all. If Armando Gonzalez can't be tied to the theft, then how did they get there? It makes Salazar's involvement in an organized crime ring, if not convincing, at least plausible.

Dixant keeps hammering away at Salazar's *so-called,* as he puts it, working relationship with Gonzalez. What other items had he helped his friend deliver? Where did the stuff come from? Did he ever see a bill of sale? Did he ever question their legitimacy? He's a machine gun of interrogation.

For someone who has never been on the field of a courtroom battle, Salazar holds up well. He stammers and fumbles a bit, but he doesn't lose his temper or his train of thought, and he doesn't try to lie his way out of anything. He states that he believes that people are basically good, and he lives his life by that credo.

"Even you, Mr. Dixant," he says, after answering a particularly harsh question from the prosecutor.

"Even me what?" Dixant asks, taken aback.

"Even you are doing the best you know how," Salazar answers. His tone of voice is so calm it would be infuriating to me if he were not my client. He must be a true believer—no one can lie this convincingly. "But you are wrong about me." He smiles at Dixant, almost beatifically. "You are wrong."

Because Salazar was on the stand for most of the day, Judge Rosen decides that the rest of my witnesses will testify tomorrow. After a hurried consultation with them, all of whom are willing to come back, I nervously acquiesce. It's a tribute to their devotion to him that they will return. They have already lost a day's pay. Now they will have to give up another. But they all promise that they will show up, so we agree to adjourn.

I spend a few minutes bucking up my client. I assure him that he was great, and so does his rich sponsor. "You did an excellent job," Amanda tells him. "I was watching the faces of the jurors. They believed you."

He smiles shyly. "Thank you."

That bugs me, her saying that. She has no expertise in this. Even an experienced courtroom observer knows you can't tell the verdict from the way a jury reacts. Even if they like you, most of the time they will convict you if the facts dictate that they should. My telling him he did well is part of my job. If, worst-case scenario, he is convicted, she will have raised his hopes too high, and the fall will be more painful. But she is who she is, and no one is going to influence her. Definitely not me.

The moon is no longer full. No murders have been linked to the Full Moon Killer, so the streets are safe for another thirty days. The scuttlebutt around the courthouse is that if another month passes without a killing, the task force will be shut down.

If that happens, it will be a bittersweet conclusion for the police, particularly for my new friend Lieutenant Cordova. The cops want the residents of the city to be safe, of course, but they will be left with an emptiness in their gut, because they didn't bring the case to the needed conclusion: the killer won't face justice. Detectives exist to solve crimes. When they don't, they feel hollow, useless. I've heard of cops who ate the gun, sometimes years after they retired, because of an unsolved case that stymied them for their entire career.

I got a late start on my run this evening, but since the window of danger is closed, I'm not worried. My route is a combination of the old and new, along Palisades Park, then through the leafy blocks north of Montana Avenue, up to San Vicente, then back on a zigzag course through various quiet residential streets. As I run I mentally rehearse tomorrow's program. Now that Roberto has finished testifying, I'll put on my character witnesses. They are an appealing group, solid citizens the jurors will be able to identify with.

Back at my house I stretch, shower, throw a beef Stroganoff Lean Cuisine in the microwave, pour myself a glass of Syrah, and talk to Jeremy while my dinner is heating up. Next week's concert will be the end of the season. After that, the orchestra goes on tour for six weeks, Europe and Asia. I plan to go over and spend a few weeks with my man after I run the marathon. I've never been to Europe, Asia, anywhere. Jeremy, in contrast, has circled the globe. I've been going over the itinerary, where they'll be when I'm free. Prague, Vienna, Saint Petersburg, Kyoto, Sydney, among other locations. This is going to be the vacation of a lifetime.

We'll get together tomorrow or the day after, as soon as I'm done with the trial. I drink my wine and enjoy the best microwave dinner I've ever had.

I want to win this trial. My client is innocent; he should not go to prison. But I also know there is life outside the walls of the courtroom. I want it. I'm going to have it.

SIXTEEN

ALL MY CHARACTER WITNESSES have returned as promised, and each one is a champ. To a man and woman, they have nothing but praise for Salazar. Dixant doesn't even bother to question most of them. He sits at his table, scowling darkly, making a show of looking at his watch, as if he has a more important date following this one, and doesn't want to be late. Some of the jurors notice his boorishness, and it seems to annoy them. It reminds me of the televised debate between Bill Clinton and the first Bush, when the older man kept looking at his watch, as if he couldn't wait for this crap to be over. Some people say that cost him the election. Maybe Dixant's rude behavior will help me win this contest.

I don't call Amanda Burgess as a witness. She doesn't fit in with the other witnesses, and her appearance might be off-putting to some of these working-class jurors. Dixant would certainly exploit the noblesse oblige angle. I also don't call Salazar's wife. She is overwhelmed by the workings of the state's vast machine, which are Kafkaesque to her. Dixant would rip her apart if I put her on the stand. It's also been my experience that spouses often do more harm than good. In their desire to help, they exaggerate, overdramatize, or flat-out lie. If they are caught in a lie, an entire case can go down the tubes. And juries view family members more skeptically than they do other witnesses, because the personal stakes are higher. If I had needed her to provide a critical piece of information that only she could testify to, I would have put her up there. But it wasn't necessary, so she sits in the first row behind us, rigid with nerves. Amanda, next to her, calms her from time to time with a warm pat on the arm and a sympathetic smile.

"This concludes my case," Your Honor, I tell the judge.

A questioning look crosses her face, as if she's surprised (and disappointed) I'm not calling Amanda Burgess as a character witness. That passes quickly, and she turns to Dixant. "Any rebuttal?"

"Yes, Your Honor. I have one additional witness."

Rosen gives him a sour look. If he is springing a surprise, she's going to be one unhappy lady. But not as unhappy as me.

"Is he on your witness list? I'm assuming it's a man."

"It is a man, Your Honor," he confirms, "and he isn't on the list."

Now she's even more irritated. "Approach," she orders us.

Dixant and I walk to the front of her podium. She turns off her microphone so the jury can't hear our discussion. Leaning over, she asks him, "Why wasn't this witness on your list? You know the rules." She's angry and she wants him to know it.

"We just found out about him last night, Your Honor," he explains. He's trying to sound contrite. I don't know about the judge, but he isn't convincing me, because I know how low he can go. "He got lost in the jail. You know how that is."

We all know how that is, which gives his explanation credence. The jail is a city unto itself, except much more uncivilized and brutal. The veneer of order is tissue thin, and the organization can be chaotic. I've had clients I couldn't find for days because the jail genuinely didn't know where they were located.

I have a sinking feeling I know where this is headed: a jailhouse confession, one of the slimiest tricks in the book. Even when they're legit, they reek. Too often they're phony, a contract with the devil between a prisoner looking for a break on a tough sentence and a cop or prosecutor too zealous in wanting a conviction. If that's what's going down here, I'm going to be very suspicious because of Dixant's prior attempt to game the system.

"Your Honor . . ." I begin to protest.

She puts a hand up to silence me. "Go on," she says to Dixant. She, too, knows how hard it can be to keep track of thousands of transient felons in that vast pit.

"This witness is critical to getting to the truth of this case," Dixant continues. "I wouldn't be asking the court's indulgence if he wasn't."

Judge Rosen presses her fingers to her temples. I know what is going on in her mind. On one hand, this is a violation of discovery. All witnesses have to be disclosed to the other side, before trial. On the other hand, if this witness knows something that could be critical to the outcome, it would be a miscarriage of justice to deny hearing his testimony. And of course, she has to look out for her political future. If she doesn't let this new witness testify, and Dixant goes public with what could be damning information, she'll be out on the street come next election.

"Your Honor," I try again, more forcefully.

She shakes her head at me. "Wait your turn." To Dixant: "What is the crux of his testimony?"

"He was with the accused in the jail the night the accused was arrested."

I was right. Goddamn it!

The judge ponders her options for another moment, but it's for show. She has to allow this witness in. "All right," she says. "I'll let him testify. But if I see that this is not completely on the up and up, I'll stop it and declare a mistrial, and I will recommend that the charges against the defendant be dropped," she warns Dixant. "Is that a consequence you are willing to accept?"

That's harsh; she's trying to be fair, as much as the circumstances will allow her.

Dixant doesn't hesitate. "It is, Your Honor." he says.

"And defense counsel will be given ample time to prepare her cross," she adds.

"Whatever you decide," he agrees. He seems awfully smug, which causes me even more worry.

"Let's move on, then," she says, concluding our sidebar.

I go back to the defense table, and Dixant takes his place at the lawyer's podium. "Call Alfonso Calderon," he announces. He nods to Ike, the bailiff, who opens the side door that leads to the small holding cell. A moment later Ike emerges with a man who is dressed in jailhouse orange. The man is cuffed, but not shackled. Both of his arms are tattooed from the wrist on up, and there are tattoos on his neck as well. I'm sure his body is a tableau of body art too. Most are jailhouse renderings, crude handmade ink drawings, but some are wildly colorful, professional work. His face is badly pockmarked, a telltale sign of a meth freak. Everything about him has the look of habitual criminal, a man who will spend more of his life in prison than in the free world.

The jurors' reaction to this new addition to the trial is palpable—they are immediately put off. That's understandable, because this man's aura is scary. He looks like a predator, a human coyote who doesn't give a shit about anything except his own self-preservation.

"State your name for the jury, please," Dixant instructs his witness.

"Alfonso Juan Calderon," the man answers in a voice of understated hostility.

I look at Salazar. He is staring at the man, but there is no panic in his face, and no recognition. "Do you know this guy?" I whisper to him.

Salazar shakes his head. "No," he whispers back. "I have never seen him."

I turn to the front as Dixant begins his examination. "Where do you reside presently, Mr. Calderon?"

"In the main county jail," Calderon answers, indicating the direction across the street with a flick of his shackled thumbs.

"For how long?"

"Four months, give or take, I ain't sure to the day. They took away my Blackberry."

"So you were in the jail on the night of . . ." Dixant reads off the date Salazar was arrested.

"Yeah, I was there. They don't give no weekend furloughs." Behind his canine smile, his teeth are yellow and rotting.

"Is there anyone in the courtroom today you met in the jail that night?" Dixant asks.

"Yeah." Calderon points to my table. "Him."

Everyone looks at us. I turn to my client, whose jaw is slack with surprise. "Uh-uh," he says under his breath, to himself. "No."

"Let the record show that Mr. Calderon was pointing to the accused, Roberto Salazar," Dixant states.

I start to stand to object; then I stop. I need to save my ammo for when it really counts.

Dixant continues. "What were the circumstances you two met under?"

Calderon fidgets in his seat, as if he's trying to get comfortable. Or else he's trying to remember his lines. He says, "The night he was arrested, he was put in with me."

"In your cell?"

Calderon shakes his head like a dog shaking off fleas. "No, man. Fresh fish like him who they don't expect to keep long don't get put in individual cells. Jail's too overcrowded. They bunked him in the cafeteria. Where I was, too. They put up cots there, or sometimes they just roll the mattresses out on the floor." He scowls, as if thinking about the indignity of not even having a bed to call your own. I wouldn't like it either.

Dixant nods, as if in sympathy with this poor guy's plight. "So you were in the cafeteria when the accused was brought in."

"Yeah."

"Was he assigned to a space near yours?"

"Real near. Any closer and we would've been spooning."

Next to me, Salazar is in a rage. This is the first time I've ever seen him show anger. "That is not true," he whispers harshly. "This man was not near me. I remember who was. He is lying."

I can't answer, because I have to listen to my opponent, who might be mashing my case into pudding, if he's believable (or truthful). "Later," I whisper back. "We'll discuss this later. Keep quiet now," I hush him, rudely. I'm on edge, and my temper is fraying.

"Did you and the accused talk?" Dixant continues.

"Oh, yeah." The handcuffed man gives his shoulders a shrug, as if working out the kinks. He looks at the jurors, who are looking back at him in morbid fascination, the way you look at an exotic animal in a zoo. One that's safely behind bars, which is where they keep people like this. "We had a most pleasant conversation."

"What did you talk about?" Dixant prompts.

"Everything," the prisoner replies airily. "The war in Iraq. I got some homeboys over there, it's scary shit, man. Worse than where I'm at. At least they ain't shooting at me. Not yet, anyway. So what else. The usual shit. Sports. Pussy. What guys talk about when the ladies aren't present."

When he hears the word "pussy," Salazar turns beet red. I glance behind him to look at his wife, who is staring straight ahead. Her face is frozen. She has never heard her husband described like this. It must be mortifying, especially since this is all happening in public.

I can feel Salazar's tension building. "Don't let him rile you up—that's what they want," I whisper in warning.

Judge Rosen raps her gavel sharply. "Please instruct your witness to refrain from profanity," she admonishes Dixant.

"Sorry, Your Honor," he answers with proper meekness. "You understand?" he puts to Calderon.

The prisoner nods. "Clean up my act. I'm down with that." He turns to Rosen. "Sorry, Judge. Don't get to spend much time with decent people. I'll be good, don't worry."

He smiles ingratiatingly at her. She shakes her head in repugnance and looks away. "Keep it going," she says to Dixant.

"What else did you talk about with the accused?" Dixant asks.

"What he did."

"The crime he committed?"

"Yeah, the crime."

"What did he say? As closely to the actual words as you can remember."

It's like those old E. F. Hutton commercials. Everyone—judge, jury, spectators—leans in toward the witness chair.

"That him and some other bozos hoisted a bunch of television sets and he got caught with them," he says. "Plasma Sonys, the fifty-inch model. That they had been running this scam before, but this was the first time he got caught," he adds. "He was pretty shook up, because he said he had never got caught before."

Now I'm on my feet. "Objection!" I yell, louder than I want, but I'm steamed. "There has been nothing presented here about any other crimes my client has committed, or attempted." We're in water over our heads now, because the precise model and size of the stolen television sets was never made public. Either this douche bag was given that information by the police or Dixant, or he's telling the truth. Either option is chilling to me.

"Sustained," Judge Rosen says. "Please stick to the issue at hand, Counselor," she tells Dixant.

"Yes, Your Honor," he answers, barely covering his smirk, the little shit. "What else did the accused say about these television sets he stole?"

"That he got stupid and didn't watch his butt closely enough," the career convict says. "That he had made a dumb mistake, and that he'd be more careful the next time."

"More careful the next time," Dixant repeats the phrase. "In other words, he was saying he was going to do it again?"

"Objection. Calls for speculation," I call out.

This time, Rosen doesn't answer immediately. Finally, she sustains me. But I feel that I'm losing her.

"Did you say anything to him about what he should do?" Dixant asks his witness.

"Get a good lawyer," the scumbag answers, as he looks over at me with a lascivious smile on his cracked lips.

I have been mentally undressed before, but never so rawly. My skin is literally crawling, as if I have been invaded by a horde of bugs.

The witness runs his tongue across those putrid lips. "Looks to me like he picked a winner."

As I slowly get to my feet to begin a cross-examination that is going to be scattered with land mines, any one of which could blow me up, Judge Rosen throws me a life preserver. "We'll recess for lunch," she declares.

Dixant jumps up in dismay. "Judge, can't we finish the cross-examination before lunch?" he complains. "How long can it take?"

She looks at him archly. "I didn't have breakfast this morning, and I'm hungry, Mr. Dixant." She turns to me. "Any objections from the defense?"

As if I'm going to object to a gift that is all wrapped up in a pretty bow. "No, Your Honor. No objections."

"Cross-examination will begin when we come back, at one-thirty," she pronounces. "After that, closing arguments, unless someone else decides to pull another rabbit out of a hat. I want to charge the jury so they can begin their deliberations before the end of the day," she informs Dixant and me. Meaning, keep your summations short, this isn't the trial of the century. She hoists herself out of her chair and quick-steps through the back door.

I turn to my client. "The truth. Did you ever talk to this man? Anything, one word?" My tone is harsh, but I can't worry about mollycoddling his ego. Time is flying.

"Never," he insists, taken aback by my abruptness. "I never talked to him, I never laid eyes on him." He's really worked up. "You told me not to talk to anyone, and I didn't."

I warned you about that *after* you were arrested, not the night of, I think. But I have to trust him. I've believed him so far; I can't crap out on him now, or on myself. I have too much invested in this case to let a slimeball like Dixant pull a stunt like this and get away with it.

"I need to get back to my office and do some checking up on this situation," I inform him. "I'll see you back here at one-thirty. Don't be late."

As I'm leaving, Salazar joins his wife, who is huddled in Amanda Burgess's protective shadow. Amanda says something encouraging to him, and gives him a reassuring hug. He smiles bravely. The three of them leave the courtroom together. Salazar and Amanda are talking. His dutiful wife follows, half a step behind.

We're back in court. I stand at the podium and face Dixant's new star witness. My first question is a grenade thrown right at his head. "How much did they pay you to lie?"

Dixant erupts from his chair. "Objection!" he screams.

"Sustained!" Rosen is livid. "Approach the bench, both of you."

Dixant and I walk to the side of her platform that is opposite the jury box. Judge Rosen stares daggers at me. "Ms. Thompson . . ." she hisses.

"Sorry, Your Honor," I jump in quickly, before she can really lay one on me. "I got carried away. I won't do that again."

"See that you don't." She has been trying to help me ever since Amanda Burgess made her regal entrance into this courtroom, but she's making it clear that I've exhausted my chits now. "Don't make me hold you in contempt," she warns me.

I don't have to look at Dixant to know he's lapping up my smackdown. "I won't, Your Honor," I promise, sounding properly chastised.

"All right. Resume."

I take my place at the podium again. "I'll rephrase my question," I say to the prisoner in the dock. "Did the District Attorney's office offer you anything in exchange for your testimony?"

Calderon tries to look puzzled, but his performance won't win him any Oscars. "I don't know what you mean," he says, fumbling for a tolerable answer. "They ain't paying me a dime, if that's what you're asking. Not one thin dime," he repeats himself.

"That's *not* what I'm asking," I correct him. "Did they offer you anything in exchange for coming in here and telling us about your so-called conversation with Mr. Salazar in the county jail on the night he was arrested? It doesn't have to be money."

He starts to answer, then hesitates. "I don't know what you're talking about," he says, casting an eye at Dixant, looking for cover. Dixant, stone-faced, turns away.

"Let me help you out," I volunteer, almost gleefully. I walk back to the defense table, pick up a sheet of paper, and return to the podium. "You are days away from being sent to Soledad. For aggravated assault, isn't that correct? It's your second strike, which means one more and you're down for the count. And the only reason you are still here in the county jail is because there isn't a space available for you up there, and the court won't allow any more transfers until there is one, which apparently . . ." I glance at the paper in my hand ". . . is imminent. That's true, isn't it?"

Behind me, I hear Dixant exhale. It sounds like he's choking. He had me on the ropes, and I slipped away.

"I don't know what imminent means," Calderon stalls.

"It means very soon," I school him. "You are going to Soledad very soon. Unless . . ." I pause, hoping he'll bite.

He doesn't take the bait, so I set the hook myself. "Unless you can cut a deal."

Dixant objects without getting out of his chair. Judge Rosen shoots him down. "Overruled," she says. A blind man can see where this is going, and she has excellent vision. "Continue, Counselor," she says to me encouragingly. It's nice to be in her good graces again.

"Thank you, Your Honor," I respond. I turn back to the witness. "Did the District Attorney's office offer you a deal for testifying against my client? A lesser charge, so that second strike wouldn't be on your record? A reduction in your sentence? Anything?"

The snitch isn't so cocky all of a sudden. He looks at Dixant again, who grouses, "Your Honor . . ."

"Overruled," Rosen snaps, before he can finish his sentence. She stares at Calderon from her perch on high. "Answer the question," she orders him. "And answer it truthfully."

"They . . ." He gives up all pretense. "Yes."

SEVENTEEN

"Good afternoon, ladies and gentlemen. I know that I speak for everyone in this courtroom in commending you for serving on this jury. Our legal system, which is the best in the world, only works because of citizens like you, who sacrifice their time to do this."

It's a few minutes after four. Most of the witnesses and other spectators who were here earlier are gone. They did their duty; it's up to me now. Salazar's wife is still present, of course, and so is Amanda Burgess. It seems wacky to me that this rich woman would spend all this time here. None of the jurors know who she is, so her presence won't affect the outcome. She is comforting to Salazar's wife, but so what, really? They aren't friends; I don't think they'd ever met until this trial. When it's over, regardless of the outcome, they may never see each other again. I can't help but wonder, what is her motive? She is good-hearted, obviously, but enough is enough. She actually freaks me out a bit. Her presence in the row behind me is like water dripping from a faucet—it's maddeningly relentless in a passive-aggressive way. And I can't help but feel as if I'm still auditioning for her, that I still have to prove I'm a good-enough lawyer to get Salazar off.

It's stupid for me to think that, but I can't help it. I've done my best, and my work has been good, no one can say otherwise. My one big regret is that we never located Armando Gonzalez, whoever and wherever he might be. A good private detective with an open checkbook from an expensive law firm probably would have found him, assuming he exists (which I have to, because if he doesn't, my client is a liar and a con man, and I'm the real dupe). The more money you have, the better the results. Our funds are limited. So be it. You learn early on in my office to play the hand you're dealt. Bitching and moaning won't get you anything but an ulcer and a negative comment in your file.

"Roberto Salazar has led an exemplary life. I'm not the only one who is telling you that. Everyone in the community is. His friends, his neighbors, his customers. He is a devoted husband and father. His résumé is spotless. Not only has he never been convicted of a crime, even a minor misdemeanor, but he's never been arrested for one. His record is absolutely clean. Cleaner, I would wager, than most of us in this room.

"He did, what we now see in hindsight, a stupid thing. He agreed to deliver some stolen television sets. He got caught with them. He was arrested, and now he's here in court, pleading his case before you.

"But . . . and this is what's important, ladies and gentlemen. He didn't know they were stolen. At the time, he didn't think what he was doing was stupid. He thought he was doing the right thing. He was helping a friend in need."

I take a moment to let that sink in and gauge how I'm doing with the jurors. Their expressions tell me I'm doing okay. They're waiting for me to convince them, if I can, of Salazar's innocence. That's the best you can expect: a jury whose mind isn't already made up.

"How many of us would do that?" I continue. "Get out of bed in the middle of the night and drive all the way across town to help a friend who was in a desperate situation? Honestly, I don't know if I would." I smile apologetically. "I probably wouldn't. Maybe some of you wouldn't either."

A few sympathetic nods tell me I'm right. Most of us aren't that self-sacrificing.

"When you judge someone's guilt or innocence, which is a

very heavy burden, you consider motive, you consider opportunity, you consider timing. But you also consider character. If character did not count in helping you come to your decision, I would not have been allowed to bring in all those witnesses who have spoken about Mr. Salazar's integrity. But it does count, because it tells us about a person's history. And your history tells us about who you are today.

"All of us live our lives in predictable patterns. Good people don't all of a sudden become evil, nor do bad people suddenly become good. We may remember that Saint Paul was converted from evil to good on the road to Damascus; but unless you are a saint, such an immediate and powerful personality change doesn't happen. We are who we are. If and when we do change, it is a long, slow process. People simply do not change their core beliefs, philosophies, and ways of living overnight."

The Saint Paul allusion does not come from my own beliefs, but it is an apt one, and there are always some jury members who are churchgoers. That is an analogy they understand and empathize with. Not only is it about change, it speaks of forgiveness, a concept I want to plant in their minds.

"Roberto Salazar made a mistake. But he did not commit a crime. The prosecution did not bring forth any witnesses who testified that Mr. Salazar stole those television sets. They couldn't, because there aren't any. They did not offer any witnesses who testified that Mr. Salazar was involved in any burglary ring, because again, there aren't any. They did not connect Mr. Salazar to any other crime of any kind, because there aren't any. Zero. Mr. Salazar has never committed a crime. His record is spotless."

I take a quick glance at my notes. I know where I'm going, but I don't like to forget anything. I haven't, so I plunge ahead.

"There are two main witnesses against Mr. Salazar in this trial. The officer who arrested him, and the jailhouse informant who squealed on him."

Out of the corner of my eye I spot Dixant half rising out of his chair, as if to make an objection to that last remark. But Judge

Rosen immediately shakes her head *no,* so he sits back down. He can rebut me in his own closing argument. Examining witnesses has to be as factual and truthful as possible, but opening and closing summations are appeals to both the facts and the heart. *If the glove does not fit, you must acquit* was only tangentially about a marginal fact; it was really an appeal to feelings—about how the system prematurely assumes guilt about certain people, especially, as in that infamous case, a member of a historically oppressed minority. More subtly, that's where I'm going now. Not because I want to exploit the race card, but because in this situation, it's appropriate.

"Let's take each of these witnesses one at a time," I say. "First, the police officer who arrested Mr. Salazar. Did he stop Mr. Salazar because he had reason to believe there were stolen television sets in Mr. Salazar's truck? He testified he did not. Then why did he stop him? According to his sworn testimony . . ." I pluck the appropriate page of transcript from my pile of notes and read: *"One of Mr. Salazar's tail-lights was flickering, and he had run a stop sign."*

I pause for a moment to let the flimsiness of those accusations sink in. "It was three in the morning. Maybe Mr. Salazar made a rolling stop through that sign instead of coming to a full stop. You stop someone for that, when there isn't another car on the road for blocks around? Over a thousand murders occur in Los Angeles county every year, but people are being pulled over for not coming to a complete stop on a deserted street in the dead of night? What kind of misguided priorities are those? Either this officer is an overzealous martinet, or he was looking for an excuse to pull Mr. Salazar over. You saw him testify. Did he look like he was over the top? He didn't to me. He looked like a calm, cool, in-control peace officer. Which leaves us with the other possibility: that he was looking for an excuse—any excuse, no matter how flimsy—to pull over Mr. Salazar."

I glance at my notes again. "Oh, I forgot. The flickering taillight. He wanted to make sure Mr. Salazar's truck wasn't going to have an electrical short. What if there were people inside that truck? People who had been smuggled into this country illegally. What if a fire broke out in the back of that truck because of faulty wiring, and they burned to death? That officer didn't want to search Mr. Salazar's truck, without due cause and without a proper warrant, because of an actual infraction of the law. He was performing a humanitarian act. He was an angel of mercy, if you will."

I shake my head in bemused disbelief. "Unfortunately, there weren't any human beings in the back of Mr. Salazar's truck. Only a bunch of television sets. That officer must have been pretty disappointed. But he recovered and did his duty. He arrested Mr. Salazar."

I smile in mock chagrin. "Okay," I admit. "They were stolen. Not by Mr. Salazar—we all agree to that, including my opponent, Mr. Dixant. But he had them, so he's guilty by association."

I leave the podium and walk toward the jury box. "I want to give you folks a premise you can all relate to. Your daughter is a teenager, a junior in high school, seventeen. She's a good girl, stays out of trouble, gets good grades. She has this new boyfriend. He's older than her, a little wild. Maybe he's in college, working, in the army. You disapprove of the relationship but you're not going to stop it, because she has to learn to make her own decisions, and because if you do, she'll resent you, and probably keep seeing him behind your back. And the boy isn't a bad guy, he's just a young man sowing his oats, as guys do.

"One night, they're out at a party. She doesn't drink, but he has a couple of beers. On the way home a cop stops him, because he's driving erratically. When they pull him over, they think, or claim, that they smell marijuana smoke, so they search the car. They don't find any marijuana in the car, but they do find a vial of crack cocaine. They don't just arrest the boy, they arrest your daughter too, because she was there. That's the law."

I take a long pause, because I really want the jurors to absorb this. From their expressions and fidgeting, they are. I wait long enough so that they're uncomfortable with this malignant seed I've just planted, then I start up again.

"Your daughter didn't know the crack was in the car. She's never done drugs in her life, she doesn't even drink beer with her friends. But the law is the law. She was in a car in which there was an illegal substance, so she is guilty by association.

"If you and she are lucky, the District Attorney will make the sensible decision, and not charge her with a crime. If you are *unlucky,* he will, and her life and yours will be hell to pay for a long time, even if she doesn't get convicted. And if he does *not* charge her," I continue, "what will the reason be? It will be because he researched her history and learned that she is a good person. A person of character."

I walk back to the podium. Behind me, I hear them stirring— I've touched a nerve.

"At least the officer who arrested Mr. Salazar was doing his duty by the book, more or less," I say. "But their other key witness, the jailhouse informant, is a different story. He had no legitimate reason to come forward with his story—none whatsoever. You think he did it because he's a good citizen? To make that claim would be an insult to your intelligence, ladies and gentlemen. The man is a career criminal, he's never walked a straight line in his life. He testified for one reason, and one reason only: to get a break on his sentence."

I shake my head in anger. I can really get worked up over a case—sometimes too much. You have to be in control. But a little righteous indignation, properly channeled, can be an asset. In their guts, jurors can tell honest passion from manufactured baloney, and they respond to it.

"That's all that we have here. A convicted felon's word that Mr. Salazar confessed his crimes to him. No corroboration, no other witnesses, nothing. Well, I don't know about you, but I didn't believe him, not for a second. And the fact that the prosecution brought him on at the last possible moment makes me even more suspicious. The man was in the county jail, right under their noses, and it took them more than sixty days to find him? I'm sorry, but that doesn't smell good to me. In fact, it stinks.

"Jailhouse informants—let's call them what they call themselves, snitches—used to be used by prosecutors much more than they are today. There is a very strong reason that they aren't. It's because they have been proven, time and time again, to be unreliable. Part of the reason the Los Angeles Police Department is currently under federal supervision is because they used jailhouse informants who they knew were lying. Dozens of convictions have been overturned because of an unholy alliance between the police, the prosecutors, and these jailhouse liars.

"This case should never have been brought to trial. Anyone looking at this objectively would see that this man sitting before you . . ." I turn and sweep my arm toward Salazar ". . . is not a criminal. He is a good man who made a bad mistake. He has suffered for that. But he did not steal those television sets, and he didn't know they were stolen. He was being a Good Samaritan, trying to help a friend. And because he's a good man—better than most of us, frankly—he has gone through pain, suffering, humiliation. Even if you find him not guilty, which I believe you will and should, what has happened to him during the past three months has scarred him for life. He is never going to be as trusting of authority as he was before. He is never going to be as open to helping others as he was before. He is going to retreat from fully engaging, and all of his friends and neighbors and parishioners and others are going to be the worse for it."

I fire my parting shot. "There is a difference between committing a crime and making a mistake. You do not send someone to jail for making a mistake. You teach him a lesson, so he won't make that mistake again. Well, believe me, ladies and gentlemen, Mr. Salazar has learned his lesson, and then some. There is justice in this world, and there is injustice. You all know the difference. And you know, in your hearts, that sending Mr. Salazar to prison for making a mistake would be a terrible injustice. I trust you will not do that. You will find him not guilty, and will send him home to again be with his wife, his children, and all of the people in his community he so lovingly and selflessly serves."

Wayne Dixant doesn't waste any time buttering up his audience. "Do you people remember Kenneth Lay, the CEO of Enron, who swindled thousands of people out of hundreds of millions of dollars? Some of you may have lost money out of your bank accounts or retirement funds because of him. The citizens of the state of California—you and me—lost billions of dollars, not millions but *billions,* because of his shady, illegal, and immoral manipulations." A quick break, then: "I see your heads nodding. You all remember that scandal. But here's something you may not know about it. At Ken Lay's trial, scores of people, many of them well-known, famous men and women, including several clergymen, swore to his good character. What a good father he was, good citizen, Eagle Scout, benefactor of the downtrodden, all things good and true. A saint on earth to rival Saint Augustine himself, the way some of his character witnesses laid it on. But he was convicted anyway, because he broke the law, and the jury who decided his fate was able to separate the facts from the emotional appeals that were made to them.

"That is the choice we have here: facts versus emotion. Fact: the accused, Roberto Salazar, was caught red-handed with a shipment of stolen goods. That is not in dispute, even by him. Fact: he had no legal documents for them. He couldn't, because they had been stolen less than six hours before he was caught with them. In the back of his truck. Which was locked. Which he frantically tried to stop the police from searching, only yielding when they threatened to arrest him."

Dixant sighs. It's a very theatrical sigh, too heavy-handed for my taste, but that's his style. The jury, which I felt was leaning in my direction, now seems to be on his wavelength, a cause for concern to me. The guy is a scumbag and bullshit artist extraordinaire, but he's putting on a good summation.

"That was a great performance my esteemed opponent just put on," he says, without a trace of sneer. "She should take her act across the street to the Mark Taper Theater, I hear they're auditioning actors for their next show. A comedy, I'm told." He is dripping in earnest sarcasm now, it's puddling at his feet. What really fries my butt is that the jury is buying this lame's bullshit. Some of them are even smiling at his crappy jokes. I force myself not to slump in my seat as I listen to him rip me. "In Ms. Thompson's view of how our legal system works, facts don't matter; the testimony of the policemen of this city who dedicate their lives to protect and serve you doesn't matter; the truth doesn't matter. All that matters is whether or not the accused is a nice guy. Well, ladies and gentlemen, facts *do* matter, because they are indisputable truths. Everything else is subjective. Which is why, when we decide whether a defendant is innocent or guilty, we examine the facts and put our emotions aside."

He looks over at Salazar and me again, but this time, his look is one of distilled venom, which he takes no pains to conceal from the jury. "If ever a summation was a textbook example of grasping at straws, you just witnessed it. Ms. Thompson had no facts on her side—none. Let me give you one glaring example. If, in *fact,* the accused was making a legitimate delivery, why didn't the defense bring as a witness whomever those television sets were supposed to be delivered to? If that delivery was on the up and up, whoever was supposed to receive them would have said so. He would have provided documents to show it was, *in fact,* a legal transaction. In *fact,* if the accused's lawyer had taken that simple and obvious step before this trial began, the people might not have prosecuted Mr. Salazar, because there would be proof—*facts,* again—that at least part of the transaction was legitimate, and given the accused's prior good record, we might have given him the benefit of the doubt. But that person was never called to the stand.

"That omission could have been a case of brain lock on Ms. Thompson's part. We all drop the ball sometimes. In this situation, though, I don't think so. It's too obvious, and Ms. Thompson is too smart not to have followed that up. The real reason, which is apparent to all of us, is that whomever these stolen television sets were being delivered to was not legitimate, either. He was part of the overall crime picture. There is no other logical explanation."

Dixant got me on that one. I was hoping he wouldn't connect those dots, but he has. He's an asshole, but he's not stupid. Of course I didn't try to find out who was on the receiving end of those television sets, because I knew from the get-go they had been stolen, even if Salazar didn't. If I had contacted the man he was supposed to deliver them to and asked him to come forward on our behalf he would have told me to shove it and five minutes later he would have shut down his operation and joined Gonzalez in deep hiding. And without any paperwork from Salazar to back me up, I would have had no way to force him to help us. So I never tried.

"Let's review the timetable," Dixant says, as he walks to an easel his assistant has set up next to the jury box. There is a large artist's pad on it, upon which a simple map and time line have been drawn. Picking up a pointer, he starts to trace the sequence of events.

"We know the television sets were stolen from San Pedro a few hours before the accused was arrested," he says, pointing to the first set of figures. He traces the pointer down the line. "The accused was arrested in West Los Angeles, which is twenty miles away on the freeways, at three in the morning." The pointer moves again. "According to the accused, he left his home in East Los Angeles . . ." The pointer skips across the drawing to the opposite side. ". . . At approximately one o'clock in the morning. We only have his word for that. No one else has corroborated that, not even his wife. If she had, it might be easier for us to believe him. But she didn't testify for her husband, so we only have his word for that."

Hoisted on another petard. Salazar's wife might have confirmed the time frame if she was awake at the time Salazar got the call. But she would also have fallen apart, and might have hurt her husband more than she could help him. I couldn't take that chance; and I couldn't, out of basic decency, put her on the stand to be ripped to shreds. Now, of course, it looks as if we have something else to hide.

"He drove clear across the entire city and met the aforementioned Gonzalez in Wilmington, at about two in the morning." Dixant traces a line from where Salazar lives to Wilmington. It's a long distance, even on paper. "Gets out of bed, drives all the way across a huge city. To help a friend. And we know, because the defense has driven this down our throats with all their character witnesses, that the accused is a wonderful human being, the salt of the earth.

"And what does he find when he gets there, thirty miles away from his warm bed and the comfort of his wife at two o'clock in the morning? A truck with a faulty generator." Dixant turns away from the easel and faces the jury. "Let me ask you something, ladies and gentlemen. With all due respect to the accused's goodness of heart, does this make sense to you? That a man whose truck broke down in Wilmington . . ." He taps his pointer on the Wilmington spot on the map. ". . . Would call for help from someone who lives all the way over in East L.A.?" The pointer moves across his diagram again. "I'll grant that Mr. Salazar is a fine man, who helps his friends when they are in trouble. But still, think about it. Does that make sense? It doesn't to me. Especially if you're sitting on a truck full of hot television sets, right off a freeway exit, where any police officer driving by is going to stop and ask you what the problem is, then offer to help, which is the last thing you want: a cop's interference, no matter how well intentioned. You're going to want to get your vehicle to a safer, more secluded place. Wouldn't it make more sense to think that Mr. Gonzalez, assuming he actually exists, would have called a tow truck? In the amount of time it took the accused to drive halfway across the county and load those television sets from one truck to the other, Gonzalez could have gotten his truck fixed at an all-night garage and gone on his way."

Dixant walks back to the podium, flips through his notes, and extracts a sheet of paper. Holding it up, he declares, "There is a twenty-four-hour garage less than three miles from where this alleged transfer took place. Wilmington is a heavily industrialized area. It gets a lot of truck traffic, and this station has to make repairs around the clock. Any tow company would have known that. They would have taken Gonzalez's truck there and a new generator would have been installed in less than half an hour, it's a simple repair to make. I know, because I checked that myself."

A cardinal rule in preparing a case is to analyze it from the other side. I didn't do that thoroughly enough, and my lack of anticipating the prosecution's moves is biting me on the butt.

Too late now for regrets, unfortunately. You make choices and live with them. Or die with them. The more convincingly Dixant lays out his case, the deeper I'm sinking. I steal a glance at my client. He is listening attentively, but he doesn't seem overly worried. From the very beginning he has trusted me to pull his fat out of the fire. I hope he'll still believe in me when this is over.

"Salazar and Gonzalez transfer the television sets from one truck to the other," Dixant continues. "In plain sight, where anyone could drive by and see them. But luckily for them, these two men make the transfer without any trouble. They finish by two-thirty." He taps his time line again. "Salazar leaves, and Gonzalez waits for a tow truck to come get him. *Now* he waits for the tow truck, after he's off-loaded his hot goods. If anything bad happens after this, he's in the clear."

Dixant's pointer moves up the 405 freeway, tracing Salazar's route. "The time is three o'clock in the morning. The accused pulls off the freeway. According to him, to go to the bathroom. I'll accept that. When you gotta go, you gotta go," he cracks.

A few of the jurors smile at his dumb joke, more to relieve the tension than because it's funny, since it isn't. Dixant doesn't care; he's rolling, and he knows it.

"Anyway, he figures he's home free, right? The transfer of the stolen television sets was made, they're locked up tight in his truck, all he has to do is drive over the pass, deliver them, and go back to his warm bed."

He turns and looks at Salazar and me, which draws the jury's attention to us. Their stares at Salazar aren't friendly, as they were earlier. Dixant waits for them to get a good look, then says, "But he never gets home, because he carelessly runs a stop sign, an officer is passing by, he is lawfully stopped, the officer notices a faulty tail-light, he inspects the truck, finds the stolen television sets, and arrests him. What terrible luck. I mean, who would ever think an officer would be driving by at that precise moment, so late at night? Obviously, not the accused. Which was a bad mistake to make. Because the Los Angeles Police Department and Sheriff's Department is always out there. To protect and serve the honest citizens of our community. You and me."

Having finished his physical presentation, Dixant leaves his display and walks back to the podium. "I want to take a moment to talk about the prosecution's witness, Mr. Calderon," he says. "Ms. Thompson was very aggressive in denouncing this man and attacking his story and his credibility. She had to be, because if it's true, there can be no doubt that her client is guilty. So she has to tear Mr. Calderon down, and convince you that he was lying. If I were her, I would do the same thing. And she was right to denounce the abuses of the past that came from using jailhouse informants as witnesses. As a public official, I am ashamed and embarrassed about those abuses. Everyone in law enforcement in Los Angeles County, policemen and prosecutors alike, is ashamed of this record. Which is why we are much, much more careful now about using these informants, because we know, from painful experience, that there have been grievous abuses. We are very careful not to let that happen anymore. If there is any question about such witnesses today, we don't use them. That is official departmental policy, and it is strictly enforced.

"You may not believe that this corrupt behavior is over. I can understand your being suspicious. We lost your trust, and we're trying our best to earn it back. But let's take a step back and examine these particular circumstances logically. Mr. Calderon was in the jail when the accused was also in the jail. That's in the record. Calderon testified that they were in close proximity. The accused said they weren't. One of them is telling the truth, one is lying. We don't know which one. Calderon told you that the accused confessed to him. The accused said he didn't. Again, one is lying and one isn't. Which one, we don't know.

"But there is one thing we do know. The details that Calderon talked about are true. That is not debatable. Everyone, including my esteemed opponent, agrees about that. Calderon could only have known about those details in one of two ways. Either the accused told him, or I told him. I, meaning me, one of my associates, or a police officer. Because no one else knew."

He's thrown down the gauntlet now. All the chips are on the table.

"If you think this witness was coached by me or anyone associated with this case, you should find the accused not guilty. You would be derelict in your duty, not only legally but morally, if you didn't. But if you don't think we did, then you have to believe my witness, because there would have been no other way for him to know what he told you, other than finding it out from the accused."

The courtroom is as quiet as a tomb. Not even the air is moving. Some of the jurors might not even be breathing. I can barely catch my own breath.

Dixant squares up his notes into a neat stack. The finish line is in sight, and he races toward it. "Do you believe his story? *Can* you believe his story? I can't. I don't see how anyone, thinking logically, can believe his story. He was caught with a shipment of stolen goods. That is a fact. Everything else is conjecture.

"My opponent claims that people don't change. We are who we are. Basically, I agree with her. That's human nature. But circumstances change. An opportunity presents itself, and you take it. That is human nature, too. Even good people do bad things. No one is a criminal until he commits a crime, regardless of whether he's twelve, eighteen, thirty-five, ninety. There is no statute of limitations on becoming a criminal, no age ceiling that says once you are this old, you will never commit a crime. Kenneth Lay was in his fifties before he committed his crimes.

"When you go into the jury room to decide your verdict, you will have two choices: guilty, or not guilty. You will be instructed by Judge Rosen to make your decision based on the facts that have been presented to you. *Facts*, ladies and gentlemen, not emotions. Please do not let your emotions cloud the facts in this case. If you do, you will be doing our system of justice a great disservice. We are a nation of laws, not men. And thank God for that."

He has made his case. Now he can let the air out of the balloon. "The facts in this case speak loud and clear. They say, beyond any reasonable doubt, that the accused, Roberto Salazar, transported stolen goods. That is a crime. I believe in our system of laws, and I know you do, too. Make your decision with your minds, not your hearts. And when you do, the only verdict you can arrive at under the laws of the state of California will be that the accused is guilty."

EIGHTEEN

U SUALLY, THE LONGER A jury is out, the better it is for the defense, and if it brings in a fast verdict, the tendency is they have found the defendant guilty. There are plenty of exceptions, of course: O.J.'s jury came back fast and Scooter Libby's dragged their heels, but the theory is true more often than not. I'm always happy when a jury plays it slow. In a case like this, where there is only one count and the choices aren't complex, if they go more than two or three days, it generally means they are deadlocked, and a hung jury has to be declared. I'll settle for that. Given the ill will between the D.A.'s office and ours because of Dixant's crude chicanery, I doubt the state would try this case again. They'd lick their wounds, and move on.

Judge Rosen charged the jury at the end of the day yesterday and sent them home. They were back at nine this morning to begin deliberating. It's noon now; they'll break for lunch soon, then they'll return for the rest of the afternoon. Dixant and I, as well as Roberto Salazar, are on notice. I'm in my office, catching up on work that has piled up while I was in trial. I made sure Roberto understood that when the jury reached its decision and we are recalled to the courtroom, he should be on time, and presentable. He's waiting at home; he can be here in less than an hour.

I spent last night rehashing the trial, fretting over what I could have done differently. I probably should have had Salazar testify that he had been a delivery boy for Gonzalez before, and had been paid for his labors. And I should have leaned harder on Calderon, Dixant's jailhouse snitch, citing specific cases of previous witnesses like him who had been discredited and whose testimony had not only been thrown out, but had also caused mistrials or outright dismissals. I also could have asked for a longer adjournment to scrounge up an expert (the best ones are former cops and prosecutors) who would have had experience in eviscerating jailhouse informants with more authority than I had. I thought that exposing the Dixant-Calderon quid pro quo would be enough, but it may not have been. His bullshit was obvious to me, and would have been to any trial lawyer or court observer, but a layman serving on a jury might not have seen what a lying piece of shit he was. I'll know when the jury brings back its verdict.

I'm sure there are other things I could have done better as well. But the *fact,* as Dixant rammed down the jury's throat, was that Salazar was caught with those stolen television sets, and the only witness who could get him off was never found.

I did my best, and given the circumstances, I put up a good defense. That's all you can do: give it your best shot. You have to live with that and accept it, or you'll eat your guts out.

No matter how good a case I put on at trial, I'm always in a worried state of mind during deliberations. If the prosecution loses, it's a bad mark on their record. If a defense lawyer loses, his client loses his freedom. Most of the time, my side loses; but even if we expect it, it's a shitty feeling. If I lose this one, I'll feel worse than usual, because I do believe, in my heart, that the only crime Roberto Salazar was guilty of was gullibility.

High noon. I didn't pack a lunch today, so I'll grab a salad someplace close by and bring it back up here. I'm swamped; I'll eat while I work.

My phone rings. Judge Rosen's clerk is on the other end of the line. The jury has reached a verdict, she informs me. We're to be in the courtroom at one-thirty sharp.

I hang up in a daze. Immediately, my stomach starts churning.

I didn't expect this, not this soon. They've been deliberating less than three hours. This is way too fast.

I dial Salazar's phone number and force myself to project confidence as I give him the news. "Leave right now," I adjure him, "in case there's heavy traffic."

He doesn't sound worried; he doesn't know about my quick-jury rule. "This is good, isn't it?" he asks. His tone is genuinely cheerful. "We convinced them. You convinced them," he corrects himself. The man is self-effacing to a fault.

"Let's not get ahead of ourselves," I caution him. "I'll meet you outside the courtroom. Drive carefully."

I replace the receiver in its cradle and slump back in my chair. Forget lunch now—I wouldn't be able to keep anything down. Blindly, I pick up a random case file from the pile and try to force myself to read it. This is going to be an interminable ninety minutes.

The jurors shuffle into the courtroom and take their assigned chairs in the box. They all avoid eye contact with Salazar and me. My heart drops. They went with their minds, not their hearts. They did their duty, as the law required. I can't fault that, but I am dismayed about it.

I steal a glance over at Dixant. He's trying to mold his face into a neutral mask, but he can't hide the gloating expression that's fighting to burst out. I want to win this case for my client, but I also want to kick that smug bastard's ass. I have a sinking feeling I'm not going to do either.

Next to me, Salazar seems calm in his skin. I wonder what he's been doing while we have been waiting. Praying, maybe? Is a personal triumph the sort of thing a religious person prays for? I suppose a saint would pray that the jury will not feel remorse with their decision, especially if it goes against him. Since I'm no saint, I don't know. I wouldn't feel altruistic, that's for sure. More like the opposite. I hope this man sitting here beside me isn't such a nice guy that he would turn the other cheek all the time. And yet, if I compare my life to his in terms of satisfaction, ease with yourself, giving and getting love, he's way ahead of me. A sobering thought.

Sitting in the row behind us, Salazar's wife is his emotional opposite. Her nerve ends are so raw it's as if she's stuck her finger into a light socket. And next to her, the ever-present rock of ages, Amanda Burgess. Does this woman have a life? I'm glad she's here to keep Mrs. Salazar from completely falling apart, but isn't there a limit to what I can only think of as noblesse oblige?

She smiles at me as our eyes meet. Good luck, she mouths silently. I give her a tepid nod of thanks in return. I can't help myself, but I still feel as if I'm auditioning for her.

Judge Rosen turns her attention to the jury box. She asks the dreaded question: "Has the jury reached a decision?"

The foreperson, a middle-aged elementary school teacher, stands up. "We have, Your Honor." Her voice is a low contralto, heavy and dusky. A Sunday church-choir voice.

She hands the verdict sheet to the clerk, who carries it over to Rosen. The judge unfolds and reads it. Her expression doesn't give anything away. She hands the paper to the clerk, who conveys it back to the foreperson. "The defendant will rise," she says.

I put a hand on Salazar's elbow to prompt him to stand up. I stand next to him. Across the aisle, Dixant and his assistant also get up. It's an act of respect, not for the people present, but for the system. When we are all in place, Judge Rosen asks, "What is your verdict?"

My muscles tighten. I'm glad I remembered to go to the bathroom before coming in here. I resist the urge to take Salazar's hand.

"We find the defendant not guilty."

There is a moment of silence while the verdict sinks in—then I feel a rush of relief wash over me, as if I had bobbed to the surface of the ocean after being caught in a fierce undertow. I break into a wide, happy smile as I turn to Salazar, who is also smiling, but not as effusively, more as if he's just glad it's over, and he can get on with his life. Behind us, his wife rushes forward and hugs him over the railing. Amanda Burgess, standing in place, gives me her own smile, one of satisfaction and approval.

Judge Rosen brings down her gavel. "The defendant is free to go," she announces. Nodding at me, she reminds me, "Fill out the necessary documents." I nod back that I will. But as she is turning to the jurors to thank them, Dixant's voice rings out abrasively. "Poll the jury," he demands rudely.

My head whips around. Jesus, this guy really is a jerk. But it's his right to ask. He's pissed and he isn't taking any pains to conceal it. His face is livid red, like a ripe beet. If you gave his temples a good squeeze, his brains might pop out of his ears, he's so uptight.

Judge Rosen lifts an inquisitive eyebrow. It's over, she wants to dismiss the jurors and lay this to rest. "Mr. Dixant . . ." She's giving him a moment to reconsider, to abate his stubbornness for once.

He doesn't budge. "Poll the jury, Your Honor," he repeats his request.

"If you insist," she answers tartly. He'll pay for this down the line, when he comes up against her again. She looks at the jurors. "I'm going to ask each of you to say your verdict out loud, individually," she explains. She looks at the nearest one. "Juror number one."

"Not guilty."

"Juror number two."

"Not guilty."

Each juror in turn is asked, and each gives the same not-guilty response. Dixant glares at them as they speak, as if to dare them to say the words out loud. Some of the jurors make their pronouncement with authority, but others are less forthright. A few sound downright reluctant, casting their looks to the floor. But they all say the two words their foreperson had pronounced.

As soon as juror number twelve utters her response, Rosen

brings her gavel down, more forcefully than necessary. "The defendant is free to go," she says, staring ice cubes at Dixant. She thanks the jurors for their diligence and effort, and with a flourish of robe thrown over shoulder, she calls out as she stands to leave: "Court is adjourned."

We mill around for a few minutes—Salazar, his wife, Amanda Burgess, and I. His wife is in tears; she expected the worst. He comforts her with hugs and caresses. Amanda stands to the side, like a proud parent at a wedding or confirmation. She sidles over to me.

"Congratulations," she tells me. "You must feel good."

"Of course. And relieved," I admit.

She nods in understanding. "Yes. I must admit, when Mr. Dixant finished giving his summation yesterday, I was nervous. His argument was more persuasive than I would have expected."

"The jury believed Roberto," I say to her. "They saw his decency."

"Virtue does have its own reward, sometimes," she answers with a wry smile. She puts a friendly hand on my forearm. Her touch is feather light—she could hold a bird in her hands without harming it. "Roberto will thank you, of course, but I want to thank you too. If there is ever anything—"

I stop her, nicely. "I should thank *you*," I say. "Your support made a real difference."

"This was important to me," she says. "I'll let you go, but there is one thing I want to say. Please take this in the spirit in which it is given, which is with appreciation and generosity."

I freeze inside. A phrase like that is usually a prelude to a slap in the face.

"I know you love your work here, and thank God for that. I don't know if another lawyer would have gotten Roberto off. The facts were against him, but your skill and passion carried the day. Watching you, I really came to appreciate how talented you are, Jessica." She hesitates for the briefest of moments.

I wait for the "however," but she surprises me. "If you ever decide to go into the private sector, I would like to help you. I'm well connected, as you know. I have many friends in big law firms in this city. Any of whom would be happy to have you join their firms." Her hand touches mine. "You would make a fortune. And you would be associating with the top echelons of your profession."

As opposed to grubbing in the dirt with civil servants is the unstated but clear implication. Part of me is annoyed that she would take such an attitude—what I do with my life is none of her damn business. But another part of me can't help but be flattered. The air Amanda Burgess breathes is rarified. She's offering me a chance to climb up on the mountaintop with her.

"Thank you," I say. "I'll think about it."

"Good." One more hand on mine. "Stay in touch, please. And allow me to do the same."

Roberto Salazar and I have our final good-byes. "I usually tell my clients to stay out of trouble," I say to him, "but with you, I don't have to. I know it will be hard, because your inclination is always to be helpful, but the next time someone calls you in the middle of the night and asks for a favor, turn him down."

He smiles back at me. "That will depend on who calls," he chides me sweetly. "And what the favor is."

I watch as he and his wife leave the courtroom, arm in arm. Lovebirds, they broadcast it to the world. It must be wonderful to be in such a soulful relationship.

"The system doesn't always work."

I look over my shoulder. Wayne Dixant is behind me, hovering like a turkey vulture. I don't reply to his sour grapes. I could be magnanimous, throw him a bone of consolation, but he fucked with me too much for any post-trial civility.

"You won, that's all that counts, right?" he says bitterly, with nary a grace note of conciliation. This guy is the sorest loser I've ever gone up against. "But we both know the truth."

He spins on his heel and marches out. Loser.

I wait a few minutes until I presume the coast is clear; I don't want to have to share a corridor or elevator with Dixant. But as I leave the courtroom, a couple of the jurors, both women, approach me. It's obvious they have been waiting to talk to me, which is fine with me. I like to get jurors' reactions, to find out what worked, what didn't, and why.

Although they smile at me, they are clearly uncomfortable. "Mr. Salazar is a good, decent man," one of them says by way of initiating our conversation. "You presented those qualities of his very well."

"Thank you." I accept their encomium with good cheer. "I agree—he is a good man. And thank you for the compliment."

"You're welcome." They look around nervously, as if afraid someone (like Wayne Dixant) might be eavesdropping. The speaker leans in closer. "We had to find him not guilty," she confides to me in a low hush, "even though he was."

My body jerks involuntarily. "Excuse me?"

"The judge instructed us to reach our verdict based on the facts, not feelings or emotions," she says, as if she has to remind me of what I know by heart, having heard it at every single trial I've been in or witnessed. Which Judge Rosen did, in her instructions to them. It's what judges always tell juries: *Your job is to decide the facts of a case, not to cloud it with your own moral judgments.* (An instruction that often goes in one ear and out the other, because juries dance to their own music.) "But we couldn't, because if we did, we would have had to find him guilty, and send him to prison." she says. "Nobody wanted to do that."

"Hmm," I vamp. I want her to keep explaining, specifically.

She does, because on behalf of all of them, she needs to explain their motive for subverting the rules. "Anybody can make a mistake. And it wasn't like he was selling drugs, or pulled a gun on someone. He got a little greedy. We all do. Him less than most, but still . . ." Her voice trails off, then starts up again. "Sending that man to jail wouldn't have done anyone any good," she tells me with staunch conviction.

"It was my idea," the second lady horns in. "Everybody agreed, right off the bat."

The first lady gives her a mild look of pique, then finishes what she wanted to say. "He deserved a second chance. He won't do that again, we're sure of it."

She looks around the hallway again, then leans in conspiratorially. "And we didn't want to disappoint you. You're so nice." Her face wrinkles in disgust. "Not like that Dixant man. He is foul. He had a good case, but he needs a personality transplant."

I fight back a laugh; they might take it the wrong way. After all the preparation and trial, the whole ball of wax came down to who was likable and who wasn't. I don't always win those contests, because I can be prickly, but this time Salazar and I were the good guys and Dixant was the heavy, a role he was born to play. Which proves, once again, that appearances can be more important than truth.

I usually don't like subjective qualities like character to win out over objective, verifiable truths, because to do so is a perversion of justice, and I believe in justice. But in this special situation I take comfort in knowing that character does matter, and that truth can sometimes be greater than a collection of dry and heartless facts.

NINETEEN

IN LESS THAN FORTY-EIGHT hours I will run my marathon. It's in San Diego. I'll drive down tomorrow, Saturday afternoon, check into my hotel, go to the prerace dinner, where I'll carbo-load like crazy, and try to get some sleep, although I'm sure I'll be too restless to get much. I've been antsy about this for weeks; the anticipation is like an itch that can't be scratched. It's one of those experiences, so I've been told, that you can't really understand until you do it. Like giving birth, my other major goal for the near future. Not that I'm equating the two, but both are a leap of faith into the unknown. You don't know how you'll handle these challenges until you're actually doing them.

The only downer is that Jeremy won't be waiting for me at the finish line with a cold drink and a hug. The orchestra left on its tour three weeks ago. Last night they performed in Krakow, Poland. The next few days they are in the Baltic countries, then Finland. Salonen is Finnish, so they'll have a rousing reception in Helsinki. That would be a concert I'd love to make, but our schedules didn't permit it. After that they're going to Moscow, Saint Petersburg, then back into the heart of Europe. I'm flying into Prague a week from today. I can't wait.

Tonight is the first night of the full moon. The police are on high alert. The killer hasn't struck for the past two months; if he doesn't claim a victim this go-around, the task force will be disbanded. The LAPD is understaffed, and they can't tie up many of their elite detectives indefinitely. I haven't seen my newly minted pal Cordova this month, but I'm sure he's wound up super tight. He doesn't want another murder on his hands, but he doesn't want the killer to vanish into thin air, either. His ambition is to catch the killer before he strikes again, which is impossible, basically. I don't know many of the specifics of the crimes—they are a tightly held secret known only by those directly working on the murders—but I do know that the victims weren't murdered by some grotesque means. The scuttlebutt around the courthouse is that the women were killed by strangulation, probably with gloved hands—no fingerprints were found anywhere. The killer does not have a telltale signature, like a razor slash, bite marks, or foreign objects inserted into various cavities—the kinds of fetishistic markings these sick animals often leave in their wake, like animal scat.

They may have been raped; that's less clear. Some of them exhibited bruising around their genitals, but there was no semen residue found in any of them, which means there was no DNA left behind. Either the killer used a condom, which seems bizarre, given the violent nature of the murders, or sex wasn't involved, and the marks found on the victims were coincidental, from previous consensual sex. A technician looking for foul play could read more into the physical evidence than actually exists. People see what they want to see, especially when they are predisposed to come to a certain conclusion.

It's seven-fifteen. The westbound traffic on the I-10 was brutal, bumper to bumper every car length of the way. It took me more than an hour to get home, the price you pay for living in the City of Angels. I change into my running outfit and hit the street. Tonight's run will be short and slow, a three-mile jog along Palisades Park to keep my muscles loose and oily. Tomorrow I rest, Sunday I race. After that, who knows? I could give up running completely and take up kayaking, swimming in the ocean, or Tai Chi. Or maybe I'll get hooked on long-distance running and start to plan the next one. They say pain has its own rewards if you can tolerate it and get beyond it. Pretty soon, I'm going to find out if that's true for me.

Sunset isn't for another hour, but the police are already out, melting into the Friday evening beehive of activity. They're more inconspicuous this time around, in shorts, jeans, other casual clothing. Some are as gnarly looking as surfers or dealers. I can spot them, though, because I've seen some of them in the courthouse. A few have testified against clients of mine.

On impulse, I break off my jog and approach one of them. He sees me coming and gives me an almost-imperceptible head shake—don't bust my cover. I look around to make sure no one is watching us, and approach him anyway. He's cute, in a beach-bum dissipated way, wearing a Hawaiian shirt over OP cargo shorts. I could be a thirty-something groupie trying to turn his head, a not-uncommon variety of female seen along these beaches.

"I've seen you around," I say, to break the ice. I finger his shirttail—rayon, the real deal. "I like this look. Suits you." I smile at him flirtatiously. "I'm Jessica."

If he had ever heard my last name, he wouldn't remember it; there are thousands of us in the system. But he can't help but flirt back at an attractive lady who is almost five-eleven, wears her black hair in a long braid down her back, and is wearing running shorts and a tight singlet. "I like yours too," he lobs back at me, his eyes going to my legs. Not the most scintillating of come-ons, but he is a cop.

I check around us again. We are two pebbles in the ocean here, nothing more. "How's my pal Lieutenant Cordova?" I ask him.

He stares at me with suspicion, and some nervousness. "How do you know Cordova?"

"From work," I placate him. "That's all. I know he's in charge of the task force."

He relaxes. "He's wound up tight as a nun's you know what. We all are. Waiting for lightning to strike, when you don't know where, when, or if—that's the worst."

I nod in understanding. He's a cop. Cops live for action.

His cell phone rings. He flips it open. "This is Cavanaugh." He listens. "Nothing yet. Later."

As he's about to hang up, he interjects, "You near Lieutenant Cordova? Hey, put him on."

He waits a moment, then says, "Talking to a friend of yours, Lieutenant." He thrusts the phone at me. "Here."

I take his cell reluctantly. "Hello?" He asks who this is. "Jessica Thompson," I tell him. "You know, the runner," I say, trying to make light of what is an embarrassing moment to me. These men are out here on a very serious mission, and I'm playing games with one of them. "Ocean at Wilshire," I answer, when he asks where we are. Feeling stupid, I add, "Your officer is really on the ball. No one would ever spot him." I listen again. "Only because I know him from the courthouse. If he was any funkier, you'd arrest him." I pause for a moment as I listen again. "Sure," I tell him reluctantly.

I hand the phone back to Cavanaugh. "He's swinging by to say hello."

The detective scowls. He's opened a can of worms that should have been kept shut.

We stand in awkward juxtaposition, with nothing more to say to each other. The evening throng flows slowly around us like a clogged river. Cordova drives up in his plain wrap, gets out, and walks over to us. He's dressed casually, as he was the first night I saw him in this part of town. Jeans, an alligator-logo golf shirt, K mart running shoes. He waves to Cavanaugh in greeting. "I dig the threads," he says, teasing his subordinate. He's not a prima donna, I like that about him. "What's the shirt," he asks, "Nat Nast?"

Cavanaugh grins as he shakes his head. "Tommy Bahama, on sale at Costco."

"You must be pulling a shitload of overtime to afford those shirts," Cordova quips. "Even at Costco. You had dinner?"

"Not yet."

"Grab some now, while it's still light out. Gonna be a long night, I'm afraid."

"Okay, Chief." Cavanaugh is happy to be let off the leash. "See you," he says to me, keeping his guard up with his boss right there.

"See you," I respond.

He walks away, disappearing into the crowd. Cordova gives me the eye. "You're like a bad penny, always turning up," he says dryly. I can't tell if he's pulling my chain or not.

"I live here," I say in my defense. "What's your excuse?"

He shakes his head. "Wrong joke, wrong time."

I feel chastised. "Sorry."

"You're not going to be out later tonight, I hope. You of all people should know better."

"No," I tell him. I can't help feeling as if he's the principal and I'm the first-year English teacher. He wears the weight of authority like a second skin. "Or the next two nights, either. I won't be here."

He cocks a questioning eyebrow.

"I'm going to San Diego. My run."

He's slow on the uptake, but then he gets it. "Your marathon is this weekend?"

"Yes. Sunday."

He whistles in appreciation. "You're really gonna do it."

"I'm going to try." Of course I'm going to do it; I'll crawl across the finish line on two broken legs if I have to.

"Good on you." He pats his gut. It's big, but firm, like the rest of him. I'm sure he's fit, but a man his size would have hell to pay running twenty-six miles. He's more the shot-putter type.

"Do you think . . ." I catch myself. I don't want to interfere in this.

"Don't know." His eyes are restless, scanning the crowd. "He's missed the last two . . ." He doesn't finish his thought. He doesn't have to.

There is nothing further to say. I need to finish my run before I stiffen up. That's all I need, to pull a muscle the day before the race of my life. "Good luck," I tell him.

"Thanks. Same to you." He smiles. "You'll do good."

He's saying that to be kind, because he has no idea how hard I've trained, or my fierce resoluteness; but it's a nice gesture. I know his mind is elsewhere, but he looks me in the eye when he says it, and he seems to really mean it.

"So will you," I respond, trying to sound as positive about his mission as he does about mine. "So will you."

TWENTY

MY RACE GOES SWIMMINGLY, right from the beginning. The start was insane—the Tokyo subway system at rush hour cubed—but I expected that, so I was mentally prepared to go with the flow. Even though they use a staggered start, depending on your self-predicted time to finish (I had confidently written three hours and fifty-three minutes on my entry form, but I was hoping to go a few minutes under that), it takes a couple of miles with all those bodies tightly packed together before the sea of humanity begins to break up and we are all able to run at our individual paces.

I'm not very buttoned-up (except when it comes to work), but the tactics I laid out for this race were as precise and controlled as a mathematical formula. My two longest training runs had been twenty miles, and my times for both of them were within a minute of each other, even though I had run them over separate routes: two hours and fifty minutes, a rock-steady eight-and-a-half-minute mile. I was tired at the end of both of those runs, but I wasn't exhausted; I could have kept going. And my legs felt okay. They were sore, and I didn't run for a couple of days afterward, but there wasn't any bad cramping, no muscles turning either to jelly or concrete. I stretched, iced, took hot tubs, iced some more, gobbled Advil, and on the third day after each long run I was doing my usual ten miles again.

So here was my plan: I would run the first twenty-one miles at my usual pace, which would take three hours, plus four or five minutes extra because of the bunching up at the beginning. I knew the last five miles would take their toll. Everyone I talked to—runners who had done it, trainers, coaches—all told me the same thing: a marathon is two races, the first one twenty or twenty-one miles, and the second one, five or six miles that can feel like another twenty. You run the last fifth of the race on guts and determination. And unless you are an elite runner, you run it slower. So if you have set a time you want to make, you have to be under your average when you hit mile twenty-one.

Which is exactly how my race unfolds. At the end of the first hour, I have run six and a half miles. At hour two, I'm up to thirteen and a half. I have more than half the race under my belt and I'm cruising, clicking off those 8:30 miles as if I have a metronome in my head. The first half of the race was advertised as being harder than the second, because there are more hills and inclines, so although I know I will be in for pain later on, I feel great.

On the stroke of hour three, I am halfway between the twenty- and twenty-one-mile markers. By now, I'm passing other runners who had started way ahead of me. Most of them are really hurting—I can see the pain in their faces as I glance at them in passing. Poor bastards, I think, trying not to feel too smug and self-satisfied. Probably didn't train hard enough. Not like me—I've trained harder than Oscar de la Hoya trains for a championship fight.

Half a mile later, when I hit the twenty-one-mile sign, my watch reads three hours, five minutes, and a handful of seconds. I'm home free. I can run the last five miles and change to a ten-and-a-half-minute pace and still break four hours. I hope I don't slow down that much, but even if my pace drops a full minute, I'll achieve my goal with time to spare. I begin imagining myself spreading my arms wide as the finish line draws close, and smiling for the camera as my toe hits the magic line.

My muscles have been tightening gradually, and I am beginning to feel fatigued, but I know that feeling—it isn't that different from how I feel at the end of a thirteen-mile training run, or even the twenty-milers. There's no panic in my mind, just the realization that here it comes, the race within the race: suck it up and keep pushing. Maintain your form. Five miles is nothing. I can run five miles backward, I can hop five miles on one leg, I can . . .

Hit the wall. At twenty-two and a quarter miles, the gods of hubris wrap my legs in steel bands so tightly it feels as if I'm losing the circulation in them. I've had clients complain that the police handcuffed them so tightly any feeling was gone from their hands. That's what this feels like.

I don't totally stop running, thankfully. If I do, I might not be able to start up again. All around me, casualties are falling by the wayside like dead leaves off autumnal trees. I don't want to be one of them. I will not allow that. I am going to complete this race, even if I have to crawl to the finish line.

Luckily, this catastrophe happens at a relief station, so I have an excuse to slow down (I know no one is watching me, but I am mortifyingly self-conscious anyway). Moving at a snail's pace (the slowest snail in the world), I grab a cup of water and drink it in one swallow. Then another, another. I pour water on my head, down my back, on my legs, which by now are beginning to feel as if they are two blocks of cement.

I begin to run again, but now my gait is unfamiliar to me; it's as if I have been transformed by some devilish alchemy into a tree stump. An eighty-year-old dowager could run circles around me, a toddler has a longer stride than mine has become. My body is begging me to stop, but my mind, that stubborn muscle, won't let me. It rants at me, mocking my feebleness—weakling, wuss, *loser*.

Mind over matter. I have never understood the profundity of what I had always thought was a sophomoric aphorism, until this moment in time. My goal now is simple: one foot after the other, then another.

Mile twenty-three approaches. I pass the marker like the tortoise who will never catch the hare. Now I am the runner who is being passed by the others, I am the one whose face registers her agony, the one to feel sorry for and be happy that you trained hard enough, because she didn't. Push, I rail at myself, you've come so far. Only three miles to go. You can do this. Thousands of others are doing it—so can you. Don't quit, you'll never forgive yourself.

Three miles. I can hop three miles, I can run three miles carrying a piano on my back. Which is what this feels like.

At mile twenty-four, I look at my watch and almost throw up. I have slowed to a crawl. I am now running at a twelve-minute-mile pace, which won't get me close to my goal of breaking four hours. At this rate I'll be lucky to finish by sundown, I think, as I further indulge my self-pity.

And then, miraculously, I catch my second wind. I thought that only applied to breathing, but I discover it can pertain to muscles rebounding as well. I am still in a world of pain, but now it's bearable—just.

By mile twenty-five, I am feeling better. The sensation is relative, of course, I still feel awful, but the end is in sight. I steal a glance at my watch. I've picked up my pace—my time is three hours, forty-nine minutes. I am running through my pain, and coming out the other side.

Push. Push like you've never pushed before. You took a bullet and lived. You can run a mile and a fifth in eleven minutes. Forget the pain, it's going to be there whether you run fast or slow. So run fast.

I run as fast as I can. I cannot run one second faster. I've done my absolute best. But on this day, my best isn't good enough. It takes me twelve and a half excruciating minutes to run the last mile and a fifth. I still throw my arms out and force a smile for the camera as I cross the line, but inside I am grief-stricken.

A cheery volunteer rushes up to me and throws a thermal blanket over my shoulders. "Congratulations," she says with a big, wide smile. "Great run."

"Thanks," I gasp. And then I collapse into a pile of bodies, alongside hundreds of other sufferers.

My official time is four hours, one minute, fourteen seconds. If I had run each mile three seconds faster, I would have broken four hours. Three measly seconds. But it might as well have been three minutes. I wasn't going to make it. Not this day.

But: I finished. And I fought through the pain, a triumph in itself. When I undertake a marathon again, which I have already decided I will do, one of my training runs will be a full four hours, so my body can undergo the experience before the actual race. That is a cardinal rule in training and I paid the price by neglecting it. It's similar to trying a case: preparation is critical. The next time, I'll be better prepared.

I was going to go home this afternoon, but there is no way I can be immobile in a car for the drive to L.A. in the Sunday evening freeway traffic. I would freeze up like a statue, so I extend my stay until tomorrow. I have sick time coming; in the morning I'll call in and take the day off. I don't have a court appearance or client meetings scheduled, so I won't be missed.

The bathtub at my hotel has Jacuzzi jets, so I'm up to my neck in a hot-tub bubble bath. The crisp, dry white wine I'm sipping is helping to leech the pain as well. Later, I'll treat myself to a massage. My room-service dinner will be a New York filet, charred medium rare, a baked potato smothered with butter, crisp-fried onion rings, creamed spinach, and a good bottle of Syrah. Topped off with a hot-fudge sundae, followed by another hot soak.

I'm not in training anymore.

TWENTY-ONE

W E'VE FOUND ANOTHER VICTIM."
      This must be how it feels to be hit by lightning.
"Where?"

The experienced detective, trained to be calm, is rattled; Cordova can hear the tremor in his voice. "Off one of the service roads that leads into Brentwood Country Club, where Montana meets Yale. In the bushes."

"Who called it in?"

"Couple of kids looking for a secluded place to do something they didn't want their parents to know about."

"No mistake? Not a random killing, or a copycat?"

"No, sir. It's our man." An uncomfortable cough. "He left the same signature."

Which no one but the selected members of this task force are privy to, under strict confidentiality.

Here we go. "Secure the area, but don't do anything until I get there. Except cover her. Don't let anyone near that body. And keep those kids under wraps until I can talk to them. Any media show up yet?"

"No, sir. We're on secure channel, like you instructed."

A small victory. Maybe the only one. "I'll be there in five minutes."

He hangs up. Sonofabitch!

It is Monday morning, one-thirty. The last night of the full moon. In a few hours, the sun will come up. The ordeal would have been over. Now it isn't.

Cordova stands next to the murdered woman's body. The ligature marks around her neck are already beginning to darken. Her shorts—culottes, technically—have been pulled off, revealing her vagina, buttocks, and thighs.

He hunches down to confirm his detective's quick analysis. Forced penetration is not what he's looking for; that will be for the medical examiner to determine. It's what is not there.

Same MO as the others. Cordova feels bile rising in his throat, swallows to keep it down. He pulls the blanket over her, to preserve her modesty. It's the least he can do. Find her killer—that is what he has to do.

He conference-calls the entire task force, all one hundred of them. He tells them: "You know what you're looking for."

Three AM. The medical examiner arrives and checks out the crime scene. The victim's wallet is still on her, in a pocket of her shorts. He hands it over to Cordova, who has not touched the victim, because LAPD policy stipulates that no one touches the body until the coroner has inspected it.

The coroner finishes his work and the body is taken away. The woman's next of kin have to be notified, always a horrible assignment. Some high-ranking official, maybe even the mayor, will do the honors this time.

The press, rapacious vultures, have already found out there was a killing—they always do—but the details are withheld from them. There will be a public skewering for that later, but for a few hours they have to keep a tight lid on this. That killer is out there, and they don't want to blow whatever slim chance they have of finding him because the crime was blabbed publicly. By this afternoon, though, the decibel level of the talk-radio shows will be deafening.

A few false leads about possible suspects come in, but they

are all quickly checked out and dismissed. It's like trying to hold water in a sieve, Cordova thinks morosely; they've lost him. The fallout is going to be brutal.

Six-fifteen. The sun has been up for more than half an hour. It's over—he's slipped through their fingers.

His phone rings. He snaps it open. "Cordova."

"Just got an anonymous tip," the detective on the other end says. "Don't know how credible it is. Fits the profile, kind of."

The profile being a description they got from an eighty-year-old man, what he saw from a block away, in the middle of the night. Cordova thinks: I should have had the old codger's vision checked. Might have saved them some grief. But it's all they have. "Where?"

"Saltair, a couple blocks north of San Vicente. The tipster says there's a Chicano-looking guy in work clothes sitting in a dark blue Nissan pickup."

A working-class Latino in that neighborhood at this hour of the morning—that's funky. Still, he could have a perfectly valid reason.

"Want us to check it out?" the detective asks. "We're right nearby."

"Hell, yes. Call me back."

Cordova hangs up and waits. Christ, this is nerve-racking. A minute later, his cell rings again. "Anything?" he barks out.

"It's like the caller said," the detective tells him. "Male Chicano. Looks to be in his early to mid-thirties, in a truck."

"What's he doing?"

"Just sitting there."

"Where are you now?"

"Around the corner. He hasn't spotted us."

"I'm on my way."

"Good morning."

Roberto Salazar, reading *La Opinion,* L.A.'s major Spanish-language newspaper, looks up with a startled expression; he didn't hear anyone approaching. A big man is standing outside his truck, looking at him through the driver's-side window, which is rolled down. He's trying to appear friendly, but he's a cop, you can smell it on him even though he's dressed casually. A *hermano,* but still a cop.

Having recently been on the wrong end of an encounter with the police, Salazar is immediately on guard. He replaces the lid on his half-drunk cup of McDonald's coffee and puts the cup in a cup holder. The wrapper from his Egg McMuffin is crumpled up on the passenger-side floor.

"Hello," he replies, trying not to sound nervous. But why should he be? "What do you want?" he asks this man, who is crowding his space.

Cordova thinks: the description, although not specific, fits. Dark-colored Japanese truck. Work clothes. And he's wearing a Dodgers hat. Lots of coincidences.

He flashes his badge. "Police, sir. We're investigating an incident nearby. Have you seen anything out of the ordinary?"

Salazar shakes his head. "I haven't seen anything."

"May I see your driver's license, sir?" Cordova holds his hand out, palm up.

Not again. "Have I done something wrong?"

"No, sir. I just need to check."

Salazar sighs. You don't resist these people, they'll come down harder on you if you do. "All right." He reaches into his back pocket, pulls out his billfold, takes the license out, and hands it over. "It's up to date," he points out.

"Yes, sir. I can see that." Cordova glances at the address. East L.A. "Just a minute."

He walks away ten yards to where two of his men, the ones who spotted Salazar's truck, are holding down the fort, leaning against the side of their unmarked Chrysler 300 sedan, the model with the big V-8 engine. Cordova hands the senior detective the license. "Run this."

While the detective gets on his radio, Cordova walks back to the truck. "Won't take long," he says affably. Two fellows shooting the breeze. "Whatcha doing 'round here this early in the morning?" The threat is not in his tone of voice, rather in his authority.

"Waiting."

"What for?"

Salazar cocks a thumb toward the back of his truck, which is loaded with his gardening equipment. "To start work. Can't cut the lawns until seven o'clock. City rule."

"Gotcha." Cordova looks behind him. His man is still checking on the driver's license. "So how come you're here so early?"

"Beat the traffic. By six-thirty, the 10 freeway don't move. I would be late."

Cordova scrutinizes the man. He doesn't seem nervous. And his explanation for being here is plausible. He's sat fuming many a time on the freeways himself.

"Boss." The detective who is checking Salazar's ID calls over.

"Be right back," Cordova tells Salazar.

He joins the other detectives, who look disturbed. "What do you have?" he asks.

"This man was in trial last month. L.A. County Superior Court. Grand theft."

What the fuck? "What's he doing out?"

"He was acquitted." The detective hands the license back to Cordova, who looks at it more closely.

"Humph." Acquitted or not, this casts a new light on things. "Stay put," he instructs his troops, "but stay sharp. If he makes any sudden move . . ." He doesn't have to finish the thought; they know.

He walks back to the truck, Salazar's driver's license in hand, which he is not ready to give back yet. "I need to ask you some questions, sir," he says through the open window. "Step out of your truck, please."

Salazar has a pained expression on his face. "Why?"

The fun and games are over. He will still be courteous, because he always is, but he'll be firm now. And careful. He has known officers who were careless with suspects and then were shot to death. "Step out, sir."

Salazar sighs. Slowly, he folds his newspaper and lays it on the passenger's seat. He gets out and faces Cordova. "What do you want?" he asks.

"I'm going to search your person. Turn around, put your hands on the roof of your vehicle, and spread your legs. Empty your pockets, please."

Salazar does as he is told. Cordova pats him down. He's clean.

"You can put your possessions back in your pockets, sir. Just step over there." He points to the sidewalk. "We need to search your truck."

There is nothing illegal in his truck this time, only his gardening equipment. But still, Salazar is offended and angry. No wonder there is so much rage and hatred toward the police. And this man is the same as him, Chicano. No pride, he thinks. He has sold his soul.

Cordova motions to the other detectives, who join him. "Search the back. I'll do the front." He pulls on a pair of latex gloves. His men do the same.

"Be careful," Salazar cries out, as the detectives begin taking out his lawnmower, weed whacker, other tools of his trade, and place them on the ground. "That is my livelihood," he says indignantly.

Methodically, the detectives unload the bed of the pickup truck. They climb up onto it, get on their hands and knees, and look for whatever they can find. "Got some rope," they call to Cordova, who is checking behind the seats.

Cordova looks at the specimen they show him, then shakes his head no. His men want to solve this so badly they're not thinking clearly. "Too thick, too coarse," he explains. That rope is what a tree trimmer would use to secure a branch he was cutting off. If it had been the weapon used to strangle the woman, it would have torn the flesh of her throat. But her throat was not cut, only crushed. The other victim's necks weren't ripped either. If a rope had killed them, it would have been a finer weave.

The detectives toss the rope aside, start searching again. Salazar, standing on the sidewalk, watches with growing anger. But they are the police—you don't mess with the police. You have to wait them out.

Inside the cab, Cordova opens the glove box. It's crammed full with junk. He pulls items out: tune-up bills from Jiffy Lube, receipts for supplies, other odds and ends. The usual crap you find in a workingman's car or truck. Methodically, he checks each item out. Nothing here to indicate any contact with this new victim, or any of the previous ones.

Salazar can't hold off any longer. He needs to get to his first job. If he falls behind, his schedule will be messed up for the entire day. He walks to the front door of the truck.

"I know why you are doing this," he says to Cordova, who has finished rooting through the glove box and is now rummaging with his hands under the seats.

Cordova looks at him. "Please step back, sir."

"It's because of my trial," Salazar says. He's growing more and more upset. All of his equipment is out of the truck bed, strewn about the street. These men are pigs, they have no propriety. "Because I was innocent," Salazar continues. He is whining, and is upset with himself for sounding like a woman, but he can't help it, his emotions have gotten the better of him. "My lawyer warned me that the police would hassle me. I didn't believe her, I thought you people did your jobs fair and square." Bitterly: "But she was right."

Ms. Thompson had warned him about being on the Westside early in the morning. But if he didn't leave his house while it was still dark out, he would never get here on time. He had to make his living. It was unfair to stop him from doing that.

But she was right. He should have done what she told him. He could have rearranged his schedule. Now he's paying for trying too hard.

Cordova doesn't respond, because he isn't going to get in a spitting contest with this man, and also because the man is right. They *are* hassling him because of his prior arrest. Not the fact that he wasn't convicted—some are, some aren't. Your job is to arrest and gather evidence, the rest of the process is out of your hands.

"How much longer will you be?" Salazar asks, in a voice of mounting impatience. He has taken a step back, but he's still closer than Cordova wants him to be.

"We're almost finished," Cordova answers. He's pissed off, because this has turned out to be a blind poke, and because this suspect isn't docile. "Now step back, please. Don't crowd me."

Reluctantly, Salazar retreats to the sidewalk. He checks the time on his cell phone. He's going to be late to his first job. He'll have to cut corners to catch up, which he hates to do. He prides himself on giving every client a thorough job.

From the back, one of the detectives calls over to Cordova. "Finished here, Lieutenant. It's clean."

Cordova grunts. He's almost finished too. A fast look under the floor mats, and that will do it. "Put his stuff back. Carefully," he reminds them. Even though the man was recently arrested, which is a cloud on his credibility regardless of the verdict, he is a public citizen. Until proven guilty, he has to be treated properly.

The floor under the driver's side mat is oily, grimy. A few gum wrappers and other small bits of detritus have been squished into the floorboards. Cordova flops the mat back down and lifts the one on the passenger side.

The floor under the mat on this side is cleaner. He gives the space a cursory look. Then, as he's about to drop the mat, some-thing catches his eye. He squats down and looks closer. "What is this?" He actually says the words to himself out loud.

He almost missed the small item, because it's dark under there. Very cautiously, he reaches down, picks it up, and exam-ines it carefully, to make sure it's what he thinks it is. Holding it by the fingertips of one gloved hand, he reaches into a pocket and takes out a small Ziploc bag. He drops the item into the plastic bag, climbs out of the truck, and walks over to his men, who are almost done putting Salazar's equipment and tools back into the truck bed. "Look at this," he says. He raises the bag so they can see the contents.

The two other detectives peer at the bag. One of them swears softly. "Where did you find it?" one of them asks.

"Hidden under a floor mat." Cordova says. "We have to be super careful. Call for backup."

He puts the plastic bag in his car, locks it, and returns to Salazar.

"Now can I go?" Salazar asks. "My day is already messed up." He holds his hand out. "I need my license back."

Cordova looks at him. This has to be the coolest operator I've ever encountered, he thinks, or he's a true psychopath. Or, God forbid, he's innocent, and the evidence won't be what we think it is.

Behind them, three unmarked cars drive up. Six detectives get out and approach the two who are assisting Cordova. One of the detectives whispers something to the new arrivals. They stare at Salazar, stunned.

"I'm going to have to take you in for questioning," Cordova tells Salazar brusquely; no more Mr. Nice Guy. "Turn around and place your hands behind you."

Salazar jumps back. "No!"

"It's a precaution, sir," Cordova explains, firmly. "We have to question you in a controlled environment." He doesn't want a public demonstration, in case this turns out to be a dry well, so he makes an executive decision. "We won't cuff you if you come with us voluntarily," he offers.

"Not again!" Salazar wails. "What about my truck? What about my customers?"

"We will make good for you," Cordova says. A promise that

can't be kept, but he doesn't want this to get physical. Some ass-hole secretly filming this on his cell phone puts it on the Internet and it's Rodney King and MacArthur Park all over again.

"What if I don't want to talk?" Salazar asks belligerently. "What if I don't want to come with you?" He is surprised (and frightened) by his belligerence, but enough is enough. He is sick and tired of being a punching bag for the police. "I have a business to run!" he wails. "What have I done wrong?"

Cordova keeps his cool. "Are you going to come with me voluntarily, or not?"

Salazar is shaking. What choice does he have? If he says no, the policeman will pull his gun out, handcuff him, and arrest him. Either way, he's screwed.

"I will come with you," he gives in. "You don't have to arrest me. Whatever it is you think I did, I did not do it."

TWENTY-TWO

T HE SUN IS SHINING, the birds are singing. Amazingly, I don't feel as much pain as I was afraid I would. Yesterday afternoon and evening I gobbled Advil by the handful—that, a deep Swedish massage, and ice bags on my back and thighs knocked the soreness down pretty well. It's ten in the morning and I'm already on the road, heading home to the accompaniment of Diana Krall on the CD.

My cell phone rings. Jeremy? He didn't call last night. I was hoping he would so I could cry on his shoulder. Coordinating our schedules with the differences in time zones is difficult—the window when we're both available is small. I don't know how many hours apart there are between here and wherever he is, but it would be night, and the concert might be over.

I have to pay attention to traffic, so I don't check the caller ID—it's too small to read while driving at seventy miles an hour. "Jeremy?" I answer optimistically.

No such luck. "It's Joe Blevins, Jessica. Where are you?"

I look at the oncoming freeway sign as I whiz by. "Passing through Oceanside."

"Oceanside?" he repeats, as if surprised. Then he remembers: "Your marathon was yesterday. How did you do?"

"Great," I tell him. More and more, that doesn't feel like a lie. "I called a day off into your voice mail, didn't you get it? I have weeks of sick leave piled up, Joe." I'm a workaholic and he knows it; I shouldn't have to defend myself about taking off one day.

"I know you did. But you need to come in." He sounds apologetic, almost frightened. "You're not listening to the news, are you? Any of the talk shows?"

"No. I don't listen to that garbage."

"Good. Don't. And don't stop for lunch. If you're hungry, we'll order in."

"Joe, what—"

He cuts me off. "I'll explain when you get here. Come straight to our floor." Joe is a cool customer; he never sounds desperate. But now he does. "Don't stop to schmooze or get a smoothie or powder your face. Just come see me. I'll be in Pakula's office."

Adrian Pakula is the number-two person in the entire office. Mike Judge is the official head, but he's appointed by the county board of supervisors. His position is executive and political, rather than administrative. On a practical level, Pakula runs the show. Everyone reports to him through the chain of command. I might go a month without seeing Pakula, unless I bump into him on the elevator. If I'm meeting Joe in his office, something big has come up. My mind immediately goes on speed recall, inventorying everything I've been doing to see if I can find something I've fucked up. Off the top of my head, I can't.

"Joe—"

The phone goes dead.

The lemmings are streaming in from their lunch break as I enter our building and pass through employee security. There's a sense of electricity in the air I don't usually feel, but my head is in my own space, so I don't think about what's causing it. I spot a couple of prosecutors and other court personnel I know, but they barely acknowledge my presence—they're in their own spaces, as I'm in mine. That's comforting; whatever Joe's problem is, I'm not the cause. So why the cloak-and-dagger hush-hush?

I ride the elevator straight to the nineteenth floor and go directly to Pakula's office. As befitting his status, he has his own secretary, Maude Lomax, a fixture in the department going back to
the Coolidge administration, according to office lore. A matriarch
of her church, the First AME Church of Compton, she is always
attired in a dress, a girdle, support hose, and fashionable heels,
even though, at her weight of close to three hundred pounds, her
feet must be killing her in those shoes.

She greets me with a grandmotherly smile. "Nice to see you
again, Jessica." Thousands of lawyers and staff have passed by
her desk, and she remembers each of them, which is one of the
reasons she'll have her job until they carry her out on a litter.
"They are waiting for you." She opens the door without knocking and ushers me in, closing the door behind her.

Pakula, wearing a well-cut pinstripe suit befitting his status, is
standing behind his desk. Joe, rumpled in shirtsleeves, is to the
side. "Have a seat, Jessica," Pakula says by way of greeting. He
indicates a captain's chair on the opposite side of his desk. "Joe
tells me you ran a marathon yesterday."

"Yes, I did." I try not to sound too full of myself.

"How'd you do?"

"Good. Finished, ran a respectable time, especially for my first
one." I hate it when people brag about themselves, but I can't help
doing it now. "I was in the top ten percent of women." Shut up,
you twit, I admonish myself, as I add, "Top three percent in my
age group."

"Very impressive. Was it hard?"

I'm not going to lie. "Yes."

"Well, congratulations. You're a better man than I am." He
smiles; then he abruptly drops the chummy camaraderie. "You defended a man named Roberto Salazar last month." He picks up a
file that I recognize. It's Salazar's case file.

"Yes, sir."

"You won. Even though, so I'm told, the evidence was against
you. Pretty good evidence."

"Yes. I did win. Sometimes there's more to a case than factual evidence, as you know better than me," I say deferentially.

"I do know that," he agrees. "The man was a pillar in his community, had great character references, and so forth. Which carried the day, as I understand it."

"That was what did it," I confirm. "Some of the jurors even told me so, afterward. They felt that one mistake shouldn't ruin a good life, so they gave him a break. Which, in my opinion, he deserved. He's a good man, and he learned his lesson. I can vouch for that."

Pakula looks at me strangely as I say that. He's always reminding us not to get emotionally attached to clients. That can drain the life out of you, as I know, which is why I almost never do it. Roberto was the exception that proves the rule.

"You have a winning style, Jessica," he compliments me. "You're going to do well in this office, if you stick with us."

"Thank you, sir." I sit patiently, waiting for the other shoe to drop. The chief public defender didn't call me into his office on my day off to congratulate me on what, in the grand scheme of things, was a minor victory.

"There was another Full Moon Murder."

I slump. "Oh, God, no. When?"

"Last night."

I look at Joe. He is more upset than I've ever seen him. "Is that why you didn't want me to listen to the news?"

"Yes," he says heavily. "The police have it tightly under wraps, but rumors are flying around like a swarm of hornets."

Now I understand why I felt that sense of tension and expectation when I came into the building.

"There's going to be a press conference in a couple of hours," Pakula says. "It will rock this city."

I shudder. This is beyond awful.

"But that's only half of the story." He hesitates for a second, as if to gird himself. "The police have made an arrest. Which is also being kept secret, until they are absolutely certain. We're getting our information secondhand from friends in the D.A.'s office, but it sounds as if they have their man."

"That's great!" I exude. "I mean, it's terrible there was another murder, but at least the police have the killer."

Something in both their faces, almost a mournfulness, brings me up short. "Isn't it?" I ask. "Great?"

Pakula takes Salazar's picture out of his file and shoves it in my face. "The man they arrested is your client."

You would think the pope, the Dalai Lama, or Bill Clinton were standing on the steps of City Hall, the crowd is so big. I'm there, too. I rudely elbowed my way almost to the front. I'm sure my breath is rank, because as soon as I left Pakula's office, I threw up last night's dinner. God's punishment for my gluttony. I couldn't care less about how I look or smell. All I care about is having my worst fear officially confirmed.

It's two-thirty. The press conference is being held now to make sure the story hits the prime television news audience. Not only local, but national. Violence in Los Angeles is a spectator sport, like the WWE, meant to be entertaining not only to us, but to the entire country. Because the newest victim and the suspect were found in the city's jurisdiction, Chief Bratton gets to be the bearer of these great tidings. Sheriff Baca stands so close to him they could be Siamese twins. Mayor Villaraigosa is with the two top cops—he's not going to let them have the spotlight to themselves. Sharing the stage with them are the five members of the county board of supervisors, all fifteen of the city council men and women, Steve Cooley, the D.A., and a bunch of others I don't recognize, but who have enough juice to horn in.

I spot Cordova way in the back of the crowd, buried behind the dignitaries. He looks tired, but he also looks relieved. I don't stare at him; I don't want him to see me.

Bratton has his game face on: grim and in charge. A well-tuned political animal (both his present and former wife have been TV court reporters), he checks to make sure all the cameras are ready to roll, then steps to the cluster of microphones.

"Early this morning, the Full Moon Killer claimed another victim," he begins.

Immediately, the hue and cry rises up. Bratton waits for the hullabaloo to fade out, then continues. "Her family has been notified, and the entire city mourns their loss. Every time there is a murder in this city, it's a dark day," he declares. "But today, there is also some good news. A few hours after the latest victim was discovered, a special task force of detectives from the LAPD and the county sheriff's department, which Sheriff Baca and I created to investigate these murders, arrested a suspect, who is now in custody. The evidence we have against him has convinced us, with a strong degree of certainty, that he is the Full Moon Killer."

The clamor, almost deafening when the announcement of the murder was made, now verges on hysteria. Reporters shriek questions at Bratton and the other luminaries. "Who is the killer?" "How did you find him?" "Where is he now?" This crowd is fast becoming an unruly rabble. I can feel its pulse, its raging heart. This is how a lynch mob forms, I think as I stand trapped among them, feeling the collective tension and anger.

"We are in the process of securing a lawyer for this suspect, so we can legally interrogate him," Bratton says. "Once he has legal representation, we will release his name and whatever other information we have."

Someone cries out: "How soon?"

"As soon as we can," the chief promises.

All along Spring Street the television reporters and their crews are jockeying for position, to have the money shot of City Hall in the background behind them while they do their live stand-ups. I don't pay attention to them as I drag myself back to my office. I'm emotionally wasted. I thought I was tapped out yesterday after I finished the marathon, but that was nothing compared to how I feel now. How could this have happened? Salazar is a poster boy for upward mobility in the barrio. That he has killed these women doesn't compute. But if Luis Cordova arrested him, he must have very solid evidence. This case is too big, important, visible, to play games with. And Cordova is an honest cop—I'd bet the farm on that.

I really thought I had a handle on my former client, but now it's obvious that I didn't. Was his story about helping out his friend a sham after all? He had me completely convinced he was telling the truth. But I have to admit, as much as I don't want to, that there are holes I'm only now seeing. We never found the mysterious and elusive Armando Gonzalez—couldn't even prove he actually existed. On the night Salazar was arrested, a woman was found murdered no more than a couple of miles away. His excuse for being in that location—he had to go to the bathroom—seems flimsy now, contrived.

This is the price you pay for getting emotionally involved with a client—you lose your objectivity. I'm still proud I got Salazar off—that was my job, and I did it well. But I went beyond that. I gave him a piece of my heart. Now I understand Pakula's unhappiness. Not that he isn't pleased whenever we win a case. Lord knows, we don't have many victories, so we savor every one of them. But you prefer to win a case on the merits. Playing the emotional card is a double-edged sword. I won; but now, it seems, I didn't.

This is going to bite our department in the ass, big time. Don't drink the Kool-Aid; meaning, don't buy into your own hype. A lesson that has to be relearned, over and over again.

The elevators in the main hallway seem to be in gridlock; I stand in front of them, waiting impatiently. I've had enough angst in my life over the past twenty-four hours to fill Dodger Stadium. I'll run up to my office, check my messages, and get out of here. Everyone

I look at seems to be shimmering. It's as if we were all hit by a bolt of lightning. Or maybe I'm projecting my own feelings of guilt onto a bunch of people who don't have a clue.

"Are you happy now?" The scream comes from behind me.

I know that voice, too damn well. I turn and face Wayne Dixant, who is standing behind me. His face is so crimson with rage I'm scared he could rupture an artery. That's what I need to complete the trifecta—be the cause for this asshole to actually blow out his brains.

It feels as if the whole world is watching him tear the flesh from my bones. They recoil from us like the parting of the Red Sea.

"Are you happy now, Thompson?" Dixant rants. "A woman was murdered because of you. That poor girl would be alive today if you hadn't gotten that bastard off!" He points a biblical prophet's damning finger at me. "I hope you're proud of yourself today. Because her blood is on your hands."

Too late now, an elevator arrives. I rush in. Behind me, no one moves—it's as if I have typhoid. I stand there, utterly alone, until the doors slide to a close, sealing me inside, a wounded animal seeking refuge in the deepest recess of a cave.

PART
TWO

TWENTY-THREE

T HE DOCTOR'S OFFICE IS in Toluca Lake, which is near Warner Bros. Studios, off the Cahuenga Pass. I can jump on the 101 a block from my office, drive over the hill into the Valley, and be there in twenty minutes (avoiding rush hour, of course). It's my lunch hour. This is my first visit.

Dr. Schwartzman is about ten years older than I am. She wears rings, engagement and wedding. Pictures of two healthy-looking teenagers adorn her desk, in Tiffany frames. She is direct, professionally friendly. Although she did flinch at the old bullet-wound scar when she examined me.

Dr. Schwartzman isn't my regular ob-gyn, so she doesn't know my history. I got her name from a coworker, in casual conversation. Everything will change now, including my doctor, because I want to start a fresh, clean slate.

"Have you ever been pregnant before?" she asks.

"No. I didn't think I could."

"Because of being shot? You thought that prevented your ability to conceive?"

"Yes." This conversation is uncomfortable, but of course, she has to ask. "I never have been, so at some point I assumed I couldn't."

"So you don't use birth control?" She's making notes on a form.

"No."

"Does the father know you are pregnant?"

I look up at the ceiling. It's covered with those ugly foam panels that dampen the soul, and the spirit, which you see in every doctor's office.

"Not yet," I tell her. "He's been out of town, on business."

"It's important for him to know, as soon as possible," she counsels me.

"I know. I'm going to."

What will Jeremy's reaction be, I wonder? We've never talked about having a family. Will he be happy? Will he feel trapped? Both those things, probably. And other strong emotions as well.

This is uncharted territory for me. I have no model for family, for relationships. I'm sailing in unknown waters. No map, no compass, no life preserver.

I stand up. Inexplicably, I feel heavier. I know that's idiotic; if the fetus just beginning to form inside of me has any weight, it's a few ounces, barely registering. But I'm an entirely different person now.

My pheromones are overpowering tonight. If I stepped outside, I'd cause a twenty-car pileup. I'm wearing a black silk Chinese sheath that has a slit all the way up the thigh. Fuck-me Jimmy Choo strappy sandals with four-inch heels. When you have long legs, flaunt them. My hair is in a braid coiled up on my head— Jeremy's favorite style—to show off my slender neck, another one of my better features. A touch too much eye shadow, but I'm going for seductiveness, not subtlety. I even dabbed perfume behind my ears, Chanel No. 5. If it was good enough for Marilyn Monroe, it's good enough for me.

The dinner that I'm preparing is going to be an all-out assault on Jeremy's emotions. Flowers, candles, French champagne. Coltrane on the Bose, the ballads album with Johnny Hartman. We'll dance while sipping from our champagne flutes. Then, his favorite meal: oysters on the half shell (I shuck my own), vichyssoise, lobster, wild rice, grilled asparagus. Brewer-Clifton Pinot

Noir from the Santa Ynez Valley. Heart-attack-inducing brownies from Sweet Lady Jane's for dessert. A modest meal at home for two that will cost me three hundred dollars, but it will be worth every penny, because by the time we've finished this decadence and I drop my bombshell, Jeremy will be so overwhelmed with love and emotion he'll sweep me in his arms, proclaim his undying love to me and our unborn child and the other one we'll have (hopefully) in three years, and we'll adjourn to the bedroom, where I will melt the marrow from his bones.

That's my fantasy, please God. The reality, recently, hasn't been anything that special.

First of all, I didn't go to Europe. After Roberto Salazar's arrest and the inevitable rage of hostile publicity, all I wanted was to hide under a massive boulder. I was so looking forward to getting on that Lufthansa plane to Prague, I could barely wait for the day of departure. But forty-eight hours before I was scheduled to go, Jeremy called me from Vienna, the orchestra's last stop before the Czech Republic. Six in the morning, I was still brain soggy from sleep.

"I don't know how to say this, Jess," he began. It sounded as if his words were slurred, as if he had been drinking too much, but it could have been the connection. "We have to change our plans."

That woke me up. "What?"

The change was that Jeremy had met these incredible jazz musicians, real avant-garde artists, who were about to cut an album and wanted him to be on it, playing his baritone saxophone. They had even composed a couple of tunes specifically featuring him. They (including a woman, the keyboardist), were poised to be the new smoking-hot thing in music. It was an incredible opportunity, one he would never have again.

He knew how much I wanted to travel to Europe, and how awful my life was in L.A. If I really had to come, he would put this chance aside and we would have our vacation as planned. He would abide by my decision. And of course, if I did agree to this, it would only be a postponement, not a cancellation. We would come in the fall, before the symphony season started, when the weather would be better and there wouldn't be the crush of summer tourists.

What could I say? Give up a dream so I can cry on your shoulder because I screwed up? Love is, among other things, about not being selfish, being more considerate of the other than of yourself.

"If you want to think about it . . ." His voice came over the line from six thousand miles away. From the moon, it could have been, I felt so disconnected.

"I don't have to think about it," I told him. "This is an incredible chance for you. We can go to Europe any time."

"Thank you so much, Jessica." He sounded like a little boy whose mother had finally relented and told him he could try out for the football team. "I think we can get a refund on your ticket, since we'll be going later. If we can't, I'll cover it."

So practical so quickly? I didn't think that then, but I did later. "Don't worry about that," I said. "It'll all work out."

"It will," he vowed. "I promise. Listen, I probably woke you, and I have to go, the bus is about to leave for the airport, but I'll call you later. And Jessica . . ."

He paused, so I filled in the silence. "What, Jeremy?"

"I love you."

"I love you, too."

Which I did. And still do. But now, not only with passion, but with desperation.

There's another reason I'm putting on the Ritz tonight. Things have been kind of iffy between Jeremy and me since he got back from Europe. To begin with, he stayed an extra two weeks to finish the album. And since he's been back, there has been some distance between us. I think he feels guilty that he cancelled our trip for his own personal needs, at the very time I was so needy myself. When you feel that kind of guilt, you breed resentment toward the other person. That doesn't make sense logically, but it's human nature. I've been there in other circumstances, so I recognize the signs. I haven't been a barrel of laughs either, which adds to the strain. Roberto Salazar's arrest, and the shitstorm of anger that followed it, was a deep cut to my psyche. I've been wanting Jeremy to take care of me, protect me, and ward off the blows. But he hasn't done that. He feels my pain, but he isn't going to ride shoulder to shoulder with me into battle. He has no interest in the whole business of law and courts and the system, because he thinks the system is corrupt and rigged (often, I can't blame him). He tolerates what I do because he's with me, not because he believes in what I do. And even though he's a liberal on paper, he doesn't get it that scumbags deserve as good a defense as nice people.

It's been that way with us since the beginning. He's an artist. His art, and me, is his life. He has blinders on about everything else, and he's comfortable with that, he likes being narrowly focused. That's how an artist has to live, I know, but it can cause friction with those of us who have to live in the real world.

Tonight, we're going to shed all that stress, like a snake shedding its old skin for the new one. I'm going to will that to happen. That old homily about today being the beginning of the rest of your life? Well, tonight, that will really be true. There is no other path for us.

He brings a bottle of wine, a decent Chardonnay that sells at Trader Joe's for about fifteen dollars. I have to be careful not to drink too much, now that I am with child. Besides, I don't want to screw up dinner. I did open the oysters already; they're on ice in the fridge. Drinking and handling a knife, even a dull oyster blade, is dangerous to your health. I did that once and wound up in the emergency room, getting my hand bandaged. Hurt like hell. And a bloody palm would really spoil the mood.

We'll drink champagne, smooch, feed each other oysters straight from the shell. We'll be the way we were when we first started courting and couldn't keep our hands off each other. In love and lust again, which conquers all.

But first, we have to talk.

I curl up on the sofa, shoes off, legs tucked under me. Jeremy, drink in hand, sprawls out next to me, stretching out his stork-like arms and legs. His looks are unconventional, but to me he's rakishly handsome, always has been.

Now that the moment of truth is upon us, I'm like a cat on a hot tin roof. What I'm about to spring on him is monumental. "I have something to tell you," I say. "It's important."

"Me, too." His knee starts jiggling, a nervous gesture.

That he also has something important to tell me throws me off. This entire evening has been exquisitely orchestrated to get us to this moment. I don't want any distractions. But I know that whatever it is he has to get off his chest, it won't be as critical as what I'm going to tell him. So I graciously say to him, "You go first."

"No, you."

"Jeremy." I stroke his arm. "Come on. Tell me."

He shakes his head. "Jessica . . ."

Enough with beating around the bush. We have to get this over with. "All right," I say. I'm the one who set this up—I'll take the initiative. I'm bursting from holding back my news anyway. I pause, then take the plunge. "I'm pregnant."

And as the words are halfway out of my mouth, hovering phantomlike in the air, he blurts out, "I'm leaving you."

We stare at each other in shock and disbelief.

He reacts first. "You're pregnant?" He's normally pale anyway, but now he looks like a ghost.

I feel as if I'm drowning. "Why?" I blubber.

"It's . . ." He shakes his head and waves his hands in the air, as if trying to ward off an incoming evil spirit. Then he collapses into himself. "I've met someone."

Oh, man. I never saw that coming. "Who? Where?"

"It's . . . she's . . ." He gets up and starts to pace. He's too nervous to sit, he needs to put space between us. "The woman from the group I recorded the album with," he informs me forlornly.

I'm shaking. This was going to be the most wonderful night

of my life, the payoff for all those years of misery I endured. Now everything is ashes in my mouth.

"That's why you didn't want me to come," I say, thinking out loud. Jesus Christ, it was right there in front of me. How could I have been so blind?

"Not exactly," he temporizes. "I mean . . ."

"Yes, *exactly*!" I throw in his face. "You went to Europe, you met this woman, she seduced you, you serenaded each other with your stupid fucking instruments, and that was it! Three years of a life together, down the drain!"

"Jessica, it's not like that." He's bleating like a baby. "Listen, please."

"To what? Some excuse that will explain everything, so we can skip away laughing and singing?" I'm over the top, screaming at him through my tears. "I love you, you bastard! And I'm carrying your child! Our child!"

He stares at me, so miserably. Then he looks away. The coward can't even face me.

"Why?" Now I'm begging, which infuriates me, I feel so small, so impotent; but I can't help it, the pain is excruciating. "Why, Jeremy? What did I do?"

"Nothing, Jess. You didn't do anything."

"Then why?" I plead. "There has to be a reason. What is it? What did I do wrong?" I'm on my knees in front of him. Screw my ego, you can't worry about shame at a time like this. "Tell me. Whatever it is, I'll fix it. Just tell me what to do, because I can't lose you." I'm sobbing uncontrollably. "I can't. Not now. Especially not now."

He extracts my hands from the death grip they have on his legs. "There's nothing to fix. We had a great time together, but now it's over." He stands up. "I have to go."

He grabs his coat and heads for the door. I waylay him, putting my body between him and escape.

"You can't leave me, Jeremy. I'm having a baby. *Our* baby. You can't leave now."

"I don't want a baby. I've always been clear about that." He groans. "You're going to have to have an abortion, Jessica. Because we . . . you . . . are not having this baby. Any baby."

I stare at him, slack-jawed. "An abortion? Are you crazy? I've wanted a baby for years. Now I'm finally pregnant and I'm going to get rid of it?" I grab his arm in a death grip. "I'm thirty-five years old. If I don't have this baby, I'll never be able to have another one. I can't abort it. I won't."

"Then you'll have to raise it yourself." He's so cold now. In the blink of an eye, it's as if we barely know each other, or ever did.

"But you're the father. You're going to be involved." Defiantly, I throw in his face, "Whether you want to be or not."

Jeremy steps back. And then he says the five words no woman, no matter how awful the circumstances, can tolerate: "Are you sure it's mine?"

I'm the one who ran fifty miles a week for six months to train for the marathon. I'm the one who lifted weights, made a fetish of Pilates, crunched three hundred sit-ups a day on the exercise ball. I take a step back, to get traction. And as I scream at him, "You son of a bitch!," I throw a right cross that Muhammad Ali in his prime would envy.

Jeremy has a long, delicate, aquiline nose. Millennia of selective breeding by his forbears went into the crafting of that aristocratic Hebraic schnoz. Now, as my enraged fist slams through the delicate flesh into the spongy cartilage, his nose flattens across his face like a collapsed soufflé.

Immediately, blood gushes out, all over. "Jesus Christ!" he screams. "Are you insane?"

"So what if I am?" I fire back. I grab a dish towel and shove it at his face. "Don't drip all over my rug."

He holds the towel to his ruined nose. His face is swelling, especially around the eyes. His entire head is going to be black and blue tomorrow.

"You could have messed up my embouchure," he hurls at me, barely able to speak. "You could have ruined my entire career."

If my punch had landed two inches lower, it would have. Damn, I wish I had thought of that. "Cry me a river." I throw open the front door. "Get out, you asshole. Your fucking embouchure," I taunt him. "Who gives a shit about your embouchure?"

He staggers outside, almost tripping on the front steps. "You didn't have to do that, Jessica," he moans in parting. "That wasn't necessary."

What a baby. He's so into his own cocoon, it's laughable. "Do you want me to call the paramedics? For your embouchure?"

"No."

He weaves down the sidewalk to his car, fingers the keys out of his pocket, remotes it open. "You shouldn't have hit me," he lisps between cracked lips. From the sound of his voice, I may have knocked out some teeth. I hope I did.

"So sue me. If you have the guts, which you don't."

He gets into his car and drives away. I go back inside and slam the door. Then I collapse in a sobbing heap on the floor. I'm pregnant, I'm alone, and I just blew three hundred dollars on a dinner I'm about to throw into the garbage.

TWENTY-FOUR

ROBERTO SALAZAR IS IN the Los Angeles County Men's Central Jail, charged with the last Full Moon Killing. He is being held in the jail's special maximum-security section, where they house the most dangerous and notorious prisoners. These inmates are under twenty-four-hour surveillance, visually and on camera, to ensure that there will never be any question that they have been mistreated, and that they don't kill themselves before the state can do the job. The lights in their cells are always on. They can't even pee without being watched as closely as if they were under a microscope. Because of the extreme surveillance requirements, and to prevent their being prey to any crazed psycho craving his fifteen minutes of fame, they are totally segregated from the general population. O.J. was locked up in this section. So were the Hillside Stranglers—Buono and Bianchi, the Menendez brothers, and other figures of grisly notoriety.

Normally in murder cases it takes years to get from the initial arrest to the actual trial. Phil Spector, to cite a recent example, walked around a free man for four years before the state managed to wrangle him into a courtroom. Finding and dealing with witnesses, sifting through mountains of evidence, setting up experts, defense lawyers leaving, new ones coming in (who have to be brought up to speed)—it's a slow slog, like swimming through a sea of molasses. But the District Attorney is ramming this one through. He wants to keep it fresh in the public's mind. And Roberto Salazar is not a deep-pockets celebrity who can pay a battery of high-priced lawyers to delay his day of reckoning. He's a nonentity off the street who has to take whatever legal representation the state is willing to give him.

Which is going to be us: the Los Angeles County Public Defender's office. Salazar will be defended by us, a decision that generated considerable debate. Michael Judge, who has to navigate petty, perilous, and pernicious political waters, thought it might be better (meaning less controversial) if a private lawyer was brought in to defend him, and some of the other top brass supported that idea. That's not unusual. For example, anytime there is a trial where there are multiple defendants, only one can be defended by our office. The others must have outside lawyers to avoid any possibility of conflict of interest. (The state foots the bill.) The reasoning behind off-loading this case was not because an outsider could do a better job, but because of Salazar's previous history with us. Specifically, with me. By getting him off in his earlier trial, I had, through my association with him, become an accomplice in this latest murder. Unwittingly, certainly, but still an accomplice.

No one has ever said that to my face. No one had to. Wayne Dixant was a bullying asshole for calling me out the way he did, but he was right. It didn't matter that I had done what I was supposed to do, what every lawyer is supposed to do—give the client the best defense possible. It was the perception that mattered. I had put a killer back on the street, which had allowed him to kill again.

After a few days of hand-wringing and dithering, the powers that be decided our office should try the case. Part of the decision, to be cynically frank, was economic. The lawyers in the Public Defender's office are already on salary. It won't cost Joe Taxpayer any extra money for us to defend Salazar. Even though private lawyers who are assigned cases like this are paid less than their regular fee, the cost can still be astronomical, in the hundreds of thousands of dollars. Why waste that kind of money on a nobody everyone knows is guilty anyway?

The other reason we're doing it is purer and better. It's our job. This is why we exist: to defend those who can't afford to defend themselves. If we passed the buck every time a controversial case crossed our doorstep, we would lose our reason to be. There are thousands of counties and dozens of states around the country that either have lousy public defender offices or don't have them at all. The maxim *equal justice under the law* is laughable. In those places, if you are indigent, you are going to get a bad defense, if you get one at all. I'm not saying there are a lot of innocent people in prison in Texas, for example, but if you are poor, that's not the state you want to get arrested in—especially if you're poor and a member of a minority. We are far from perfect here in the Golden State, but every defendant gets a competent lawyer, at least every defendant who uses a public defender. (I won't comment on the quality of private lawyers except to say that they're like apples—every barrel has a few rotten ones.)

What was surprising is that I was selected to be one of Salazar's lawyers. I'm not the lead, I don't have the experience. I have never tried a capital case; this will be my first one. My superior, Joe Blevins, one of our best and most experienced trial lawyers, is the front man. I'm sitting second chair. But I'll be there, every day, for all the world to see.

My assignment was not only unexpected, it was controversial, as you can imagine. Some people in the office were afraid it would look as if we were rubbing salt into a wound. Others worried about the public's reaction. There has been blowback on talk radio, Steve Lopez's column in the *L.A. Times,* even some national forums. Mostly it's been the usual windbags—Nancy Grace has thrown in her two cents, Larry King, some of the geniuses from Fox News.

None of this is affecting me, because I've put blinders on. I don't read anything about the case, I don't listen or watch any news shows that touch on it. I could be living on the world's most remote desert island as far as any news about this case reaching me. I have a job to do, and I'm going to do it the best I can.

I'm on this case for two reasons. The first is that my boss wanted me on it. "This will be a defining moment in your career," he told me when the idea was initially broached. "You're a good lawyer, and this department needs all the good lawyers it can get. I'm hoping you'll stay for a long time, and if you do, you'll be handling many cases like this one. You need the right training for them, and you'll get it with me."

The second reason is personally gut-wrenching. Salazar wanted me to represent him; he requested me specifically. When I was told he had made that request, I panicked. The prospect of defending him again, this time on a charge of such magnitude, scared the shit out of me, particularly since my gut reaction, like everyone else's, was that he actually is the Full Moon Killer. Rationally, I wanted him to be properly represented, but emotionally, I didn't want to be the one to do it.

I had to put those feelings aside, too. My job is to defend people, not judge them. I can do that in the private recesses of my heart, but not in the open world. All my life I've fought against that, because for me, it's personal. So many times, in so many situations, I could have been (and was) judged unfairly, wrongly. Starting with my mother, who was always reminding me I was a loser, then to the schools where I didn't fit in; until I was out of my teens, I was an outcast. I was judged not for who I was, but what people thought I was. That was a long time ago, but I still feel those stings.

So after I got over my initial shock and panic about being Salazar's lawyer again, I realized I had been doing to him what I hated for others to do to me. A heavy recognition that jolted me back into balance.

He probably is guilty. If he is, and the state proves it and a jury convicts him, so be it. But I will defend him the best I can. It's not about him—it's about me. My self-esteem, my dignity. I want to keep them as intact as I can. Doing this will help me.

Still, the prospect of getting back into the lion's den has been tough. And that was before Jeremy dropped his bomb on me. But I have to stay strong. Self-pity is an easy emotion to fall into, but it's deadly, like falling asleep in a snowstorm—your body wants to, your mind wants to, but you know that if you do, you will never wake up.

TWENTY-FIVE

JOE AND I WALK from our office to the county jail. It's only a
few blocks, and it's faster and easier to walk than drive and
hassle the parking. We present ourselves at the appointed time,
and they whisk us right in. They are not going to diddle us on a
case of this importance; they don't want to give us any reason, no
matter how trivial, to cry foul. Moments later, Roberto Salazar,
escorted by two jail deputies, is brought into the interview room.
He's handcuffed and shackled, so his gait is like a ninety-year-old
man's brittle shuffle. He looks us over with eyes that have gone
dull and guarded from confinement. No longer is he the sweet,
naive, optimistic lover of humanity I defended earlier. Now he's a
sullen, angry prisoner who has no faith in the system or trust in
anyone who works for it, including Joe and me. I understand why
he feels this way, but it hurts to see it. The bastards grind you
down. That's their objective, and they do the job well.

"Unlock him," Joe instructs the jailers. "He's going to need to
use his hands."

Wordlessly, one of the deputies uncouples the handcuffs and
waist-shackles. Salazar slumps into the chair across the table from
us and flexes his arms to get the circulation going.

"I'll buzz you when we're done," Joe tells the guards. "It's going to be a while."

The deputies close the door behind them as they leave. It's a
metal door, built like a tank. You can hear the locks engage, seal-

ing us in. It's a chilling feeling. To add to the claustrophobia, there is the nagging worry that our conversations are bugged, at least some of the time. That's illegal, of course, but bending the rules in the so-called pursuit of justice has never been a deterrent for the police. We have to hope they're playing fair and square, and we try not to discuss critical information or strategy within these walls.

"My wife is falling apart," Salazar says by way of greeting. "The whole community is shunning her. She can't even go to the grocery store without being ripped apart. And my kids are tormented at school." He buries his face in his hands. "They don't deserve that, they didn't do anything." He raises his head and stares at us. "I didn't, either."

He has been maintaining his innocence from Day One. There has not been a chink in his armor, not one tiny crack. Usually, when a lawyer thinks (or knows) that his client is guilty, he doesn't ask him if he is, not directly. He doesn't want to know that truth, because it will be a psychological straitjacket. But in this case, Salazar has been outspoken and consistent: he did not kill that woman. He did not kill any of those women. He acknowledges (bitterly) that the police found damning evidence in his truck, "*but I did not put it there.*" He swears that on the heads of his children.

The evidence. God, it's horrific! That needle in the haystack Cordova found under the floor mat of Salazar's truck, which blew his normally imperturbable mind, was a pair of underpants that belonged to the most recent murdered woman. She had apparently been wearing them when she was killed, and because stripping the victims of their panties was the killer's ugly signature, it linked all the murders to one another. In every killing, the victim was naked from the waist down, and her underpants were missing. The murderer, it seemed obvious (and odious), wanted a fetishistic souvenir of his work.

That a pair of underpants was taken from each of the victims had been a closely guarded secret. Only those cops and prosecutors directly involved in the murder cases (and the killer himself) knew about it, and not one of them leaked. The media never got wind until after the fact, a point of pride for the LAPD, the L.A. Sheriff's Department, and the D.A.'s office. Once the DNA evidence confirmed that those panties belonged to the latest victim, the state's case against Salazar went from good to virtually airtight.

The panties had been sent to two labs that test for DNA—one in Northern California, where the L.A. Coroner's Office normally sends their DNA work, and a second in Maryland, which has a national reputation. The District Attorney's office wanted to be super careful with the DNA, because even the best labs make mistakes. So they doubled up on the testing, which is almost un-heard of.

The results from both labs, which positively identified the panties as having belonged to the victim, came back in thirty days, a minor miracle, because DNA tests usually take months. It's a complicated process, and the labs are jammed with samples sent in from jurisdictions all over the country. That the Los Angeles Coroner's Office got this one back so fast was testament to the im-portance of this case. The rumor, which I believe to be true, is that Governor Schwarzenegger personally interceded to expedite the testing.

I was sick to my stomach when I found out about the results. Although I was never absolutely sure whether Salazar really was a dupe about those stolen televisions or was in on the fix, I still liked him as a person and was impressed with his considerable achievements. But if he is the killer, and this evidence overwhelm-ingly points to that, it means that he's not only a murderer, but he's also really fucked up, a real sicko.

The only glimmer in this sky of black clouds, if there is one, is that Salazar's DNA is not on the underwear. For the purposes of defending him, though, that is pretty much irrelevant. The au-topsies of the murder victims didn't indicate that they had been sexually assaulted, so rape isn't part of the charges against Salazar. Murder is more than enough.

The police didn't know that rape wasn't an element in the

killings when they busted Salazar, though, so immediately after his arrest they scoured his house, inside, out, and backward. Anything that might be incriminating was taken. What they were looking for—hoping for—were other sets of women's underwear that could tie him to the previous victims. Anything that had been washed would be useless, but they did take all the soiled female laundry from the family's hamper. Each article was analyzed for DNA content, but they all turned out to belong to Mrs. Salazar. So that was a dead end, thank God, because if there had been a match, there would be no point in having a trial. They could take Salazar to the nearest public forum and hang him, after he was first drawn and quartered.

The police also tried to reexamine his cube truck to see if there was evidence in it they had overlooked, since when they arrested him the first time they were interested in television sets, not women's underwear. But between that arrest and this one Salazar sold the truck, and it can't be located. It's probably in Mexico or was crushed for scrap, because it wouldn't have been worth any money on resale here. His reason for selling it was that since the police had that truck in their records, they would stop him again for other phantom infractions, and would try to pin another bogus charge on him. (That the sets were stolen didn't count in his reasoning, since he didn't know they were contraband; a dubious distinction, even to me, but I understand his thinking.)

The bottom line is that no other pairs of underwear belonging to any of the other victims has been found.

Joe and Salazar did not get off on a good footing when we first started working on this case. Right off the bat, as soon as Salazar insisted he hadn't left the incriminating evidence in his truck, Joe interrupted him. "Who did?" he demanded brusquely, almost dismissively. "The tooth fairy?"

Salazar jumped when Joe attacked him that directly. So did I. But I knew where Joe was coming from. He doesn't want clients to play head games with him, what we're doing is too serious.

But Salazar didn't back down. "No," he declared. "The tooth fairy exists only for children. I am not a child."

"Who, then?" Joe demanded.

"The police," Salazar shot back, "or—"

"Stop right there," Joe ordered him. "We're not getting into any police conspiracy theories. At least not until someone shows me absolute proof, which I'm not going to hold my breath for. That is an insane defense, and all it would do is tighten the hangman's noose around your neck. For one thing," he pointed out, "where did they get them? The victim wasn't wearing them, and a few hours later, they were found in your truck. That won't wash, so drop it."

The police do plant evidence—that's a fact. But in this situation, with the players involved and the timing between finding the body and arresting Salazar, if we so much as hinted that that was the case, we would be pilloried. Even staunch civil liberty groups, such as the ACLU or the Mexican American Legal Defense and Educational Fund, wouldn't back us on that.

"You were about to say something else," Joe asked Salazar. "What was it?"

"That the real killer could have planted it in my truck."

Joe rolled his eyes at that idea too. "When? Again, let's remember the time line. Meaning there was no time."

"There was, a little," Salazar disagreed. He explained that he'd left his house early that morning while it was still dark out to beat the crosstown traffic. Because he was early, he stopped at a McDonald's on Bundy to get an Egg McMuffin and coffee. He bought his newspaper out of a rack outside the fast-food joint. He was inside the McDonald's for a few minutes. The real killer could have slipped the panties in then. He never locked his truck.

"Of all the trucks in all of Los Angeles, the *real killer* (Joe leaned heavy on the sarcasm) picks yours. Man, what a piece of bad luck that was for you." In other words, forget about it.

Salazar didn't have a comeback for that.

So we're stuck. Salazar insists he didn't kill any of the women, and didn't leave the panties in his truck. He also made the point, as proof that he isn't the killer, that the police hadn't found any articles of underwear from the other murdered women. "If I kept one pair of underpants, like they say I did," he demanded, "why didn't I keep all of them?"

That was another easy pigeon to shoot down, which Joe did, and not gently. "Because she had just been killed, and you didn't have time to get rid of them. That's the logical answer, which the D.A. would throw in our face," he bluntly told our client. "Leave this alone, for now. We have other matters to deal with."

We are going to do our best for Salazar. We always do. But this is going to be a brutal case to defend, and we are not going to let ourselves look like fools or jerks. Whatever defense we decide to put on, it will be as logical and reasonable to the twelve men and women who will be on our jury as we can make it.

So here we are, in the present. "We got your appointment book back," Joe tells Salazar, reaching into his hand-tooled leather briefcase, which his wife gave him for his tenth anniversary in the office (twenty years ago). He takes out a dog-eared notebook, the kind with the dappled black-and-white cover used by kids in elementary school. This beat-up appointment book, which Salazar carried with him, had been taken from him at the scene, along with everything else. Joe smoothes a hand over the frayed cover as if to buff up the contents, like a genie rubbing a magic lamp, hoping for three wishes. "The police made a copy, and if there is incriminating material in it, they'll use it against you. There's nothing we can do about that. But hopefully, we'll be the ones who can use it to your benefit, and not them."

Several of the pages in the book have been marked with Post-its. The date on the first flagged page conforms to the night the first victim was murdered. The coroner had pegged the time of death between two and five in the morning, so Salazar's whereabouts between midnight and dawn that day are critical. The same holds true for all the other days when one of the murders was committed. Salazar is only being tried for the latest crime, because that's the one that has direct evidence linking him to the victim, but in reality, he will be on trial for all of them, because it's a given that the murders were the work of a single man. If we can prove that he could not have been where one or more of those crimes were committed, that will be a huge boost for us.

We already have one strike against us in that regard, a big one, because of Salazar being in the vicinity of one of the earlier murders the night he was arrested with the stolen television sets. So far, the police haven't proved he was near any of the other killings on the days and dates they occurred, but we know they're working their butts off to find another connection. If they do, it will be more gasoline they can throw on the pyre.

"Let's get started," Joe says. "We have a lot of ground to cover." He dives into his briefcase again and pulls out a large manila envelope. He sets it on the table next to Salazar's appointment book, opens the flap, and pulls out a stack of eight-by-ten color photos of the murdered women. Details about each one, including where she lived and where her body was found, are stapled to the backs of the pictures. They have been stacked in sequence, from the first victim to the last.

Joe lays the top picture in front of Salazar. "Do you recognize her?" he asks. "Take your time."

Salazar scrutinizes the photo carefully. Then he looks up. "No."

"You're positive?" I ask him. I'm suspicious now of everything he tells me, no matter how innocuous. I wish that weren't the case, but I can't help it. Fool me once, shame on you. Fool me twice, shame on me. I'm not going to be hoodwinked again.

"You've never laid eyes on this woman?" I pick the picture up, turn it over, and scan the information. "She lived on Medio Drive. Do you have any clients on Medio?"

I pick up his logbook to look for myself, but he stops me. "Yes," he says. "The Shapiros. Sixteen-twenty."

"You know the address by heart?"

"I know the addresses of all my clients," he says with a proud voice. "Over fifty of them." He taps his temple with a finger. "I don't need the book to tell me where they live."

"So you might have seen her," I press. "If only in passing."

His forehead wrinkles in concentration. "I suppose so," he grudgingly allows. "But I don't remember her."

Joe and I exchange a concerned glance. If the prosecution hasn't already made this connection, they will.

I put the picture aside, pick up the next one, and put in front of him. "What about her?" I ask.

Salazar looks at this picture with the same intensity with which he viewed the previous one. "No," he says firmly. "I don't recognize her, either."

I check the information on the back of the picture. "South Marino Avenue, in Brentwood. Do you have any clients who live there?" I ask.

"No," he answers. But before I can relax my guard, he says, "but I have two clients on Alta Avenue, around the corner. The Steins and the Lomaxes."

"So it's possible you had seen her, too," I state. "And she, you."

He shakes his head in exasperation. "Yes, it is possible," he admits. "But I do not remember her. When I am working, I am not looking at people walking up and down the street. I don't have time to sightsee. Besides, I am a married man. I don't look at other women that way."

"What way is that?" Joe asks.

"Checking them out," Salazar says in exasperation. "Which is what I would have to do to remember them." He picks up the picture, stares at it. "She is a pretty woman . . ."

"Was," Joe corrects him. "She's dead. She was murdered."

"Sorry," Salazar says. He sounds as if he's really contrite. "Was. But what I was going to say is, she is not special looking. You would not remember a woman who looks like this unless you actually knew her. Which I did not," he states emphatically.

"If you say so," Joe gives in. Like me, he's skeptical. He's also worried that if Salazar is lying about knowing these women, it could backfire on us. "Let's move on," he says, dismissing this line of inquiry, for now.

Salazar does not admit to knowing any of the murdered women. This is important, because the cops' main witness stated that it appeared to him that the victim knew the man she was talking to, shortly before she was murdered. The man who may well have been her killer.

That's the good news. The bad news is that all the victims lived, and were killed, in proximity to one or more of Salazar's gardening clients. He was in their space on a steady basis, whether he ever actually saw them or not.

As far as we know, the police only have that one witness. An old man who thinks he saw a man and a woman talking, late at night, on a dark street, from a full block away. That's not going to hold up well in court. I don't know if the prosecutors will even use him. He certainly can't identify Salazar—they've already tried that. They brought the old gent in and showed him Salazar's picture, along with other men who fit Salazar's general description. To his credit, the man would not give them even a maybe.

One for our side. But in the overall scheme of things, not very important.

Joe's and my fear, which we have discussed at length, is that another witness will emerge who will more clearly link Salazar to one of the murdered women. If that happens, we'll really be screwed.

"Let's go back to the night before you were arrested," Joe says, as he puts the pictures of the slain women back in the envelope. "From the time you left your house."

"We've been over this a million times," Salazar complains. "I've told you everything I can remember."

"So we'll go over it again," Joe scolds him. "What, you have something better to do?"

Salazar scowls. "Funny."

"That's me, the class clown," Joe says. He puts his tape recorder on the table, turns it on, takes out a notebook, and opens it to a clean page. I do the same, and lead off with our first question, the same one I asked him the last time: "What time did you get up?"

Salazar's commitment to his businesses, rather than being a positive, is turning out to be a huge thorn in our side. He often stayed up late and woke early, doing his bookkeeping or other obligations, which means that most of the time his wife was asleep when he got into bed, and was still asleep when he got up. Often he was gone from the house before she and their kids were awake. So she won't be able to verify his schedule.

At least she's still in her husband's corner. I've seen marriages shipwrecked on rocks far less treacherous than these. I think of my own situation—a single woman, newly pregnant, whose long-time relationship has collapsed. If Salazar's wife had bailed on him, I would not have blamed her. But despite everything, she's still behind him. He has declared his innocence and that is good enough for her. No matter what happens to him, they have a lasting marriage. I'm jealous.

"I woke up at four-thirty." His voice is weary with repetition and with the strain of having to cope with being in jail.

"You're positive," I challenge. I look at my notes from our previous session to check his answer.

"Yes."

"Because?"

"I looked at the clock."

Same answer as before, which is good. He has to be consistent in every detail. If one little item turns out to be contradictory, everything he says will be suspect.

"Okay," I say, looking at Joe, who nods that he's satisfied. "Then what?"

He got dressed. He went into the kitchen and read through his appointment book, to make sure there weren't any changes to his schedule he had forgotten about—there weren't. He drank a glass of apple juice and a cup of instant coffee that he heated in the microwave. He washed and dried the glass and cup and put them away. He turned on his computer, which was in the kitchen nook, and skimmed his e-mail in case he had a last-minute message from a client. There weren't any. He checked the voice mail on his cell phone. No messages.

Five-fifteen. He went into his children's bedroom, kissed them good-bye, but didn't wake them. He went outside, got into his truck, which was parked in the driveway (the small garage is used for storage), and drove off. He took the 60 to the 10 west, exiting at Barrington. He drove north to Wilshire, then west to the McDonald's near Bundy, where he got an Egg McMuffin and a cup of coffee to go. His first job was nearby, but he couldn't start work that early, so he ate his fast-food breakfast and read his Spanish-language newspaper while he waited until he could start. He was at his first job, minding his own business, when he was arrested.

Joe signals the jailers that we are done. They unlock the door, come in, cuff and shackle Salazar. They are not tender with him, but they aren't abusive, either. They wouldn't be with his lawyers present.

"Is there anything we can do for your family?" I ask as they are leading him out.

His composure breaks, and he starts to shake. "Get the world off their backs," he pleads. "I don't know how much more hurt they can take."

Joe pays for our lattes at the Starbucks down the block from our office. I offer to kick in for mine, but he declines—for three dollars he'll be a big spender.

We sit at a quiet corner table and compare notes. "We're spinning our wheels," Joe says. He's not being overly glum, just realistic. That there has not been another killing since Salazar was arrested lends more weight to him really being the killer. That there had been an earlier, similar lull in the murders is considered to be an unimportant anomaly.

Something's been eating at me, and I finally figure out what it is. "From the little we know," I say, thinking out loud, "the victims knew the killer. At least one of them did. That's what the eyewitness said." We have the police report.

Joe gives me a look that says don't go chasing in blind alleys, but I press on. "And let's assume Salazar really didn't know them, as he claims. And for the sake of argument, let's say he isn't the killer. So, what if the panties weren't put in the truck that morning, but sometime earlier, when an opportunity presented itself? They could have been there for weeks. Salazar is in and out of his truck all day long, and he doesn't lock it. If the killer knew the victim, he could have taken a pair of her undies long before he killed her."

Joe doesn't respond, but he doesn't shoot me down, either.

"The police got an anonymous call at six in the morning, tipping them off to Salazar," I continue. "Doesn't that seem the least bit suspicious to you? Pretty damn coincidental, wouldn't you say?"

Joe ponders the ideas I've thrown at him for about a second. "It's still a molehill. We can't base our defense on wild suppositions."

"But at least it's a hill, it isn't completely flat ground." Another idea comes to me. "We need to find out if these women knew one another. And we also have to find out if they all knew some John Doe in common, even if they didn't know one another."

"How are we going to do that?" Joe asks me. It's a reasonable question.

"Talk to people who knew the victims, for starters."

"We're defending the man who's accused of killing them. We're the last people they're going to want to talk to."

"They will be reluctant, yes." Like climbing the Berlin Wall. "But some might, if we—I—can convince them that maybe Salazar isn't the killer, and the real one is still out there."

Joe smiles. "You'd better polish your tongue."

"I will. But it's possible," I argue. I'm trying to convince myself of that as much as I'm trying to sway him. "Woman to woman. It could have been one of them." I sip my latte. "It could have been me. I was out late in those neighborhoods some of those nights."

"You would have outrun him," Joe says. He's chiding me, but underneath, we're both serious. "But what the hell. Give it a shot," he gives in, knowing I'll grind him down until I get my way. "We have to try everything." He finishes his latte. I point to his upper lip. He wipes off foam with a napkin. "You actually think there's a chance this guy is innocent, don't you." It's a rhetorical question.

"A tiny one," I admit. After putting in all that time, elbow grease, and passion defending Salazar the first time, I'm not completely ready to throw him overboard yet. "Maybe five percent. Do you? Have any, even an ounce?"

"I'm not thinking about that, because it's a waste of time, and spinning what-ifs in the air is not going to help." He gathers up our cups and drops them into the trash. "What's important is Salazar's time line for those nights. And a credible alibi witness."

He's seeing the forest, not the trees—forget sentimentality, concentrate on reality. The best chance we have to win is if we can come up with a solid alibi for Salazar for one or more of the nights the killings took place.

But we're still going to have to confront those panties that were found in his truck.

TWENTY-SIX

AMANDA BURGESS LIVES IN Rustic Canyon, my favorite neighborhood in all of Los Angeles. It is north of Santa Monica, not far from the ocean. Nothing commercial, only houses. In a city that's obsessed with celebrity and exposure, the people who live there are vigilant in protecting their privacy. It is a rich community, but not fussy like Beverly Hills or Bel Air. If I could afford to live anywhere, that is where I'd be. But since the median house cost is over four million dollars, I'll only live there in my dreams.

Even by the lofty standards of this wealthy enclave, Amanda's house is special. Redwood, rock, concrete, and glass block, reminiscent of the style of Frank Lloyd Wright. The floor plan is open, with an indoor/outdoor flow that makes you feel like you're in the coolest tree house ever. Looking out to the back through floor-to-ceiling windows I can see a koi pond, a black-bottom lap pool, a low-slung pool house. Next to the pool there is an old-fashioned wooden hot tub on a raised platform. Hundreds of exotic plantings and trees populate the property. The inside furnishings are spare but classy Herman Miller and Japanese style. The art on the walls is modern American—abstract and pop. This house is clearly an expression of Amanda's personality—one side of many, I'm sure.

I've never been here before. I separate business from pleasure. I don't socialize with clients. I don't want to know about their wives, kids, parents, boyfriends, girlfriends, anything that isn't directly about the case; and when it's over, it's over. My wish is to never see or hear from them again. Nothing personal, but in my job, I don't get to pick my clients; they are assigned to me. My friends, conversely, are my choosing. I don't have friends who get into trouble with the law, unless you count traffic violations or DUIs.

Which is why I have steadfastly resisted Amanda Burgess's entreaties to pay her a visit. But she is like water dripping on a rock, a steady, nonstop ping, ping, ping. Sooner or later, the rock wears away. She has been on me to come and talk about Salazar, and will not take *no* for an answer. I don't think the word is in her vocabulary when it pertains to something she wants.

It took her more than two months of phoning, e-mailing, even some personal letters written by hand with a fountain pen to break through my defense. (Her penmanship is excellent, elegant and strong.) So here I am on a Saturday, a day off. A day I could be spending at the beach, an art museum, shopping, going to the movies, or just lazing around.

She did promise me a terrific lunch.

I got here shortly before noon. A maid in an informal white uniform opened the door and invited me inside. She left me in the living room with the great views and went to fetch her boss. I've been here for about a minute, more than enough time to be impressed. I'm sure that's the intention.

"Thank you so much for coming, Jessica."

Amanda entered on cat's feet—I didn't hear her. Now I turn. She is wearing lightweight cotton overalls over a short-sleeved blouse. Canvas flats. Almost no makeup, no jewelry. A sensible outfit to garden in or go shopping at the Farmers Market. I'm glad I dressed casually.

She comes to me and takes my hands in hers. They have been recently lotioned. "I know I'm imposing on your weekend, and I really appreciate your doing this."

"I had to," I tell her. "You wouldn't give in until I did."

Her laugh is low, throaty. "You're a tough nut to crack. Tougher than most." She withdraws her hands from mine. "Can I get you something to drink? I make a mean Bloody Mary. You don't have to work today, do you?"

"No," I answer. "I'm off. And water will be fine, or juice." I'm pregnant now; I can't drink alcohol. Not for months, maybe even years. Are you allowed to drink if you're breast-feeding? Another question to ask my doctor. I've been keeping a list. It's getting long.

"I have fresh-squeezed orange juice."

"Yes, thank you."

"Come with me."

She leads me through the house into a kitchen that could be straight out of *Martha Stewart Living*. It is bigger than my living room; hell, it's almost as large as my whole house. A Guatemalan family of ten could live in here comfortably. The Wolf stove has six burners and two ovens, and there is a microwave and a separate convection oven. Sub-Zero refrigerator/freezer, of course. An in-kitchen barbecue. Rows and rows of shelves and drawers, all custom-built. The look is not ostentatious, but the cumulative feeling is one of power. I've been in similarly munificent kitchens before, and I'm always in awe at what money can buy. Not only every gadget you could ever dream of, but with understated taste as well.

"How many people live here?" I ask her. "Besides you."

"Just Isabella." She nods toward the maid/housekeeper, who is at the far end of the room, chopping lettuce. "And Jorge, her husband, who does a bit of everything. Anyone else comes in as needed, including my secretary and bookkeeper. And the gardeners, pool maintenance, the usual. I don't like having a large permanent staff underfoot, I enjoy my privacy."

She takes a pitcher of orange juice out of one of the refrigerators and pours me a glass. I take a sip. It tastes freshly squeezed, all right. Like ten minutes ago. "Yum," I say.

"We have our own citrus trees," Amanda says, as she pours

for herself. "I forgot to ask you," she says. "You're not allergic to shellfish, I hope."

"I'm not allergic to anything," I assure her. Except selfish, self-centered musicians. And clients who lie to me. And street beggars. What else can't I tolerate? "No food allergies."

"Good." She tops off my glass. "Let's go outside. I'll give you the tour."

She has four acres. There used to be another house on two of them that belonged to someone else, but she felt hemmed in, so she bought it and tore it down.

The pond has several beautiful koi in it, some of which are close to four feet long. Keeping koi is an expensive hobby. I know someone who keeps them—you can spend upward of forty or fifty thousand dollars on a really good one. Several hundred thousand dollars worth of fish are swimming around in Amanda Burgess's pond.

The fish sense her approaching and rise to the surface. She tosses some food into the water. They swarm to it. "Beautiful, aren't they," she says in admiration.

"Very," I agree.

"They're like parrots. Parrots of the sea. Not only because of their beauty, but they live long lives, sixty to eighty years. They'll be here long after I'm gone."

We meander around. She knows every plant, every tree, every piece of vegetation. The overall feeling is random harmony. I'm enjoying the tour, but I'm wondering when she's going to bring up the real reason she asked me to come here. I'm not pushing that; it will come in due time. I hope she takes her time, being here is wondrously pleasurable.

Amanda checks the time. "I think Isabella will be ready for us now," she announces. "Let's eat."

Lunch is terrific, as advertised. A lump of caviar the size of a tennis ball sits on a porcelain platter. A seafood salad, beautifully presented. There must be three or four pounds of lobster in the salad, plus crab, shrimp, oysters, mussels, and several kinds of fish.

"Dig in," Amanda says. She piles my plate with food, then spoons up a big dollop of caviar on a side plate. "You wouldn't know it to look at me," she says, helping herself to an equally hearty portion, "but I have the appetite of a lumberjack. Fortunately, I have the metabolism of a hummingbird, so I burn it off." She smiles. "Working out every day helps, too. Which you know, being a top athlete yourself."

She uncorks a bottle of white wine and presents the label to me for inspection. It's French. I'm sure it wasn't $2.99 at Trader Joe's. "Should I inspect the cork?" I quip.

Her laugh is genuine. "If we don't like it, we'll send it back."

"I don't know if I should be drinking," I tell her, as she's about to pour some wine into my glass.

She stops. "Do you have work to do later on?" Then: "That's right. You're in training. But a glass, or two?"

I'm not in training. I'm pregnant. Barely, but even so . . . "I'm not in training anymore," I declare. Screw it. I'm not going to give up everything, at least not today. "I would love to drink your wine."

Dessert is sorbet and fresh fruit. As the housekeeper is clearing our plates, Amanda says, "We'll have our coffee in the study. It's comfortable there, and private."

Unlike the rest of her house, Amanda's study has an old-fashioned, almost formal feel to it, as if it is a sanctuary from the outside world. Two of the walls are floor-to-ceiling bookshelves, and they're stuffed with books. Judging by the spines, many of them are very old. "Great library," I compliment Amanda. "Have you read them?"

She shakes her head. "I buy them by the yard. Makes me look like an intellectual. Most of them were my father's and grandfather's. Both avid readers."

The coffee service has already been set up. Amanda pours for both of us. She asks if I take sugar and cream, and I tell her just some milk.

"I have a confession to make," she says, as we settle into comfortable armchairs. "About the books. I'm mildly dyslexic. Einstein, Churchill, and Edison were, too, so I'm in good company. I've learned to overcome it, but reading never came easy to me." The smile she flashes at me now is almost apologetic, as if she's sorry to burden me with this secret. "Not many people know this about me, but I feel a kinship with you, Jessica. And I am impressed with your intelligence, as you already know." She cocks her head, as if better to gauge my reaction to what she's saying. "I'm not embarrassing you, am I?"

"No." I feel a slight flush on my neck. Is it embarrassment, or is it pride, that a woman of her standing would take to me? Old insecurities never die, and they never fade away, either.

Finally, she gets to it. "How is Roberto doing?"

"He's acclimating okay," I tell her, "which is a shame, because you have to become hard to survive, and he's surviving. One good thing is that he's completely isolated from the other prisoners, so he doesn't have to watch his back all the time."

"What's happened is horrible," she says, shuddering. "I literally can't sleep some nights, it so dominates my mind. How could he have done such a thing?" She rubs at her temples with her knuckles. "How could I have misjudged him so badly?"

"You're not the only one," I remind her. "We all did."

She puts her cup down. Her hand is shaking. "So you think he actually did it."

"I'm his lawyer, so I'm not going to answer that question. But the evidence against him is strong."

"I have such a profound sense of betrayal," she says. Now that Pandora's box has been opened, her tightly controlled emotions are roiling. "Which, of course, makes me angry. And guilty! My God! Four young women, brutally murdered. I know it's irrational, but I feel complicit in those murders. That I should have somehow . . ." She slumps back in her chair.

"Stopped them from happening? How could you have done that? You're not a mind reader. And you're assuming it is him."

She looks at me sharply. "So you aren't positive."

I have to be careful about what I say to her. She could twist my words into implications I don't mean. "That's up to a jury to decide. What I mean is, no one—you, me, anyone—is responsible for those killings except the person who committed them. We can be our brother's keeper sometimes, but we're not his facilitator, for sure not in a situation like this."

She clears her throat. "I guess you're right," she allows; grudgingly. "What is really eating at me is that I can't accept that he's the killer. I mean I'm not absolutely convinced. It's an emotional reaction, I know, but I can't help it."

She scoots forward in her chair to get closer to me. "He's not a stupid man. You know that. So why would he have been so dumb as to leave that evidence in his truck? That's idiotic!"

"There's a simple explanation for that," I contradict her. "He didn't have time to get rid of them. It was only a few hours. And maybe he didn't want to get rid of them. Maybe he wanted to keep them, as a reminder."

She shudders. "That's a sick thought."

"There are a lot of them."

"But if that is the case," she argues, "why weren't any found from any of the other victims? I understand the police searched his house, his truck, his church, everywhere. Wouldn't they have found something?"

"I can't answer that. Maybe they're stashed somewhere no one except him knows about. Again, that's speculation. I'm not convicting him in a conversation, let's be clear about that, Amanda."

"I understand. But I have to talk about this with someone, and you're the only one I can do it with."

I've had the same concerns she's voicing, but I've kept them to myself. As time passes, though, my belief in Salazar's possible innocence, sad to say, has been plummeting. That theory about the panties being planted in his truck seems more unbelievable by the day. Too many coincidences would have had to happen to make that in any way credible.

Joe's and my bigger worry, and it is major, is that we haven't been able to find any alibi witnesses for Salazar for any of the other murders. You would think that if he is innocent there would be a confirmation of his being somewhere else, witnesses who could attest to that. But so far, not a single one.

Amanda breaks into my thoughts. "What should I do?" she asks me.

I'm startled. "About what?"

"This—God, I hate to call it an obsession with Roberto, but I can't let it go. What should I do?" she asks again. "What *can* I do?"

"Nothing, that I know of," I answer. "But let me ask you a question of my own. Why are you so worked up about this? I could understand your support for him before, because we both thought he was duped in that television deal. And I know you like him and his family, and have been impressed by his good works. But I don't get why you're so emotionally involved with him now. Or is there something that I'm missing?"

Shit, did I just put my foot in my mouth? My question, if taken the wrong way, could imply there is more to their relationship than she lets on.

Fortunately for me, she doesn't take offense, or perhaps the implication didn't register. "It's hard to explain," she says. "Let me ask you something, Jessica. You aren't married, are you."

"No."

"Have you ever been?"

"No."

She smiles. "But you are engaged, so one of these days . . ."

I don't answer. Jeremy, you bastard! I'm still crying myself to sleep over him.

"So I assume you've never had children."

I could say *a bun in the oven,* but that is a tightly guarded secret, and will be until I'm showing and can't finesse it. "No," I tell
her. "No children."

Her eyes get a faraway look in them. "I do. A daughter. She's
about your age, I think. Thirty-five?" she guesses shrewdly.

"Exactly," I confirm.

"If you ever decide to have children, you'll want to get tested,"
she advises me in a strange, melancholy tone of voice, one I've
never heard from her. "The unforeseeable consequences of having
children as you age can be heartbreaking. I know, from my own
experience."

Her look wanders across the room, where some photographs
in silver frames are arranged on a side table. They are too far
away for me to make them out.

"For a woman of my generation, I married late," she says. "I
was your age, which in those days practically made me an old
maid. I didn't care, because before that, I had too many things I
wanted to do. And I hadn't met the right man.

"Then, I did. Or thought I did. James Burgess. Opposites attract, they say, and I was attracted to him. I come from money,
and he didn't. He didn't care about things material, which I found
refreshing, since my family was all about making money. He was
an academic, a professor at Pomona College. American history. A
nice man, not a cutthroat, like the men I had always been around.
He was happy to let me take the lead in our relationship, which I
was used to doing. Still am, as you may have noticed.

"With James, the attraction was more about compatibility
than passion. We were never passionate for each other, at least I
wasn't for him. Until shortly before we got married, I was still involved with another man. He wasn't someone I wanted to have a
life with, but the attraction was too strong to resist."

My face must be registering my astonishment, both at what she
is telling me and the candor in her casualness. "Have I shocked
you?" she asks.

"Yes," I admit. "Not that you slept around—plenty of people

do—but most people keep that kind of information to themselves. I'd never tell."

"It's not something I've broadcasted freely," she says nonchalantly, "but at this time of my life, who cares? It's ancient history. And once James and I got married, I was faithful."

She continues. "Immediately, I got pregnant. It could have been on our wedding night. We were both a little tipsy, so I don't remember the details. Our daughter, Elizabeth, was born nine months later. We lived in Beverly Hills then."

She crosses the room to the shelf that has the photographs on it, picks one up, and holds it out to me.

The picture is a formal sitting. The girl in it is a teenager, or slightly older; it's hard to tell—there is a lack of focus in her expression. Her hair is fine and straight, falling limply down the sides of her thin, delicately featured face. I see a bit of Amanda in her, around the eyes. Those eyes are looking toward the camera, but they seem not to be seeing it. The feeling I get is that she is not in the moment but is somewhere else, in her own special world.

You look at Amanda Burgess, you see strength. There is no strength in her daughter's face.

"I can see the resemblance," I say politely. "Does she live here in Los Angeles?"

Amanda shakes her head. "Paso Robles. In the countryside."

"That's a great area," I exclaim. "Lots of cool wineries." Jeremy and I spent a long weekend there last year. We stayed at a wonderful bed and breakfast on the Justin Winery property. I'll never go there again. "Do you have grandchildren?" I ask.

Amanda's face contorts into a fist, as if I had punched her in the gut. "Elizabeth isn't married. Nor will she ever be." She takes the picture from me and stares at it with tenderness. "My daughter was born with severe birth defects. She is a virtual encyclopedia of them. She can't talk, walk, can't sit up by herself. She might have the IQ of a six-month-old. It's impossible to know."

Christ. What do you say to that? "I'm sorry."

She looks at the photograph again. "A severely handicapped

child is a real test of a marriage," she says, her eyes on her damaged daughter's uncomprehending face. "Which James and I failed. For a marriage to work when its feet are held to the fire, compatibility isn't enough. There has to be passion, because passion is the real glue. Compatibility doesn't hold up under that kind of stress. At least, it didn't for us."

I'm flattered that Amanda is comfortable enough with me to share such personal information, but I wish she wasn't. We are never going to be friends. She's twice my age, and we come from different social classes. I could make a gazillion dollars and I would never be in her league. I don't feel bad about that, her stature is not something I aspire to. And I have enough real worries of my own without taking on anyone else's, even by the indirect osmosis of merely knowing about them.

Besides, what does any of this have to do with Roberto Salazar?

"We never brought Elizabeth home," Amanda continues. "It wasn't a question of money. I come from a wealthy family. We could have turned our house into a permanent-care facility—around-the-clock nurses, aides, medical equipment. The decision was one of commitment. Were we willing to alter our lives, in a fundamental way, to raise a vegetable? A child who probably would never even know who we were?" She lays the photo aside. "James was willing to try. I wasn't."

She takes up the coffee pot and pours herself another cup. I decline a refill.

"Elizabeth was in the hospital for several months while the doctors tried to figure out what her long-term prognosis might be. In the end, the conclusions were bleak, as I knew they would be. We found the finest facility for someone with her needs, and she was brought there before her first birthday. She's never left."

Her sigh comes from some pit buried deep within her. "My marriage didn't last much longer. Too much stress, too much guilt." She looks at me, then abruptly turns away. "Because there was another element in the equation, which you can probably figure out."

I can; but no way am I going to say it.

She does. "Was James her father? Or was my lover the real biological father? James didn't know about him, but a blind man could see there was nothing of him in Elizabeth. I think he suspected something, but that didn't stop him from loving her. He loves her unconditionally. He goes up to Paso every month to see her, religiously."

She puts her cup down, untouched. "I don't. A couple times a year is all I can take. Not that it matters, because she doesn't recognize us. She doesn't know her mother from the man in the moon. But that doesn't buy me any solace from having abandoned my flesh and blood. That's an emptiness inside me I'm going to live with forever."

Merely listening to this is painful. I can't imagine what actually living with it must be like.

"I took off like a scalded rabbit. I went on a retreat for a year, to try to find my lost soul. If I had one. To my surprise, at the end of that year I found out I did, so I came back. I sold the house in Beverly Hills and bought this one. It was the most tranquil place I could find, short of moving to Big Sur, which I didn't want to do. I knew I wasn't going to have any more children. I wasn't in a relationship, and even if I had been, I didn't want to take that risk again.

"Whatever mothering instincts I had, I channeled into serving others who are less well off and need a helping hand. I mentor young people, I assist families who have financial troubles, I support minority businesses. If I find someone I think is worthwhile, I do what I can to help that person fulfill a greater potential than he or she would without my help. Don't get me wrong, I'm not some selfless saint. Mother Teresa would kick me to the curb in two seconds flat. My motives are selfish. If there's a heaven, I want to get in—at least have a fighting chance. What I do is for redemption—my own."

She takes one of my hands in both of hers, the same warm inclusionary gesture she extended to me when I arrived. "Which brings me, by way of Timbuktu, to Roberto. As soon as I met him, I saw this innate decency and honesty. I could literally feel it, it radiated from him. His warmth toward people, his optimistic spirit, the way he is with his wife, children, everyone. I fell for him." She gulps, and hesitates. "Not how that word is normally used, of course—I'm more than old enough to be his mother. But some people, you know they're good, and you want to bask in their light. Do you know what I mean? I'm not rambling too much, am I?"

"I know exactly what you mean."

"Good. So many people don't. When I was your age, I didn't. It took a life-changing catastrophe to wake me up."

She lets go of my hands. They're hot from her warmth. "I have known Roberto for three years, but it feels as if I've known him much longer. In some ways, forever. And I know that in what is an unfair, perhaps even unhealthy way, I've subliminally, or maybe not so subliminally, adopted him. The replacement child for the one I lost."

This is heavy stuff. I've never unburdened myself to anyone like this, let alone to a virtual stranger.

Amanda shakes her head as if there are cobwebs in it. "You must think I'm batty."

"I think you're caring."

"That's generous of you. The crux of the matter is that I have a bond with this man, and now it's broken, and it hurts. It hurts like hell."

She sits down, deflated. "So there we are. What happens now?"

"About the case?"

"Yes."

"We keep working at it. So far, we're not making much progress."

"What do you need?"

"A good alibi witness. Someone who will swear under oath they were with Roberto during the time one of the murders was committed, and can prove it. We know there won't be one for this latest murder, because we know his time line, and he was alone all that time. But someone from an earlier one."

"Have you asked him?"

"Yes. He's given us a few leads, but so far, none of them have checked out. It's hard, because these killings happened in the dead of night. Not many people are around during those hours. We're still looking, and we will until the bitter end, but it's frustrating."

"I'm sure it is." She glances at her watch. "I've imposed on your time for too long, Jessica. You must have more things to do on a lovely Saturday than listen to an old woman's sob story."

"Actually, I don't." Now that Jeremy has dumped me, I have plenty of free time—too damn much. "The lunch was great. And you're good company." *When you aren't wringing me out emotionally.*

"Thank you. So are you."

She walks me through the house to the front door. "I value our relationship. You have a good head, Jessica. And heart."

We say good-bye to each other. I walk down the pathway to my car and pull out, watching her through my rearview mirror. She waits until I'm gone before she goes inside.

Maybe I was wrong. Maybe money can't buy happiness.

TWENTY-SEVEN

LOS ANGELES IS VAST, vast, vast. You can live your entire life here and never set foot in huge chunks of it. I can count the number of times I've been in East L.A. on the fingers of my hands; I don't have to remove my shoes to add more digits. A couple of times a year I go with friends, after work, to La Serenata de Garibaldi, a very good Mexican restaurant on First Street in Boyle Heights, which specializes in seafood. It's a hop, skip, and jump from our office, an easy jaunt. That's about it. Most of the best Mexican restaurants, like the Tapazola Grill, my personal favorite, are in West L.A. or the Valley, so for a *gringa* like me, there's nothing over there that draws me in, particularly since my Spanish is rudimentary at best. I could get lost and vanish, never to be seen again.

So here I am, driving deep into the heart of this city within a city. I am heading for Roberto Salazar's church in East Los Angeles, where I will meet with the few people his wife has been able to round up who might be able to alibi him for one of the nights that one of the murders took place. Not nearly as many people have come forward as she had hoped; some are afraid of dealing with the system, from bad personal experience, while others have turned their backs on their former friend and pastor. He has brought shame on their heads, and they are upset, angry, and scared about it.

When you're on a murder trial, the department takes you off

your other cases. That's the good news. The bad news—one piece of many—is that even for the toughest cases, including murder with the possibility of the death penalty, we don't get a full-time investigator. That is one of the big differences between a private-firm defense and one done by the government. We don't have the money or the resources to bring in the big guns. No forensic specialists like Henry Lee, no Barry Schecks to add nuance (and confusion) for our side. Our team consists of Joe, me, and Tori Higgens, a very good investigator in our office who is spread thin over many cases, because our budget can only fit in a limited number of support staff. She has done some of our interviews, but she isn't always available. She isn't today, for instance. And I want to do these particular interviews myself, because even if she did a good prelim, which she would, Joe or I would have to follow up. We have to look these people in the eye, read their body language, use our own bullshit detectors to determine if they are for real and can help us, or will blow up in our face.

I like getting out and doing this stuff. Confinement in the office is becoming claustrophobic. I can feel my baby inside me, growing every day. So far, I've been able to hide my pregnancy, but soon I'm going to show. I've already constructed an elaborate fabric of lies to cover my real situation. My boyfriend/fiancé/partner and I aren't getting married, at least not yet. Plenty of people don't get married, and they raise fine, healthy, well-adjusted children. Look at all the lesbian and gay parents out there. The single women who adopt. Life is a mosaic, a multilayered tapestry of arrangements. We're one more patch in that enormous quilt.

I cruise down Whittier Boulevard. I have XM Satellite Radio, which I've tuned to a classic soul station. I'm in a Smokey Robinson mood today. The air-conditioning in my car is blasting cold air, which is vital for my well-being. Since I've become pregnant, my body has started overheating, a hormonal reaction, I assume. I'll ask Dr. Schwartzman on my next visit.

I turn off Whittier, drive north, then left at the side street I've written down. Garfield High School, a megacampus of almost five thousand students, is a couple blocks away. Half a mile past that is East Los Angeles Junior College. Both, high school and college, are almost completely Latino, predominantly Mexican with smatterings of other Central American countries—Guatemala, El Salvador, Honduras—mixed in. A city within a city, a country within a country.

I'm a stranger here, an interloper. It's a weird feeling to have in the place you have called home your entire life. Not queasy or threatening, but definitely foreign. I wonder how I would feel being here at night, especially if unescorted. Nervous, I'm sure. I don't plan on coming here after dark, so I won't find out.

Salazar's church is a hole-in-the-wall converted store in the middle of a block of similar buildings and small apartment houses. It reminds me of the dozens of little Orthodox Jewish synagogues in the Fairfax-Melrose section of midcity that serve a tiny community living within a few blocks of their sanctuary. Ironically, or perhaps perversely, this place used to sell appliances, including television sets. The old logo, fading but still visible, is etched on the front windows.

I find a parking spot across the street and parallel park with only three back and forths, an accomplishment for me—I'm a lousy parker. I gather up my briefcase, which contains my notes and other necessary information, and get out.

The three-digit heat hits me as if I'd stepped into a sauna. I gasp for breath. According to the radio, the color of the air index today is orange—kids and asthmatics are warned to stay inside. I look both ways to check traffic, dash across the street, and push the door open. They have air-conditioning, but it's a single window unit in an opening above the entrance, inadequate for little more than lowering the temperature from scorching to uncomfortable. No cross-ventilation; the air in here hangs heavy and still. I pause in the doorway for a moment, taking in the scene.

One blocky room, about twenty by sixty feet. The plastic folding chairs you buy at Target or Home Depot are set up in orderly rows. In the front, at the opposite end from the entrance where I'm standing, there is a small stage on which a portable pulpit rests. The stage is on casters, so it's movable. The pulpit is draped with a bright woven tapestry that looks Oaxacan. Against the back wall, a guitar and an accordion rest side by side, like images in a Cezanne still life. On the side walls, there are stock paintings of Christ performing miracles. One of the crosses mounted behind the pulpit features a bloody Christ wearing his crown of thorns. The other cross is bare. My guess is that they are hand-me-downs from other, more prosperous congregations.

The three people standing in the front, anxiously awaiting my arrival, have long, mournful faces: Salazar's wife, and two men. I don't recognize either of them, they weren't at the earlier trial. One is dressed in the work clothes of a mechanic or common laborer. He looks as if he is in his mid-thirties, about Salazar's age. The other is younger, early twenties. He sports several tattoos on his beefy forearms and biceps. His head is shaved, and he's wearing a wifebeater and low-slung khakis. A gangbanger, probably. His face is incongruously sweet, like a stuffed carnival panda.

"Hola, señora," I call across the room to Salazar's wife in greeting. "Hola," she answers back in her low, almost inaudible voice.

The two men eye me with caution as I approach them. Mrs. Salazar introduces them as Carlos and Juan. I don't need any more information about them yet—last names, phone numbers, and so forth. If they prove to be useful, I'll get it. My objective now is to find out if they're credible. If one or both are, that will be a huge boost for us, because these men are the only two possible alibi witnesses we know about, at least so far.

"Do you speak English?" I ask them, mentally kicking myself for not having thought to ask Mrs. Salazar about that earlier, so I could have brought a translator with me in case they didn't. To my relief, they both do. One has a thick accent, so I assume he's foreign-born, and might not be here legally. The other man's inflection is the pure Southern California Mexican accent you hear from every homeboy's lips.

"Thank you for coming to meet with me," I commend them. They are here voluntarily; it's a brave thing they are doing. They mutter *de nada* in response, and stare at me from under hooded eyelids.

"I have to speak to each of you individually," I tell them. I can't have one listening to the other's story, it could later be construed as coaching the witnesses. "Who wants to go first?"

They look at each other, then the older one says, "I'll do it. I must return to work as soon as I can."

There is a coffee shop around the corner. Mrs. Salazar and the other man will wait there. I'll call Mrs. Salazar on her cell when I'm finished with the first man. I fish a ten out of my wallet and hand it to her. "On the state," I say as I press the bill into her reluctant palm. "The least we can do." Which isn't much.

They leave. I sit down with the first man, and begin to ask him questions.

On the night before the early morning discovery of murder number two, Carlos and Salazar drove a local youth-group soccer team to a game in Alhambra. Salazar had driven to the Boys and Girls Club, the pickup location, straight from work, all the way on the other side of the city. They played under the lights at an outdoor rec center. The game was over at nine-thirty, then they took the boys to a local Jack in the Box for a late meal. The tab came to almost one hundred dollars, which Salazar paid for out of his pocket. He shrugged off the expense, telling his friend Carlos that he could afford it, and these kids couldn't. He did that often, Carlos informs me. A notorious soft touch.

By the time they got back to the Boys and Girls Club in East Los Angeles, it was after eleven (the game was on a Friday night, so the kids didn't have to get up early the next day for school). Most of the boys' parents were waiting for them, but a few kids had been left to get home on their own. Although Salazar had been on the go since five that morning, he insisted on driving each boy home. He wasn't going to leave any of them alone on these dark streets at night. Carlos had gamely accompanied him. After they dropped the last boy off, Salazar drove Carlos back to the club, where he had left his car. Carlos recalled checking the time on his cell phone: twelve-forty-five. It had been a long, tiring day.

"So you went home and then what?" I ask, rummaging through my files to find the coroner's estimated time of death for that victim. One to three in the morning, more likely closer to one. If she had been murdered at one, or half an hour to forty-five minutes later, it would have been impossible for Salazar to drive clear across the city, even if the freeways were deserted, accost the victim, and kill her in that time frame.

"I went to sleep. My wife waited up for me; you can check the time with her. She was angry that I was so late, but when I explained the reason, she forgave me. Roberto has such a big heart, you can't be mad at him for keeping you out late."

What he's told me is all well and good, but it isn't good enough. The window for Salazar to have committed that murder is narrow, but it's still open. This isn't the airtight alibi we need. We won't be able to sway a jury to our side if this is the best we have. I will check with Salazar's wife to find out if she was awake when her husband got home, although she might not remember.

"Thank you," I tell Carlos. "You've been very helpful." I shake his hand and take down his last name, phone number, the other information I'll need. "I'll be in touch. You can go now." I open my cell phone and start to punch in Mrs. Salazar's number.

"Don't you want to hear the rest?"

I close the phone. "What else is there?"

Carlos gets a sheepish look on his face, as if he's embarrassed over what he's about to tell me. "The next morning, me and Roberto met up at the club at six-thirty. There was a girls' softball game in Exposition Park, at eight. Roberto was their coach too."

"You must have been exhausted," I say, writing these new details down.

"I was. But I promised Roberto. I had to keep my promise." He smiles shyly. "He drove the van. I slept on the way over."

Getting better. "When Roberto showed up, how did he look?"

"Tired. We both were."

"I mean, what was he wearing? Had he changed clothes? Taken a shower?"

"He was wearing clean clothes, and his hair was still wet, so he must have showered," Carlos confirms.

Now the window is really narrow. Salazar drives to the Westside, accosts his victim, who probably knew him. Some time has to pass before he kills her. Then he drives all the way back home, goes to bed, wakes up, takes a shower, and shows up back at the club five and a half hours after a witness says he left it. Maybe Superman could have made that schedule, but Roberto Salazar is not faster than a speeding bullet. Certainly not in the crappy trucks he drives.

"You're sure of these times?" I question Carlos. "Both late that night and early the next morning."

"I checked on my cell phone, both times. So, yes."

Everyone tells time from their cell now. It's as accurate as DNA, and you don't have to hire a five-thousand-dollar-a-day expert to explain it.

Juan, the younger man, is less helpful. He was with Salazar the night of the first murder, but they parted company early enough that Salazar would have had time to get over to the Westside, kill that victim, and be back on his home turf before sunup. So that's a bust.

He does, however, give me a startling piece of information we could use if the prosecution is allowed to introduce Salazar's earlier arrest as corroboration of his being at the right time and place (for them) when victim number three was killed.

"Armando Gonzalez. Shady little asshole. I wouldn't trust him to clean my toilet bowl, but Roberto, man, he trusts everyone. I'm always warning him: don't be so trustful; but he always smiles and says that's how he is. Which is true, and it sometimes backfires on him. Like with Armando. Armando left Roberto holding the bag on that deal. Sucker skipped town so fast he left a vapor trail."

"So you knew Armando was dealing hot goods? And that he really does exist."

"Oh, yeah. He definitely exists. Except, see, his name ain't Armando. It's Reynaldo. He uses Armando as an alias, so the pigs can't track him. Got some fake ID down at MacArthur Park, sails right through."

MacArthur Park. Where my own fake ID came from, all those years ago. Some things never change. "Do you have any idea where Armando is at present?" I ask Juan.

He shakes his head. "If he had come back, he would have taken off again when Roberto was arrested for these murders. Guilty by association, if you know what I mean."

Of course I do. That's why half the people in jail are there. "Why didn't you come forward with this when Salazar was arrested for those stolen television sets?" I scold Juan. "It really would have helped."

He gives me a half-assed grin. "Wasn't available."

I get it. "County or state?"

"Lompoc. Aggravated assault. Got out the month before last."

Ex-cons make bad witnesses, but I may have to use him anyway. "Do you have a job now?" I ask him. Rehabilitation can be a mitigating factor. The odds are that some of the jurors will have had a friend or relative who's done time.

He nods. "Mechanic. For the MTD."

"I didn't know they hire ex-felons."

"They need good mechanics. A friend of my mother pulled some strings. But I've got to stay clean, that's the deal."

"Are you?"

"So far." He shrugs. "Who knows what the future will bring?"

My sentiments exactly.

TWENTY-EIGHT

W̲HAT?"

"Nothing." Joe turns away and stirs sugar into his coffee.

"You were giving me this weird look."

"You look different, that's all. More . . ." Groping for the diplomatic word: "Filled out."

"Are you telling me I'm fat?" I don't drink coffee anymore—just green tea, organic, loaded with vitamin C and antioxidants. My eating habits are so healthy now they're disgusting.

"No, no. You look fine, great. Never better."

"I'm not running sixty miles a week anymore. I would expect to put on a few pounds, here and there."

"Of course. You look great, you really do."

It's time to let the world know I'm pregnant. I can't fake it much longer, and covering it up is wearing me out. "Thanks," I say, not too sarcastically. "You cut a dashing figure yourself." For a fifty-seven-year-old man whose most strenuous exercise is lifting his finger to push the elevator button.

We're in his office. I'm giving him a rundown on my latest interviews. He listens attentively, but nothing I tell him is cause for celebration.

"Close but no cigar on this Carlos fellow," he pronounces after I'm done. "We'll use him if we can't come up with anything better, but he doesn't close the window. Narrows it, but it's still open." He rocks back and forth on his heels. "We're spinning our wheels. Trying to prove a negative. That Salazar can't account for every second of his time when those murders were committed makes him guilty. Ipso facto."

Ipso facto. A phrase not of my generation, although I know what it means in this context. It means we're screwed unless we get Salazar a better alibi than we have so far.

"Those goddamned underpants. Why the fuck did he hang on to them?" Joe laments for the umpteenth time.

"He says he didn't put them there," I remind him. My role is to play devil's advocate. His is to be real.

"Here we go round the mulberry bush again," Joe lashes out in exasperation. "They were there. In his truck. And stop already with the conspiracy stuff, you're hurting my ears." He's fed up with our banging our heads against the wall.

"That's all they have," he says. "That one lousy piece of evidence. No DNA to connect him to them, no motive. They have no real proof, at least that we know of, that any of them knew him. No eyewitnesses putting him and any of them together." He's working up a head of steam, which is out of character for him— an indication of how frustrating this has become. "This should be a slam dunk for us, but it's the opposite."

He sticks a finger in his coffee to test for heat. Satisfied, he licks the digit and sips from his cup. This is office coffee he's drinking, he does it for energy rather than flavor.

"Which is why we have to work the plant angle," I argue. "It is conceivable."

"Except—" Joe raises a finger in rebuttal.

"What?"

"No more murders since he was arrested."

"I'll grant you that." I sip my own liquid refreshment. It's tasteless. "But there was a lull between this last one and the ones that came before too," I remind him. "If the real killer's still at large, he could be changing his pattern. Or now that someone has been arrested, he backs off, lets Salazar take the fall. Isn't that how it happened in the Zodiac case?" I had put that hypothesis to Cordova, during the earlier lag in the killings. It didn't fit then; it probably doesn't now either. But a possibility is a possibility even if the odds are basically zilch.

"They never managed to make any charges stick in that case," Joe says. "This is different. They have their man, and they're hanging on to him for dear life." He makes a sour look as he drains the dishwater that passes for coffee from our machine. "We need something that absolutely clears him of one of these killings. Otherwise, we're fried. And we better hope like hell nothing else comes out of the woodwork."

He tosses his paper cup from three-point range toward the recycling basket. It clanks against the lip and spins out, onto the floor. Now even more irritated, he bends down to pick it up, squashes it in his hand before dropping it into the bin. "Those fucking panties. What the hell was he thinking?"

"Come in, please." Cordova ushers the woman into his office. "Have a seat." He shuts the door and sits down at his desk, opposite her. "You have something to tell me?"

She does. He listens until she's finished. Then he picks up the phone and orders the suspect book to be brought up to his office. It arrives right away. He begins turning pages, slowly, so she can get a good look.

"Him," she says, putting her finger on a photograph among others on the page. "This man."

"Are you sure?"

"Positive."

Cordova keeps a poker face. "Wait here, please." He exits his office and motions for one of his senior deputies to come over. "This could be the big enchilada," he says, his voice low but quivering with excitement—that's how important this is. "Set up a lineup."

Salazar and seven other men. They look pretty much alike— none of the old days of five blonds and a brunette, or five midgets and a giant. These men are all Latino, and all are about Salazar's age and size.

"Take your time," Cordova tells the witness.

She doesn't need much time. "Second from the left," she declares emphatically.

"Are you positive? Take your time," he says again. Always err on the side of caution. "Make sure you're certain."

"Second from the left," she repeats. "I'm sure."

Cordova picks up the phone and calls Harry Loomis, the District Attorney's number-one murder-trial lawyer, who is the lead prosecutor on this case. Cordova's usual façade—the stoic, impassive, emotional armor of the career cop, which buttresses him against the too-true axiom that anything that can go wrong will go wrong—doesn't hold this time.

This is what he says when Loomis comes to the phone: "Your ship just came in."

TWENTY-NINE

G ODFUCKINGDAMNIT!"
Joe hurls the document to the floor as if it is radioactive, which, for our purposes, it is.

I pick the offending pages up and place them on Joe's desk: an eyewitness's statement linking Roberto Salazar to one of the murder victims. The witness has positively identified Salazar—first through his picture in the cops' suspect book, then by looking at him in a lineup—as someone she saw the victim with on the same night the victim was murdered. Her ID of him is 100 percent sure, no equivocation. And according to what is transcribed on these pages, his contact with the victim wasn't happenstance; they obviously knew each other. Reading between the lines, a sexual relationship is a possibility. The D.A. will try to make that supposition explicit.

We just got the document today, as part of the discovery process. The police have had it for more than a month, but they took their sweet time forwarding it to us. The usual MO—withhold as long as possible. Sometimes we don't get important material until we're actually in trial. It was misplaced, lost, they had a brain cramp. The courts will rap their knuckles, but rarely will a judge throw out anything. Mistakes happen. That should not blur the bigger picture, that justice be served. If the defense plays the game the same way, though, they hear about it, loud and clear, particularly if our office is conducting the case, because we don't have the clout to fight back strongly. Our clients are poor, anonymous, and disadvantaged. No one gives a shit about them except us. They're guilty anyway, so why split hairs?

We will investigate her to see if there are chinks in her armor. Sometimes there are. Eyewitnesses are notably undependable. There can be intrigues—jealousies, resentments, slights, gamesmanship—that color the supposed impartiality of the truth. The blindfolded lady sometimes sneaks a peek. The witness won't talk to us, but we can learn a lot about her without her cooperation.

"A month to go," Joe says, flipping pages on his desk calendar. "These last days are going to fly by like minutes." He sighs heavily. "The odds are always against us, Jessica, but this one eats it on a stick. Not one damn alibi witness worth a shit, nothing that can help us with reasonable doubt." He picks up the new material. "And now this." He crams the pages into his already overstuffed valise—his reading material for tonight. Snapping the case shut, he smiles and shrugs, a *what, me worry?* gesture of futility. "Whatcha gonna do? You do your best, that's all you can do. Am I right?"

"You're right, Joe."

"Don't lose sleep over this." He glances at my extended belly, which is swelling more by the day. "You're sleeping for two."

"And eating for four," I crack. In the past month I've had these ravenous cravings, like in the old jokes about expectant mothers. To my shock, they're true. If I didn't have stupendous willpower, I'd eat a pint of ice cream every night, scarf a bag of tortilla chips, wolf down two double-doubles from In-N-Out Burger—don't hold the fries. I succumbed to the god of temptation and had one last week; it was delicious. From now on, I have to avoid those places like the plague.

We leave the office, take the elevator down to the ground floor, and walk to the parking lot. The sun is still high, the air hazy—as if the sky were covered with brown gauze. I wave goodbye to Joe, get into my car, a laborious feat in itself now, and head for home. I have a ton of material to read through tonight, and I tire more easily, so it's a struggle. But I have to do it—if I ever start letting things slide, that will be the day I pack it in. I'm tempted sometimes to do that: let this shit go and practice another type of law, where your emotions aren't engaged, but I'm not ready to do that; not yet.

I wonder how I'll feel when this trial is over.

I'm loaded down with shopping bags. I have just come out of the Whole Foods market on Gayley, in Westwood. I've gone organic, an insurance policy against the poisons that I am convinced are inherent in regular food. And it tastes better. I should have made this change earlier, when I was in training. I might have shaved those precious seconds from my marathon time.

"Jessica?" The voice comes from behind me. I freeze, but my legs shake involuntarily. Slowly, I turn. Jeremy and I stare at each other from a distance of ten feet, like two animals in a zoo, each on our respective side of the bars. It's the first time we've laid eyes on each other since our violent breakup. His nose has healed, but it's a bit flatter than before, not as refined. That makes me feel good.

His jaw drops as he takes in my new body. "Jesus. You're pregnant."

Immediately, I'm pissed off. "Like you didn't know?"

"I mean . . ." He swallows, his Adam's apple bobbing up and down in his long, swanlike neck. I never noticed the resemblance to Ichabod Crane before, but it's definitely there.

"That I'm going to have it? I told you I was."

He looks at me with incredulity; or maybe it's an unwillingness to face reality. "Aren't you awfully big for how far along you are?"

Oh, Jeremy, you always say the exact right thing, you schmuck. "Huge. I'm going to have a brontosaurus. It will be in *The Guinness Book of World Records*."

"I didn't mean . . ." He's stammering and backtracking like a schoolboy caught peeking into the girls' locker room.

"That I'm not svelte and sexy, the way you like me?" I set my bags down on the sidewalk and spread my arms wide. "Take a look. This is who I am now. A woman who is pregnant . . ." I pause for dramatic effect. "With your child."

He shrivels before my eyes. "Look, Jessica . . ." His eyes dart back and forth, as if he's looking for an escape from this nightmare.

"*You* look. Look hard. This is what a pregnant woman looks like, Jeremy."

People are stopping to watch us, a freak show on the sidewalks of Westwood, Los Angeles, California. Jeremy summons up the courage to face me head-on. "You look beautiful," he says. "I could never visualize you being pregnant, but you look fantastic."

My antagonism melts. "Really?"

His head bobs up and down. "The most beautiful pregnant woman I've ever seen."

Where do I go from here? "How are you?" I ask.

"Okay. Getting along."

"Are you still . . ." I can't finish my sentence.

He nods stiffly. "Yes."

I bend over and pick up my plastic grocery bags. They feel as if they're stuffed with bowling balls. "Good luck with her. I hope it works out for you." I hope you catch the plague, too.

He takes a baby step toward me. "Can we get together, Jessica? We have to talk."

I back away. I can't let him into my space, I'm too vulnerable. My hormones control me now, not the other way around. "I'm busy. Work, planning for the baby, the rest of my life. Maybe later." Or maybe never.

He doesn't press me further. "I hope we can."

"We'll see." I heft the bags in my arms. "I have to go."

"Do you need any help?"

He means carrying the groceries to my car, not any help I really need. "No. I can manage." The way I always do, you weasel.

"It's good to see you, Jessica."

I don't reply. He stands in place, not knowing what to do next. Finally he says, "Take care of yourself."

Who else will? Certainly not you. "You, too."

Another awkward moment; then I turn away from him and walk toward my car. I want to look back to see if he's still there, but I force myself not to.

THIRTY

W E ARE HAVING A skull session, one of the last ones before the trial starts, which is coming at us like a freight train without brakes. Joe and I along with Adrian Pakula, Siobhan Flynn, another lawyer who is our office's DNA expert, and Tori Higgens, our investigator. We have reviewed the prosecution's case ad nauseam. There don't seem to be any surprises. They don't need any; they have enough evidence to get their conviction without pulling any underhanded bullshit, as they sometimes do when their case is shaky. That the victim's panties were found in Salazar's truck is their hole card, but they can also place him close to where and when another of the murders took place. And they have two eyewitnesses: the old man who saw a victim with a man who fit Salazar's basic description, which by itself would be worthless, but in the mix will have an effect, and most important, their other witness, the woman who saw a victim talking to Salazar the night she was killed. The witness had picked Salazar out of a legitimate lineup. We will have tough sledding trying to challenge that with any success; the police bent over backward to go by the book.

What we can offer in rebuttal is pathetic: Salazar's friend Carlos, who will tighten the time frame of one of the killings (but by itself, not tightly enough); the lack of DNA evidence linking Salazar to the evidence; some character witnesses; and Salazar himself. We are not going to have as strong a character-witness presence as in his previous trial—most of them have been scared off by this latest accusation and will not come forward. I don't blame them. There is a huge difference between speaking up for someone who may have been sandbagged on a charge of transporting stolen television sets and saying a good word for someone who may be a mass murderer. We will not use Salazar's wife, for the same reasons I didn't use her in the first trial.

Putting Salazar on the stand runs the risk of convicting him through his own words and actions. The D.A. will treat him like he's an Inquisition heretic. But unless a miracle happens, we won't have a choice. He'll have to speak in his own defense. The jurors, along with public opinion, will demand it.

The purpose of this meeting is to finalize who's going to do what. We have our game plan. This is one more review to make sure we are all absolutely, positively in synch. Joe is the lead attorney and I'm his second, but I'm going to play a more active role than what is normal for a lawyer of my experience.

There are three reasons for this. Number one, Joe and Pakula want me to. They feel I'm ready for the big time, and they want me to spread my wings. I'm grateful for their confidence, and I'm not afraid of it. I've been in this office for six years—if I'm not prepared for center stage now, I never will be. The second reason is my relationship with Salazar. I defended him successfully once, and the hope is that some of the magic will rub off onto this trial. And he is comfortable with me, which is vital. A client who is uneasy with his lawyer is a bad client. The jury can read the tension in the relationship, and will subconsciously develop negative feelings toward the defendant.

The third reason I'm going to be taking a prominent role is because of my condition. Juries respond to pregnant women, and am I ever pregnant. My maternal glow will fill the courtroom with a warm bath of light that we hope will shine down beatifically on Roberto Salazar. In particular, the women on the jury will bond with me—it's the strongest glue in the world, so our task in jury selection will be to seat as many mothers and grandmothers on the panel as we can squeeze in. The danger is that they will sympathize with the murdered women. We are taking the risk that that emotion will be offset by my Madonnaesqe (the Virgin, not the diva) appearance before them, in the flesh.

The baby inside me grows and grows, and so do I. By the day, the hour, the minute. By the time the trial begins, I will look like Baby Huey in heels. I have bought three new suits and the necessary accessories to fit my changed profile (out of our petty cash stash, Joe insisted on it). I ordered them two sizes bigger than I am today; hopefully, I won't be any larger, because if I am, they will have to bring me into the courtroom with a construction crane.

Adrian Pakula, who has seen it all, appreciates the dilemma my pregnancy poses for our opponents. "If I were in their shoes, I would have gone the other way. But they can't, because the decision has been taken out of their hands, even though they'd deny it," he declares, with relish. He punctuates this pronouncement with a laugh; one of the few, I suspect, we will have at the prosecution's expense.

The "other way" would have been to request a postponement, which is standard in a case of this importance. As I have noted, it usually take years before a death penalty trial takes place. But this is not a usual case. This case is as much political as it is legal; in the real world, more. The state has to bring this case to trial as quickly as possible, while the memories of the killings are still fresh in the public's mind. Even the most grisly of murders lose their potency to shock and produce anger when they get lost in the fog of time. So to trial we will go.

We talk for about an hour. No disagreements, we're locked in. Pakula wraps up the meeting. We've all heard this pep talk before, but it bears repeating. "Start positive, and stay positive. Keep your energy up. We know this is not a good case for us, but the jurors don't. You convince them that we're confident, and it will rub off. We can win this, but you gotta believe. And one last thing. Do your best, and live with that, no matter what."

I believe. I believe in myself and my partners. I believe in cuddly puppy dogs and warm summer rains and chilled margaritas with salt on the rim. But in Roberto Salazar, not so much anymore. But no one will see that. I will do my best. And if that isn't good enough, I will live with it. I've lived with much worse. I sure as shit can live with the outcome of this trial.

THIRTY-ONE

D AY ONE OF THE People of the State of California versus Roberto Salazar. The courtroom is standing room only. This is the biggest trial of the year, the legal community's equivalent of a Hollywood premiere, so opening-day attendance by the media and trial junkies is mandatory. All that's missing is a B-list celebrity, an omission compensated for by the blanket of grisly publicity that has covered this case for more than a year.

The jury is brought in and seated. We all rise as the judge is announced, enters, and climbs to the bench; then we sit again at the bailiff's command—puppets on a string. Judge Hiro Suzuki, an experienced jurist who runs a tight courtroom, gets right to it. "Is the prosecution ready?"

Harry Loomis, the lead prosecutor, buttons his suit coat as he stands at his table across the aisle from ours. It's a Brooks Brothers charcoal-gray pinstripe. The tie is Harvard crimson. Old school, like the man wearing it. Seated alongside him are two other lawyers from his office. Younger, snazzier, but lacking his air of authority. These two are the tip of the iceberg; a big staff has been assigned to this case. This is one trial they absolutely cannot afford to lose.

When they make a movie about Loomis's life, he'll be played by Tom Hanks, the most honest, trustworthy man in the world. He reeks of integrity. I'm sure he can be as cutthroat as anyone else—you don't get to be the top criminal prosecutor in the largest district attorney's office in the country without breaking some eggs. But you would never have an inkling of that from his demeanor. To the eye he is calm, unflappable, capable, and nice.

"We are, Your Honor."

He sits down. Suzuki turns to us. "Is the defense ready?"

Both Joe, who buys his suits at Macy's, always on sale, and I, wearing an expensive Donna Karan maternity dress, stand up. There are two reasons we're both on our feet. The first is to imprint on the jury, from day one, that we are equals. The second is to remind them, yet again, that I am great with child. From the looks I'm getting, it's working. Their eyes are not only on our faces, but on my belly, which is sticking out as if I've stuffed a prize-winning watermelon under my dress. Some of the women can't help but smile. That's a good beginning.

Joe takes the lead. "We are, Your Honor."

We sit down. Suzuki nods at Loomis. "Proceed, Counselor."

Loomis takes his place at the podium and faces the jury box. With the self-assurance of a celebrated orchestra conductor, he works without notes.

"Last year, four women were murdered in this city over a period of seven months. All the murders were committed during the full moon, which is a small window: seventy-two hours. The evidence we have found proves, without a doubt, that they were all killed by the same person. That killer is sitting in the courtroom today. His name is Roberto Salazar."

Salazar's eyes are fixed on a spot on the wall above Judge Suzuki's head. He does not look at the jurors. Joe and I do. The jurors are staring at us—it's instinctive, human nature. They are curious, but I don't see anger or predetermination in their faces. I've been in trials that were over before they began. For the moment, at least, this doesn't seem to be one of them.

"The accused is on trial in this courtroom for the last of those four murders. But make no mistake, ladies and gentlemen—he committed all of them. The precise way these murders were executed, the specific signature the killer left behind, and the time frame for when these murders took place clearly and unmistakably reveal that they were all the work of one person."

Tying all the crimes together, which will ratchet up the fear factor against Salazar, was a battle we fought and lost. Since Salazar is only on trial for one of the murders, we argued that only the evidence relating to the last killing should be allowed.

Judge Suzuki did not agree. Because the methods and styles of all four killings were so alike, and so unique, he decided that they could be linked together. Not only could be, but should be. As always, so justice can be properly served.

We didn't expect he would rule in our favor, but his decision was a kidney punch nonetheless. Four murders carry much, much more emotional and psychological weight than one. You murder one person, you're a killer. You murder four, you're a monster.

"We will present evidence to you, ladies and gentlemen," Loomis continues, "which will show that the accused was seen, by unimpeachable witnesses, at the scene not only of the last murder, but at others."

Another battle we fought and lost. Not only will the two eyewitnesses place Salazar at different crime scenes, but Suzuki will allow the prosecution to bring up Salazar's arrest for the stolen television sets in order to put him at the location of that earlier killing. The arrest itself cannot be cited by them—the judge made it clear that that is off-limits. But the cop who stopped him that night will be allowed to testify as to where and when the encounter took place.

There will be other battles like these, and we are not going to win any of them. The deck is stacked against us, we knew that going in. We will fight the good fight, but it will be a Sisyphean grind all the way.

"We will connect DNA evidence directly from the victim to the accused," Loomis tells the jurors. "DNA evidence that will be accurate, unbiased, irrefutable. Evidence that only the victim's killer could have had in his possession."

In the past decade, DNA has become the new Holy Grail. I believe in DNA; every lawyer I know does, especially defense lawyers, because DNA has gotten hundreds of innocent people out of prison. But I have wondered if it can be manipulated, or more likely, misinterpreted. In this trial, the DNA evidence is going to be the most damning piece of evidence against us, the one thing for which we will have no rebuttal.

I text message Siobhan about whether there is anything known about DNA manipulation, or the misuse of it, that resulted in a verdict that was later discovered to have been screwed up because of it. She isn't here today; being our office's sole expert, she is all over the map. Today she's at a trial in Downey, one of our satellite offices. When we get to the DNA section of our trial, she will do the cross-examination of the prosecution's witnesses.

"This is not going to be a long, drawn-out trial," Loomis says, "because this is not a complicated case. But it is an important one. Four young women in the prime of their lives were brutally and sadistically murdered. For almost a year, hundreds of thousands of women in this city lived in fear that they could be the killer's next victim. And if it weren't for the diligent work by the police task force that was set up to catch this killer and, to be perfectly honest, a lucky break, this killer . . ." he pivots and points to Salazar, who does not look at him, doesn't even flinch, ". . . would still be out on the street, and other innocent women might be dead. Probably would be dead. Fortunately, we will never know."

He continues. "One thing we do know, because we have multiple and credible witnesses to this—the killer knew his victims. He was seen with some of them shortly before they were murdered, and it was clear that the parties were familiar with each other. That solves the mystery of how the killer was able to entice his victims to their death—they knew him, and trusted him. Mr. Salazar is a gardener by trade," he explains. "He has clients in every one of the neighborhoods where these victims were killed. In most of the cases, on the same block, almost next door. The victims would have seen him around, and would have come to trust him.

"I don't know if the defense has any real evidence on their side. What I do know, because I've been down this road before, is that they will try to bedazzle you with slight of hand, fake you out so you can't see the truth. It's what defense lawyers do when they don't have a case, and these lawyers do not have a case, ladies and gentlemen, they are holding an empty sack. Not their fault—they are good lawyers. Joe Blevins wins cases lesser lawyers couldn't." He smiles. "To the chagrin of our side. But when he does win, it's because he has evidence to back him up. Evidence, facts. The other defense lawyer, Ms. Thompson, is not someone I have yet had the pleasure of sharing a courtroom with, but she has an excellent reputation. I know this because she recently won a case against a good lawyer from my office. So this is going to be a fair fight."

He leaves the podium and approaches the rail that separates the jury from the rest of the courtroom. "This is a capital case. That means if the people win, which we fully expect to do, the death penalty will be an option. That carries a huge weight, which will be on your shoulders. It's a great burden to ask of anyone, and I thank you in advance for being willing to take it on. Not everyone has the guts to do that. I admire and applaud each of you for being on this panel."

He gives them the eye-to-eye treatment, engaging each juror down the row, one at a time. "Having accepted that burden, you have made an agreement with the state—a covenant—that if the facts and evidence convince you that the accused, Roberto Salazar, is guilty of murder, you will find him guilty. That is why we have trials in this country, why we have juries, why we have laws. I am not going to determine innocence or guilt. The other lawyers aren't going to, the judge isn't going to. You are."

Loomis steps back, so he can engage all twelve jurors with a single look. "It's going to be hard for you to send a man to his death. If you do, that decision is going to be on your consciences for the rest of your lives." He turns and points at Salazar again, and again Salazar does not look at him, or the jurors. "Tragically,

for those four dead women, it was not hard for him to send them
to their deaths. He did it with ice water in his veins. Even now, as
he sits here before you, there is no remorse on his face."

He walks back to the podium and grips the sides with both
hands. Rocking forward on the balls of his wingtips, he says,
"You will have remorse. But you will also show courage. When
this trial is over, you will render your verdict. You will not bring
forth that verdict lightly; you will have heavy hearts. But you will
do it, because you will have no choice. The evidence and your human sense of moral outrage can lead you to only one conclusion.
And down the road, when it's over, that will soothe you, that you
did the right thing."

He rocks back. "If only Roberto Salazar had done the right
thing, none of us would be here today. None of us want to be here
today, but we have to be, because justice demands that we be. The
same justice that will demand a verdict of guilty of murder in the
first degree."

Joe hoists his bulky frame out of his chair, gives himself a waggle
like an Old English sheepdog shaking off the rain from a summer
cloudburst, and shambles to the podium. Against Loomis's polished urbanity he might appear to be cast for *Mayberry R.F.D.*,
but that's a calculated deception. He's a good, smart lawyer who
knows how to connect with a jury.

He jumps right into the deep end. "This trial is a rush to judgment. No murder trial, not one that has the possibility of the
death penalty, has gone from arrest to the courtroom this fast in
more than twenty years. Not only in Los Angeles, anywhere in
California. That's because this trial is not about whether Roberto
Salazar is guilty or not—he isn't—but because this trial is about
politics. The actual guilt or innocence of Mr. Salazar is a means to
a greater end." Quickly: "When I tell you that, I don't mean it
with any disrespect. Four young women were murdered. Whoever
killed them should be brought to justice.

"What I mean," Joe explains, "is that the reason this trial is

happening so quickly is because of political pressure, not because
of the pursuit of justice. Let me share something with you I
learned recently. The average murder trial in California—I know
this because I looked it up—takes three years from the time a suspect is arrested until the first day of jury selection. More than five
times what this one is taking. Some take even longer."

I looked it up. Nice homey touch. The old warhorse is pulling
out the stops. During our prep days he didn't show this kind of
engagement.

I swivel in my chair and look around. Joe has pulled off his
first objective: he has the courtroom's attention. Judge Suzuki
stares down from his platform. The reporters and spectators, including Amanda Burgess and Salazar's wife, who are in the first
row of civilians behind us, are on the edges of their seats. Across
the aisle, the prosecutors are paying closer attention than they
normally do when the other side delivers their opening remarks.
Loomis appears to be calm—he can weather any storm, that is
one of the reasons he's so good—but his associates are visibly
aroused. If they expected this to be an easy smackdown, they have
now been officially disabused of that notion.

Joe continues. "When Judge Suzuki questioned you to find
out if you could serve on this jury fairly and impartially, some of
you admitted that you had read or seen some publicity about this
case, but had not formed an opinion. That's all we ask, that you
keep an open mind until you've heard all the testimony from both
sides. The truth is, you would have had to have been living in a
cave or on the moon if you had not known about this. It was all
over the newspapers and radio and television for months. Everywhere on the Internet. This city was a captive to this case: the Full
Moon Murders. Not many crimes rise to the level of notoriety
where they get their own names. But this one did."

He stops and glances at the notes he was taking while Loomis
was delivering his opening statement. Running his finger down a
page, he looks up and says, "I want to touch on something the
prosecutor just told you. That the victims knew their killer. Well,

maybe they did and maybe they didn't. But if they did, this whole notion of a psychopathic killer looming out there, one who only kills during the full moon, goes out the window. You can't have your cake and eat it, too, which is what the prosecution wants to do. The killer was a crazy nut who only killed during the full moon, because of some compulsion that the moon brought forth in him, but at the same time he was a calculating murderer who knew his victims, set them up, and then killed them. Folks," he says, swaying back on his heels like a country preacher delivering a sermon, "that doesn't make sense. And we will demonstrate, by the way, that Mr. Salazar is not a psychopath. He's a regular guy.

"Let's return to the theme I was exploring a minute earlier—pressure. The pressure to find a killer. Because of the intense notoriety of these crimes, the pressure to find the killer was tremendous, on everyone. Not just the police. The politicians were under fire, too, because they set themselves up to be. The mayor was on television every week, promising results. Members of the city council and board of supervisors—same thing. There was an extreme pressure to solve this crime, from all quarters.

"When that happens, who feels the pressure the most? The police, because they are on the front line, and finding murderers is their job. The word came down from on high—solve this crime. And solve it fast."

I sense movement from our opponents across the aisle, and check them out. Loomis is whispering something to one of his subordinates, who scribbles furiously on his notepad. They have to keep their mouths shut during opening remarks, but they will hammer at us about this later. We expect that; we want them to. We want to engage them in battle, not only about facts and evidence, but over ego, and supremacy. Criminal lawyers on both sides of the aisle are rabid alpha animals. They have to be to be successful. Sometimes that hubris can bring them down. From what I have heard about Harry Loomis, he doesn't succumb to that bait very often. But he is human, and this is a high-stakes trial. We'll see.

"A special police task force was set up to find the Full Moon Killer," Joe says. "Over a hundred cops were assigned to it." He stabs a finger in the air for emphasis. "Over a hundred policemen and women were assigned to solve one case. That's how important this was to the City and County of Los Angeles. O.J., Robert Blake, Phil Spector may have had more publicity—we are the entertainment capital of the world—but this case was more important, especially to the political elites whose careers depend on producing results.

"So what happened?" Joe asks the air. "Nothing. Zero. Nada. Over a hundred officers work on this for three months, and they come up blank. No arrests, no suspects, not even any leads. They're getting desperate. The politicians from above, including their own brass, are hounding them day and night. Find the killer! Find a killer! Bring in a killer!

"But they didn't, because they couldn't. They couldn't find him. And so, they were about to be disbanded." Joe nods his head vigorously. "That's right, my friends. If one more full moon had gone by without the killer's being caught, that elite task force was going to be put out to pasture. Thanks for trying, now go away." He leans forward. "Cops are people, just like you and me. They are not robots, they have feelings. Those feelings can get hurt. If your job is to solve crimes, and you don't, you don't feel good about yourself. Why do you think the suicide rate for policemen is one of the highest of any profession in the world? Because they have such incredible pressure on them to produce results, and when they don't, usually through no fault of their own, they have a profound sense of shame. Being a policeman is emotionally and psychologically brutal, ladies and gentlemen. Unless you have walked in their shoes, you have no idea how traumatic their lives are, every single day."

I love this approach. Your opponents are now your partners. We are all being manipulated by the system. Everyone can understand that, because everyone hates the man, even the man himself.

"Finally, on the last night of the full moon, with daylight only a few hours away, another victim is found. Another horrible tragedy. And man, if the pressure was intense before, it's in the stratosphere now. They have to find that killer. No matter what, they have to find that killer."

Joe turns away from the jury box and looks at our table. Salazar sits at attention like a marine guard at the Tomb of the Unknown Soldier, but I'm uncomfortable being restricted to one position. I want to squirm around to alleviate the pressure my added weight has put on my ass and hips and bones. I would like to slip my shoes off too, because my feet are swelling in them; another side effect of being pregnant. I'm even wearing pantyhose, to keep the swelling down; and I'm a woman who hates stockings. I almost never wear them, unless I'm trying to look sexy. I feel about as sexy now as an elephant on roller skates. But I force myself to sit still and keep my shoes on. If the jurors see me fidgeting, they'll start fidgeting too, and Joe will lose their concentration.

Joe points at Salazar. "They found him. A man on his way to work. Not a blemish on his record, a solid citizen. The police had a vague description of someone who might have been with one of the earlier victims, so they rousted him. And they found a so-called piece of evidence that connected him to the crime. Later, we'll break that down to show you how flimsy it was. For now, that's all they had. And from that one piece of uncorroborated evidence, they arrested him and charged him with murder. And six months later, here we are."

A pause to slacken his thirst, and give his audience—twelve men and women—time to breathe, because he's moving fast.

"We do not have to prove that Roberto Salazar did not commit the crime he's charged with. It's the prosecution's obligation to prove that he did, and they must reach a high standard to do that—a very high standard. Which they are not going to be able to do. Furthermore, we are going to be able to demonstrate why he could *not* have committed this crime, or the others that he may not be on trial for, but has been accused of by innuendo and association. We all understand that the same person committed all the Full Moon Murders. If Mr. Salazar didn't do every one of them, he didn't do any of them.

"As I told you in my opening, this trial is a viper with two heads, both lethal. One is about whether a man committed murder. The other is about a city sweeping its fears under the rug. If this city thinks that convicting my client will solve their problem, they are wrong. All they will do is put an innocent man in jail, but they will not kill that snake, because it will be out there, still alive and able to attack again." He puts his hands together in a vaguely prayerful gesture and raises them to his lips, as if in contemplation. Subliminal, or calculated? I wonder. He may not know himself.

"Hopefully, that snake won't strike again. The real killer, if he is as diabolical, clever, and elusive as he has proved to be, could seize upon Mr. Salazar's conviction as an opportunity to steal away into the night and never be heard from again. There was a lull in the killings before, so we know his attacks can be random. If that were to happen, the city's temperature would be lowered, at least temporarily, but justice will not have been served."

He steps back. He has scored his points. It's time to exit on a high note.

"That's where you come in. Not to help this city get over their fright—that's not your job. Our elected and paid officials will do that, we hope and trust. You twelve ladies and gentlemen are on this panel for one specific and important reason—to serve justice. The way you will do that will be to listen to all the witnesses and weigh their testimony. And when you do, you will come to the only conclusion that is right: that Roberto Salazar is not the Full Moon Killer, and must walk out of this courtroom a free man."

THIRTY-TWO

RARELY DID I COOK, even in the days when I was a lean, mean, marathon-training machine. Now, swollen all over, not just my belly but my ankles, feet, ass, even my earlobes, I can barely roust the energy to boil an egg, let alone grill a steak or roast a chicken. Except for salads, which I throw together with a slapdash randomness, chopping and mincing lettuce and other innocent raw vegetables and dousing them with store-bought dressing, I eat takeout. There is a Greek deli two blocks from my house that makes the kinds of food I crave now: stuffed grape leaves, noodle pudding with raisins, chicken tamales, hummus, tiramisu. It's all good.

Amanda comes over to practice our birthing skills. Selecting her as my birth coach was a shot out of the blue. Actually, I didn't choose her; she chose herself. When I told her I was pregnant, she lost her normal composure. She broke down, literally crying for joy. What could she do for me? Name it, and it's yours. Cribs, clothes, hospital expenses, whatever. She was referring to material things, but there was an underlying desire, an emotional need to be part of this, that initially went unspoken; but when I told her I was fine, she gave up all pretense of detachment and spelled it out.

"I will never be a grandmother, I will never have a grandchild. I never really had a child. I've missed all that. If you would let me be part of your birth and baby it would give me incredible joy, and

I would support you any way you want. I know this is a huge favor to ask, and I'll understand if you turn me down. But I want you to know that I would like to be there for you, any way I can."

Talk about needy! It was as if she had opened a vein and was bleeding right in front of me. I stood there in shock, not knowing how to respond. "Thanks," I finally said. "That's incredibly gracious of you. But I don't want to be beholden to you." What I really meant was that I didn't want to be under her control. She is a powerful force, much stronger than I am. I didn't want to give up any autonomy, I've paid too much in dues to earn it.

Her answer to that was that I wouldn't be beholden, that she would do as much or as little as I asked, and that she would butt out immediately if our bond, in whatever shape it turned out, wasn't working.

I'm alone. I'm scared of the future. And she really seems to care about me. My mother fucked me over, and now Jeremy has. That's two big rejections. Here was a chance for the opposite, a chance to be cared for, accepted, and loved.

"Okay," I told her. "Let's give it a try."

She was overjoyed. So now we are practicing for the birth of my child—I as the mother, she as the coach, supporter, family member by proxy.

This is the first time she's come to my place; I usually go to hers. She arrives driving a Jaguar XKR coupe; she's a rakish woman, age be damned. She breezes in like a cyclone from the Wizard of Oz, says nothing, but lifts her eyebrows in alarm. Picking up the phone, she makes a call, and an hour later, as we're finishing our session, a cleaning crew arrives on my doorstep. Two efficient Dominican ladies, ladened with mops, vacuums, bottles of cleansers. Amanda takes me out to dinner, and two hours later, when we return to my humble abode, sated and blissed out from our meal, my house is spotless, glistening with the luster of hand-scrubbing. You could eat off the floors, the place is so pristine.

I don't bother making a pretense of offering to pay; Amanda

would be insulted. She has taken on the role of surrogate grandmother-to-be with a vengeance. A happy extreme, but formidable, like everything she gets involved with.

"Thank you," I say to Amanda as she gathers her purse and birthing mat. "You didn't have to do that."

"Of course I didn't," she chirps. "I like a clean environment. Especially for you, who must be careful not to get sick."

I walk her outside. The air is fragrant with night-blooming jasmine. "See you tomorrow," she tells me, as she remotes her car open. Pausing before getting in, she says, "Your partner did very well."

We have avoided talking about the trial. Our bond now is my pregnancy, not Roberto Salazar. "Yes," I answer. "Joe's good."

"I won't be there every day. I don't want to be a disruption. The white woman's burden," she spews, wrinkling her nose in distaste. She is repeating an implied obscenity that one of the right-wing talk-show radio bullies spat out that was picked up and commented on by some of the jaded courtroom reporters when Amanda took her seat next to Salazar's wife this morning. "But I do want to be strong for them." She purses her lips seriously. "No one seems willing to be anymore."

"Don't pay attention to that crap," I tell her. "Come whenever you want. I'll make sure you get in."

She kisses me good-bye on the cheek. "Go to sleep," she orders. "You have to be alert. For two important reasons."

She gets in her car and drives off. I galumph up the three stairs to my porch, go inside, and make myself a pot of herb tea. I need to go over the material that will be coming up in the next couple of days.

Today was pretty fireworks and sparklers—eye dazzlers. Tomorrow we start slugging it out in the trenches.

Fine rhetoric captures the mind, but 99 percent of trial results come down to proof, and they have proof on their side. The victim's underwear. Salazar's proximity to not one but at least two of the killings. His lack of an iron-tight alibi for any of the nights the killings occurred. And the prosecution's key eyewitness, the woman who will swear on her sainted mother's body that she saw the last victim and Salazar together on the very night the poor woman was murdered.

Of all the unanswered questions, that one, even more than the underwear, is my personal bugaboo: what was he doing out on the streets of West L.A., far from home, at that ungodly hour of the night? The night he was caught with the stolen television sets I can buy, but this? He has no excuse. He maintains he was in his house, but his wife can't back him up, which is very worrisome. I'm beginning to wonder if he's some kind of real-life Jekyll and Hyde, a good, pious man who is transformed during the time of the full moon into a monster. That's a scenario out of Robert Louis Stevenson—pure fiction; yet I can't think of any other interpretation that would explain it.

That is, of course, if he is guilty. The state is paying Joe, me, and the rest of our team to defend him as if he were innocent until proven guilty. We will do that, but I believe we have to think outside the box if we are going to come up with a defense for Salazar that will hold water.

I advance my beyond-the-pale hypothesis to Joe the next morning, when we reconnoiter in his office before it's time to take the elevator down to the pit that is called a courtroom.

"Not guilty by reason of split personality. Or maybe he's a werewolf," he chortles, licking the powdered sugar residue of his morning cruller from his fingertips. "Anyway, it's too late for that now; our own shrink says he's a hundred percent sane. We'd be undercutting our case if we dared bring that up, which we won't," he tells me in no uncertain terms. "The werewolf strikes. That would be a first in California jurisprudence. And the last," he adds, washing down the last bite of pure cholesterol with a swig of the motor oil that passes for coffee in our dayroom. "We would not only face disbarment, we would become legendary laughing-stocks." He crumples his napkin and drops it into the wastebasket. "We don't have to resort to witchcraft," he says. "Not for another week, at least."

Deputy Chief of Police Clarence Dupree is the prosecution's first witness. He is here to give an overview of the Full Moon Killings, from first to last, pointing out the similarities in the killing method, and the particular article of clothing that was taken from each victim. Dupree, a tall, ropy-muscled medium-complexioned African American with graying hair, who bears a more-than-passing resemblance to Morgan Freeman, is wearing his dress uniform, with all the buttons and bows on his breast.

One of Loomis's deputies, Arthur Wong, a man of Asian ancestry (Chinese), leads Dupree through his paces. In a city that has been racially polarized for generations, and is becoming even more so, that's a nice touch, one minority in friendly rapport with another. Arthur is a pretty cool guy. I've clashed with him before, and afterward there were no hard feelings on either side. He takes his work seriously, but himself much less, which earns him kudos in my book.

The details of the strangulations elicit barely a ripple among the jurors. In a city where newspapers and televisions take lurid pleasure in breathlessly screaming at their audience about eight-year-olds shot on their front porches by marauding gangs, this kind of murder is almost humdrum. I watch the seven men and five women as Dupree details how each victim was identically killed, and their reactions are muted.

When the subject of the women's missing underpants is introduced, however, the emotional temperature in the room abruptly rises. Sex is in the air now. Murder coupled with sex, a blast of searing heat from a pornographic oven. Although the secret of the stolen panties was leaked months ago, shortly after Salazar's arrest, this is the first time it has officially seen the light of day.

Amazingly to me, some of the jurors look truly shocked, as if they had not heard of this before. Sitting inches away, without looking at him, I can sense Salazar going rigid. He has read the jurors' reactions, and it isn't good for him. It's one thing to kill people, but to add a kinky and weird sexual component to their murders is much worse. Sex is still our crazy uncle in the locked room, even though there is more porn in the world now than ever, thanks to the Internet.

"In every one of these murders, that was the constant, the missing underpants?" Wong asks Dupree.

"That and the method of killing, yes," Dupree answers with easy assurance. He has done this hundreds of times, he is as comfortable here as he is at his breakfast table.

"Which lead to the conclusion—?"

"That one individual committed the murders."

"Because only a chosen few knew about this quirk, fetish, sickness, however you want to describe it."

I'm on my feet faster than Joe, which, considering my bulk, is no small thing. "Objection, Your Honor. Leading the witness, and using prejudicial and unwarranted descriptions."

"Withdrawn," Arthur declares fast, before I can be sustained. "Let me rephrase. How did the police come to the conclusion that this was the doing of one man?"

"Person," Dupree corrects him. They rehearsed that exchange, I'm sure. Makes Dupree look objective, the cop who only wants the facts, ma'am. "Because of the uniqueness of the circumstances," he says, basically repackaging the question Wong had supposedly withdrawn.

I'm not going to split hairs. That evidence is incontrovertible, we're not going to fight its existence.

"When did the police department link these crimes?" Arthur asks.

How, when, why, where. The basics.

"When the second victim was found. Same method of killing, same removal of the article of clothing."

"That's when you were sure?"

"No," Dupree demurs. "We were pretty certain, but we don't

like to make snap judgments. Two that were similar was strong evidence for us, but it wasn't until the third victim that we were convinced there was a serial killer out there."

Serial killer. Two of the scariest words in the English language. I look at Joe—should I object? A tiny head shake *no.* Don't fight battles you can't win. We cannot win this one. The same person killed four women under the same circumstances. That's the definition of a serial killer.

The remainder of Dupree's testimony is standard issue, no surprises. By the time Wong is finished it's close to lunchtime, so Judge Suzuki calls it. Our side will get a fresh start after lunch.

The bailiffs lead Salazar away. Humanely, they let him hug his wife briefly before escorting him out. That's a nice gesture, not often given.

Joe and I wait until the courtroom has been cleared. "Do you mind if I take him?" Joe asks, meaning Dupree's cross-examination. We have agreed that we will split the work. Since he delivered our opening remarks, it could be my turn at bat.

"No," I answer. Dupree is tangential to us. An older man questioning a contemporary his age is more appropriate than my doing it. "Not much to do."

"I agree. Move 'em on, head 'em out, Rawhide," Joe sings, dating himself. "But I have a few wrinkles."

"How's it going, Chief?" Joe asks Dupree.

Dupree smiles. He does have that Morgan Freeman smirk down cold. Probably practices in front of the mirror while he's shaving. "Goin' good. And that's assistant chief. Don't want to rile up my boss."

"One person," Joe says. He waits, but Dupree doesn't respond. Joe amplifies: "One person did all the killings."

"Yes."

"Because of the MO. The method and the object that was taken from each of them."

"That's correct."

"No chance of its being a coincidence?"

Dupree parries easily. "Maybe one in a million. Or less."

"But not the method," Joe pursues. "Strangulation is not that uncommon, is it, Chief? Excuse me, Assistant Chief."

"No," Dupree agrees with equanimity. He's not going to let Joe get his goat. "Strangulation isn't the most common method for killing someone, but it happens with some regularity. Usually when it's a crime of real passion." Joe has given him an opening, and he takes it. "When the killer and victim know each other, because you have to be very close to each other. Not like a gun shot, or even a knifing."

Joe isn't fazed by Dupree's expertise, nor by his bringing the supposed connection between victims and killer into play. We are going to use that ourselves, down the road. "So if that was all you had, Mr. Salazar would not have been arrested."

"Probably not," Dupree admits. "But we had more than that."

"Okay," Joe says. "You stated that one person did all the killings," he says again.

"You've asked me that question already," Dupree points out. "My answer is the same: yes."

"These strangulation marks on their necks. Were they all the same?"

"I can't answer that. You would have to ask the medical examiner."

Which Joe or I will, but he isn't going to announce it in advance. Instead, he asks, "So it's possible there may have been more than one killer. Two or more men, working in concert."

Dupree seems a bit flustered by that question. He takes a moment before answering. "I suppose so. But the pattern doesn't indicate that."

"What pattern is that, Chief?"

Dupree doesn't bother to correct Joe about his title. "The pattern that is developed in thousands of homicides over dozens of years," he answers in his best Joe Friday voice. "Serial killers usually don't work in teams."

"You mean like Bianchi and Buono did? The Hillside Stranglers? Right here in Los Angeles?"

Dupree holds his ground. "They were the exception to the rule."

As does Joe. "They worked together."

"Yes, they did."

A wedge. Small, but every inch counts.

Now Joe says, "These purloined women's underpants. The undergarments that were taken from each of the victims. Were they taken before the victims were killed, or while they were still alive?"

That question really does throw Dupree. He gives it some thought. "After, I presume."

"Why would you presume that?" Joe pounces. "If the victims knew their assailant, as the District Attorney stated in his opening remarks, isn't it just as likely that the victims could have engaged in sexual relations with their killers before they were killed? And if they did, isn't it logical they would have removed their underpants? That's usually how it's done, isn't it?"

From somewhere behind me in the gallery there comes a nervous snicker, followed by a cough to cover it. Suzuki frowns in the offender's direction, but doesn't rap for silence, so as not to bring more attention to the disruption.

"I guess they could have taken them off before they were murdered," Dupree concedes. "I can't answer that question. You would have to ask the medical examiner about that, too."

Dupree does know that all the victims exhibited signs of having had sex shortly before they were killed. He also knows that rape wasn't likely, but he isn't going to stick his neck out any farther than he has to. He has already ventured into waters deeper than he expected.

"So there could have been more than one assailant," Joe concludes, "and if there was sexual activity, it could have been consensual, so it's possible the victims gave their underpants to whomever they had sex with that night. Yes or no?"

"Theoretically, I guess," Dupree answers. He's going to hold firm as best he can. "In the real world, I would say no."

Joe executes a slow 360-degree turn, like a tourist taking in the wonder of the Sistine Chapel for the first time. "Is this not the real world?" he asks with mock naïveté, when he is facing Dupree again. "I do believe it is." With a sharpness in his voice heretofore not revealed, he says, "And in the real world, everything I have said is possible."

Loomis is on his feet, as much to protect his witness from further derision as to make a legal point. "Objection, Your Honor. Speculation without basis."

"Sustained," Suzuki responds. "Strike that last remark," he instructs the court stenographer.

Joe doesn't argue; he's accomplished his goals. "No further questions of this witness, Your Honor."

Steven Walker is the criminologist from the county coroner's office who performed the forensic investigation in the field for the first Full Moon Killing, before anyone realized this was going to be an epidemic. Now it's the prosecution's intent to show that it was. That won't be hard, everyone knows it was. Whom to pin it on—that's why we're here.

Loomis does the honors. Now that Joe has showcased his excellent interrogating credentials, Loomis has to match him or risk having his thunder stolen. Juries lock in quickly on whose side has the upper hand; you don't want to be playing catch-up with their affection. That's the real reason O.J. won—Johnnie Cochran kicked the prosecution's ass each and every day of that trial.

Walker, who joined the coroner's office after putting in twenty-five years in the army (he lost a leg in the first Gulf War), knows his stuff. I've been in trials with him before; he's a straight shooter who plays by the rules.

"You determined the victim had been murdered, is that correct?" Loomis asks.

"Yes," Walker answers. He has his notes with him in a binder to make sure he gets his facts straight. They are in his lap, ready to be referred to if necessary.

"Please explain how you arrived at that conclusion."

Walker doesn't need his notes for this answer. "She was strangled. There were visible marks on her throat that clearly showed she had been choked. Her neck was black from ruptured blood vessels. Later, when our office did an autopsy, they found out her windpipe had been crushed."

"Were there any indications she fought her assailant, such as skin scrapings under her fingernails, or something similar?"

"No. I would assume she tried to stop him, but we didn't find that."

"You said *him*. Why did you come to the conclusion the killing was done by a man?"

"Experience. Most strangulations are done by men. It takes strength to overpower someone and then choke them to death. Most women don't have that strength. Although a woman who worked out, lifted weights, could have," he modifies. "There was another reason I thought it was a man," he adds.

"What was that?"

"The choke marks on her neck indicated her killer had fairly large hands. Again, you can find women who have big hands, but not many. You put the different things together, you come to a reasonable conclusion."

"And were you able to determine the time of death?"

Walker checks his notes. "Between two o'clock and four o'clock in the morning."

"Explain to the court, if you will, how an experienced criminologist such as yourself arrives at these findings."

Walker shifts in his chair and looks at the jurors, who are listening carefully. Some are taking notes. "The body temperature of the victim is a good indicator," he says. "The manner in which the blood has settled in the body is another one. In the lab we have more sophisticated tests we run, but an experienced field inspector usually gets the time of death pretty close, particularly if the body is found within a short time after the killing takes place."

"Besides deciding that the cause of death was strangulation, and that the victim had been killed a few hours before she was found, was there anything unusual about her, or the circumstances, that you noticed?"

"She was fully dressed," Walker answers, "except for her underpants. They were missing."

"All her clothes were accounted for, except her underpants," Loomis restates the answer.

"Yes."

"What did you make of that?"

"Well, she might not have worn any. That seems to be the fashion among young women these days," he deadpans.

The courtroom breaks into laughter. Even Judge Suzuki covers a smile. Humor—the best medicine, and often the best persuader.

"But seriously," Walker continues, "my initial reaction was that there was sexual activity, and that her killer took the panties because he was afraid there would be evidence on them that could be traced back to him."

"Do you mean rape?" Loomis prompts.

I'm tempted to object, but I let it slide, because I want to get Walker over and done with, and Joe doesn't do it either, which tells me we're on the same page. The information will get in, regardless, so why bring more attention to it?

"Rape is always a possibility, yes, but regular sexual activity is also considered. Particularly in this case, since there weren't any clear signs that the victim had put up a struggle." He looks apologetic, almost embarrassed. "This is not a pleasant thing to say, but the most likely scenario is that the victim and her assailant had consensual sex, and that she was killed afterward. Maybe immediately afterward."

The air in the courtroom has suddenly become heavier, like the dank atmosphere of a sarcophagus that is opened after centuries of being shut. That the Full Moon Killer might also have been the victims' lover, and killed them during or right after having sex, adds enormous psychological weight to this trial.

I look at Salazar, who is listening carefully. If he and these women were sexually involved, you would think his body would involuntarily reveal it. But there is no show of any reaction. If he is innocent, as he swears, I can buy it. Otherwise, the blood in his veins is colder than ice.

"Did you check the victim for rape, or other sexual activity?" Loomis asks.

"Yes." Another reference to his notes. I'm sure he knows the answers—he's been prepped well—but he wants to be extra sure. One slipup can destroy an entire lifetime of credibility. "Dr. Ramos, the pathologist from our office who was assigned to this case, did that when he did the autopsy."

"What were the results?"

"The conditions of her genitals indicated that she had had sex within a day or two before she was killed. Maybe hours, or less. There was some bruising, but nothing to a level that we could definitely confirm as rape."

"Was semen present?"

"No."

"What conclusion do you take from that?"

"That whoever had sex with her pulled out before ejaculation, or wore a condom."

"Which would be another indication that the victim and her killer knew each other."

I struggle to my feet, which are killing me. I'm going to have to break down and get shoes a size larger. For a woman whose feet are already banana boats, that's hard to swallow. "Objection, Your Honor. Calls for speculation."

"Overruled," Suzuki decides without hesitation.

"That would be a reasonable assumption to make," Walker answers.

The prosecution has a tight blueprint. Next up, the cops who found the second body and the criminologist who presided over the crime scene. Another death by strangulation, another pair of missing underpants. No semen left behind. The date, thirty days from the previous murder, in which the MO and other circumstances were identical. A second killing that took place during the full moon.

Arthur Wong is running the witness. Wong is like me, a promising up-and-comer, though without the night sweats and cravings for anything pistachio. His people want him to get meaningful public face time. Loomis will do the heavy lifting: Cordova, the DNA experts, their key eyewitnesses.

Wong's witness is Richard Cavanaugh, the Hawaiian-shirt-wearing undercover detective who was a member of Cordova's task force. No casual getup today—the detective is dressed in a snappy blazer-and-slacks outfit. His hair is shorter than when I saw him out on the street, and his beard is trimmed. He still wears an earring, however. Let the jurors know they have a real live undercover cop in the house.

After he took the oath and mounted the witness chair, he glanced over at the defense table, and our eyes met. We had not seen each other since the night before Salazar was arrested, and he obviously didn't know about my condition. His reaction was a double take right out of Laurel and Hardy.

Wong leads him through the standard recitation of his bona fides, and he describes the crime scene—the murdered victim, cause of death by strangulation, the missing undies.

"Were you the lead detective at the crime scene?" Wong asks Cavanaugh.

"Yes."

"Did you notice the similarities between that victim's murder and the one that took place during the previous full moon?"

"No," Cavanaugh answers. "I wasn't on that case, so I didn't know about it."

"Did the fact that the victim's underpants were missing raise a red flag?"

Smart fellow, Arthur Wong. That's a question our side would

legitimately ask. By doing it themselves, they take the sting out of any possible benefit we might have.

"Not particularly," Cavanaugh says. "Articles of clothing are often taken from crime scenes, along with other stuff, like purses and car keys, so it didn't register with me. It wasn't until later, when the two cases were compared, that the connections began to fall into place. The third one confirmed it."

"Do you know who made those connections?"

"Lieutenant Luis Cordova of the LAPD, Robbery-Homicide Division."

"Is he your superior?"

Cavanaugh nods. "He's second in command at Robbery-Homicide. He was in charge of the Full Moon Task Force."

"Did he coin that term? The Full Moon Killer?"

Cavanaugh guffaws. "That was a media invention. Anything to sell tickets."

I stand at the podium. Cavanaugh can't take his eyes off me. I have that effect on men.

"How are you today, Detective?" I ask him.

"Fine," he answers brightly. "And you?"

"Getting along, thank you. How many homicide cases have you investigated in your career?"

He blinks. "I don't know. Probably about fifty."

"In those investigations, how many arrests were made? Percentagewise."

"Over ninety percent," he answers, managing not to sound boastful. "There are cases we never solve, but we do a good job. I'm speaking for the entire division, not just myself."

"And of those arrests, how many resulted in convictions?"

"Only one murder I have solved did not result in a conviction. When we arrest someone, we generally have good proof. We work with the District Attorney closely. Unless we have strong reasons to arrest someone, we don't move forward. We bend over backward not to arrest innocent people," he says piously. "The public thinks differently sometimes, but their perceptions are based on emotional reactions, not proof."

"In other words, you have no ax to grind," I say.

"None."

"And in all those arrests and convictions, isn't there always a motive? Jealousy, anger, retribution, money, drugs. Even if it's spontaneous, or random, like a gang-style drive-by shooting, there's usually some reason, isn't there? Some motive?"

Cavanaugh thinks about that for a moment. "I would say that's true."

"So you, and the other detectives on the task force who were trying to find the so-called Full Moon Killer, focused on motive? On why someone would want to kill these women?"

Reluctantly, he admits, "We tried to."

"Tried to? Meaning, tried to but failed?"

"Yes," he admits. "We couldn't find one."

"So as far as you know, there was no connection between these women, besides their living in the same area of Los Angeles and the fact that they were all murdered."

"All murdered during the full moon, all strangled, all without their underpants," he corrects me.

"Personal connection," I say, putting an impatient edge to my voice. He knows what I'm talking about, and he's playing a little game with me. Cops and defense lawyers, natural enemies, like mongooses and cobras.

"Were there any *personal* connections?" I come around the side of the podium, so my profile is in full view of him and the jury. "Did any of these women know any of the others?"

He shakes his head dolefully. "Not that we found. It was all happening fast, and preventing another murder was our main objective. And catching the killer, of course."

"Yes, catching the killer. That was your mandate. Catch the killer."

"That was our job," he corrects me again.

"So just to make doubly sure," I say. "The police never came up with a motive for why these particular women were killed."

"No," he answers. "The best we could figure out was they were in the wrong place at the wrong time."

"Thank you." I turn to the judge. "No further questions." I turn my back on him and walk to our table.

He's not going to leave without taking a parting shot. "Ted Bundy didn't have a motive," he says to my retreating back. "For some killers, especially serial killers, true psychopaths, the pleasure they get from killing is motive enough."

That's it for the day. Joe and I go up to his office to hash over the day's proceedings. I fall into a chair in a heap and kick my shoes off. Immediately, I feel better. If I can't get them back on I'll walk out barefoot.

"I screwed up at the end with Cavanaugh, didn't I?" I lament. "I gave him an opening and he nailed me."

"Don't be hard on yourself," Joe soothes me. He takes a couple of Diet Cokes from his minifridge, pops the tops, and hands me one.

"Roberto Salazar is not Ted Bundy, and by the end of the trial the jury will understand that," Joe says. "You made your point— the police didn't make a personal connection between any of the victims, and they never established a motive. That's going to be important down the line."

"Thanks," I tell him. "I needed that."

"You're doing fine."

He hefts his briefcase, which is stuffed with nighttime reading, and offers me a hand up. I stuff my shoes into my purse. Low-heeled, backless slides, that's what I need. I'll buy a couple pairs tonight. Nordstrom's is open until nine. I hope they carry women's size 12.

THIRTY-THREE

T HE SALESMAN HAS TO dig deep in the back shelves to find
shoes that fit me, but he manages to come up with two pairs
of low-heeled slides in size 12, which are snug but will do the
trick. They are not as stylish as I would like, but I doubt anyone
is checking out my feet these days. My belly, that's all anyone can
see.

I luxuriate in a long, hot bath, then dry off and dig into my
organic, skinless, takeout chicken breast. It tastes like a roofing
shingle. Tomorrow night, no matter what, I'm going to hotfoot it
over to Pete's Cafe & Bar after work and have a Hellman burger
with garlic-fries, two of the many goodies I denied myself while I
was in training. I still am, in a different kind of way, but I can eat
things I didn't eat then. A burger and fries once in a blue moon,
the baby can tolerate that. The baby wants Mommy to be happy.
Mommy is happy when she satisfies her cravings.

The phone rings. If it isn't Joe, I'm not going to pick up. Whoever it is can wait until tomorrow.

I check the caller ID. Amanda. Calling to praise me for my
performance today, no doubt. I can't duck her. I pick up the receiver. "Hello, Amanda. How are you?"

I listen; then I start to shake. I reach out a hand to steady myself, and lower my big body into a chair. "When?" I croak. I listen. "Where is she?"

Salazar's wife tried to kill herself. She took an overdose of sleeping pills. She's been on them since her husband was arrested the second time. Luckily, a friend found her in time and called for help. The paramedics took her to Los Angeles County-USC Medical Center, the main hospital for East L.A. She is in intensive care.

"I can't go down there," I tell Amanda. "I'm jammed, and it's too late." And I don't want to. That's not my job. Defending her husband is my job, and it's full-time work. Whatever energy I have left over is for me and my unborn child. I won't be guilt-tripped into taking on any more emotional burdens.

Amanda can't go, either. The publicity would be totally negative, totally devastating. She will make sure Mrs. Salazar gets the best medical attention available. She will call me if anything changes. Otherwise, we'll talk in the morning.

I hang up. This is horrible. I feel terrible for that poor woman. That she would do such a thing speaks to how desperate and isolated she must feel.

And something else, something more sinister. Her doing this tells me that she has lost faith in her husband. A devoted wife would not try to take her life. She has been so humiliated, so cut apart from everything in her life, that she doesn't feel there is any way out. And that is bad news for her husband.

I'm at the office by seven-thirty in the morning. Earlier, I talked to Amanda. Salazar's wife is out of danger. The suicide attempt was more a cry for help than a real effort to end her life. Amanda will keep me up to date. She won't be in court today, it wouldn't be appropriate.

"Does Roberto know?" I asked her, when we spoke at six in the morning. "Was he informed?"

She doesn't know if he does or not. That will be my first order of business today, before we go back into trial. If he hasn't been told, he'll be devastated. If he was, he'll be more remote and angrier than ever. By his lights, the system has completely fucked him over. Now that cesspool of evil has spread to his family. He has been harder and harder to reach. Now he's going to dig himself into a hole no one will be able to penetrate.

Salazar knows. I read it on his face as soon as he is brought into the courtroom. One of his jailers must have told him. They love to rub in the misery. His face is ashen, his expression cut in stone.

"She's going to be all right," I say, trying to reassure him. I had called the hospital to make sure for myself. She will be moved out of intensive care later today, but she will be closely watched to make sure she doesn't try to off herself again.

He shakes his head in disagreement. "She will never be all right again," he contradicts me.

Shit. Just as I predicted. He's in a funk blacker than the dark side of the moon. I look around. The courtroom is filling up. We have almost no time to talk before the judge and jury come in. Joe had text-messaged me that he wouldn't be here until right at the appointed time, so Salazar and I are alone—as alone as you can be when dozens of people, all hostile to you, are watching your every move. That includes Loomis and his entourage, who can't help but stare in our direction. Obviously, they know.

"Listen up," I whisper to him. "This is bad news, but you cannot show that. No one on the jury is going to know about it, they're not allowed to read or hear anything about this case or you. So if you hang a long face today, they aren't going to know why. They'll think it's because you're feeling guilty, and they'll carry that impression through the rest of the trial and into the jury room. So buck up. I know it's hard, Roberto, but you have to take care of you. Comprende?"

He stares at me, as if he's looking through me. Then he gives a curt nod. "I understand."

"We'll get through this. She's going to be all right," I say again, as much to hear it for myself as for him. If his wife had died last night, there would have been hell to pay. Almost certainly there would have been a postponement of the trial, which could have had all kinds of unknown ramifications. Even this unsuccessful suicide attempt might cause a delay in the proceedings for a few days.

Joe bustles into the courtroom and flops his briefcase on our table. I had called him earlier this morning to give him the news, so he's on board. He cocks an inquisitive eye at me, and I nod: yes, Salazar knows.

We walk away from the defense table and caucus against the wall. "How is he doing?" Joe asks, glancing back at Salazar, who is sitting motionless at the table, his back stiff, as if he had a coat hanger inside his coat. "Should we ask for a continuance until tomorrow?"

"I don't think so," I reply. "If anything, this incident is going to cause him to retreat deeper into his shell. We need to push everything forward." It isn't my job to instruct Joe on how to run this case, but I'm going to do it anyway. "I think we should get their witnesses off the stand as fast as we can. Limit our cross-examinations to what's absolutely necessary, and no more."

"Umm," Joe ponders. "You're probably right. We'll play it by ear." He shakes his head dolefully. "Let's hope the jury doesn't find out. I've been checking the media. So far, nothing in the papers or radio. Maybe we can finesse it. It isn't newsworthy unless they connect the dots."

"Or someone does it for them," I say, cocking my head in the direction of the prosecution table.

"We can't control that. We do what we can. Don't worry about the rest, it's bad for your health." He gives me a friendly belly pat. "Take care of you. The hell with the rest of them."

Judge Suzuki, in shirtsleeves, calls us and the prosecution into his chambers before the jury is brought in. "Are you going to ask for a continuance?" he asks Joe and me. "Any objections?" he puts to Loomis, before Joe can answer. He knows about Salazar's wife, and he knows Loomis does, too.

"A day or two, no," Loomis answers.

Continuances are given all the time, for reasons important and mundane. A scheduled visit to the dentist is cause to push back. Not a big deal. It will only become a big deal if the reason leaks out.

"We're not going to ask for a continuance," Joe tells the judge. "Mrs. Salazar is out of danger, and our client wants to move forward."

Suzuki shrugs. "Fine with me." He raises a cautionary finger. "If I find out this information gets out any more than it has, I will impose strong sanctions on whoever does it." He directs his remarks at Loomis. "That includes the jail personnel. I'm holding you responsible for them. I know they already told the prisoner, which was against the rules. I'll let that pass, this one time. But not twice. Understood?"

It is rare for a judge to chastise a lawyer for an infraction he didn't directly commit. Suzuki wants to make sure this case stays buttoned-up tight. Not only because he's a stickler for protocol, but because he doesn't want to give us grounds for appeal. A reversal from a higher court because the trial judge screwed up is like a lash across the back—it leaves permanent scars. Suzuki wants to sail into his retirement unblemished.

"Understood, Your Honor," Loomis says. His muted tone of voice signifies that he means it.

Suzuki shrugs into his robes. "Let's get this show on the road."

So much has happened to me in the past year that Salazar's first trial seems as if it took place in another life, until the cop who arrested him that night takes the stand, and then it all comes back in a flash. As he swears to tell the truth, he is staring daggers at me, as if to say, you got me last time, bitch, now it's my turn for payback. I return his glare with a Mona Lisa smile.

A third member of the prosecution team, Meg Rawlings, conducts the examination. I guess they figured that my performance has been so stellar they need to balance the equation with a female from their side. Meg is not pregnant, so I've got a leg up on her on that score. However, she is a very good lawyer. We've done trials together, and I like going up against her, she doesn't take cheap shots, the way her compatriot Dixant did in that earlier trial.

"Officer Talbert," she says, "tell us what happened the night of April 13, 2006."

I had forgotten his name. Michael Talbert. A name I had hoped not to hear again.

Talbert wriggles around in the witness chair. He's a beefy guy—getting his ass into a comfortable position takes a bit of shifting. He flicks open his notebook, runs a pudgy finger down the page, reads to himself (his lips move), then shuts the book and looks up.

"I was on night patrol in the Brentwood-Westwood section of Los Angeles. There had been a rash of burglaries, so the force beefed up its presence there to show the colors and to be nearby in case we got a call. Around three in the morning I was driving down Sepulveda, north of Sunset, when I saw a vehicle that aroused my suspicions."

"What was it about this vehicle that caused you to be suspicious, Officer Talbert?" Meg asks. "What kind of vehicle was it?"

Another glance at his notes. "A GMC cube truck. Small." He pauses, then remembers the other half of the question. "It ran a stop sign. Also, one of its tail-lights was flickering."

"Did you pull it over?"

"Yes, I did."

"And you asked the driver for identification."

"Yes."

"What was the name of the driver of the truck you stopped on Sepulveda Boulevard in the area of Los Angeles between Westwood and Brentwood at three o'clock in the morning of April thirteenth?"

Talbert doesn't have to refer to his notes. "Roberto Salazar." He points at us. "The man sitting at the defense table, wearing the blue blazer."

Joe is in a brown suit, and I'm the wrong sex, so there is no doubt as to whom Talbert is pointing at. Everyone looks where Talbert is pointing. I feel as if a klieg light is shining on us, the kind they use at Hollywood premieres and used-car dealership openings.

"You are certain the driver and owner of the truck you stopped was Mr. Salazar, and you are also certain of the time and location?" Meg rephrases for him.

"Absolutely. The time and place are in the records, and I testified . . ."

Joe is on his feet as if he has a rocket up his ass. "Objection!" he thunders.

Suzuki's gavel comes down like a sledgehammer. "Sustained." He glares at Meg, then past her to Loomis. Turning to the bailiff, he orders him: "Remove the jury."

The jurors, who seem confused, are ushered out. When they are gone, Suzuki looks down from his perch. "We will take a short recess," he declaims in a loud, angry voice. To both teams of lawyers: "In my chambers. The witness will remained seated where he is."

"I swear that was not our intention," Meg pleads before Suzuki. "We specifically told him he couldn't do that." She looks to Loomis for support, who nods. He steps forward, to take whatever brunt of criticism the judge will level at them, a hallmark of a good leader. "The witness did that on his own, I swear it," he says, turning to Joe and me.

"We believe you," Joe says with easy, almost insouciant equanimity. "It was a slip of the tongue."

"So you're all right to proceed with this witness?" Suzuki asks. He sounds surprised. Loomis looks surprised, too.

"Yes, we're fine with him." To Loomis: "How much longer are you going to have this witness on the stand?"

"We're done with him," Loomis answers. Talbert is radioactive to them now. "Two minutes to recap, tops."

"Good by me," Joe says. "Jessica?"

"Good by me," I parrot. I'm anxious to get my hands on Officer Michael Talbert, the sooner the better.

I'm as chipper as a chipmunk with a cheek full of acorns. "Officer Talbert. Long time no see."

I am standing at the podium in my new, unstylish but comfortable shoes. I had forgotten how piglike his eyes are, two little red beads in a sea of flesh. His entire face is swinish. If ever a cop deserved to be called a pig, it would be Officer Michael Talbert, LAPD.

"Counselor," he replies guardedly.

"Do you recall the last time we met face-to-face?" I ask him.

He doesn't answer; instead, he looks over at the prosecution table, as if he wants instructions from them. Loomis, a worried and puzzled look on his face, gets to his feet.

"Your Honor. May we approach?"

Suzuki nods. Loomis and Meg Rawlings come out from behind their table and walk to the side of the judge's bench that is opposite the jury box. I follow them; Joe joins me.

"Your Honor, you stipulated that Mr. Salazar's previous arrest and trial could not be introduced into these proceedings," Loomis complains. "We agreed to that. So why is the defense bringing it up? That is clearly a violation of the agreement."

Joe steps forward with a devilish look on his mug. It's an act of will that he isn't literally licking his chops.

"The *prosecution* agreed, Your Honor. Not the defense. Telling the jury that our client had a previous arrest record would be prejudicial against us, we all agree about that. But no one, including you, Your Honor, ever said the defense couldn't introduce it. Now we have to, because the jury is going to figure it out regardless of what officer Talbert didn't say. He opened the door, and now we're walking through it. We have every legal right to do so," he adds. His tone is calm and even, but his attitude is aggressive.

Suzuki looks at Loomis. "This is highly unusual, but I'm going to have to rule for the defense," he tells the senior deputy D.A. "Officer Talbert gave them the opening to bring up that arrest and trial. They're right—the jury will figure it out. So I'm allowing Ms. Thompson to continue her line of questioning."

Loomis scowls, but he doesn't protest. He could still get benefits from this. Salazar was arrested for a serious crime less than a year ago, in the exact place and time where a Full Moon victim was found. He's more upset about being trumped.

I take up my position at the podium again. "Would you repeat my last question?" I ask the court reporter.

She reads it back. "Do you recall the last time we met face to face?"

Talbert looks grim. He doesn't know where this is going, but he doesn't like the prospects, whatever they are. "Yes. I recall it."

"What was the occasion?"

"I was testifying in a trial."

"Whom were you testifying against, Officer?"

Talbert points to Salazar. "Him."

"Let the record show that Officer Talbert identified Roberto Salazar as the person he was testifying about in a previous case in which I was the defense attorney." I slide my feet out of one shoe, then the other. Standing still is the hardest thing I'm going through. But this won't take long, and the payoff will be worth it.

"Did that testimony have something to do with your having stopped Mr. Salazar's truck on the night you mentioned?"

He nods. "Yes."

"After you stopped Mr. Salazar, did you search his truck?"

"Yes," in a tone like a growl.

"And what did you find?"

"A load of television sets."

"Television sets," I repeat. "Where did they come from? Did Mr. Salazar tell you?"

"He said he was taking them to a warehouse in the valley, for a friend."

"Did you check that out? Was that a legitimate delivery?"

Talbert shakes his head emphatically. "His story was bogus. The television sets had been stolen from a container car in San Pedro."

"And when you found that out, did you arrest him?"

He spits out his answer. "Yes."

The jury is staring at us with fascination, their heads rotating back and forth as if they're watching a tennis match.

"And Mr. Salazar went to trial, which was when you saw me, is that correct? I was Mr. Salazar's lawyer, and I cross-examined you."

"That's right."

I walk halfway to the jury box. "Would you please tell the court, Officer Talbert, what the verdict of that trial was?"

Talbert looks as if he's been constipated for a week. "Not guilty."

"Not guilty," I repeat, looking the jurors in the face as I speak. "He was arrested for a crime, but he was not guilty of that crime. Is that correct?"

"The jury found him not guilty," he says petulantly.

"They did," I agree. "And fast. Within a couple of hours. They barely had time to fill out their ballots." I turn back to Talbert. "Because, to use your word, they felt his arrest was bogus."

He starts to come back at me, but Loomis catches his eye. *Keep your trap shut.* You can almost see the silent warning hanging over Loomis's head in big, red, neon letters.

"Let's go back to the night you arrested Mr. Salazar," I carry on. "After you found out the television sets had been stolen, you arrested Mr. Salazar on the spot and brought him to jail, is that correct?"

He's deflated now. "Yes."

"What happened to his truck, and the contents of it?"

"It was towed to a police impound lot. The television sets were removed, to be used as evidence."

"Who searched it?" I ask.

"Initially, I did," he says. "Then the impound people did."

"Did you do a thorough job?"

"As best I could, under the circumstances."

"And the impound people, later. Did they?"

"Yes."

"They're good at that, aren't they?

"Very good."

"When you searched Mr. Salazar's truck, and later on, when the detectives at the impound yard searched it, did they look for anything else that should not have been there? Guns, drugs, anything else that might have been used to further incriminate Mr. Salazar?"

Of course they would have looked for that kind of stuff. They would have gone over that truck with a fine-tooth comb. If they had come up with anything, especially drugs, that would have really nailed Salazar's ass to the wall.

"No," Talbert admits. "They didn't find anything like that."

I leave the podium and walk to the witness box. I rarely do that, I like to keep my distance. But sometimes, proximity is useful. When I am just out of what I hope is spitting range, I ask, "Did you or anyone else find a pair of women's underpants in that truck?"

I don't have to look behind to know that Loomis is cringing. It's all there, in Talbert's face.

"No," he answers. "We did not."

"Not when you arrested him, and not later. In fact, you never found a pair of women's panties in Mr. Salazar's truck, did you?"

He looks me in the eye and takes his medicine like a man. "No. We never found any women's underpants in that truck."

THIRTY-FOUR

AGAINST MY BETTER JUDGMENT, I go see Mrs. Salazar in the hospital after court is adjourned for the day. Somebody has to report back to Salazar about his wife's condition, and I'm the only candidate except for Amanda, who is making herself scarce. If word gets out, there could be nosy tabloid or television reporters lurking about, fishing for something juicy to titillate their customers, and she can't handle that kind of publicity. But the place is devoid of the press, fortunately. It's enough that I have to run that gauntlet every day at the courthouse. To see their jackal-like faces anywhere else would cause me to blow a gasket, which I can't let happen. I have to stay calm. The baby doesn't like turbulence, it's a great governor for my emotions.

It takes me a while to find Salazar's wife; County-USC is an enormous facility. Anyone who isn't familiar with its layout would be well advised to leave a trail of bread crumbs to find the way out.

I finally locate her. She has been moved from an intensive care unit to a semiprivate room. She looks completely desiccated, as if the liquid has been drained from her body, and all that is left is dry flesh and skeleton. I've seen mummies in museums who looked healthier. The other bed is occupied by an old lady who is out of it; tubes and hoses are sprouting from every orifice of her body.

A couple of Mrs. Salazar's friends are with her; two of the

women who came to Salazar's first trial. When Mrs. Salazar sees
me, she cringes. "Oh, Mrs. Thompson, I am so sorry!"

It's Ms., but I don't correct her. "Sorry for what?"

"For causing all this trouble," she keens. "For everyone." Her
voice is raspy and pinched.

Her friends sit on either side of her, holding her hands. They
make clucking sounds, that are meant to be soothing and supportive. One of them puts a small ice cube in her mouth. She sucks
on it.

"How are you feeling?" I ask.

She waggles her head, as if to say, *Not bad*. One of her friends
answers for her, "She is tired, but she is much better now."

"Who is watching your children?"

"Her sister," the go-between tells me. Lowering her voice, she
confides, "They do not know. They think she had a bad stomach-
ache."

Mrs. Salazar pushes herself up a little on her elbows. That
small effort seems to take all her energy. She asks me, in a low,
hoarse voice, "How is Roberto?"

I'm not going to baby her. Her husband is in a shitload of
trouble, and this compounded it. "Not too good. He's freaked out
that he can't come see you." I sit down on the edge of the bed.
"He counts on your support," I tell her. "You need to get better
fast, and start coming to court again."

She nods; then she starts to cry. "I have no more strength for
that. It is all too terrible."

"It is terrible," I agree, "but you have to get it together to be
there for Roberto. However you manage to do it, but you must
do it."

Her visitors, uncomfortable with hearing me haranguing her,
announce that they are going to take a break, but will be back
soon. After they leave, I scoot closer to her.

"Why did you do this?" I question her. "You must have a reason, besides feeling overwhelmed."

She turns her face away and stares at the wall. After holding her tongue for a moment, she says, still not looking at me, "I do not believe him anymore."

That sends a tremor down my spine. "What do you mean?"

She turns back to me. Her mouth is quivering. "He goes out at night sometimes. He thinks I am asleep, but I am not."

Shit. I didn't need to hear this. But now that she's broached the subject, I have to hear the rest of it. "How many times has he done that, that you know about?"

She shrugs her bony shoulders. "Five, six, maybe. I do not remember."

"Do you remember when?" I take the plunge. "During the full moon?"

"I am not sure. Maybe." She starts to shiver with agitation. "He comes back while it is still dark out and gets into bed. He pretends he was there all night, but I know he was not."

Oy. "Did you ever say anything to him about it? Ask him where he was?"

Her eyes widen. "No, no! I would never do that."

Because you didn't want to know where he was—getting it on with some floozy. A natural reaction. Since Jeremy dropped his bomb on me, I've had searing fits of jealousy, so I know the emotion.

I have to bring that fear into the light. Once you expose them you're on the road to recovery. "You thought he was seeing someone."

She bobs her head. The tears start flowing again.

Men of God are as human as anyone else, so of course that's what she would think—what any woman would think. "Do you still believe that's the reason?"

She chokes down her sobs. "I do not know what to think anymore. I don't know if he . . ." She can't finish the thought. She doesn't have to. If he really is the killer. "I have lost faith in him," she tells me. "Without him, what do I have to live for?"

Oh, you poor, wretched woman whose world has been turned so upside-down. "Your children."

Her sigh sounds like a death rattle. "I know. What I did was wrong. *Stupido*. I was not thinking."

Social worker is not part of my job description, but there are times you have to enlarge your portfolio. "You need to get out of here, go home, and be with them." I take my card out of my purse, scribble my cell phone number on it, and hand it to her. "Call me tomorrow. I'll put you in touch with someone you can talk to about this. Free of charge," I add. She won't go if she has to pay. She might not go anyway, but I'll push her; she needs professional help. "Someone who speaks Spanish, if you would prefer that."

She looks at my card, then lays it on the bedside table. "All right," she says in a small voice, falling back on her pillows. She's wiped out. And I've learned all I need to know—more.

"And once you feel better, you have to come back to the trial," I nag her again. "Even if you don't want to. The outcome might depend on your being there."

She lowers her eyes. "I will try."

That's all I can ask for.

Omar Chatterjee, M.D., is the coroner's office DNA expert. Although he came here from India thirty years ago, he still speaks with an Indian-British accent. He knows his stuff cold, and unlike the celebrity pathologists who hog the headlines, he doesn't trumpet his knowledge. His word is impeccable. I've never known him to mess up.

Siobhan Flynn, our DNA specialist, is at the defense table with Joe and me today. She'll do the cross-examination. Chatterjee puts on a pair of latex gloves and takes the evidence—the panties that were found in Salazar's truck—out of the evidence bag.

"Are these the woman's undergarments that were certified as belonging to the victim, Cheryl Lynn Steinmetz?" Arthur Wong asks. Cheryl Lynn Steinmetz was the Full Moon Killer's last victim, the one whose underpants were found in Salazar's truck.

"Yes," Chatterjee answers. He's a man of few words.

"Is there any doubt at all that they could have belonged to someone else?"

"No. These are Ms. Steinmetz's panties. The DNA evidence confirmed it."

Siobhan and I have gone over the test results very carefully. The panties were compared to DNA taken from the corpse at the autopsy, and they matched. These panties belonged to the last Full Moon victim. We won't contest that evidence, it is beyond question.

Wong asks a few more questions to cement the fact that the panties found in Salazar's truck belonged to the victim, and that there is no possibility they could have been anyone else's. He puts the panties back in their container and returns it to the evidence table.

Siobhan replaces Wong at the podium. This will be her only appearance at the trial, unless something else about DNA comes up. "Besides finding Ms. Steinmetz's DNA on those panties, did you find anyone else's?" she asks Chatterjee.

Chatterjee is direct and explicit. "No."

"Not Mr. Salazar's?" Siobhan sounds surprised. I look at the jurors. They seem a bit surprised, too.

"No."

"What about fingerprints? Did you find Mr. Salazar's fingerprints on the panties?"

"No."

Siobhan looks even more surprised. "Isn't that unusual? If Mr. Salazar took them and put them in his truck, wouldn't his fingerprints be on them?"

"Not necessarily. Not all materials pick up fingerprints," Chatterjee explains. "That's a common fallacy. Or they may be smudged so that they cannot be identified. Or Mr. Salazar could have used gloves to pick them up. If he was the assailant," he adds. A careful scientist, he deals with facts, not suppositions.

"There are several plausible reasons why his or anyone else's fingerprints weren't found on those panties."

"Were the victim's?"

"Yes. But they were her undergarments. She would have handled them many times while wearing them, such as pulling them down to go to the bathroom. Touching an article multiple times increases the possibility of leaving prints."

Siobhan nods, but looks skeptical. She picks up the Ziploc bag containing the panties from the evidence table and holds it up, squinting like a jeweler examining a gemstone as she looks at it. "Let me ask you something else, Doctor. Can you tell how recently Ms. Steinmetz's DNA was left on these panties? Was it definitely on the night she was killed?"

"Not necessarily," Chatterjee answers firmly. "That would not be possible to know, because DNA lasts a long time. Months, even years. Although once the panties had been washed, the traces would be gone, so you would assume the samples were recent. But to specifically answer your question, the answer is no, we can't pinpoint when the DNA was deposited onto them."

"Then it would be possible," Siobhan continues along that line, "for the DNA that was recovered to be weeks or months old."

"Yes."

"If that's so, then it would also be possible that those are not the underpants the victim was wearing on the night she was killed at all. They could be a different pair altogether, and could have been put in Mr. Salazar's truck long before Ms. Steinmetz was killed."

Loomis bolts to his feet. "Objection! This isn't questioning, it's editorializing."

"Sustained," Judge Suzuki agrees. "Strike that last comment from the record," he tells the court reporter. "The defense will save their opinions for their summation," he cautions Siobhan, at the same time casting a reproving eye at Joe and me.

"Yes, Your Honor," Siobhan answers. "No further questions."

As she walks back to our table, I check the jurors' reactions.

From the looks on their faces, they aren't buying her speculation. We didn't expect them to. But you have to try everything, especially when you're on the defensive. You never know when you might get water from what you thought was a dry well.

During the short recess before the prosecution's next witness takes the stand, Amanda Burgess slips into the courtroom and takes her customary place behind our table. She gives Salazar an encouraging smile and mouths "She's okay." Salazar digests that information stoically, not a muscle moving in his face.

Joe gives Amanda a cursory nod. "Her highness returns," he mutters under his breath. He appreciates the support she's giving Salazar, but he's also put off by the whiff of privileged condescension that is inevitable in such a relationship. I felt that way, too, until Amanda and I became closer.

"She means well, Joe." I have to defend her. We're having a baby together.

"I know. It's my knee-jerk reaction to the high and mighty."

I walk to the railing. Amanda comes to meet me. "The hospital sent her home," she whispers. "I talked to her. I think she's going to be all right." She grimaces. "What an ordeal." She touches my hand. "She told me you came to see her. That was terrific of you. I didn't have the courage. Thank you for doing that."

"I did it for him," I say in a quiet voice, nodding at Salazar. "She has to show she supports him, no matter what."

"She's awfully fragile," Amanda says. "I don't know if she can handle more public scrutiny. Having to go through that media gauntlet every day is awful, even for someone who's tough. I get the shivers every time I walk by all those reporters and cameras. Any more stress and she could have a major breakdown."

Amanda is right about that, but she and I have different agendas. She's concerned for the entire Salazar family. My only consideration is my client.

"I'll talk to her again," I tell Amanda. "I want her to see a psychologist. I told her I'd give her some recommendations. Get on her case to call me later today, after we adjourn. It's really important to show a united front."

Amanda looks doubtful. "I'll try. How is it going?"

"The DNA evidence against us is bad. Joe got in a few shots, but it was a rough morning."

"I'm glad I missed it, then. Should I stay around for the rest of the day?"

"Your call. Roberto likes having you here. You're the only supporter who comes anymore."

"I'll stay, then." Comforting fingers on my hand again. "Keep up the good fight. I'm proud of you. You're doing a wonderful job."

I'm glad she thinks so. Personally, I'm not so sure.

Aaron Lazarus, the eighty-four-year-old man who saw one of the victims on the night she was murdered, is sworn in. He stands proud and erect as he takes the oath, like a small-town Rotarian reciting the Pledge of Allegiance. Testifying in a trial is a civic responsibility that he takes seriously—I can see that patriotic look in his eye. And for a man who has been retired for fifteen or more years, without much to look forward to besides taking his dog on her twice-daily walks, having a moment in the public eye is an occasion to savor.

Loomis, as the oldest and senior member of the prosecution team, leads the sprightly octogenarian through his testimony. How he was out walking his dog, late at night. A pretty young woman walking in the middle of the block caught his eye. You're never too old to admire a lovely woman, he comments, to light chuckling and all-around smiles. What a sweet old gent, still dreaming of the possibilities of romance. Then, as he watched her, because there was nothing else to do until his dog did her business, he saw her stop at the other end of the street and talk to a man who seemed to be working on his truck, maybe checking the tire pressure. She and the man seemed to know each other; her body language was relaxed, and she seemed to be at ease while talking to the man. Lazarus recalls thinking that the man looked out of place in this neighborhood at this hour of the night, and then that he immediately felt guilty about it, because that was racial profiling, which he does not approve of. But he did get a good look at the basic elements: the man's age, basic complexion, what he was wearing, the color and condition of his truck.

"Were you able to see the man's face with any clarity?" Loomis asks.

Lazarus shakes his head. "I'm afraid not. He was too far away, and he had on that hat."

"And you were mostly looking at that pretty woman," Loomis says with a tacit wink.

As it turns out, even old people who should, by dint of their seniority, be immune to embarrassment over questions like that, can blush. Lazarus does now. "Yes, I must admit I was."

"So if you were to look at the defendant sitting over there . . ." Loomis points to Salazar, sitting next to me, ". . . you could not identify him."

"No. I could not, and would not. Unless I was absolutely certain, I would not do that."

This is a nice structure the prosecution is building. I admire their handiwork. The witness is now on record as being unable to ID Salazar as the man he saw that night, so we can't attack him about that. But the other pieces—the age, ethnicity, clothing, Salazar's truck—he's sure about them. More details to throw onto the coals, like a handful of dry twigs. You accumulate enough of these twigs, you can build a roaring fire.

"You saw this woman clearly," Loomis continues with his questioning.

"Yes."

"Did the police show you her picture? Was that how you identified her?"

Lazarus shakes his head. "No. I did see her face, but not clearly enough that I could identify her with certainty."

Loomis looks puzzled. I look at the jurors. They do, too. Jesus, did the prosecution screw up here? Joe leans forward in his chair. He's thinking what I'm thinking.

"Then how did you know the woman you saw was one of the victims of the Full Moon Killer?" Loomis asks. He seems to be off-balance.

"By her clothing. She was wearing a light blue sweat-outfit. UCLA colors. I am an alumnus of UCLA," Lazarus says with pride, "I know those colors well. And she was wearing casual shoes called Crocs. Pink ones. My wife has a similar pair. I kid her about them, because they are so silly looking. So I was aware of the woman because of that."

My bad. Loomis was heading in this direction all along. He let his line out, the jury and everyone else, including Joe and me, took the bait, and now he's reeling them in.

"You came to the police voluntarily, is that correct?" Loomis asks.

"Yes. I felt I had to."

"And when you spoke to them, did they in *any* way, directly or indirectly, give you any hints or clues about these articles of clothing you saw the victim wearing?"

"Oh, no. Quite the contrary. They were skeptical about me, until I brought that up."

"So you initiated the discussion about what the victim was wearing. The police did not lead you on about that."

"Not at all. I had to prove myself before they would take me seriously." He allows himself a satisfied smile. "I believe I convinced them of my seriousness."

Loomis asks a few more questions of his witness, then he turns him over to us. He sits down, having established that a man who resembled Salazar in many important ways was seen talking to one of the victims shortly before she was killed, almost right on the spot. Not a home run, but a solid double.

Joe smiles at Loomis from the podium. "It was around midnight when you saw this encounter between the victim and the man she spoke to?"

"Shortly before. I took my dog out after the eleven o'clock news, which ends at eleven-thirty-five," he says with precision.

"And you were how far away?"

"About thirty yards."

"Thirty yards. A third of a football field. Close to midnight. How well is that street lit, Mr. Lazarus?"

"Not very well. There is one street lamp in the middle of the block."

"So it was dark out."

As Lazarus smiles, I groan to myself. I know what's coming. Joe let one slip by, and he's going to pay for it.

"Actually, it was bright out," Lazarus says, refuting Joe. "It was the night of the full moon, you see, so there was quite a bit of light."

Joe winces. Across the aisle, Loomis smiles. Any time you bring in a witness of this age, you're courting trouble. But it looks as if this old man is going to score for their side.

Joe's foundering. He ought to cut his losses and get off the stage, but he decides to try another approach. "Do you wear glasses, Mr. Lazarus?" he asks the witness. Impute the witness's vision, one of the oldest ploys in the book. You would be surprised how many times it works.

"I wear reading glasses." Lazarus pulls a slim pair of glasses out of the breast pocket of his sports coat and holds them out to Joe. "Would you like to see them?"

"No, thanks, I have my own," Joe says. "I mean for distance."

"No."

"No distance glasses. Contacts?"

"No."

"Did you have LASIK?"

Yet another *no*.

Joe steps back. "That's remarkable, Mr. Lazarus. You must be truly blessed."

"Actually," Lazarus says, as if about to confide a secret, "I always had terrible vision, all my life. The lenses of my glasses looked like Coca-Cola bottoms. I could barely see my hand in front of my face. Then I had cataract surgery, ten years ago. The doctor replaced my lenses with silicone ones. I have twenty-twenty vision now, and no astigmatism. And not only that," he exclaims, "I have UV protection!"

His energy level, almost manic there for a moment, drops back to level. "So I don't need glasses to see clearly anymore. I can see as well as anyone in this room. Better than most."

Joe's been around the block too many times; he doesn't take his losses too hard. "These old codgers live to trip you up. It's better than a good bowel movement."

We're in his office. I have my feet up on a chair, shoes off. I wiggle my stockinged toes. "He got you good," I agree.

"When you swing for the fences, sometimes you hit a home run, sometimes you strike out," he says philosophically. "We're going to need some home runs, because we aren't doing very well."

That he says so out loud is a sign. We're going down. He puts a period on that point. "It's not only that we don't have anything in rebuttal," Joe says. "The tide is against us. I've been around long enough to have a feel for that. By now, you should, too."

I nod in assent and drink from my carton of juice.

"So there weren't any panties in the cube truck. He got rid of them. You can bet your Lotto money Loomis will drive that home, that Salazar usually got rid of them. For some reason, he didn't in this last case. Maybe he wanted to be out of the neighborhood before he dumped them. Who knows?" He sits down heavily on his couch. "That old man gave them cause to search Salazar's truck, which was what they had him up there for, and he delivered the goods." He drains his Diet Coke and takes another one out of his fridge. Thank God diet sodas were invented, Joe would be a type-2 diabetic by now if they hadn't been, he drinks twenty Diet Cokes a day.

"We need something better than what we have," he says. "There has to be an alibi witness out there. There just has to be."

That's if Salazar is innocent, a thought neither of us wants to voice. Our belief in him, what portion we had, is flowing down the drain.

"Tori is still out beating the bushes," I remind Joe. "We have time."

"Not much. If she hasn't found one by now . . ." He throws up his hands, as if to say: she isn't going to.

THIRTY-FIVE

CAN I BUY YOU dinner?" Amanda asks me. "I know you have work to do tonight, but you have to eat, too."

It's early evening. We went straight from the courthouse to our birthing session, which is over now. We walk to our cars, which are parked next to each other in the parking lot. Like their owners, they reveal their class, or lack thereof.

"If we can do it fast. I'm taking some of the cross tomorrow."

Our birthing class is in Santa Monica, midway between our houses. We agree to meet at Chinois on Main. It's usually impossible to get into on short notice, but Amanda calls them on her cell and we're confirmed, table for two in fifteen minutes.

"Rank has its privileges," she smiles. She doesn't mind tossing her weight around.

We're immediately seated and order a dinner of assorted appetizers. One thing about hanging out with Amanda, you eat well. We talk about how I'm feeling: good, no complications; the trial: not so good, we don't have a base to build our case around. That is what lawyers have to do, come up with a thesis, an idea, and base their trial philosophy around it. We don't have one. None of the character witnesses I used last time will speak up for him now, they're too frightened and distrustful. They would probably be irrelevant anyway; I doubt Judge Suzuki would allow any of them in, because they would have nothing to contribute to this case.

"Don't you have a fellow who says he was with Roberto almost all night when one of the murders took place?" Amanda probes, as she chopsticks a piece of sashimi into her mouth. I'm passing on that; raw fish is a no-no when you're pregnant. There's plenty of other good stuff for me to savor.

"That's the problem," I answer. I swallow and wash my food down with an Arnold Palmer, which is a mixture of iced tea and lemonade. "Almost is not the same as the whole time. There's a window Roberto could have exploited."

"If he is the killer," Amanda says pointedly. "We can't stop believing in him."

She says that more as if it's a wish than a conviction.

"We have to be realistic," I say. "Positive, but realistic."

"You sound like you're throwing in the towel," she reproaches me.

I shake my head. "I never quit until the end. And there is always the chance of an eleventh-hour surprise. But I know what evidence they have and I know what evidence we have, and they have the goods."

"So you think there's no chance those underpants were planted."

"By whom?" How many times do we have to beat this dead horse?

She gives in. "I have no idea."

"This isn't *Perry Mason,*" I remind her. "We're not going to pull a rabbit out of the hat. Not when there isn't one in there to begin with."

The dispatcher who took the telephone call stating that a suspicious-looking Latino was near the location where the last murder had taken place is sitting in the witness chair. Ever since 9/11, people are much more sensitive to anyone in their neighborhood who doesn't fit in, so the police get a lot of calls like this one. She had contacted the closest undercover officers on the scene, and they followed through.

"Who made this call?" Joe asks her, when he starts his cross.

"I don't know."

"Don't the numbers automatically come up on your system?"

"Yes," she answers, "but this call came from a pay phone, so we don't know who made it, just the location." She has the evidence slip of the record of the call in her hand. "An AM/PM Mini-Market in Brentwood," she reads off.

I make a note to discuss this with Joe. In an age when everyone has a cell phone, pay phones are almost as anachronistic as dinosaurs. Whoever placed that call may have made it from a pay phone to hide his identity. I also make a note that we should ask Cordova, when we cross-examine him on the stand, if that pay phone was checked for fingerprints. How many people would have used it between the time the call came in and the time they arrested Salazar? Not many, I would think. Maybe only one.

"Was it a man or a woman who called this in?" Joe asks.

"A man," the dispatcher answers.

"Did he have any kind of accent you could make out?"

"I don't remember. We get hundreds of calls every day."

"Do you tape these calls?" Joe asks.

"Yes, we log them in and tape them."

"Does that tape still exist?"

"Yes. We keep them for five years."

I make another note to subpoena the tape. We can get it by the end of the day and listen to it tonight. This is an oversight— that we didn't do it earlier—although in truth, I can't see how it will help us, unless the "real" killer made the call, because he had planted the panties in Salazar's truck, and this was part of his grand scheme to frame an innocent man.

Venturing down that road is a great way to make yourself crazy. As I told Amanda over dinner last night, we will stay positive, but we also have to be realistic. And that idea is not realistic. I may go nuts at times, as I did with Jeremy, but I am not insane.

The detective who alerted Cordova to Salazar's being in the area is on the stand. Arthur Wong has the honors.

"You and your partner took the call from dispatch?"

"Yes," the detective answers. Another sports coat, slacks, and crisp white shirt ensemble. Half-Windsor knot in the tie, American flag pin in lapel. Do these guy buy their clothes from the same place? Like teenage girls, do they call each other in the morning and check on what the other members of their unit are wearing, so they don't repeat, but don't stand out, either?

"How far were you from the suspect's location?"

"A couple of blocks. Took us no time to get there."

"When you got there, what did you see?"

"A man sitting in a truck, reading a newspaper."

"What did you do then?"

"I called Lieutenant Cordova and told him what we were looking at."

"What was his response?"

"Keep an eye on the man, but don't approach him. Which is what we did."

"Okay," Wong says. "What happened then?"

"Lieutenant Cordova arrived a few minutes later."

"Upon which time you and your partner and Lieutenant Cordova searched the suspect's vehicle, found incriminating evidence that linked him to the Full Moon Killings, and arrested him?"

"That is correct."

Wong gathers his notes. "No further questions."

That was short and sweet. The prosecution is holding back getting into the meat of the search until Cordova is on the stand. He's the main man, he carries the weight. They want the jury to hear about what happened from the big dog. This witness, and others like him, are along for the ride, to add extra ballast.

I take my place at the podium. "Good morning, Detective Killebrew."

"Good morning," he greets me.

I consult my notes for the third name. "You and your partner,

Detective Mayweather, searched the truck, along with Lieutenant Cordova."

He crosses one leg over the other and straightens the knife-sharp crease of his trousers. "That's correct."

"Which of you three actually found the panties?"

"Lieutenant Cordova."

I look at my notes again. "Under the floor mat in the cab of the truck?"

"Yes."

"Where were you at the time Lieutenant Cordova found those panties? Were you searching in the cab, too?"

He shakes his head. "No. I was in the back of the truck. Me and my partner were searching through the suspect's implements."

"His tools? Lawnmower, shears, that sort of equipment?"

"Yes, that's right."

"What were you looking for?"

He seems surprised at the question. "Evidence," he answers.

"What kind of evidence?"

"Something that would tie him into the killing that had happened earlier."

"Specifically, what kind of evidence, Detective Killebrew?"

"What I just said—anything that could tie him to the victim."

"Anything meaning underpants? The victim's missing underpants?"

"Anything that might have belonged to her. A wallet, some other means of identification—"

"Was her wallet missing from the crime scene?" I butt in. I look through my notes again. "I don't see anything here that states her wallet was missing."

"I don't know," he backpedals. "I used that as an example."

I lean as far forward on the podium as my stomach will allow, which isn't much. "Is it not true that you were hoping to find a pair of underpants that had been taken from the crime scene? The panties that had belonged to the victim that were missing when her body was discovered? Isn't that what you were specifically looking for, Detective?"

He uncrosses his legs. "Yes."

"Okay," I say. A small point, but they all help. They had a preconceived idea when they conducted their search: a predisposition to find the panties that would tie Salazar to the victim. "And in fact, those panties were found, weren't they? Lieutenant Cordova found them."

He bites off his words. "Yes, I've already said that."

He's a bit testy now, which is good for us. The jury will pick up on that, which down the road will subliminally help me. Civilians, meaning everyone who isn't in law enforcement, have a love/hate feeling toward cops. They want them to be there for protection, but they are afraid they will use their position and authority to screw them over. This is more true in Los Angeles than in some other cities. It's not that your average Los Angeles policeman wants to be menacing; usually it's the opposite—they want to be helpful and nonthreatening. But the history of this city, going back decades and continuing on to the present time, doesn't allow that, emotionally and psychologically. Too much confrontation, too much casual, even unconscious, intimidation. There are people sitting on this jury in front of me who have had a bad situation with an LAPD cop, or had a close friend or relative who did. They will trust the police to a point, but if that line is crossed, they won't.

"Lieutenant Cordova found them," I repeat. "So then he did what? Called you and the other detective to come see what he had found?"

Killebrew licks his lips, an involuntary, nervous gesture. "No. He showed them to us."

"Showed them to you? How do you mean?"

"He put them in a plastic bag and showed them to us," the detective says.

"Outside of the truck cab?"

"Yes."

I look at the jury. A few of them have picked up on the distinction. They sit forward in their chairs.

"So you never actually saw those panties in Mr. Salazar's truck, is that what you are telling us, Detective Killebrew?" I continue. "Mr., excuse me, Lieutenant Cordova took them out of the truck, where he found them under the floor mat, put them in a plastic evidence bag, and then showed them to you?"

"Yes."

"What did he say?"

"That he had found them stuffed under the passenger side floor mat."

"But neither you nor your partner saw them there yourselves. You did not see them under the floor mat of Mr. Salazar's truck, or anywhere in Mr. Salazar's truck."

"No," he answers. "We didn't actually see them inside the truck."

The unknown man who called in Salazar's location to 911 sounds as if he either had laryngitis or is deliberately trying to camouflage his voice to prevent identification. Joe and I listen to the recording several times.

"Fishy," Joe concedes, after we put it back in its case. "But not enough."

"Can't we use it?" I ask.

"How?"

"To show that whoever called that tip in didn't want to be identified." I'm getting juiced about this. "It could be evidence of a cover-up."

Joe throws cold water on that notion. "Or the connection could be bad, or most likely, the caller didn't want to be involved."

He has his finger on the pulse there. People don't want to get involved. It's a hassle. You waste your time talking to the police, maybe have to give up a day's work to testify in a trial. It is also scary, because what if the criminal you fingered comes after you? We have all heard horror stories about witnesses becoming victims themselves. Better to emulate the three monkeys: see no evil, hear no evil, speak no evil. A hands-off attitude that even extends to people who have had family members murdered by gangs. This is how we have come to live today—we are not our brothers' keepers.

"But it does support the possibility that there's a conspiracy here," I insist, like a dog chewing on a meatless bone but out of instinct won't let go. "Some bozo, who shall forever remain nameless and faceless, happens to see Salazar's truck parked on the street at six in the freaking morning and calls the police to report it. And they take it seriously enough to send someone to check it out? Isn't that pushing it?"

Joe isn't biting. "Another victim had just been found. The cops were on a hair trigger. We can't chase after this, Jessica. The jury won't bite on it. It could work against us."

He's right—but still, this tickles the back of my brain. Who was out there at that hour of the morning, saw the truck, and called the police? Whoever it was could not have known there had been another murder, so there was no linkage.

Unless, of course, there really is a conspiracy, and the caller was the real killer.

Enough of this, Jessica, I warn myself. Stop thinking about this crazy shit. If we follow up this theory, we would wind up digging a dry hole, and using up precious energy.

Okay, I suppose if you canvassed the neighborhood for blocks around, you might come up with something, but we don't have the time, resources, or energy to chase after such flimsy leads. The call was made, the truck was searched, the panties were found. Those are the facts. We have to deal with the facts.

Cheryl Lynn Steinmetz was single. She lived in a rented condo in Brentwood with a roommate, a college friend named Sasha

Koontz, who is now sitting in the witness box, testifying for the prosecution. She's another one of their witnesses who is gilding the lily, to show how thorough and intense their investigation was.

Meg Rawlings is at the podium. "Tell us what happened on the morning of Cheryl Lynn's murder," she says. Her voice is calm and mellow, one woman being nice to another.

The witness's voice quivers with nervous vibrato. "Lieutenant Cordova came to our house. It was early, he woke me up. He wanted to know when the last time was that I had seen Cheryl. I told him that she had gone out after dinner and that I had gone to bed before she'd come home. I thought she was having an affair that she didn't want me to know about, so I didn't ask her where she was going or who she was seeing. I didn't even know she hadn't come home. Then he told me she had had an accident, and he had to notify her relatives. Next of kin, I think he said."

"An accident," Meg interrupts. "Not that she had been killed?"

Sasha Koontz shudders. "Not then. I think he wanted to tell her parents first."

"Okay, go on."

"I gave him Cheryl's mother's phone number. Then he asked if he could look into her room. He wasn't in there long, a minute or so. Before he left he gave me his card, and told me he would be back in touch with me after he had talked to Cheryl's mother."

"And that was it?"

The young woman, who is obviously scared about being here, nods. "He called me back later to tell me that he had talked to Cheryl's family." Tears well in the woman's eyes. "And that Cheryl was dead, that she had been killed."

She breaks into full-blown tears, and Meg hands her a tissue. She dabs at her eyes. "I'm sorry," she apologizes in a small voice. "I still have nightmares about that night."

"I understand," Meg says sympathetically. "You don't have to apologize for that." Turning to the bench, she tells Judge Suzuki that she has no more questions.

I take a pass. There is nothing I can gain by questioning this poor woman. Her raw emotion is terrible to see. Get her off the stand and out of the jury's eyes. "No questions for this witness at this time, Your Honor," I announce from our table.

We break for lunch. Coming up this afternoon and tomorrow, the prosecution's two star witnesses: Lieutenant Luis Cordova, head of the Full Moon Task Force, which found and arrested the city's most feared and notorious killer since Richard Ramirez, the Night Stalker, and the eyewitness who picked Salazar out of a lineup as the man she saw with the last victim right before she was killed.

If I weren't pregnant, I'd skip lunch, because the prospect of these two coming up, who will be good, strong witnesses against us, has dampened my appetite; but the baby is moving inside me, and I have to nourish her. I've stopped doing the girl/boy thing in my head. Unless I give birth to a boy, I'm thinking of it as a girl. A woman, like me.

I join Joe in his office. Lunch is takeout from the cafeteria downstairs. A salad and yogurt for me, pastrami on rye and cream soda for him. He wolfs down his sandwich, finishing the last bite with a satisfied burp. He doesn't have a queasy stomach in anticipation of the ass kicking we're about to get, as I do.

"Who's going to do who?" he asks me, referring to the two key witnesses. We're both prepared to cross-examine either one, so the choice doesn't matter. What matters to me is that from the very beginning, Joe has treated me as an absolute equal.

"I'd rather you take Cordova," I request. Joe knows about my nocturnal encounters with Cordova when I was out late at night, training for my marathon. "I think it would be cleaner."

"Fine. You'll take the eyewitness. Man against man, woman versus woman. Nice symmetry." He finishes his cream soda, takes the ubiquitous Diet Coke from his fridge, and sucks down half the can in one swallow. "This is why we tolerate all the bullshit, Jessica. For times like this." He finishes the Diet Coke, and smiles. "Let's get ready to rummmmble!" he bellows, as if he's announcing a championship fight in Vegas.

Two gladiators primed for battle, we pick up our briefcases and head down to the courtroom.

THIRTY-SIX

T HE TIME FOR UNDERLINGS growing and learning is over. Loomis will ride this horse to the finish line. "Tell us, Lieutenant Cordova, about the events that led to the arrest of the accused, Roberto Salazar, for the murder of Cheryl Lynn Steinmetz."

Cordova goes over everything in painstaking and convincing detail, prompted every so often by a fat one down the middle tossed by Loomis. By the time he finishes, it's four-thirty, so Judge Suzuki calls it a day. Cross-examination will start in the morning.

Joe and I both scribbled copious notes while Cordova was talking, which we will pore over tonight to see if there are any discrepancies in his testimony in comparison with his previous statements about the murders. We will also burn a few bucks out of petty cash to get an expedited court reporter's transcript. Cordova sounded airtight to me; he's been prepped for months. He and the eyewitness are the essentials of their case, along with the recovered panties. He had to be infallible, as will she. But there are always differences between now and then, small shadings that can be exploited, if you can find them. And if they matter. Usually, they don't. But you keep looking.

"What did you think?" Joe asks me when we're back upstairs again.

"He was solid. I was watching the jury. They trusted him."

"Yeah," Joe says glumly. "You know, he didn't do everything exactly by the book, which actually makes him more credible.

Humanizes him." Another Diet Coke out of the fridge. Diet
Cokes to Joe are like cigarettes to a chain-smoker; the more upset
he is, the more of them he drinks. His stomach lining must resemble a lace doily on the arm of your grandmother's sofa.

"We knew going in that this was a tough case. And even though
we've scored a few points, we were right. Their game, their ball,
their court. That fucking anonymous phone call," he grouses.
"What shitty luck."

"Yes," I agree. "If they hadn't gotten that call, the Full Moon
Killer would still be on the loose." As Joe shoots me a disbeliev-
ing look, I say, "Assuming Salazar is the killer. Which, let's face it,
we have. You have, anyway."

He falls onto the couch. "Life's a bitch."

"And then you die."

"So make the most of what's between," he says, pointing to
my ginormous belly. "That's what you live for. A damned good
reason."

"Good morning, Lieutenant Cordova."

"Good morning."

Joe is at the podium. His suit, a dark blue, light-weight wool,
is freshly pressed, his white dress shirt is right out of the dry-
cleaner's box, his shoes are spit shined to a high gloss. He's wearing oxblood wingtips today, for him the height of fashion.

"You were in charge of the task force," Joe starts out.

"That's correct."

Everyone in this room knows that. Like a good chess player,
Joe is setting his pieces in place, hopefully for a mate thirty moves
later.

"When the latest victim was found, you automatically made
the assumption that she was a victim of the so-called Full Moon
Killer?"

"That is correct." Cordova is at ease, but alert. His outfit is a
variation of what he always wears when he's dressed up—blazer
and slacks. He probably doesn't own a real suit.

"Isn't is possible that it could have been a random killing, and that the victim just wasn't wearing underwear?"

"Absolutely, it was," Cordova agrees. "But we had to go on the assumption that it was another Full Moon Killing. Not only were her panties missing, but there was a full moon. One coincidence too many, for me." He goes on without prompting. "Later, if that had turned out not to be the case, we would have gone in another direction. But we had to go on the assumption that this one was connected to the others."

"An anonymous caller phoned the police department and told them about Mr. Salazar's whereabouts, is that correct?"

"Yes, it is."

"So you went to where Mr. Salazar was parked, waiting to go to work."

"Yes."

"What aroused your suspicions that he was in any way connected to the murder that had occurred a few hours earlier?"

"His description," Cordova answers.

"The description that Mr. Lazarus, who has testified previously, gave you?"

"Yes."

"A Latino driving a pickup truck."

"That's right."

"If he had not been Latino, you would not have been suspicious of him, is that correct to say?" Joe asks.

A hesitation. Then Cordova says, "Yes, that is correct."

"In other words, racial profiling was the reason you suspected Mr. Salazar."

Racial profiling is the bogeyman of current policing, all the way up to the federal level. It's not supposed to happen, but it does, every day. The reason airport security guards search seventy-year-old nuns of northern European extraction is because they have to bend over backward to avoid the accusation of racial profiling. But if the police didn't do it, guilty people would slip through their fingers. That's not a politically correct attitude to take, particularly from someone who considers herself to be on the liberal side of the fence, but it's true.

Cordova, however, isn't buying into that. "No," he answers. "We suspected him because he fit the description the eyewitness had given us. If he had said the man was blond and blue-eyed, we would have been looking for a blue-eyed blond. That has nothing to do with racial profiling."

A nifty dodge. Joe presses on. "While you were interrogating Mr. Salazar—"

"I was questioning him," Cordova interrupts. "I was not interrogating him. In fact, what I specifically asked him was whether he had seen anything or anyone suspicious in the area."

"What changed your mind? His prior arrest, wasn't it?"

"Yes. That was the reason."

"Even though he was found innocent at trial. In other words, he had not committed the crime for which he had been accused."

"He was found not guilty," Cordova corrects Joe. "The verdict was not guilty."

A small distinction, but to a layman it could be critical. Innocent and not guilty have different meanings, especially emotionally. Cordova knows that. I'm sure he's made that distinction at other times when he's given testimony.

"But that was why you decide to search his truck."

"Yes, it was," Cordova answers forthrightly.

"Is it not true, Detective Cordova, that when you learned about Mr. Salazar's prior arrest, you did not know where or when that arrest had taken place? That is true, isn't it."

"Yes."

"So there was no connection to Mr. Salazar and those previous killings, was there?"

"Nothing direct," Cordova admits.

"In other words, you were on a fishing expedition," Joe declares. "Some vague resemblance to a description given you months before, but with no real basis in fact."

Cordova sits up taller in the witness chair. "You're right," he says. "There was no basis in fact." He turns so that he is now looking both at Joe and the jurors. "If you want to call it a fishing expedition, I will accept that. I did not have a warrant. I was going on my gut and my experience. And if those underpants had not been in that truck, I would have apologized to him and sent him on his way. But . . ." He leans forward, to physically emphasize his point. ". . . If I had not searched that truck, and there was another killing later, or multiple murders, and the accused was later found to be the killer, that would have been far worse than my technically violating his right against unreasonable search and seizure. I would never have been able to live with myself if that had happened. Who knows how many more innocent women might have been murdered if I had gone strictly by the book," he says. "Sometimes you have to err on the side of caution, and that can mean bending the rules." He leans back. "I bent the rules. I don't apologize for that. I'm thankful that I did."

You're too damn good, I think, watching this performance. I look at the jury. They're eating him up with a spoon. He has natural charisma, and he's milking it.

That was a bust, and Joe knows it, so he shifts gears. "You found the incriminating evidence in Mr. Salazar's truck, is that correct?"

"It is, yes."

"And you removed it from where you had found it and showed it to the other detectives who were there with you."

"Yes."

"So they did not see you actually find it," Joe says. "They were not in the truck cab with you."

"No," Cordova agrees, "they weren't."

Joe takes a moment before asking his next question, because he wants the jury to pay special attention to it. "Why didn't you leave it where you found it, and call them to see it there? Isn't that the way collecting evidence is usually done? The way it's supposed to be done?"

"Yes, it is," Cordova says. "I messed up. It was dark in there. I wasn't sure what I had seen, so I picked the underpants up to make sure." He gives a too-bad shrug. "Once I had done that, I had violated the crime scene, technically. So it didn't matter." He leans toward the jury box again. "I was a little excited, I'm sorry to say. I didn't go by the book. I let my emotions get the better of me."

He sits back. I look at the jurors again. They have fallen in love with him. If you went to Central Casting and asked for the perfect credible police officer, this is the one they would send over.

Joe, thwarted with this approach as well, changes direction again. "You went to the woman's home?"

Cordova had talked about that during his direct examination. His testimony and that of the victim's roommate had matched, almost word for word.

"Yes, I did."

"Did you have a warrant?"

Cordova shakes his head. "No. We were moving too fast. And the victim's roommate let us in voluntarily, so it didn't matter."

Joe looks at the notes from yesterday. "You went there to get the phone number of her family, next of kin, is that what you stated?"

"Yes, that's right. I . . . we . . . had to tell them before they heard about it through the media. That has happened before, and it's devastating to the family."

"Her roommate gave you that information?"

"Yes. She was upset, of course, but she was very helpful."

"You went into the victim's bedroom, is that correct?"

"Yes."

"With her roommate, Ms. Koontz."

"No," Cordova says. "Ms. Koontz was distraught. She had collapsed onto the living room couch."

"So you went in there alone."

"Yes."

Joe looks up from his notes. "What were you looking for? If you were there to get the name of her parents, you already had it, didn't you? Ms. Koontz had given it to you."

"She did. I was looking for something that might tie the victim to the suspect," Cordova says.

Joe looks at him suspiciously. "Like what?"

I'm watching this and I'm thinking, a pair of underpants? Is Joe actually going down that road? Man, what balls. I steal a glance at the jurors. From the way they look, they haven't connected those dots.

Cordova hasn't either, or is ignoring the implication. "A note, something like that," he explains. "People write things on their calendars. I thought maybe she had done that, something about meeting a man. A name, a place. Something to tie her directly to Salazar."

"Did you?" Joe asks.

"No. I was only there a minute or so, I had to get back into the field. All hell had broken loose. It was a shot in the dark that didn't pan out, so I left."

Joe rifles through his notes. He glances back at me—is there anything he's missed?

I could remind him to ask about fingerprints on the pay phone, but that would be useless, and would prolong Cordova's time on the stand. We have to get him off the stage—he's blowing us away.

I shake my head: no. Joe nods. "No further questions of this witness at this time, Your Honor," he tells the judge.

Suzuki gavels the session closed. After the lunch break, the prosecution's key eyewitness will make her appearance. I can hardly wait.

A surprise awaits Joe and me when we reenter the courtroom after lunch. Salazar's wife is there, sitting next to Amanda in their customary front-row seats. She looks up at me sheepishly as I walk over to them.

"Hello," she says, in a tiny voice. She still looks like death warmed over, but better than when I saw her in the hospital.

"Hello," I answer back. "I'm glad you're here. I'm glad you're better."

"She's much better," Amanda chimes in. "Getting better every day." She pats a frail hand. "Aren't you?"

"Yes." She has a tissue in her hand that she is wringing as if she's killing a chicken. "How is Roberto?" she asks nervously. They haven't seen each other since she tried to off herself.

"All right," I answer, keeping my tone neutral. "He'll be glad to see you. Make sure you give him a big smile." I lean over the railing and whisper in Amanda's ear. "Thanks for bringing her."

"It's important that she be here," Amanda whispers back. "Especially now. He needs all the support he can get."

"Amen to that."

The side door opens, and Salazar is brought in. His eyes widen when he sees his wife. She smiles wanly at him, but he doesn't smile back. He stares at her intently for a moment, as if trying to read her mind. Then he gives her a curt nod and sits down in his chair at our table.

"It wouldn't be the end of the world if you gave her a smile," I admonish him. "Her coming here in her condition is a big deal, Roberto. I know you're angry with her, but this has been hard on her."

His hands are gripping the edge of the table so tightly his knuckles are white. "My kids would have had nothing," he hisses between clenched teeth. "She had no right."

"Cut her some slack, damn it!" I hiss back. "She's human, okay?"

He inhales sharply. Then he lets go of his grip on the table and turns around to look at her. He closes his eyes, as if in prayer, then opens them and smiles at her. "Hola, dulzura," he says.

"Hola, mi amor," she whispers back.

"All rise."

Judge Suzuki enters the courtroom. The climax of this wretched tragedy is about to unfold.

The eyewitness, a middle-aged floozy with hair bleached so blond-white it almost shimmers, is wearing a short skirt. She crosses her legs as she sits in the witness chair and flashes a large portion of thigh as she does so. A couple of the male jurors who have a nice view of the pot of gold at the end of the rainbow can't help but gape. She looks like a Pamela Anderson knockoff. Her plastic surgeon didn't spare the silicone on her. Women like this are a dime a dozen in Los Angeles, where every other one is an actress, model, or singer. Only in their dreams, almost all of them.

Loomis guides her through her story. As we all listen, I feel Salazar tensing alongside me. I lean over and whisper in his ear. "You have to relax. You're sending the jury the wrong message."

He bites his lip, takes some deep breaths. I turn my attention back to the witness.

"You came to the police with this information," Loomis now says. We could object on the grounds that he's leading the witness, but he would rephrase the question, and our calling attention to it would only tighten the noose around our necks.

"Yes," she answers. She has a baby-doll voice, which goes with the rest of her persona. She must think her image is cool, she has obviously spent years cultivating it.

"What happened?" Loomis continues.

She describes the process. First, you look at pictures in a book. If one of them looks like the person you saw, you look at them for real, in a lineup, protected by the well-known one-way window.

"Did you pick someone out of the lineup?"

"Yes, I did."

"You positively identified a man in that lineup as the same man you saw with Cheryl Lynn Steinmetz right before she was murdered."

"Yes."

"And is that man in this courtroom today?"

Here it comes: the left hook that will knock us to kingdom come. My stomach is in such a knot I fear for my baby's health.

"I'm not sure."

All the air has suddenly been sucked out of the courtroom. Judge Suzuki's jaw literally drops like a cartoon drawing. Twisting to look at the jurors, I see that they are in shock, too. As is everyone else.

A few reporters dash out, cell phones in hand. The rest of the audience stares at the witness in amazement. She couldn't have blown everyone away any more if she had poured gasoline over her head and lit herself on fire.

Loomis, Mr. Ice-water-in-his-veins, looks as if he's been poleaxed. He leaves the podium and walks to his witness. I look at his hands. They are trembling.

"I'm sorry, Ms. Morganne." That's her name: Marlene Morganne. Obviously, made up. She must have wanted two Ms, and Marilyn Monroe was already taken. "The man you picked out of the lineup. He is in this courtroom today, isn't he?" There's an edge in Loomis's voice now, an implied threat.

Her answer is the same. "I'm not sure."

Loomis turns to Judge Suzuki. "May I ask the defendant to rise?" he asks.

The *defendant,* not the *accused.* The first time he's said it that way.

Suzuki nods. "The defendant will rise," he orders Salazar.

I touch my client's elbow. He gets to his feet. I stand next to him. Joe stands as well. "Look right at her," I whisper to Salazar.

He turns his face to the woman, and stares at her unblinkingly.

"The defendant, Roberto Salazar," Loomis says, in a voice that could cut glass. "Isn't he the man you picked out of the police lineup?"

The woman's lip is quivering; she's on the verge of tears. She shakes her bleached tresses. "I can't be positive," she says. Her voice sounds like Shirley Temple, when she was six or seven.

"But you identified him!" Loomis has lost his cool. He sounds almost hysterical now. "You positively identified him."

"I know," she whimpers. "But I was looking at him through that mirror. In person, I'm not sure." She squints her eyes, as if that will bring Salazar into sharper focus. "It could be him, but I'm not a hundred percent positive. So I can't say it was him absolutely." She looks up at the judge. "I can't lie, can I? If I'm not positive it's him, I shouldn't lie that it is, should I?"

If a judge is God in his courtroom, this is a very wrathful God. "No," Suzuki commands her. "If you are not sure this is the man you saw that night with the victim, you must not testify that it is."

She looks down at her hands. "Then I can't."

Loomis, the color drained not only from his face but, from the look of his hands, his entire body, asks for a recess. Suzuki grants it and retreats to his chambers. The bailiff escorts the witness, who is shivering with anxiety, out of the room. Loomis retreats to the prosecution table. He and his team begin to confab in furious rage and bewilderment.

I'm emotionally wrung out. This beats anything they could concoct on *Perry Mason* or *The Twilight Zone*. The television talking heads will be in a frenzy tonight.

Sitting alongside me, Salazar is like a sphinx. I look behind me, at Amanda and Salazar's wife. Amanda has her arms around Mrs. Salazar. She shakes her head in amazement and gives me a smile that is equal parts surprise and joy.

I turn back to Joe. "Can you believe this?" I ask him in astonishment.

"Someone got to her."

I feel like I just touched the third rail. "*What?*"

"Someone got to her," he repeats. His voice is muted, so only I can hear him. "Either threatened her, or bought her off."

"Who would have done that? Who *could* have done that?"
He cocks his head toward the gallery. "Who do you think?"
I turn and look at Amanda again. She's still smiling.

The prosecution team, clumped together at their table, look as
if they have just attended a funeral. Maybe they have. Maybe it
was their own.

Their witness used the recess to refresh her makeup. There is
a trace of mascara smeared on her cheeks, as if she put it on in a
dark closet. My stomach feels like a kettledrum—the baby has
been kicking up a storm, protesting being emotionally disturbed.
I can't help that, she'll have to bear it a while longer. Her mother
is a gladiator, girded for battle in an expensive maternity dress.

"This man you saw with the victim, the night she was killed.
How far were you from him?" I ask the witness from my place at
the lawyer's podium.

The witness thinks a moment, squeezing her eyes together to
concentrate better. This must be something she learned in Acting
101, how to look serious convincingly. She isn't convincing me,
but the jurors sure are fascinated by her.

"Ten feet, about," she ventures.

"Ten feet." I leave the podium and stride to the witness box.
I'm so close to her I can smell the Altoids on her breath. They
didn't completely mask the halitosis that comes from a dry, frightened throat. I turn around and walk four steps away, turn back
and look up at the judge.

"I would like the defendant to come stand next to me," I request.

"Go ahead."

I motion to Salazar. He gets up, adjusts his coat, and walks
over to me. I turn to the witness again.

"About this close?" I ask.

She swallows, trying to raise some saliva. "Yes," she says, in
a voice that sounds as if she's been eating sand.

I walk to the stand and hand her the glass of water that is provided for witnesses. She grabs it from me and gulps it down. When she has drained it, I take the empty glass from her hand, because if I don't, she might drop it, cut herself, and bleed to death—the only act that could top her performance so far. Then I go back to Salazar, take him by the arm, and march him a step closer. Now we are about six feet from her. If she had been ordered not to fire until she could see the whites of his eyes, her guns (if she had any) would be blazing.

I take a step to the side so Salazar is alone in the center of the floor, standing in a figurative spotlight. "Can you say, with one hundred percent certainty, that this is the man you saw that night?" I ask.

She shakes her head. "It looks a lot like him, but I can't swear to it."

"Do you want him to come closer?"

"No!" she cries out in alarm, recoiling against the back of her chair. "I can see him fine. It doesn't matter how close he comes. I can't swear it's the same man. I'm telling the truth. What else do you people want from me?"

THIRTY-SEVEN

SOMETIMES YOU WIN, SOMETIMES the other side loses. That's what could happen here. Loomis, on redirect, tried to bully his witness into recanting, but she held firm. Salazar might be the man she saw, but she won't swear to it. Judge Suzuki finally has to step in and save her from the prosecution's hounding. Their own witness, their star.

She was their last witness, so they rest their case. A feeling of gloom pervades their half of the courtroom, even though we haven't presented our side. They still have powerful forces behind them, the panties being the strongest, as well as Salazar's proximity to at least two of the murder sites. But a witness who turns like that can poison the well. We will have to wait for the verdict to find out if she did.

Tomorrow, we present our side. It will be short. We only have a few witnesses—Carlos, Salazar's friend who was with him the night of and the morning after one of the killings, a couple of Salazar's customers who will establish his working habits, a psychologist we hired to evaluate Salazar, and finally, Salazar himself. He will testify in his own defense. He has to. If we don't put him on the stand, he will be judged guilty by omission.

I sit at home, reading over the transcripts of the prosecution's case, to see if there are any glitches. As I'm about to call it a night, a few lines of testimony from two of their witnesses catch my eye.

I read them over again, and compare them to each other. Then I pick up the phone, and call Joe.

"Recall Sasha Koontz," the bailiff says in his clear, loud voice.

Cheryl Lynn Steinmetz's roommate comes forward. As she has already been sworn in, she is still under oath, so she doesn't have to do that again. She sits down and looks at me with a puzzled expression.

This will only take a few minutes. Either I guessed right, or I didn't. I lay the relevant page of her testimony on the top of the podium and read from it. *"Lieutenant Cordova came to our house. It was early; he woke me up."* I look up. "This would have been what time, Ms. Koontz? Seven, seven-thirty?"

"Oh, no," she answers. "It was much earlier. About five."

I can feel the buzz behind me, like a swarm of bees returning to the hive. "Five in the morning?"

"Yes."

"You're sure of that."

"Yes, because when the doorbell rang, I looked at my clock. It was right after five."

"Who did you think it was?" I asked.

"Cheryl," she replies. "I thought she had forgotten her key. She did that, sometimes."

"You're absolutely sure of that time. That it was before six-fifteen." Six-fifteen was when the 911 dispatcher got the anonymous phone call about Salazar.

"Yes, I'm sure. It was a few minutes after five o'clock in the morning."

"One more question. Where did Ms. Steinmetz keep her dirty laundry?"

"In her hamper."

"Which was where?"

"In her closet."

"Her bedroom closet?"

"Yes."

Cordova is on the stand. If he's nervous, he doesn't show it. Although Joe cross-examined him before, I'm doing it now. I found the glitch, it's my right to explore it.

I have the pertinent page of Cordova's testimony in front of me. "Let me read some of your testimony back to you," I tell him. "Question: *What were you looking for?* Answer: *I was looking for something that might tie the victim to the suspect.* Question: *Like what?* Answer: *A note, something like that. People write things on their calendars. I thought maybe she had done that, something about meeting a man. A name, a place. Something to tie her to . . .*" I pause. "*. . . Salazar.*"

I look up. "At five o'clock in the morning, you had not yet found Roberto Salazar. So why did you say his name? Why did you give all of us the impression that you had gone to the victim's house *after* you had found and arrested Roberto Salazar, not before?"

Cordova remains unruffled, at least outwardly. "It was a mistake. A slip of the tongue."

"A slip of the tongue? Something that important and it's nothing more than a slip of the tongue?"

"I was hoping to find a name," he repeats stubbornly. "Nothing more."

"At five in the morning. Alone in her room. With a killer at large on the streets of Los Angeles." Before he can answer, I turn my back on him and announce in a clear and authoritative voice, "No further questions."

On redirect, Cordova explains that going to a victim's home is standard procedure, for the reasons he gave, and also in case the next of kin lived there. So he was going by the book. But my point about Cordova saying Salazar's name before the police had found him has been made, and the jury is going to remember it.

THIRTY-EIGHT

OUR FIRST TWO WITNESSES are two of Salazar's regular customers. Both swear that Salazar begins their yard work at seven o'clock on the dot, and is often parked outside their houses as much as an hour before he is scheduled, drinking coffee, reading a magazine, or talking on his cell phone. Sometimes he'll start earlier—watering the flowers, hand-trimming bushes, chores that don't make noise. Their testimony establishes that Salazar is often on the Westside early in the morning, and that his presence there on the day of his arrest was not an aberration.

A decent enough start. But then Carlos, our one good alibi witness, fucks up royally. Even though Joe and I spent days with him going over his testimony, he falls apart almost immediately. He confuses times and locations, can't remember names—the whole nine yards. It is an acute case of stage fright by a man scared to death of the system. Joe, who is conducting the examination, is constantly interrupted by Loomis's objecting to his leading the witness, which he is—he has to—and Judge Suzuki invariably rules in Loomis's favor. By the time Joe finishes, I don't think there is one person in the courtroom who doesn't feel sorry for Carlos, nor does one of them believe him. The looks on the faces of the jurors are clear they sure as hell don't.

Loomis practically sprints to the podium to begin his cross. He eviscerates Carlos, shreds him into confetti. The poor shlump is drenched in sweat.

When Loomis is finished, there is less man than hulk on the stand. Judge Suzuki, attempting to be humane, frees Carlos from his ordeal as nicely as he can while remaining impartial. Carlos is bent over almost in half as he leaves the room, like a man holding in an acute case of diarrhea. I wonder if he drinks. If he doesn't, he should start, immediately.

"That went well," Joe remarks dryly, as Carlos vanishes out the doors at the back of the room. His remark is so off the wall I can't help but bleat out an involuntary laugh. Immediately, I cover my mouth with my hands, but Suzuki heard me. He favors us with an inquisitive and unfriendly look.

I point to my stomach as if it's the culprit and I'm an innocent bystander, then make a wringing motion with my hands.

Suzuki nods in understanding. "We'll take a ten-minute recess before the next witness," he announces.

I retreat to the ladies' room for a much-needed pee. As the baby gets bigger and bigger, it's harder and harder to control my bladder. I've begun wearing two pairs of cotton underpants to absorb any errant moisture. And I've sworn off asparagus. I remind myself to talk to Judge Suzuki about my delicate situation so that if I have to ask for breaks, he will automatically grant them. He wouldn't want me piddling on his courtroom floor.

Back in the courtroom, with a few minutes left in the recess, I take the chamber's temperature. There is a roiling mood of anticipation in the air, coupled with such palpable tension you can almost physically touch it. We have one more witness left, the psychologist we hired to evaluate Salazar (it was positive, or we wouldn't be putting him on), then Salazar himself will take the stage. How he handles himself during our examination, and more important, at cross-examination, will be critical to our success or failure. All the rehearsals have gone well, but as we saw from his friend Carlos's travesty, you can throw the practice performances out the window when you actually open on Broadway.

In a corner of the room, Joe and the psychologist are talking quietly, a last-minute rehash of the questions Joe is going to ask.

Usually when a lawyer from our office uses a psychologist, it is because we have a client with some severe mental illness, and to put such a person behind bars without medical supervision is nuts; yet it's done all the time. We get a disproportionate number of mentally ill people, because we deal with society's dregs. Salazar is actually an exception.

Joe excuses himself from the witness and joins me at the defense table. "I think Dr. Silk will help with damage control," he says. The psychologist's name is Leonard Silk. "Let's face it," Joe says with a twisted expression on his face, "we have nowhere to go but up after that clusterfuck with Carlos."

To me, Dr. Silk is more cotton than silk, but that's good, because slickness doesn't work with juries—they develop a good bullshit detector for condescension, a trap many expert witnesses fall into. They fall in love with their knowledge, and want you to know how smart they are. Like that kid in school who always raised his hand and knew every answer, they can become pains in the ass fast. And juries tend to fade out when experts are talking—technical material is boring. We're putting Silk up there because, one, he's going to say good things about Salazar—that he doesn't fit any pattern of a serial killer—and, two, because he's the only other witness we have. To go directly from Carlos to Salazar could be ruinous, because the jury would still have the taste of that fiasco in their mouths. Bridging them with a more objective witness is smart. And he isn't Latino, which is also important. It might be racist to say that, but it's true. Even in this so-called enlightened age, white men carry an aura of authority about them.

The prosecution didn't have a psychologist witness, because the one they brought in to evaluate Salazar concluded that he wasn't crazy, was not faking his belief in his innocence, and didn't fit any serial-killer patterns. Silk, who arrived at the same conclusions, will present Salazar as a rational man without major hang-ups. Having our doctor testify will be beneficial to us, except for whatever tidbits Loomis can squeeze out of Silk on cross. Joe and I are not worried about that. Silk is a veteran, he knows how to avoid the prosecution's traps.

After establishing Dr. Silk's credentials, Joe addresses the issue Loomis will bring up if he doesn't—that Silk has been an expert witness in hundreds of trials, almost all of them for the defense. That's the nature of the beast. After fifty years of lawyer shows on television, jurors are sophisticated now; they know that every expert who is involved in a trial is partisan to one side or the other. But you still need to establish that your partisan witness isn't bending the truth. He may be interpreting it to your advantage, but he can't lie. On the rare occasions that they do, they invariably get tripped up. So they don't.

One thing Dr. Silk learned during his sessions with Salazar, which none of us knew, because Salazar never told us, is that he was adopted at birth. He does not know who his birth mother was, and doesn't care. He grew up in the Southwest, New Mexico and Arizona, and left home after he finished high school. He moved to L.A., went to work for a gardener, learned the business, then started his own. Both of his parents are dead, and he has no siblings. He has led two lives, before Los Angeles, and after. He loves his wife, he loves his kids, he loves his work, and he gets fulfillment in his ministry and youth work.

"Are there studies about adoptive children?" Joe asks Silk.

"Thousands."

"About their behavior in society?"

"Are they more social, less social, that sort of thing?" Silk answers with a question of his own.

"Yes. Or other characteristics that separate them from non-adoptive children."

"Not across the board," Silk answers. "If they came from an emotionally and psychologically stable family, they're like anyone else, statistically. It's all about the individual. In some ways you can equate them to children who come from families in which the parents divorce. They often are more stable, not less, because they crave stability."

Joe moves to the heart of his argument. "Do serial killers or killers in general exhibit social or psychological qualities that differentiate them from people who aren't killers?"

"If it's a crime of passion, which most killings are, no," Silk answers. "But if they aren't, the answer is yes. A person who kills in cold blood is a sociopath. They do not feel empathy or remorse toward their victims, or anyone."

"In your professional opinion, Doctor, are these murders the work of a sociopath?"

"Yes, they are."

"You examined Roberto Salazar, is that correct?"

"Yes. I met with him on several occasions."

"In your opinion as a clinical psychologist, with decades of experience in this special field, is Mr. Salazar a sociopath?"

"No."

"Does he have any sociopathic tendencies at all? Any indications of them?"

"None that I could discern," Salt answers decisively. "He has compassion, warmth, decency. In my opinion, his personality is the polar opposite of a sociopath's."

"So from a psychological point of view, he does not fit the pattern of a serial killer."

"No. He's about as far away from that as you can get."

Loomis doesn't spend much time on Silk. It's the end of the week, and Loomis knows the jurors are itchy to be released from their bondage, so he doesn't prolong their agony. Unless technical testimony brings forth something new and shocking, it goes in one ear and out the other. Two hours of back and forth and Silk is finished.

Today is Thursday. Court is adjourned until Monday morning, at which point the perfect storm that will be Roberto Salazar testifying for his life will begin.

THIRTY-NINE

I THREW UP LAST NIGHT. I would like to blame my delicate stomach on my being pregnant, but you don't bullshit a bullshitter. I have been a lawyer for seven years and have handled over a thousand felony cases, and none were as remotely important as this one. Starting today, Roberto Salazar takes the stand in his defense, and I'm conducting the direct. This will be the most important day, or days, of my career. I'm more uptight than I've been since I don't know when. Worse than the first time I took my clothes off in front of a bunch of strangers. Almost as bad as when my mother shot me and I was afraid I might bleed to death.

Joe and I spent the three-day break rehearsing intensely with Salazar; almost all day Friday, and several hours both Saturday and Sunday. He was more receptive to us than he had been earlier in the trial. He knows his life depends on convincing the jury that he didn't kill those women. It's going to be a tough battle, despite the key eyewitness's change of mind and Cordova's slipup with the timing of his visit to the victim's home. The eyewitness didn't say it wasn't Salazar, she said she wasn't 100 percent absolutely positively certain. And Cordova's record is spotless; inserting Salazar's name probably was a slip of the tongue. Still, he did say it. It's on the record.

My job is to make Salazar come across as sympathetic and believable. He has to charm the jury, make them like him, and subliminally want to protect him against the machine. If he can do that, and if he can hold off Harry Loomis, who under that velvet glove will come at him like a rabid dog, he has a chance. Slim. But slim is better than none.

Roberto Salazar is brought in and takes his seat. He is freshly barbered and his shirt is new, right out of the wrapping. I bought it yesterday. He looks like a scoutmaster, the straight kind who doesn't prey on his charges. He smiles at his wife and Amanda, who are in their customary seats, directly behind us. Amanda gives him an encouraging smile in return. His wife looks like she's scared shitless. She's probably the most realistic person in the room.

"How do you feel?" I ask him, pulling his attention away from his wife. I don't want her negative vibes infecting him.

"I'm all right," he answers, with surprising calm. If he's uptight, he isn't showing it. I would be jumping out of my skin if I were in his position. I practically am, anyway.

"How do *you* feel?" he inquires of me, as if I'm the one in need of support and he is my advocate. He's a minister—maybe he believes that God is going to take care of him. That reminds me of the old saying that probably came from the mouth of a Southern sheriff in a bygone era. *Your soul may belong to Jesus, boy, but your ass belongs to me.* God can judge us in the hereafter, but in the United States, a secular nation (at least for now), the judging is done by human beings.

"I'm as good as a woman in my condition can feel," I say, leaning in close to him, my mouth at his ear. "Answer my questions the way we rehearsed," I remind him. "Speak clearly, in full sentences when necessary, but don't add your own thoughts or ideas. You can look at the jury from time to time, but don't play to them."

"How long will this take?" he asks.

Why, you have another appointment? "All day for us, or maybe longer. We're not going to rush this, I want those jurors to get comfortable with you, and that will take time. Them, I don't know," I say, looking over my shoulder at the prosecutors sitting on the other side of the aisle. Loomis is looking at some papers, deliberately not paying attention to us, but the other lawyers are. They stare at us openly. Not with overt hostility, more like sizing us up. Are there going to be any last-minute surprises? That has to be on their minds. With cross-discovery now there aren't many, but they have already been burned by their key eyewitness, so they're skittish and ornery. What they're really wondering is how Salazar will hold up on the stand against their boss, who can eviscerate a defendant without the poor victim realizing his guts are all over the floor until he's bled to death. They hope Salazar will wither and die, leaving nothing more than a small grease stain on the courtroom floor that the custodian will wash away with Fantastik and a little elbow grease.

I've worried and wondered about that happening. The prospect makes me nervous, scared. And at the end of the day, I can't control how that will go. Roberto Salazar will have to stand and deliver.

With me deftly coaching him, Roberto Salazar tells his life story. He never knew either of his birth parents. He was adopted shortly after he was born by a Mexican American couple who could not conceive. The adoption was prearranged. His parents never told him the specifics and he never asked them, but by putting bits and pieces together he decided that his birth mother must have been a young girl, unmarried, Catholic, so abortion was out of the question. She would have been sent to a home for unwed mothers, probably run by nuns. His adoptive parents, both dead now, were older than most parents. They lived in a small town on the Arizona–New Mexico border. His father drove a delivery truck, his mother was a maid at a motel. Their social life was nonexistent. They were haphazard churchgoers, and when he was young, Salazar was not religious.

The small town he was raised in was the kind of place kids leave when they grow up, and he did. Los Angeles beckoned, through the glamour of television shows. He had a few different jobs when he first arrived—delivering telephone books, hiring out as a day laborer. He fell in with other young men like him, men who had no future plans, and lived in the moment. Which included joining a gang.

There is a stir in the courtroom when Salazar says he was a gangbanger. That is new and interesting information. The prosecution team is certainly jolted by hearing that. One of them, a female paralegal, listens to Loomis as he whispers urgently into her ear, then bolts out of the courtroom. If Salazar has a record, they will know in minutes.

But I know what they don't—he doesn't have one. This is the prelude to how Salazar came to Jesus, and turned his life around.

"How old were you when you joined this gang?" I ask.

"Eighteen. Right after I landed in L.A."

"How long were you a member?"

"Six months. I never was actually a member, it was like I was in training. To prove myself."

"Did you prove yourself?"

He shakes his head. "No."

"Why not?"

"I quit."

"They let you?"

A nod and a shrug. "They didn't care that much. I didn't fit their image. I moved to another part of town, to make sure they wouldn't hassle me, but they never did."

"While you were in this gang, did you ever commit a crime?"

"No."

"Beat anybody up? Get into fights?"

"A few," he admits. "Nothing serious. Just fists and feet, no weapons."

"So you were never arrested."

"No."

At the prosecution table, Loomis puts on a sour face. He says something to another assistant, who scurries out. To catch the first one and tell her not to waste her time, I'm sure. It's fun to watch your opponent chase his tail.

"What did you do then?" I continue.

"I went to work for Mr. Bayani." He looks at the jury as he explains. "He was Filipino. Bayani means hero in Tagalog, which was his ancestors' language." He smiles. "It was a good name. He was a hero to me."

"Mr. Bayani was the gardener who taught you the business?"

"Yes. And more."

"He taught you other things besides gardening?"

"Yes." He sits up straight. "He taught me to be a responsible man."

And with that simple, declarative sentence, the atmosphere in the courtroom changes. I can feel it. Everyone can. I steal a backward glance at Joe. He gives me a tight smile and an invisible nod.

Harry Loomis has felt that tectonic shift as much as anyone. He gets to his feet. "I fail to see where this is going, Your Honor," he says. "Mr. Salazar is not on trial here because of his life story, no matter how compelling or heartwarming it might be. He is on trial for murder, and the questions to him should relate to that. Otherwise, we are going to be here until Los Angeles falls into the sea."

Judge Suzuki gives me an inquiring eye, inviting me to explain where I'm going with this line of questioning.

"I'm not going to belabor this, Your Honor," I promise. "But when you accuse someone of murder, especially when it isn't committed in a split second of mindless passion, you are attacking his moral code, or lack of one. Mr. Salazar has a strong moral code, it governs his entire life. I think it is relevant that the jury understand that."

Suzuki's nod of acquiescence is lukewarm. "I'll allow you to pursue this a bit longer," he tells me. "But then we have to move on to what we are here for."

"Thank you, Your Honor. We'll be there real fast. But first . . ."

I don't have to spell it out. "Ten-minute recess," the judge announces.

I leave and make a beeline for the ladies' room. With the frequency of my piddling, pretty soon there is going to be a groove worn in the floor from the courtroom to the ladies' room.

Back in action, refreshed and relieved, I take up my questioning again. "You are a minister?" I ask Salazar.

"Yes. A small church, in East Los Angeles. We have about a hundred members."

"Not a Catholic church, I assume. You are not a priest."

He smiles at that. "Oh, no. I am not officially ordained by a denomination." He closes his eyes for a moment, then reopens them. "If I was ordained by anyone, it was by God. And Mr. Bayani."

Salazar's conversion and ascension to his rump pulpit came about because of his mentor, the Filipino gardener. December had come up on the calendar. This would be the first Christmas Salazar would spend in his new city. He had no plans for celebration. Grab a six-pack and some take-out food and watch football on the television in the small room he rented, over by MacArthur Park, in a house he shared with ten other young men, all of Mexican and Central American heritage. He would be alone, because the others were going back to Mexico for the holidays or spending the day with family. He was not religious, and he had no family or close friends to celebrate with. Beer, Taco Bell, the Dallas Cowboys on the tube. Christmas in Los Angeles.

On Christmas Eve, Salazar and Mr. Bayani finished their last gardening job shortly before dark. It was almost five o'clock. They loaded Mr. Bayani's truck and climbed in. Mr. Bayani lived in Filipinotown, which is northwest of downtown L.A., near Echo Park. Not too far from Salazar's flophouse. He would detour by, drop Salazar off as he always did, then go home for Christmas Eve dinner with his wife.

But this night, Mr. Bayani didn't drop off nineteen-year-old

Roberto Salazar at the dump he called home. He waited while Roberto went upstairs, showered, and changed into clean clothes. Then the two of them drove to Bayani's house. They feasted with Bayani's neighbors, all Filipinos. Roast pig, goat stew, turkey, dozens of side dishes, wine and beer (San Miguel, of course), pies and cakes. The meal had been three days in preparation. When they were finished, Salazar was as stuffed as the turkey had been, for the first time since his arrival in L.A.

He was ready to go home and sleep it off, but Bayani had more in store for him that night. They packed the extra food (there was plenty) into Tupperware containers and drove to the Union Rescue Mission on San Pedro Street, in the center of L.A.'s homeless population. Their leftovers would be an important part of tomorrow's Christmas dinner for the hundreds of homeless people who would flock to the mission for a free meal. It was late, so there were people everywhere, including many families. Salazar looked at the little kids gathered on pallets on the floor who had nothing—no home, hardly any clothing, no food. He had never had much, but this hit him in the gut.

The people in charge knew Mr. Bayani. They thanked him and Salazar profusely, praising them for their generosity. Mr. Bayani shrugged the praise off with his typical modesty. If you have, you give. That was his credo.

Roberto Salazar didn't know it, but that would become his credo, too. The next morning he was all spic and span, waiting outside his place when Mr. and Mrs. Bayani drove up to take him to church. He had not been in a church in years and had forgotten what little about the mass he had learned. But that didn't matter, because they were not going to a Catholic church.

The Bayani's church was Pentecostal. It was in a converted furniture store off I-5, near Dodger Stadium. The congregation was a mixed bag. All races, sexes, ages. They had one thing in common—they felt God, alive inside of them.

"I accepted Jesus as my savior that morning," Salazar says, "and from that moment on, everything in my life changed."

Loomis is on his feet again. "Your Honor, I again have to object. With all due respect to the accused's religious beliefs, this is irrelevant and—"

"Your Honor, this man is on trial for his life!" I interrupt, cutting Loomis off. "He should be allowed to tell us who he is and how he got that way. That is not irrelevant or immaterial, it is critical." I turn and face Loomis. "What are you afraid of?"

Loomis drops his jaw and gapes at me. Lawyers directly attacking each other is considered verboten. When it's done, it's usually by innuendo, death by a thousand cuts. Frontal assaults can turn a trial into a mudslinging brawl. Sometimes they do, anyway, but you try not to get down into that gutter.

Loomis is boiling; he's high atop our legal community's totem pole, and he's not used to being confronted head-on. But he masks his anger well; the jury doesn't pick up on it. I do, though, and I know Joe and Judge Suzuki do, too. Suzuki stares down at me from his perch on high.

"Ms. Thompson—"

"I'm sorry, Your Honor," I say hastily. "I apologize to my worthy opponent. But my client is on trial for murder. I take that seriously. Which we all do, of course. But please give me a little more time to establish Mr. Salazar's history before we deal with the case in hand."

"Ten minutes," Suzuki gives me, grudgingly. "Then we're moving forward."

I rush Salazar through the rest of his personal narrative. He met his wife, got married, had children. He took courses in landscaping and horticulture in community college. When Mr. Bayani decided to retire, he bought the business, which meant he took over Mr. Bayani's customers. He quickly doubled them. He puts in long hours, but he still takes time to be with his family, work with other kids, and preach. Every Sunday morning, his little church is filled with worshippers.

The jury has been listening sympathetically. Now it's time for me to wrap this up and move on. "What has happened to your church since your arrest and confinement?" I ask.

"It's falling apart." He sounds more sad about it than anything else. "They are going to other churches. Even when this is over, I don't know if they will come back."

"Well, I hope they do," I commiserate. "For them, and for you."

We break for lunch. I approach Loomis, who gives me the fisheye.

"I apologize. I lost my head."

I'll give him this—he doesn't hold a grudge. "Apology accepted." He looks past me to Salazar, who is being led out by his deputy escort. "Hell of a story," he comments. He starts to turn away, then turns back to me. "But it wouldn't be the first time a man who claims to have found God broke His most important rule."

FORTY

THE NIGHT OF THE last Full Moon Murder, and Salazar's arrest, early the next morning. We go over everything in painstaking detail. I want to cover every base I can think of, and I also don't want Loomis to be able to start his cross-examination today, so I take my sweet time. Not that I wouldn't anyway—how Salazar comes across is pretty much our entire case. When we get to that fateful morning, he tells it the way he told Joe and me months before, when we were interrogating him again and again. No deviations, no hesitations.

He was sitting in his truck, minding his own business, when the police accosted him. Having been arrested before, for a crime for which he was ultimately found not guilty, he was wary and hostile—a natural reaction.

I see a few jurors flinch. They may have been stopped and questioned for something they didn't do. It's a natural reaction to be leery of the police when they do that.

"Did they tell you why they were searching your truck?" I ask him. We're on our third hour of direct now, I've already taken two bathroom breaks. The clock reads a few minutes after four. By the time I finish we will be done for the day, as I've planned it.

"No," he answers.

"They didn't give you a reason?"

He shakes his head. "No."

"Why did you let them?"

He stares at me as if I have suddenly grown another head. "They are the police. You do not say no to the police."

Some people do. People who are savvy about the police, people who know that if you stonewall them, you can blow them off. Those people are the ones who have had dealings with cops— criminals. Salazar only had the one encounter, and it had turned out disastrously. But there were no television sets in his truck this time, so he had nothing to worry about, as far as he was concerned.

"What did you think was going to happen?" I ask.

"Nothing," he answers. "I did not know what they were looking for, but I was not hiding anything," he says with conviction.

"The woman's underpants that Lieutenant Cordova found in your truck. Did he show them to you?"

"No. He did not."

"He just arrested you. Did he say why?"

Salazar corrects me. "He did not arrest me, at first. He told me he wanted to take me in for questioning."

"Questioning," I repeat. I know how everything went down, of course, but I want the initial evasiveness of the police to register with the jury. "Did he say what for?"

"No."

"But you went with him anyway. Voluntarily. Of your free choice," I clarify.

He stares at me balefully. "You do not have free choice when the police want to talk to you."

"So at the time, you had no idea why you were being brought in to be questioned?"

"None."

"And when did they formally arrest you?"

"Later that day."

I leave the podium and walk over to him, so that we are a few feet apart. "Mr. Salazar. Did you know any of the women you are accused of killing?"

"No."

"Had you ever seen them? Even if just on the street?"

"No."

"Never spoke to them? A friendly hello in passing?"

"No."

"So you never, under any circumstances, had any contact with any of these women whatsoever? Not the latest victim or any of the previous ones?"

"No."

I walk back to the podium, turn, and face him. "Mr. Salazar. Did you kill Cheryl Lynn Steinmetz?"

His face darkens. He shudders and closes his eyes for a moment. When he reopens them, he looks at me without blinking, without twitching a muscle.

"No, I did not. I have never killed anyone."

The courtroom is quiet. I take a moment to let everything we have done over the past four hours sink in. Then I turn to the judge. "No more questions, Your Honor."

It's windy tonight. Santa Anas are blowing in from the desert. I sit on my tiny front porch on my weathered green Adirondack, eating butter pecan ice cream out of the container. My baby kicks, stops, kicks again. My back is sore, I squirm around, trying to find a comfortable position. There isn't one.

After we adjourned for the day, Joe critiqued my performance. He was pleased with it, and he was pleased with Salazar's, as well. Our boy was not furtive, nor was he slick or slimy. He sounded believable; he sounded as if he were telling the truth. It is always a calculated risk when you put the defendant on the stand. If they come across as lying, you're doomed. Salazar came through. Tomorrow, Loomis will hammer at him. But we have done as well as we can, and having spent all these months with Salazar, I think he will stand up to the cross-examination.

There is nothing more I can do. I scrape the dregs out of the carton and lick the spoon. A pint of ice cream, down the hatch. I push myself out of my chair, and go inside.

Loomis, at the podium, holds the section of the police murder book that details everything they took out of Salazar's truck.

"When the police searched your truck, they found a box of condoms. Contraceptives. Why would you have contraceptives in your truck?"

Salazar has a ready answer. "My wife and I cannot afford to have any more children."

"So they are for birth control. With your wife."

"Yes."

"You didn't have them so that if you had sexual relations with some other woman you would not get her pregnant? Or so you would not leave a trace of yourself inside this other woman? Or women?"

Man, that was a bomb! I can feel the reverberations in the room. I twist to look behind me, at Mrs. Salazar. She is staring at the floor.

A cold wash comes over me. Salazar didn't have those condoms because he was practicing birth control with his wife. She didn't know anything about them.

I study the audience. No one else in the courtroom, including Loomis and the jurors, seems to have come to that same conclusion, fortunately. Still, I silently curse myself. Joe and I had not paid that much attention to the rest of the contents in Salazar's truck, because we were locked onto the panties. Now the idea has been planted: Salazar, the God-fearing married man, was getting some on the side.

Salazar maintains his self-control. "I do not have sex with other women," he answers calmly. "I am faithful to my wife."

"Good for you," Loomis comments pithily.

I'm on my feet. "Objection!"

"Sustained," Judge Suzuki says without passion. "Save the editorializing for your summation," he tells Loomis, who shrugs the warning off—he's made his point.

Loomis puts the murder book aside and picks up a printed sheet of paper—the names of Salazar's clients. There are times and dates attached to the list. We have an identical list, which I place in front of me. Loomis runs his finger down the names until he comes to the one he's earmarked. "You have a weekly routine, is that correct?" he asks. "You work for different people on different days of the week."

"Yes."

"Each one is scheduled for a certain time. The same time, every week?"

"Yes."

"One of the reasons would be so that if one of your customers wanted to talk to you about some specific work they wanted you to do, they would know when you would be there."

"Yes," Salazar answers. "That is one reason."

Loomis looks at the schedule again, then looks up. "The first customer whose property you were going to work on the morning you were arrested. You always worked for that client on that day, at that time?"

Salazar shifts a bit in his chair. "No."

Loomis brandishes the schedule. "In fact, you had just changed your schedule. Normally, your first customer that day would be . . ." he trails his finger down the list. "The Clothiers. Who live several miles from that location. Is that correct?"

Salazar nods. "Yes."

"But you switched them with the Brownlees," Loomis reads. "Until that week, you did your landscaping for them on a different day, and at different time. Is that correct?"

"Yes."

Loomis purses his lips, as if trying to figure out this anomaly. "Why did you do that? Isn't keeping to the same schedule week after week important? You just said it was."

"It is," Salazar says. "But sometimes you have to make changes. I switched other clients that week as well."

"Why? If maintaining routine is so important?"

"It was more convenient for me to change some of the times and locations around."

"And it was also convenient that these changes happened the exact same week a woman was murdered a block from where the police found you, wasn't it."

You never saw a woman this pregnant get to her feet so fast. "Objection!" I bellow. "That is absolutely out of order!"

"Sustained." This time Suzuki's rebuke carries some heat.

Loomis is unruffled. "I'll rephrase. You rearranged your schedule on the same week the murder victim was found, is that correct? Would you like me to refresh your memory as to the dates?" he asks with an undertone of sarcasm.

"I remember," Salazar says. "Yes, it was that week."

"What a coincidence," Loomis remarks. "An unlucky one for you." Before I can object or Salazar can try to answer, he says, "Let's move on. I'll keep my opinions to myself," he tells the judge. Changing direction, he asks, "What time did you go to bed the night before you were arrested, Mr. Salazar?"

"About eleven o'clock."

"Was your wife awake?"

"No."

"When did she go to bed?"

"Around nine-thirty. She goes to bed early."

"Was she asleep when you got into bed?"

"Yes."

"And she was still asleep when you woke up the next morning?"

"Yes."

"She didn't hear your alarm go off?"

"I don't use an alarm," Salazar says. He points to his head. "My alarm clock is in here."

Loomis fiddles with his notes again. "So let's make sure we

have this time line correct. Your wife went to bed at nine-thirty on the night before you were arrested. She was not awake when you got into bed, she still was not awake when you got out of bed, and she was still not awake when you left. Is that correct?"

Salazar nods in the affirmative. "Yes."

"Between the time you went to bed that night and the time the police approached you the following morning, did anyone see you? How about at the McDonald's, where you bought your coffee and Egg McMuffin? The server at the counter?"

"I did not go inside."

"You used the drive-through window?"

"Yes."

"So are you saying that whoever handed you your bag of food and took your money wouldn't be able to remember that you were there then?"

"I don't think so," Salazar agrees.

"Was it a man or a woman?"

"I don't remember. I wasn't paying attention," Salazar answers doggedly. "There wasn't much light, and you can't see good into there."

This line of questioning is bullshit, because it's irrelevant, but I don't object. Brick by brick, Loomis is building the case that Salazar has absolutely no alibi for the critical hours in question, not even a kid handing out bags through a McDonald's take-out window. From nine-thirty the night before until six-fifteen the following morning, his whereabouts are known only to him. That is not evidence of guilt, but it's harmful.

Loomis looks up from his notes. "How did the victim's underpants get into your truck, Mr. Salazar?"

Salazar hangs tough. "I don't know."

Good on you, man, I cheer him silently. For someone who is on trial for his life, he is handling himself very well.

"Who do you think did?"

Salazar shakes his head. "How would I know? It wasn't me, that's all I know."

"Quite a coincidence, isn't it, Mr. Salazar, that you were hang-ing around a couple of blocks from where the victim was found, isn't it."

"Yes."

"And that was the week you changed your work schedule. That same week. Another coincidence."

Salazar shrugs. "I guess it is."

"And that when you were arrested before, you were less than two blocks away from where that victim was murdered. Another coincidence."

That isn't a question, so Salazar doesn't respond. We drilled that into him—only answer questions. Don't let them bait you into responding to anything that isn't a direct question.

"Was that a coincidence, too?" Loomis asks the question now.

"If you say it is."

"An awful lot of coincidences. A reasonable person could conclude there are too many of them, don't you think?"

Joe is up before me. "Objection! Baiting the witness." He scowls at Loomis.

"Sustained," Judge Suzuki rules. "Questions, Mr. Loomis, not hypotheses."

Loomis, buying time, flips through his notes again. Then he gives up. "No more questions for this witness, Your Honor." He turns and walks back to his chair.

Suzuki looks at us. "Redirect?"

I struggle to my aching feet. Standing in place, I ask Salazar, "Do you lock your truck, Mr. Salazar? When you are at the dif-ferent locations where you do your work?"

He shakes his head. "No. There is nothing valuable in it worth stealing. Only my equipment in the back. I try to keep an eye on that. Where I work mostly, I don't worry about my stuff being stolen."

"So anyone could get into your truck if they wanted to."

"I guess. There's nothing in there worth anything," he reiter-ates.

That was the last point I had to make. Now we're done. I turn to Suzuki.

"The defense rests."

Suzuki turns to Loomis. "Do you have any more questions for this witness?" He's already gathering his papers, prepared to adjourn for the day.

Loomis stands behind his chair. "No, Your Honor. But we do have one additional witness of our own we wish to call."

Joe gets up and walks around to the front of our table. "What's going on?" he demands. He's pissed, and confused. I am too.

Judge Suzuki is upset as well. "The jury is excused," he announces. "The court will stand in recess until tomorrow morning."

We all wait until the jurors file out of the room. Then Suzuki asks Loomis, "Who do you have?"

"A witness who will establish that some of the victims knew each other."

Joe and I look at each other in confusion. No such name was on the list. "We have not received any notice of this, Your Honor," Joe protests.

"I apologize to the court. We just discovered this witness," Loomis says. "We will be happy to share our information with defense counsel."

Suzuki sighs. He wants this to be over. "We will discuss this in chambers."

Before we go back to the judge's office, Joe and I congratulate Salazar on doing a good job. He exchanges a smile with his wife, who still looks like death warmed over, and another with Amanda, who presents a more optimistic visage. Then he is led away, and we go into Judge Suzuki's office.

The prosecution's eleventh-hour witness is a trainer at a women-only health club in Brentwood. Two of the murder victims had been members of the club. The trainer had coached both of them.

"It shows that they knew each other," Loomis argues. "Which could lead to their having contact with the accused."

"How does it show they knew each other?" Joe argues back. "When I belonged to a gym and had a coach, I didn't know any of his other clients. This is a fishing expedition, pure and simple."

Suzuki takes off his robes during this back and forth. He hangs them up and gets himself a beer from his refrigerator. He doesn't offer us refreshments. He wants to get us out of here, go home, and have his dinner.

"Maybe the witness can tell us something that connects them," Loomis says, retreating from his brash assertion, but only somewhat. He wants to push every link he can muster. Build up a body of circumstantial evidence to bolster his physical evidence.

"I'll let your witness in," Suzuki decides without enthusiasm. "But only this one. And stay on point. Give the defense whatever new information you have." To us: "If you tell me tomorrow morning you need more time, I'll give it to you."

Loomis hands Joe and me a slim folder, and gives one to the judge. "See you tomorrow," Suzuki says. "Be prepared to begin closing arguments after lunch."

Joe intercedes. "If we have to spend tonight going over this, we won't be able to prepare properly. I want another day."

Suzuki nods in agreement. "That's fair. Okay, then. The last witness tomorrow, then closing the following day. Barring any unforeseen circumstances, I want to charge the jury by the end of the day after tomorrow."

FORTY-ONE

THE WIND IS FIERCE tonight, gusts blowing in from the high desert at forty miles an hour. Too strong for me to enjoy my usual evening sojourn on my porch. I sit at my dining-room table munching organic baby carrots instead of sugary ice cream, like a conscientious mama to be is supposed to do, and read up on Loomis's last-minute witness, the trainer at the women's gym.

There is nothing on these pages that connects the victims to Salazar. But this new information implies that it is possible they might have known each other, which could lead to the assumption that if they did, they may have known their assailant. But unless the trainer is going to testify that they also knew Salazar, I don't see how this can hurt us.

If she does, of course, it will be an awful blow to us. But a witness that critical would have come forward long ago, so I'm not too worried about it.

That the victims might have known each other does worry me, though. If the trainer confirms they did, that information will reinforce the prosecution's theory that they also could have known their killer, and they will hammer home the idea that the killer is Salazar. Yes, their key eyewitness repudiated her identification on the stand, but only partially—she didn't say it *wasn't* him, she just could not swear that it was.

Juries are unpredictable, but most of the time they believe the authority's story, not the defense's. Why would someone be arrested if he is not guilty? The defense is always fighting to overcome that instinctive reaction.

My other underlying fear, besides that, is that all of this circumstantial evidence is going to sink our ship. Our main bugaboo, besides the underpants, is that Salazar was in the wrong place at the wrong time too often. Way too often. Where there is smoke there is usually fire.

The gym trainer is one of those superbuff women who strut around in their latex body-hugging workout clothes and shame the world, even those of us who are fit as marines, as I was when I was in training. Okay, your ass is tighter than a snare drum. Get over it.

Her name is Dimitra St. Clair. She looks to be in her early thirties, a few years younger than I am, but fighting hard to stay young, like the women on *Friends*. Came to L.A. from wherever to be an actress—no, not really an actress, a television star. A celebrity. Didn't make it, like the millions who came before her, so she found a new niche that had cachet. Trainer to women who have time and money to hone their bodies. Women married to guys who make money, women who have good jobs, or students who come from families that have money. The gym is in Brentwood, so it is populated with such rich women. Older ones, too, who want to keep up. They know they have to so they don't end up on the sidelines, replaced by trophy wives.

The initiation fee at her gym is a thousand dollars, and the monthly dues are two hundred. That's stiff, even by L.A. standards. (An acquaintance of mine who is a member gave me those figures.) So the clientele is posh, and can afford the rates Dimitra and her fellow trainers charge: a hundred dollars a session. You can live in a nice condo off Barrington and drive a Mercedes C280 racking in that kind of income.

She is dressed demurely. Loomis would have told her to. He doesn't want her to come across as low rent, even if she can pay the bills.

I hate women like this on sight. I told Joe I had to do the cross. I can read her mind—this is her shot at fifteen minutes of prime time. Who knows? If she sparkles, maybe she could parlay this appearance into spinning the wheel on a game show, or becoming a contestant on *Survivor*.

Loomis leads her through a brief explanation of what she does, particularly how she relates to her clientele. Each one has a different routine, depending on what they want to accomplish and their fitness level. Nothing cookie-cutter; it's all about that special person.

"You were Cheryl Lynn Steinmetz's trainer?" Loomis asks.

"Yes." The woman has been massaging a tissue. She brings it to her eyes, which are misting up. No wonder she couldn't make it as an actress, her gesture is patently phony. "She was a doll to work with. Really worked hard to stay in shape."

"How long were you her trainer?"

"About three months. Right up until she . . ." She stops and dabs at her eyes again.

"Would you like to take a short break?" Loomis asks solicitously.

She shakes her head. "No. I'll work through this." Another eye dab.

"Until she was murdered," Loomis finishes for her.

"Yes." She shivers. It's impossible not to notice that she's had her breasts done, and probably some more work too, but in L.A. that's normal, so she doesn't lose points on that. A girl has to stay current.

Loomis mentions the name of one of the other victims, who had also been a client of Ms. St. Clair. She had moved on before she was killed, so their connection wasn't as strong as the one St. Clair had with Cheryl Lynn.

"Do personal trainers such as yourself become friendly with their clients?" Loomis asks.

"Oh, yes. Not with all of them, but some of them, for sure."

"Were you and Cheryl Lynn Steinmetz friends?"

"Yes."

"Did she confide in you? About her personal life?"

"All the time."

"Sort of like how some women confide in their hairdressers?" Loomis suggests.

"Exactly!" She perks up. "Did you ever see that movie with Warren Beatty? *Shampoo?* Sometimes it gets that personal." Quickly, she frowns. "I don't sleep with clients. That's a no-no. Anyway, mine are all women, and I don't swing that way. Not that I have anything against anyone who does," she adds. She's covering all the bases.

"But they do tell you their secrets."

"Yes. Often. They have to tell someone, and I'm a good listener." She looks up. "And discreet. They know they can trust me."

"Was there something specific Cheryl Lynn confided to you, shortly before she was murdered?"

Joe and I exchange a worried glance. What the hell is this? I make a move to get up and object, but Joe stops me. Let's see where this is going, he's signaling me.

"Yes," the witness answers.

"What was that?" Loomis asks.

The words come out in a rush.

"She had been having an affair with a married man. She wanted to break it off, but he didn't want to. She was afraid he might become violent because she was rejecting him. The way she talked about him, it was like he was beneath her, like from a different class or background. She was afraid she would look bad if it became known she was sleeping with a married man who wasn't up to her standards," she concludes breathlessly.

Now Joe jumps up. "Objection! This is hearsay! I—"

He doesn't have to finish. Suzuki turns and glares at the witness, then at Loomis. "Sustained," he declares, his voice echoing through the big, high-ceilinged room. He is royally pissed. "That is the end of this line of questioning, Counselor. Am I clear?"

Loomis nods. He can take a punch, and he has made his point. "Yes, Your Honor."

Suzuki turns to the jury box. "The jury will disregard that last series of questions and answers," he tells the jurors. To the court reporter: "Strike everything from when the witness began talking about personal conversations she had with the deceased."

Despite being smacked, Loomis got his innuendo in, so he wraps up his questioning and turns the floor over to us. I waddle to the podium, a sheaf of notes clutched in my hand. I smooth them on the dais and look up.

"Is Dimitra St. Clair your actual name?" I ask, out of left field.

She jerks. "What do you mean?"

"Is that the name on your driver's license? Is that the name you were born with?"

Chagrined: "No."

"What is your real name?"

Her face turns crimson. "Noreen Borkowski. I can explain—"

I step on her line. "You don't have to. You moved to Hollywood to become an actress, and you took on a fresh name, to have a fresh start. The way Norma Jeane Baker became Marilyn Monroe. It happens all the time, nothing to be ashamed of."

Which, of course, she is, particularly since I have set her up to be, so score one for me. "How long have you been a personal trainer, Ms. Bor . . . Ms. St. Clair."

Her eyes, so wide a moment ago, are slits now. "Three years."

"And before that you were . . ."

Oh, man. She is so pissed at me. Just where I want her. "I did some modeling. And acting." She pauses. "Waitressing, bartending."

"Escort service?"

She squirms as if she has the hives. "Some. But strictly legit."

"Of course." I let her twist for a few seconds, then ask, "How long have you worked at your present place of employment?"

"A year and a half."

"How many members are there in your club?"

She frowns. "I don't know. Hundreds, I'm sure."

The answer is over five hundred, as of a week ago. We learned that last night.

"How many do you train a week?"

She has this answer down. "At the moment, twenty-two."

"Sessions or clients?" I ask.

"Clients," she answers. "Some train with me more than once a week. I actually do about thirty-five hours of training. It's hard work."

More than three grand gross. Even after the house takes its cut, it's pretty good money. As much as I make with my fancy law degree.

"You say the club has several hundred members. Besides providing workout facilities, does the club sponsor social events? Get-togethers?"

She shakes her head. "No. We're a health club, period. You come to get in shape, not to socialize."

"A serious gym."

"Yes."

"Are there classes as well as individual workouts?"

"Of course," she says. "All health clubs have classes. I teach some of them."

I look at my notes. "To your knowledge, or from memory, did the two victims who belonged to your club take any of your classes? Or any classes?"

"Yes. They both did."

"With you?"

"And other instructors. I encourage my clients to take classes. They are free—I mean they come with the monthly dues—and it helps supplement the individual workouts."

I home in. "Did these women have any classes together with you?"

She thinks for a moment. Another bullshit pose—she knows the answer. "Not that I recall," she admits.

"Or with any other instructor, to your knowledge?"

She looks at Loomis, as if for guidance, then comes back to me. "They couldn't have," she says. She explains. "They weren't members of the club at the same time. By the time Cheryl Lynn joined, Marta (the other victim) wasn't a member anymore."

"So if these two women knew each other," I continue on that line, "it would not be because they had met at your club?"

"No. They would not have met at the club."

I look at Judge Suzuki. "No further questions, Your Honor." I begin to walk back to the defense table, then I change my mind and take the podium again. "I'm sorry. I do have another question. A few more, actually."

Suzuki nods. "Go ahead."

"When did you meet with the police and tell them about this?"

"Last week," she says. She plays with her tissue. Crosses her legs.

"Just last week? This case has been all over the media for months. Why didn't you come forward before?"

She squirms some more. "I didn't know about it."

I practically laugh in her face. "You didn't know about it until a week ago? Don't you read the newspapers? Watch the news on television?"

"I don't read the papers," she snaps. "They're a pack of lies. And I do watch some news, but it's usually too depressing. I don't like to be depressed. I believe in having a positive outlook."

"Weren't people talking about it at your health club? It was about women they knew!"

"Yes." She moans, as if this is such a waste of her time. "But I didn't put it all together. I messed up, I know. But when I did learn it was Cheryl Lynn, I came to the police right away." I've got her on the defensive, so her instinct is to strike back at me. But she doesn't know how, so she sounds like a whiner. "I didn't have to," she simpers. "I knew some sharpie like you would try to trip me up. But I did it anyway, because it was the right thing."

"Yes, it was the right thing," I spit back at her. "Too bad it took so damn long."

Loomis stands in place. "Your Honor—"

"Yeah, yeah, I know," I wave him off. "Withdraw the last comment."

The witness has completely lost her composure now. She sits slumped over, and there are dark moons of sweat under her bra line. "Before you went to the police, Ms. St. Clair, had you ever heard the name Roberto Salazar?"

She shakes her head. "No."

"No one ever said that name to you? Cheryl Lynn Steinmetz never said that name to you?"

"No."

I turn to our table. "Roberto, would you please stand up?" I ask him.

He stands in place. I look at the hapless witness again. "Do you know this man?"

"No."

"Have you ever seen him before today?"

"No."

"Not once?"

"I have never seen him," she snaps. "Okay? I've never seen him."

The prosecution rests. The defense rests. Tomorrow, closing arguments. Then twelve men and women will decide whether Roberto Salazar goes free, or dies.

FORTY-TWO

HARDLY GOT ANY SLEEP last night, and it wasn't because the baby was kicking up a storm inside me. She was relatively quiet, for once. I'm giving the closing summation for the defense. My first in a murder trial. Obviously my most important, ever.

My taking the leading role was Joe's call. Increasingly, as the trial has progressed, he has turned over more and more of the work to me. It's not that he's lazy or indifferent—he is neither. He has seen me grow as a courtroom advocate, and he's decided it's time I was kicked out of the nest. Fly or die.

There is another reason I'm doing it. We don't have a case. We have won some specific battles, but any objective observer would say we have lost the war. If betting on the outcome was legal, we would be heavy underdogs. So our defense will be an offensive barrage, a give-no-quarter onslaught. A young woman in her third trimester attacking the system can get away with much more than a rumpled, middle-aged man.

I've been rehearsing my speech for days, changing details as new stuff comes up during the last days of the trial, but it's basically set. I will have a conversation with the jurors. It is one-sided—I talk, they listen. But it's still a conversation, a connection. The last one you make, and usually the most important one.

There is a faint hum from the air-conditioning. Otherwise, all is quiet. The courtroom is packed. Amanda and Mrs. Salazar are in their accustomed seats. Scattered throughout the chamber are witnesses who gave testimony, including Cordova and the members of his team. They occupy part of a row halfway back, on the prosecution side, a monolithic, foreboding force. All the spectators—in the gallery, in the jury box, at the prosecution table—are leaning forward in their chairs, as if waiting for a symphony orchestra to start the music.

Earlier this morning, Arthur Wong gave the prosecution's opening statement. They go first, we follow, then they rebut. Harry Loomis will carry the ball to the goal line for them, and he will bring the real fire, so Wong's presentation was relatively dry. He laid out the facts, crisply, cleanly, and concisely. We recessed for fifteen minutes, and now we are back in session.

I stand at the podium. One deep cleansing breath, and I begin the most important summation of my life.

"The police needed to find a killer. They were desperate for one. The city was in a panic, paralyzed. Month after month, during the period of the full moon, a woman was killed. One woman per month, three months in a row. The police were sure the killings were all the work of one man.

"A police task force was formed. The best detectives from all over the city and county, from the LAPD and sheriff's department and the other involved jurisdictions, were assigned to it. They had one job, and one job only: find the killer." I repeat the last phrase, but change the article. "Find *a* killer.

"But then the killings stopped. That caused a different kind of panic. If there were no more killings, the task force would be disbanded, and the killer might never be caught. He might vanish forever, like the Zodiac Killer in San Francisco did, back in the 1960s.

"Nothing is more frustrating to a detective than an unsolved crime. That is his life—to solve crimes. When he doesn't, his life, or at least his work, which for a conscientious detective are almost one and the same, loses meaning. Not solving a crime is failing. And cops don't like to fail. They hate it. Their essence, their ego,

is tied up in solving crimes. And I say this with praise, not accusation—a good detective has a strong ego. He or she has to. You
can't survive out on the street without one.

"But then comes a fourth killing. Same time frame, same
method. The police are horrified, of course, but secretly, they are
also relieved. Because they still have a job, and they still have a
chance to catch their elusive quarry. They would never admit to
this, but it's true."

I pause to drink some water, because my mouth is dry.

I continue. "The pressure on the task force to find the killer is
enormous now. There had been a false sense of security, because
people thought maybe the killing was finished, and it was safe for
women to go out at night again. The latest killing shattered that
illusion."

I repeat what I said earlier. "The police had to find the killer.
They had to find him. No matter what. And they had to find him
now.

"It's early in the morning, but the clock is ticking. The public
doesn't know about this latest killing yet, but they will, very soon.
And when they do, all hell is going to break loose. The talk shows
and the poll-driven politicians are going to have a field day with
this. Disasters sell tickets, and this disaster is off the Richter scale."

Again, I say, "The police have to find a killer. But they don't.
And now it's daybreak. They're stymied.

"And then, a fantastic coincidence. A phone call comes in, an
anonymous tip. Not from a cell phone, which you would expect,
coming from an area of the city where everyone has a cell phone,
or multiple cell phones. It comes from a pay phone." I take a step
toward the jury box. "A cell phone is traceable," I say. "But a pay
phone is not. I want you to remember that, ladies and gentlemen.
What kind of phone this anonymous tip was made from.

"This anonymous tipster, who has never come forward, tells
the nine-one-one operator that a suspicious-looking man is lurking. What makes him suspicious? He is Latino, and is driving a

pickup truck." I throw up my hands. "Think about that. Today, in Los Angeles, a Latino driving a pickup truck is suspicious."

I shake my head at the absurdity of that. "That is so idiotic it defies any credibility. It's not even racist, it's just dumb. Drive around any part of the city or county, from San Pedro to Chatsworth to Valencia to Santa Monica to Pasadena. You see Latino men driving pickup trucks, all hours of the day or night. It's such a common sight that no one would think twice about it. But for some reason, this sighting arouses suspicion.

"So the police investigate. The man in the truck has a perfectly valid reason for being where he is. He is there to work. He has to wait until the proper time, because he doesn't want to disturb the neighbors, so he eats his breakfast and reads his newspaper and doesn't bother anyone.

"But the police, for some reason that is absolutely unbelievable, decide to search his truck. The reason they give is that he had been arrested before. They know he was found not guilty of that charge, but in their minds, an arrest is reason enough.

"Later on, they will point to the coincidence that this man's earlier arrest happened in the vicinity of one of the previous killings." I step closer to the jury box. *But they did not know that at the time they demanded he let them search his truck.* All they had was an eighty-year-old man's vague account of maybe having seen one of the victims talking to a man who had a pickup truck. He didn't even know whether the man was Chicano. He was dark in complexion, that's all he could say. An eighty-year-old man, looking at a pretty young woman, from almost a block away, in the dark of night."

I walk back to the podium. "And that was the only excuse the police had to justify searching Mr. Salazar's truck. That sounds like an awfully flimsy excuse to me. But they did it. Better safe than sorry, that was their excuse." I give a little who-knows shrug. "Okay. I'll buy that."

I pause, and raise a finger. "But now here is something I am sure you remember. One of the detectives who searched that truck had already been to the victim's home. He had been in her bedroom. He was in there alone. No one else was with him. He was alone in the room where the victim kept her soiled clothes, in her clothes hamper. Her soiled clothes, which included her worn underwear."

It's as if I have suddenly pulled the pin from a grenade and am holding the live grenade in my hand. Somebody might get maimed, and fast. You had better duck for cover.

"The detective who had been in the victim's house, in her bedroom, is now the same detective who is searching Mr. Salazar's truck. This is not an ordinary detective, by the way. This is the head of the task force. More than anyone, finding the killer is on his shoulders."

Once again, I say, "He has to find the killer. He has to find *a* killer.

"Lo and behold, what does he find in Mr. Salazar's truck? Buried under a floorboard? A pair of the victim's panties." My eyes widen. "My God, he did it! He found the needle in the haystack. A one in a million chance, and he pulled it off!"

The buzz in the room is electric. I can almost feel the floor vibrating under my feet. I would love to sneak a peek to see how Cordova is handling this, but I don't dare. Instead, I sip some water, so that I keep my rhythm steady, and don't rush.

"So what does he do? Does he leave the evidence in place, where he found it, so the other detectives who are searching the back of the truck can see where it was hidden?" I shake my head. "No, he doesn't do that. He picks it up, puts it in a plastic bag, gets out of the truck, walks around to the back, and then shows it to his partners." I catch myself. "Excuse me, not his partners. He is the boss. The other detectives work under him. They take his orders."

Yet again, I say, "They had to find the killer. They had to find *a* killer."

I stare at the jurors, turn to look at Salazar, then give my at-

tention to the jury again. "And they did. They found him." I point
to Salazar, who sits in place, motionless and expressionless. "They
found a killer.

"They take him to police headquarters, initially, so they say,
for questioning. But later, they arrest him and book him for murder. Because of a pair of underpants that were in his truck. Hidden in his truck. Found by the police detective in charge of the
task force. Who had been in the victim's apartment, hours before.
Who had been in her bedroom. Alone."

There is a stirring behind me. I can't help but turn and look.
Cordova is on his feet, pushing his way past the other cops in the
row where he is sitting. He quick-steps down the side aisle to the
back of the room, pushes against the door, and leaves. Everyone
in the room watches him.

I wait for the interruption to subside, then take up my story
again.

"One thing that has been established, and this we don't dispute—the victims knew their killer. They may have been having
an affair with him. Some of them, anyway. Serially or at the same
time, we don't know. But I think both sides agree that there was
prior contact, a prior relationship."

I pivot, turning my body toward the defense table, so the
jury's eyes go with my movement toward Salazar. "Here is a man
who works from dawn to dusk, doing hard, physical labor. Out-
doors, where it is hot most of the year. He goes from job to job,
barely taking a moment to grab lunch. He spends evenings and
weekends with youth groups, church activities, and his family." I
practically roll my eyes. "When in the world would he have time
for an affair, let alone several? It's a preposterous idea. And let's
put our cards on the table—Mr. Salazar and the victims of the Full
Moon Killer live in different worlds. I have the utmost respect for
my client, but he does not mingle in their world. That's life. He
would be the first to agree with me, and my saying that isn't going to hurt his feelings. He doesn't need to have affairs, his life is
already filled to overflowing.

"The only piece of physical evidence against my client is the pair of underpants Lieutenant Cordova found—so he says—hidden in Mr. Salazar's truck. No other evidence was found. No other pair of panties from any of the other victims. When he was arrested earlier his truck was scoured from top to bottom, because there really was a reason for that. And did any underpants turn up? No. They did not. And this, remember, was right after that previous victim was found. Long before daylight. Doesn't it make sense," I argue, "that if his peculiarity is to remove the panties from his victims and keep them in his truck, as was the case, *supposedly*, a pair would have been found in that truck? But there were none.

"Let's return to the theory, which, as I said, both sides agree on, that the victims knew their killer. That some, if not all of them, were having affairs with him. Would it not have been easy for the killer to take a pair of underpants at any time during that affair? And then later, when the heat is on, stash them in Mr. Salazar's truck? I think that is a possible way this happened. Mr. Salazar did not lock his truck. It was unlocked all day long. He's out back in someone's yard, tending to their garden, and a pair of panties is hidden under the floorboard of his truck."

I pick up a sheet of paper, part of the court transcript. Holding it in front of my face, I say, "This is the testimony of the DNA expert. The prosecution's expert, Dr. Chatterjee." I look down, and read. "Question: *Can you tell how recently Ms. Steinmetz's DNA was left on these panties? Was it definitely on the night she was killed?* Answer, from Dr. Chatterjee: *Not necessarily. That would not be possible to know, because DNA lasts a long time. Months, even years.*"

I put the document aside. "It lasts months, even years." Crossing to the evidence table, I pick up the plastic bag that contains the panties that were taken from Salazar's truck and show it to the jury.

"There is no evidence, not one shred, that proves or even implies that this pair of women's underpants was worn by the victim on the night she was killed. None. Zero. They could just as easily have been worn days, weeks, or months before."

I walk to the table and place the evidence back. "Just as easily," I repeat.

"Now let's talk about the prosecution's other main claim against my client. The eyewitness identification. That went over well, didn't it."

Everyone in the room bursts into laughter; everyone except Loomis and his team, who sit at their table, stone faced.

"She absolutely, positively, unequivocally, without any doubt, one hundred percent, identified Mr. Salazar as the man who was with the victim the night she was killed. No doubt whatsoever. Zero. Nada. The victim and the man who obviously knew each other and were together right before she was killed. Right before. Minutes, maybe. Right before." I break into a smile. "But guess what? When she came in here and actually saw Mr. Salazar face to face, not a picture in a book, not through a one-way glass, but looking right at him, standing a few feet from her, she could not identify him as the man who was with the victim. When she finally saw Mr. Salazar in the flesh, it turned out she had been wrong!"

I shake my head in disgust. "An eighty-year-old man looking at something from a block away in the middle of the night, and a witness who recants her sworn testimony. Those are the prosecution's only witnesses." I give a knowing nod. "Boy, that is great evidence. Ironclad. I sure wish we had such good evidence."

The jury is smiling at me. They like me, and what I'm saying.

"Here's what I think is a likely scenario. More likely than anything the prosecution has presented," I say. "The police had to have a killer. We know that. Coming up empty again was unacceptable. The detective who went to the victim's house could not resist taking a pair of her soiled underpants. It was too hard to pass up such an opportunity. But now that he has them, he has to find an appropriate suspect to plant them on. He doesn't have one, and they're running out of time. It's five minutes to midnight. In five minutes their coach is going to turn into a pumpkin.

"And then, a miracle happens. A suspect falls into their lap. Some anonymous phone call comes in." I digress for a moment. "That, by the way, ought to raise a red flag in your minds. Who made this call? Why? Doesn't that feel fishy to you? It does to me. It really does to me."

Back to my thesis again. "The police respond. And there is Roberto Salazar. All wrapped up for them in a pretty pink bow. All they have to do is connect him to the victim. And they do. Her undies are in his truck. A to B to C. Guilty."

I come around the corner of the podium and lean against it. Two reasons. My back hurts, and I need to change my posture. And to bring an air of intimacy between the jury and me. I stare at their faces. They are giving me their full attention.

"The problem is, A to B to C don't add up. They just don't. There is no evidence that in any way connects Mr. Salazar to the victim. None. No other evidence was found in Mr. Salazar's truck, his other truck, his house, anywhere he might have been. None. And the prosecution's key eyewitness recanted her sworn testimony on the stand."

Another gulp of water. I'm in the home stretch now. But there are still some loose ends I have to tie up.

"The panties, and a very dubious connection to Mr. Salazar's whereabouts and the locations where the victims were found. Of course he would have been in those locations, that is where he worked. Not just for a year, the year these killings took place. For years and years before. If he is such a sociopath, why did he wait all this time before he went on his killing spree? Did something suddenly snap inside him?" I shake my head vigorously. "There is no evidence that he did, none at all. Not from any physical evidence, not from his psychological profile, which, please remember, the prosecution did not contest. Nor did they contest the findings of Dr. Leonard Silk, a renowned psychotherapist, that Mr. Salazar is not a sociopath. They couldn't, because he isn't. He is as sane and normal as you or me."

One more important note to hit, then I am done. "The prosecution is going to try to make a big deal of the fact that since Mr. Salazar's arrest there have been no more Full Moon Killings. It's true—there haven't been. But there was a break in the action before. That happens in serial killings, it is a common pattern. And sooner or later, they stop. The killer has gotten the evil out of his system, or he may have died, or there are many other legitimate reasons. That no other killings have happened since Mr. Salazar's arrest does not mean he is guilty of the ones that occurred before he was arrested."

I walk to the jury box rail. Putting my hands on it, I lean toward the jurors.

"The prosecution wants you to believe that this city is safe from this killer. But he could strike again. If that happens, they'll have a built-in excuse—they will claim that it is a copycat murder. Because the facts are known now, they are public knowledge. Any weird freak out there can kill a woman in the future, take her panties, and he'll be the Son of the Full Moon Killer, not the original killer. If it does happen, that's how they'll spin it.

"Or maybe the real killer will strike again. Either way, the man who stands on trial before you will not be that killer. Just as he is not that killer now.

"The law requires—it demands—that if Mr. Salazar, or any defendant, is to be found guilty, he must be found guilty beyond a reasonable doubt. The prosecution has not reached that bar in this case. They have a flimsy case, built entirely around one piece of evidence that could so easily have been manipulated it is virtually worthless. It is your duty, ladies and gentlemen, to weigh the facts in this case and come to a just decision. And the facts, when you examine them in the cold light of day, do not prove, beyond a reasonable doubt, that Roberto Salazar killed Cheryl Lynn Steinmetz. He is not the Full Moon Killer. He must be found not guilty, and must be allowed to walk out of this courtroom a free man."

"You did good, girl," Joe exults. He's like a proud father whose kid just won the Little League championship game with a grand slam home run in the bottom of the ninth. "Really good." He swigs some Diet Coke. "Better than I could have done." He smiles broadly. "You kicked some righteous ass."

We are on lunch break, hanging out in his office. When we reconvene, it will be Loomis's turn. He's champing at the bit. He shot me a look that could cut glass after Judge Suzuki adjourned us until after lunch.

I didn't see Cordova after he bugged out, but he will be there. I burned that bridge. I burned more than one bridge this morning. I had to. There was no other way. I want to be collegial, but I crossed the line today. I will still get along with cops and prosecutors, but not like before.

FORTY-THREE

HARRY LOOMIS, BALANCED ON his feet like a championship prizefighter, gives his closing rebuttal to my summation.

"If you believe that a decorated police officer with more than twenty years of experience, a man whose record is one hundred percent clean, who has never been brought up on disciplinary charges, who has dozens of awards and commendations—if you believe that man planted evidence in the accused's truck, you must find the accused not guilty. You must. Or if you believe that someone else murdered Cheryl Lynn Steinmetz, and planted the evidence in the truck of the accused, you must find the accused not guilty. You must do that."

He is leaning forward on the podium, gripping it hard, as if he's driving a race car. The wind is almost whipping through his hair, he radiates so much kinetic energy. Now he relaxes his white-knuckle grip and stands up straight. He smoothes his tie.

"But if you do not believe either of those things, then you must find the accused guilty as charged. Because there are no other possibilities. Someone put those underpants in the accused's truck. And it wasn't the Wicked Witch of the West. It was the accused."

He turns and points at Salazar, who is sitting in the middle of the defense table between Joe and me. Salazar stares back at him, not menacingly, but with a blankness that is almost Zen-like. I force myself to maintain what I hope is an aura of calmness. Joe, the old pro, takes it all in stride. He twiddles a pencil between his fingers, looks at Loomis, at the jurors, the judge, the other players.

Loomis turns back to the jury.

"Either it was Mr. Salazar," he repeats, "or a decorated police officer whose integrity has never been questioned during his entire career, or some unknown party who took the victim's undergarments and then planted them in the accused's truck. Out of all the trucks in all of Los Angeles, he chose that truck in which to stash the incriminating underpants. A truck owned and operated by a man who just happened to be within a stone's throw of where the victim was found. Who was found almost on top of another victim's location. Man, what an incredible set of coincidences. Out of all the trucks in all of Los Angeles County, the real killer puts the stolen evidence in that particular truck. What lousy luck for the accused.

"If you believe that's what happened."

Point by point, Loomis makes his case, and as he does, he kicks the crap out of ours. What is a married man who is faithful to his wife doing with condoms in his glove box? Do he and his wife have sex in his truck? (Mrs. Salazar winces and begins shaking when he brings that up.) Why was he right where the murders took place, not once, but multiple times? Why did he change his schedule just before Cheryl Lynn Steinmetz was killed, which conveniently, oh so conveniently, gave him an excuse to be there?

Not one but two credible witnesses saw a man who in every way fits Salazar's description with two of the victims. The truck, the baseball hat, the size, shape, age, ethnicity. Too many coincidences.

Loomis tackles their key eyewitness's recantation head-on. "Our main eyewitness . . ." He shakes his head in resigned annoyance. "That was a blunder," he admits. "She was honest—she decided she could not, with one hundred percent accuracy, swear that the accused was the man she saw. She was almost sure he is, but she couldn't swear to it. I think she panicked. People do that in court when they're not used to the pressure. But putting aside whether or not she was willing to state without any reservation that it was the accused, he still looks exactly like the man she saw with the victim."

He turns and looks at us again, specifically, at me. I feel a blast of heat coming my way, and it isn't friendly sunshine.

"The defense laid out their story. It was told well. Fairy tales usually are. Which is what that was, a fairy tale. All the elements of a good fairy tale were there—suspension of belief, creating an alternative world, concocting imaginary villains, absolving the hero of any guilt. A good story, but it isn't true. You all know that. You have good common sense. You know that fairy tales are not the truth.

"Here's what really happened. That man sitting at the defense table knew these victims. He was having affairs with them. Why else would he have those condoms in his truck? After he did, he killed them, and took a souvenir of his awful deed."

Loomis leaves the podium and starts to slowly pace back and forth in front of the jury box.

"Why did he kill them? That question may never be answered, but I have a few theories. One, he is a sociopath, despite the defense psychologist's testimony that he isn't. Sociopaths often go undetected. They pass lie detector tests with impunity. Why? Because they have no conscience, and no remorse. He killed them because he got pleasure from doing it, and because he could. They were young, defenseless women who trusted him.

"That is one possibility. Another is that these women spurned him. He was a married man, there was no future for them with him. They had sex with him, maybe once, maybe a few times, then they didn't want to anymore. And please, folks, don't judge them about that. They were single, they were not having extramarital sex, they were not betraying a relationship. The accused was. But still, that enraged him, that they would cut him off. So he killed them out of anger."

Loomis stops his pacing and faces the jury head-on. "Here is yet a third reason, and this one, I think you will agree, is the real one. He was afraid they would turn on him, blow the cover that he had so craftily concocted over the years. The family man. The youth group counselor. The man of religion. His entire life would have gone up in flames. People kill for reasons far less important than that."

He takes a step back. "You have a choice. You can believe a fairy tale, or you can believe the truth. The truth is that the accused murdered four innocent women. The truth is that the victim's underwear was found in his truck. The truth is that he was where she was murdered, when she was murdered. The truth is that he was where another victim was murdered, when she was murdered. The truth is that not one person can say he was anywhere but those places, at those times."

Loomis scans the faces of the jurors, one by one. They look back at him in rapt attention. "Part of the accused's defense is that he is a man of God, and a man of God would not kill," he says. "Well, we all know that throughout history, millions of people have been killed in the name of God, so that's not an acceptable excuse. Let me quote from scripture, to put this in the proper frame. A quotation we all know, because it rings so true. First Corinthians, chapter thirteen, verse eleven."

He speaks from memory. *"When I was a child, I spoke like a child, I thought like a child, I reasoned like a child; but when I became a man, I gave up childish ways.*

"You and I are not children. We are grownups, adult men and women. We have put away our childish things, including believing in fairy tales. Real life is staring us in the face. And in this real life, this real world, Roberto Salazar, the man sitting in front of you, murdered Cheryl Lynn Steinmetz. He must be found guilty of the most heinous crime of all, the taking of another's life. He must be found guilty of murder in the first degree, with premeditation."

FORTY-FOUR

T HE JURY HAS BEEN out for five days. Good news for us, or bad? I don't know. I'm at home, resting. I had vacation time coming. I'm in touch with the office, and can be there in an hour.

After Judge Suzuki charged the jury and adjourned the proceedings, Joe and I confabbed in his office, one last time. Our mutual consensus was that I had dazzled the audience with smoke and mirrors, but that Loomis had effectively pulled the curtain aside, revealing the little man behind the screen who was manipulating the great wizard's image. He had the evidence on his side. In the end, we had emotion. Evidence almost always trumps emotion.

We were confident that we had done our best. Now, we wait.

Amanda comes over and we practice our birthing procedure. We don't talk about the trial, or speculate on the outcome. She was very complimentary to me after it was over, congratulating me on doing what she declared was a superb job, but we have a mutual, unspoken agreement to let it lie. After the verdict, we'll talk. Right now, the concentration is on the blessed arrival. I'm less than a month away. Since this is my first pregnancy, the baby could come earlier. It is certainly big enough; I've gained almost forty-five pounds, so even if only 15 percent of that is the baby, she will be normal sized. Given my size and Jeremy's, this baby will weigh a lot more than six or seven pounds.

I have not talked to Jeremy in months. I don't want to. I don't

392 IN MY DARK DREAMS

want him there when I give birth. Maybe later, I'll let him into his child's life. But probably not. He has not pushed for that; just the opposite. He ducks my calls and e-mails, so I've stopped trying to stay in contact with him. His only connection to us may be the support check he will write every month.

Sometimes, late at night, alone in my little house, I miss him. I miss us. But more and more, he is a fading memory. A life I used to live, but don't anymore.

The judge wants to see us. I drive downtown and meet Joe in the office. It's been eight days since the jury began deliberating. Even for a trial this important, that is too long. We ride the elevator to Suzuki's floor and are shown into his chambers. Loomis and Arthur Wong are already there. Loomis looks grim.

"The jury is at a logjam," Suzuki informs us in a doleful tone of voice. "I've instructed them to deliberate some more, try to come to a verdict." He rubs his forehead with the back of his hand. "A split verdict after all this *meshugass*—what a mess that would be."

Another Yiddish-speaking Asian. What a small world we inhabit.

"From the tone of their communications, though," he goes on, "they may hang. We should know in the next twenty-four hours."

"Keep your fingers crossed," Joe says, as we ride back up to the office. For us, a tie is almost as good as a win. "A hung jury. Damn." We are alone on the elevator, so he permits himself a self-satisfied smile. "Loomis must be crazed."

"We're not there yet," I caution. I feel heavy, not only with the weight of my baby and my body, but with the emotional weight of what we have been through during the past months. "If it's only one or two—"

"That's true," Joe agrees. He doesn't want to jump the gun too much.

One or two for acquittal. What we had hoped and prayed for.

That one, possibly two, of the jurors would resist the prosecution's case and buy into our story. One or two stubborn jurors can sometimes hold out until the bitter end; more often than not, though, they are beaten down until they yield to the majority.

One more day. We have to hang in for one more day.

"We cannot come to a verdict, Your Honor," the foreperson, a middle-aged woman who works as a stock analyst, tells Judge Suzuki. They have split almost right down the middle, seven to five. Slightly in the prosecution's favor, but three or four more for our side than we dared hope for.

Suzuki's sigh is of Olympian quality. "You are positive." He knows the answer—when the division is that deep, there can't be reconciliation.

"We are, Your Honor. I'm sorry."

"Not as sorry as I am," Suzuki says in a testy tone of voice. "We have a mistrial," he announces. "The jury is dismissed." He bangs his gavel and galumphs back to his chambers without thanking them for their effort.

All this work for nothing. Well, not for nothing as far as we're concerned. Our client was not convicted of murder.

Loomis and his team leave a trail of angry smoke as they exit. Somebody is going to tie one on tonight. The whole team of them. Cordova and his group will match them shot for shot, and then some.

"What does this mean?" Salazar asks me as we stand in the fast-emptying room. "Am I free?"

"No," I answer. "You're not."

His eyes widen with uncertainty. "Am I going to have to go back to jail?"

"For now. Until the prosecution decides whether they want to try you again."

He looks baffled. "How can they do that? I thought they could only try you once."

"Not if the result is a hung jury. I'll explain it all later." I grip his arm. "Hang in a little longer. Trust me. We did better than I expected."

"How better? I'm not guilty."

I can't deal with this now, especially since the baby has decided to go bronco riding inside my belly. "We will talk it all out later."

Standing at the railing behind me, Amanda and Mrs. Salazar converge on us. The bailiff cuts them some slack, so they can have time with him. Mrs. Salazar is in shock—she doesn't know what is happening. Amanda, however, is beaming. She knows that under the circumstances, not losing was almost as good as winning.

She gives Roberto a hug of encouragement. "We'll beat this," she tells him. "Don't give up."

Joe, who is shoving his papers into his briefcase, looks at Salazar and Amanda as they embrace. He shakes his head and chuckles to himself.

"What's so funny?" I ask him. I'm thrilled for what we pulled off, but I see no humor in it.

He looks at Salazar and Amanda, still close to each other. "You ever see those pictures of dogs and their owners? How the owners and dogs wind up looking like each other? Winston Churchill and his bulldog—that sort of comparison?"

"Yes, I've seen them. So?"

"Turns out, it's true. Some ancient genetic built-in safety factor—you're attracted to those who look like you. A protective element."

"I guess. So what?"

"Her and him," he says. Meaning Amanda and Salazar. "Don't you see the similarities?"

"What?" I look at Amanda, then from her to Salazar. "No way. She's your quintessential WASP, and he's Latino. How do you get that?"

"The basic structure of their faces, particularly around the eyes. They resemble each other," he insists.

I look at both of them again, more carefully this time. *Oh, my God,* I think. I start to shake. *Oh, my God.*

PART
THREE

PART
THREE

FORTY-FIVE

BIRTH ANNOUNCEMENT

Amanda Jill Thompson
Place of Birth: Cedars-Sinai Medical Center,
Los Angeles, California
Weight: 8 pounds, 14 ounces
Height: 22 ½ inches
Color of hair: Black
Color of Eyes: Blue
Condition of Child: Perfect

FORTY-SIX

IT WAS, ALL THINGS considered, not the hardest of deliveries in the history of the world. The pain was excruciating, but I managed to bear it and get through without succumbing to drugs. Amanda, godmother and surrogate grandmother, was a wonderful coach and supporter. She broke into tears when I told her what I was naming my baby.

Giving birth hurt more than running the marathon. A lot more. Dealing with that pain will make the next marathon easier.

Mother and daughter are at home, resting and (in mother's case) recovering. I took a leave of absence. The Public Defender's Office allows six months of maternity leave, but there is no maternity pay, which sucks. We are the bottom of the totem pole. Rank has its privileges, and lack of rank doesn't.

It doesn't matter. I'm not going back.

The District Attorney revived the case against Salazar. He will be tried again, next year. Our office won't be handling the defense this time around. Frankly, there was no appetite for it. We would have if we'd been compelled to do so—that's our job—but Amanda stepped in and hired a private attorney. Abby Lench is one of the best criminal defense lawyers in Los Angeles. Salazar is in good hands.

"Abby may do better than we did," Joe said, when we found out who Salazar's new lawyer was. "He might turn up an alibi witness for Salazar."

More than anything, that was our Achilles' heel. No alibi witness. If we'd had one, the momentum, and probably the verdict, would have swung in our favor.

"Because he'll have a blank check to hunt one up," I answered. I agreed with Joe. We did the best we could, but we work for the government. Our budget and resources are limited. Amanda will pay for whatever Abby Lench tells her he needs.

Joe gave me the old fisheye then. "Because he'll buy one." He sounded tired and cynical. "Like the eyewitness who suddenly changed her story."

We did stick around long enough to petition Judge Suzuki for bail, and over Loomis's strenuous objection, it was granted. The bond was set at a million dollars. Amanda wrote the check without batting an eye. Salazar has gone back to work, although more than half of his clients dropped him, particularly on the Westside. He has picked up some new ones, but in less expensive neighborhoods. He is out of jail and walking the streets again, that's the main thing.

But not at night or early in the morning, regardless of the phase of the moon. Joe and I drummed that into his head. They are going to be gunning for you, we warned him. You have to be cleaner than Mr. Clean. Immaculate. He understood. If it means he has to fight traffic on the freeway in the morning, that's better than being locked up again.

Speaking of Joe, he came over for a visit a few days ago. He comes to the house a couple times a month. As usual, his arms were full of clothes and toys for the baby. He has adult children, but no grandchildren yet, so he carries on about her like crazy.

Not the way Amanda does, though. As far as she is concerned, this is the most special baby that has ever been born. The Christ Child pales in comparison. She has already established a trust fund for her namesake's education. Not just for college, but beginning with nursery school. My baby is never going to want for anything, at least materially.

And she will be greatly loved. I know what it feels like not to be. The sins of my mother shall not be visited on my daughter.

We fly Southwest Airlines, Burbank to Albuquerque. The baby was four months old yesterday. This is our first trip away from home. The attendants are very helpful—they board us early and give us the best seats. Amanda fusses a little during the flight, but I calm her by nursing. I pick up our rental car, a new-smelling Toyota Corolla complete with baby seat, and head north on I-25. At Santa Fe we connect to U.S. 285, and take it to New Mexico State Highway 68, which will lead us from Española to Taos.

The northern New Mexico landscape unfolds outside the car windows. The sky is clear, blue-white, virtually cloudless. Cactus, sage, brown earth outcroppings. Mountains loom in the north and west. This is a beautiful part of the world. The elevation is high, the air is thin, clean. So different from Los Angeles. You can get lost here, inside your own head. A good place for rejuvenation, rebirth. It's easy to understand why Amanda chose to retreat here, thirty-five years ago.

I pull off the paved road onto a private hard-packed dirt one that is barely wide enough for one vehicle. The dirt was oiled recently, so it isn't too bumpy, but I drive at a snail's pace. I am in no hurry. In her car seat in the back, my baby snores little bubbles.

The sanctuary is a cluster of low adobe buildings. They are almost the same color as their surroundings, so you don't see them until you are almost on top of them. I park in front of the largest one. There are a couple of other vehicles in the compound, an old Jeep and a Dodge minivan that is caked with mud. I get out and stretch my legs, inhaling deeply. A sharp smell of sage burns my nostrils. I take Amanda out of her car seat and slide her into the Snugli. She folds herself into my chest.

The nuns who run this refuge don't wear traditional habits.

The one who comes out to greet me is clad in jeans, Birkenstock sandals, wool socks, a ratty sweatshirt. Her gray hair is shapeless, almost bowl-cut. Decades of exposure to the high sun and sky have weathered her face, lines crisscrossing it like an old road map that has been folded and refolded a thousand times.

Now I know the meaning of the word *beatific*. It is her smile of greeting. She is, as I gleaned from our correspondence, more than eighty years old.

She looks at Amanda, who stares back at her. For a four-month-old baby, her stare is penetrating. "Oh, my," the old nun coos. "She is a beauty."

We walk through the compound to her office, passing other nuns along the way who are variations on the same theme as hers. All older women. None, I would think, younger than sixty. Most of them in their seventies and eighties. As they die off, they are not replaced. Attrition will close this place within a couple of decades. That's a shame—they have been providing an important service for many years. From before Amanda Burgess came to them in her time of need.

"Hundreds of women have come to us," Sister Mary Barbara tells me. "I remember most of them. I certainly remember her," she says, when we are seated in her office, two mugs of steaming green tea in front of us. "She was different from the other girls who come here. A woman, not a girl. And not poor. Educated." Another warm smile. "We take everyone who needs us. Age or race or money is not a factor."

I don't like to lie, especially to nuns, but I had concocted an elaborate set of falsehoods to explain why I was searching for information about Amanda. That I was her niece. That she was about to die and wanted to close her circles, including the one regarding the child she had out of wedlock.

That information wasn't hard to uncover. A good detective and the universal tentacles of the Internet mean there is no more privacy. The detective I hired was good. She found out what I needed in less than a week.

That was last week. Now I'm here. My daughter is nestled in the old nun's lap. I asked if she would like to hold her, and my offer was eagerly accepted. The baby lies there peacefully. She can feel that she is in safe hands.

"Or religion? My aunt isn't Catholic."

"Or religion," the sweet old nun confirms. "We have had Jewish girls, Muslims, nonbelievers. As long as they want to continue their pregnancies, we take them in. No strings attached, no questions asked."

"Do the girls' families know they have come here?"

"Some do. Some don't. We prefer that the family knows, but for some girls that is not possible. Some were victims of incest or rape. Some are running away from abusive situations. We provide a safe haven."

"And you handle the adoptions as well?"

She nods. "Yes. That is the only religious part of the process. We are a Catholic organization, and we try to put the newborns with Catholic families." She sips some tea. So do I. It's good. Lots of honey.

"We only place the children with families," she continues. "No single parents, or single-sex relationships. I hope you don't feel that makes us prejudiced," she says apologetically. "But we are Catholics," she repeats. "We follow the tenets of our church."

"I understand," I tell her.

She wants to make sure that I do, from their point of view. "We believe a child has the best chance of success in the most normal family possible. It is hard enough finding out you were adopted. That your birth mother did not keep you. There are always abandonment issues, no matter how loving the adoptive family is." She pauses. "That is one of our rules. That the child will be told he or she was adopted."

"A good one," I agree. I believe that. Sooner or later, a child would learn the truth. If the adoption was kept from them, finding out under the wrong circumstances could be devastating.

I have another question. I have so many questions. "What happens if the mother wants to keep her child after it is born?"

The old nun frowns. "We discourage that. Legally, we cannot force them to give it up, but we put pressure on them." Another sip of tea. "It isn't because we don't believe a child should be with its mother. Of course we do. But the girls who come to us don't do so because they have their lives in order. They come here because they don't. If they keep their babies, they will be taking them back into that same chaotic and dangerous life they were running away from. Too many times, the results are tragic."

I know. I've seen what happens to kids growing up in poverty, surrounded by crime.

There is a bit of hypocrisy here, because I am a single parent; but my baby will not be in that situation. And this sweet lady sitting across from me doesn't know my hubby isn't waiting back home, pining for our return. She doesn't know that the wedding ring on my finger was bought yesterday at a jewelry cart in the Third Street Mall in Santa Monica.

"Are the adoptions set up in advance?" I ask her.

"Sometimes. It isn't always possible."

"Was it with my aunt?"

"No."

Now, the question. It is a guess, but an educated one. "Because her baby was part Chicano."

She nods. "He was a beautiful boy. Almost as beautiful as this little one," she says, cradling my Amanda in her arms.

Amanda Burgess did not leave Los Angeles and come out here for a spiritual retreat after her marriage collapsed. She came here because she was pregnant with an illegitimate child, by a Latino father.

"The baby was given up for adoption."

"Yes."

"To a Chicano family? Mexican American?"

"I believe so. Those records are confidential."

"I understand. But do you keep up? To make sure the situation is good, later on?"

"Yes, we do. Not officially, but we do."

"And his situation was good?"

A vigorous nod. "It was. Which was lucky, because there aren't many qualified Latino families out there. Don't get me wrong, Latinos are wonderful family people. But they usually have their own children, or children of relatives. Placing an orphan Latino child can be difficult." She smiles. "But he was so adorable. And this family could not have children of their own. So it worked out."

"My aunt will be glad to hear that," I tell her. "She will be so very glad. I don't think she has ever really gotten over giving up that baby. But she had to."

Because he was brown, and she wasn't.

"I understand," the nun says compassionately. "Please tell her that her child had a good home. That she would be proud of him."

I don't have to tell her that. I know that she already is. And that having abandoned him once, she never will again.

FORTY-SEVEN

JOE HAS A FRESH and important piece of news waiting for me when I arrive back home. He doesn't know where I have been, and I'm not going to tell him. This is my personal crusade.

He comes over to my house to give me the news, bringing his own six-pack of Diet Coke with him.

He blurts it right out. "They found an alibi witness."

"Are you serious?" I'm glad I put the baby down for a nap, I might have dropped her.

"Serious as cancer."

"Is he believable?" I'm assuming it's a man.

His answer confirms my guess. "Seems to be."

Nothing should surprise me now, but I'm stunned anyway. "Where did Abby Lench find him? And where was this bozo when *we* needed him?"

Joe pops the top of a Diet Coke can, takes a swallow. He would offer me one, but he knows I've sworn off soft drinks while I'm nursing. "Supposedly, in Iraq. Working construction for Halliburton the past year. Didn't know or hear anything until he got back."

"Damn . . ." I sit down. This is a shock. Great for Salazar, but I have an empty feeling in my stomach. I know Joe does, too. "You predicted that," I remind him.

"Yeah, and God doesn't make little green apples. You got any vodka?"

"In the freezer."

He gets out the bottle of Smirnoff, pours some into a glass, tops it off with Diet Coke. Drinks. He sits down heavily. I look him in the face. He looks pasty. He needs to get out more. With all these drinks, and his weight, he's a prime candidate for a heart attack. I should talk to his wife about getting him off his ass and working out.

"Well, good for them," I offer without conviction. "We always said that was the one piece we were missing."

Joe takes a drink, contemplates his glass. "Someone's crossed the line, Jessica. You know it, and I know it."

I do know it, better than he does, but I'm not sharing my information. We're not a team anymore. I'm allowed to keep secrets.

"You believed in him," Joe says. "I never did."

"Which means you did a better job for him than I did."

He slumps back in his chair. "He's gonna get off." He drains his glass. "Usually I love my work, but sometimes I can't." He pops himself another soda, mixes it with more vodka, takes a long pull. I pick the bottle up and put it back in the freezer. Two is his limit in my household. I don't want him picking up a DUI.

"We don't judge our clients," I remind him, as he so often preached to me. "We defend them."

"We do." His lopsided grin turns into a grimace. "Sometimes too damn well."

The health club for women was the only connection any of the victims had to each other. The police would have looked into it, but since that knowledge was only discovered at the eleventh hour, they would not have had the time to do a thorough job. And they had their suspect nailed down (so they thought). Standard operating procedure for police work—don't go muddying the waters. You might dredge up something that doesn't fit your carefully structured game plan.

I'm not working, so I have time on my hands. And I have this itch that I keep scratching. So far, I haven't gotten all the relief I need.

The manager, Angie on her name tag, discusses the application process with me. She's in uniform—shorts, golf shirt with the club's logo over her left breast, running shoes. She is an Amazon, like the other women who work here, but she doesn't seem to have an attitude problem, which I have found is common among trainers, especially women. One reason I've never joined a gym before. When I let slip that I ran a marathon last year, her eyes sparkle with appreciation.

"That's great," she says with a touch of envy. "Being in shape is obviously important to you." She smiles at Amanda, who is propped up in my lap. "We have an excellent mother-baby program here. Gymboree, the pool, yoga. You and your daughter will really like it."

"That's the main reason I want to join."

Angie escorts me around the facility. Very high-class, everything first-rate. There are two tennis courts outside, a small track, volleyball pits. The grounds are lush and tasteful, although a bit fraying at the edges, as if the gardener has gone on vacation.

"We had to let our last gardener go," she says, as she notices me looking at the less than perfect landscaping. "He wasn't dependable. It's hard, finding a good one. There's so much competition for quality help in this area."

I know a very good one, but I'm not going to recommend him. Not to this club.

"The man who did our planting last year was terrific," she says, as we continue our tour. "We had to discharge him too, though. Some of the members felt that he was . . ." She fumbles for the right phrase. "Hitting on them. Not that he wasn't a good-looking guy, and not that some of the girls didn't like the attention, but you don't want anyone to be uncomfortable." She picks some decaying rose petals off a bush that needs trimming. "I should get him back, just to freshen up the place. He really had a green thumb. I don't know if I have his card anymore, though."

"What was his name?" As she looks at me quizzically, I explain, "Some of my friends who live in the area have good gardeners. I could find out if he works for any of them."

She shakes her head. "Robert, maybe? I don't remember the last name."

"Was he American? I mean Anglo?"

"Mexican American. Robert . . . shoot, I can't remember." She smiles. "We'll find someone. Have to keep everything looking pretty."

I follow her to the pool enclosure, where an infant/mother swimming class is in progress. My baby strains in the Snugli when she sees the other babies. She is raring to go. This is going to be fun—teaching her to swim, tumble, climb.

"Tomorrow," I whisper to her. I didn't bring bathing suits or gym clothes. "Hold your horses." She is an impatient child. She takes after her mother in that way, too.

We take the elevator down to the changing area. It's as posh as a country club. Individual lockers with combinations, plush carpeting, steam, sauna, Jacuzzi. A massage room with a masseuse available all day and early evening. You get your money's worth here.

"By the way," I say, trying to sound casual, "does an instructor named Dimitra St. Clair work here?"

Angie shakes her head. "She left us. By mutual agreement," she adds, as if tacitly telling me they canned her. "Why, is she a friend of yours?" she asks suspiciously.

"No. I just heard her name somewhere. That she was good."

"She wasn't that good." I've touched a nerve; I can hear the irritation in her voice. "She was a star fucker," the manager informs me bluntly. "We have some celebrity members, and we don't like staff cozying up to them."

"That's good to know, even if you're not a celebrity. Keep business and personal stuff separate."

"That's our policy." She pauses. "And there was that trial she testified in. It put the spotlight on us, which left a sour taste in some of the members' mouths."

It's evident this woman doesn't know who I am. One potential stumbling block I don't have to finesse. "I heard about that. One of your members was a victim of that killer, right?"

"Two were," Angie corrects me. She shudders involuntarily. "The aftershocks around this place were off the Richter scale. It was like, were we a magnet for their killer? But nothing has happened since, so that feeling has gone away."

"Good," I say enthusiastically. "I wouldn't want to be around that vibe."

Angie frowns as she suddenly remembers something unpleasant. "I had almost forgotten," she says, as she shows me an empty locker. "One of the murder victims left some clothes here. Sometimes a client will be running late and leave in her exercise outfit, and come back for her clothes the next day." She covers her eyes with a hand, as if to ward off an ugly memory. "She left them the day before she was killed." Her voice choking, she continues, "She never made it back."

"What happened to those clothes?"

"We bagged them up and put them in storage." Apologetically: "We wanted to give them to her family, but we didn't know how to get in touch with them. Should throw them out, I suppose." She laughs nervously. "It's like having a ghost in the closet."

A ghost, indeed. "I'm a lawyer for the city," I tell Angie. "I'm sure I could find out her next of kin. Because you're right, they would want her things. I could take them for you."

She doesn't have to think twice about my offer. "That would be the right thing to do," she says gratefully.

I follow her down to the basement. She pulls a plastic garbage bag out of a storage bin and looks inside. "Yes, this is it."

I look at the contents. A pair of slacks, blouse, bra, shoes, underpants. Having been enclosed for a long time, they emit a slight smell of mildew.

I take the bag from Angie. "I'm sure we'll be able to take care of this properly," I assure her.

She gives me a smile of gratitude. The sooner this ghost is

exorcised, the better. "That's nice of you. I'm really glad you're joining."

We finish the tour and go back to her office, where we fill out the application together. I give her my credit card. Nothing registers in her face as she processes it, confirming that she hasn't connected me to the trial. I have a week in which I can withdraw and get my deposit back, so I'm not worried about the money. Maybe I will like the mother-baby program. I need to start exercising again, and I want to get Amanda in the pool as soon as possible. It's never too early to protect your child against a swimming pool tragedy.

It's hot outside. I strap Amanda in her baby seat and turn the air-conditioning on. As I drive away, I think about the gardener the club let go because he was coming on to some of the women. Robert somebody.

The name for a Mexican American Robert is Roberto. Angie doesn't have to remember the last name. I already know it.

FORTY-EIGHT

THERE'S A MOON OUT tonight. It's full. I can hear the coyotes howling their dirges up in the hills of Griffith Park.

I'm here alone. Kathy Baron, a dependable high schooler who lives near me, is babysitting Amanda. She has my cell number in case of an emergency. I left two bottles of expressed breast milk in the refrigerator, so there is ample nourishment. Next week, I'll start Amanda on her first solid food. I'm told they make great organic baby food now.

The street is quiet. A few of the small houses have lights on inside, but not Salazar's. His truck is parked in the driveway. My loaded gun is in my purse. I will only use it if I have to.

It is a little after midnight. My cutoff time is one o'clock. My gut feeling is that if he is going to make a move, it will be by then, because he would have to drive all the way across town, have a rendezvous, then get back before his family wakes up. If he isn't in his house when his wife awakens, there would be trouble. She has covered for him all this time, but she is at the breaking point. I could see that etched in her face at the end of the trial.

Twelve-thirty crawls by. No movement. I'm playing a hunch. Some of my intuitions have paid off in the past. I hope this one doesn't. I should have brought coffee with me to help me stay awake, but I'm trying not to drink caffeine now, and it would make me have to pee. I don't want to leave here, and where would

411

I find an open ladies' room in an unfamiliar neighborhood at this time of night?

Quarter to one. My hunch was wrong after all. Time to go home. I am both surprised and relieved, because if I had been right, there would have been hell to pay.

I reach for the key in the ignition to turn the car on, and as my hand touches it, Salazar comes out of his house. He is dressed in dark clothes. He takes a cursory look up and down the street, but there is nothing to see except dark parked cars. Mine is one of them, but it's far enough away that he wouldn't notice me. He has never seen my car, so as far as I know, he doesn't know what make I drive.

He gets into his truck and coasts it down his driveway, waiting until he is at the street before he starts it up. A precaution not to wake up his wife, I'm guessing. That makes his behavior more suspicious to me than it already is, which is very suspicious.

He drives down the street. I wait until he rounds the corner before I start after him. There will be very few vehicles on the road at this time of night, and I know what he drives, so I'll be able to stay back and still be in contact with him.

I see him ahead of me, about a block separating us. There is another car between him and me, so I feel comfortable in this space. He drives south on Atlantic Boulevard. If he is going to West Los Angeles he can hop on the 60, which will lead him to the I-10. At this time of night, he can be in Brentwood or Santa Monica in twenty minutes.

My stomach is churning. The taste of bile rises in my throat. I feel as if I have to throw up. I brought a bottle of water with me, and I drink from it now, to keep from puking.

He crosses through a light and I follow, barely making it on the yellow. I need to stay far enough away so he doesn't spot someone tailing him, but close enough that I don't lose him. I don't know how to do this the way a professional would. The way Cordova would, for instance.

Cordova should be here tonight. I'm sure he'd want to be, but he can't. For the first two months after Salazar's release, the police shadowed his house during the full-moon period. They weren't particularly inconspicuous about it—they wanted him to know they were bird-dogging him, as if daring him to make a move. But he complained to Abby Lench, his lawyer, and Abby got a restraining order to stop the police from surveilling him. So now he can move about freely, without the police knowing what he is doing or where he is going.

They didn't get a restraining order against me, though. I'm a civilian. I can go wherever I please. Tonight my pleasure is to drive around the streets of East Los Angeles, and then, if my intuition is right, West Los Angeles. I have Cordova's cell number on my speed dial. If the shit hits the fan, I will call him. I'm brave, but only to a point.

Some businesses are still open, mostly fast-food places and bars. Jack in the Box, Taco Bell, McDonald's—all on the same block. Across the street from them, a KFC. The idea of digesting any of that carbo-loaded gunk makes me nauseated, and I take another swallow of water to calm my stomach.

Farther up, a few blocks before the freeway entrance, there is an all-night ARCO AM/PM Mini-Market. Up ahead of me, I see Salazar pull in. He parks near the front, gets out of his car, takes a quick look around, and goes into the store.

I drive past and turn onto the first side street, where I make a U-turn and park at the curb. From this vantage point I will be able to see Salazar's truck as he passes by, so I can take up my pursuit again. He didn't pull up to a gasoline pump, so he must be buying something inside. Soda, a snack. He doesn't smoke, and if he is going where I think he's going, he won't be drinking alcohol, either.

A minute passes. Two. My fear quotient is spiking. I know this is crazy, but I have to do this, because no one else can, or will. I blink to clear my vision as I stare out the front window. Since I drove by the station without stopping, I didn't notice if there were other customers inside. There could be a line at the cash register. Those stores only have one clerk on duty at this time of night.

The tapping at my side window is light, a mere knuckle rap, but I almost hit the roof, I jump so violently. My scream is from out of *The Twilight Zone.*

Roberto Salazar is standing outside my car. I never saw him coming, that's how stealthily he can move. His eyes are black coals, boring holes into me. I can feel seething rage coming off him, like a bolt of lightning shooting across the sky.

My hand snakes into my purse. I grip my gun and thumb the safety off. If he makes a move to open my door, I'll blow his head off.

We stare at each other in silence for a moment. Then, emboldened by knowing I have the power to protect myself, I crack the window an inch.

"What do you want?" I snarl at him. I can't show him that I'm scared out of my mind.

He reaches into the paper bag he's holding and takes out a package. "You must be hungry, out so late at night, and so far from your home. Do you want some beef jerky?"

He takes a piece of meat out of the package and shoves it toward my face. It looks as if it has been cut from a cadaver. I almost puke, my stomach is churning so hard.

"You should not be here," he says. His voice is low and reedy, like a cold wind blowing through tall grass. "You should be home, where you belong. Your involvement with me is in the past, Mrs. Thompson. I am finished with you now. And you are finished with me."

I start to shake. My finger tightens on the trigger of my gun.

"You are a mother now," he says in a voice that chills me to the bone. "You want your daughter to grow up to be a pretty woman. Like you are." In a whisper, he says, "I know where you live, Mrs. Thompson."

He steps back. "We are finished with each other," he warns me. "Completely. Do not forget that again."

He turns on his heel and walks away.

I watch him retreat until I am sure he isn't coming back. Then I start the car and drive away as fast as I can. I'm shaking so uncontrollably that I can barely keep the car from running off the road.

I can take blast-furnace heat. I've been a survivor my entire life. But when Salazar threatened my child, he crossed the line. Until tonight, I was not sure what I was going to do about him. Now, I am.

The street where Salazar's church is located is quiet as a tomb. No lights on, no pedestrians. I park as close to the church as I can and get out of my car. My gun is in my pocket. It feels heavy and comforting.

One thing I've learned in my years of defending hundreds of petty criminals: 90 percent of the time, breaking and entering is a piece of cake, especially into older buildings that don't have many valuables in them. A pawnshop or jewelry store will be well fortified, including a good alarm system, but the average single residence can be a bird's nest on the ground. From what I saw the last time I was here, the only thing of value in this church is the pulpit, and no one is going to steal that, there's no aftermarket for it. If the building is old, and the lock that originally came with it hasn't been upgraded, you can sometimes open it with the old credit-card-in-the-doorjamb trick. And often in a place like this, where many people come and go, they'll hide a key, usually in an obvious place. Under a flower pot, over the door frame, even under the door mat.

I walk to the door and look around. No one is in sight. Before I take out a credit card or start to look for the hidden key, I turn the doorknob to check how strong the resistance is.

There is no resistance. The door isn't locked.

I slither inside and shut the door behind me. I take a small flashlight out of my purse and shine it along the aisle, keeping it low, so I don't attract attention from the street. I'm only going to be here a very short time.

It costs a quarter to drop a dime these days. I call LAPD Robbery-Homicide from a pay phone in Mar Vista and leave a message for Lieutenant Luis Cordova. I repeat it twice, and hang up when the person who took the call asks for my name.

Forty minutes later, I am home. I check my street to make sure Salazar's truck isn't parked there, but I don't see it. Still, I have my hand on my gun when I unlock my door, which has a decent but not great lock on it, and enter cautiously.

Kathy is sleeping on the couch. I go into my room, and look into the baby's crib. She is snoring blissfully. Until this moment, I didn't realize how unbelievably scared I was. I can barely stand, my legs are trembling so badly.

Tomorrow, I will call a locksmith and have new locks installed.

FORTY-NINE

I HAVE COME TO MY office to clean out my desk and say good-bye. My friends are sad to see me go, but they understand why I'm leaving. If you can't give 100 percent all the time, you shouldn't be here. I can't do that anymore, so I'm bailing out.

My landing will be as soft as a featherbed. Beginning next month, I will be an associate partner at Bixby, Stern, and Myers, one of the top civil litigation firms in the city. My new office is large, especially compared to what I'm used to. I won't be sharing it. I have my own secretary, and two paralegals as needed. There are other perks as well, including in-house child care. I will bring my baby with me in the morning and take her home with me at night, and feed and play with her when I can grab a moment.

My starting salary is $350,000 a year, but that is a stepping-stone. In a few years I will become a full partner, and my income will triple, or better. I will buy my own house in Rustic Canyon, or anywhere I want.

Amanda set the deal up for me, of course. Arnold Stern has been her personal attorney for decades. Not that the firm isn't thrilled to have me on board—I made a nice reputation for myself in the first Salazar trial. I will do class actions, product liability, personal injury. Work that doesn't make headlines, but brings in big bucks.

Everyone in my old office is glad to see me, and they are happy for my future. But the real enthusiasm is for my baby. She is the star attraction. Oohs and aahs all around. She is dressed in a hand-stitched lace baby smock her godmother imported from a Paris baby boutique. The women can't keep from touching her, smelling her, they want to eat her up, she's so adorable. She basks in their adulation like the true princess she is.

The main topic of conversation, of course, is Roberto Salazar's arrest for the murder of the second Full Moon victim. The arrest was shown again and again on television: The police, with Lieutenant Cordova in the lead, taking him out of his house, handcuffed. Salazar being brought into the jail. Mug shots. Articles of indictment. The whole nine yards.

The police did it right this time. When they went to Salazar's church to search for the second pair of undergarments (acting on the tip of an anonymous informant), they had a police video team with them. The entire scene is on tape, so there is no question of any evidence being planted. The tape shows the police entering the church, marching down the aisle to the pulpit. Cordova puts on a pair of latex gloves and pries the cross off the wall, the one that has the crown of thorns Christ on it. He reaches behind the back of the cross and pulls out the damning evidence from where it was stuffed behind the the wooden cross.

Later, when he is interviewed, Cordova admits that the police had searched the church after they found the first set of panties in Salazar's truck, but hadn't found this second pair. There had been some squeamishness about tampering with a religious artifact. Luckily, there have been no other victims since Salazar was released on bail, but the authorities are sure it was only a matter of time before he would try again.

The police do not know who the anonymous tipster was. Maybe the same person who called in the first one. They may never know.

I have the whole dog and pony show on TiVo—the police assault on the church, Salazar's arrest, the preening politicians practically breaking their arms as they pat themselves on the back. I have replayed it several times. A fascinating piece of Los Angeles history that I was a small part of.

Joe and I go up to his office to say our private good-byes. Only officially, because we plan to continue to be friends outside the office. But as our lives are going to be separate and different now, I don't know if we'll really keep up with each other. I hope we do. He was a good teacher, a good supporter.

Joe pops the ubiquitous Diet Coke and sprawls out in his desk chair. "Abby Lench has his work cut out for him now," he says. He has a Santa Claus twinkle in his eye.

"Not my problem," I respond.

"Nor mine." He drinks his Coke, spilling some down his shirtfront. "You know the one thing I've been wondering?" he ponders. "Both the first time, and this one?"

I wait for him to tell me the rest of what he's wondering about.

"Who that anonymous informant is. Both times that was what did the trick."

I smile. "Maybe it was the real killer."

Joe gets a real belly laugh out of that. "Yeah, right."

He gives me a good-bye hug and kisses the baby on the top of her head. "Take care," he says. He walks me to the door. "We were a good team. You earned your colors, Jessica."

From Joe, that is the highest possible praise. "We'll be in touch," I promise him.

"We'd better be."

The elevator is empty as I ride down to the lobby from our floor. I don't know when I'll be in this building again. Maybe never.

The car stops on twelve. Lieutenant Luis Cordova enters. He is startled, seeing me. Then, when he realizes what the bundle in my arms actually is, he breaks into a smile.

The doors close. We're alone. I feel the familiar swoosh in my stomach as we begin our descent.

Cordova bends over and stares into Amanda's face. She stares back at him. A tiny hand reaches out and grabs his nose.

"I heard you had her," he says, after he gently disengages his honker from her surprisingly strong grip. "Congratulations. She's a doll. Like her mother."

I actually blush. "Thanks." I hesitate. "About the trial . . ."

He waves off what he knows I am going to say. That I almost outright accused him of planting evidence.

"I didn't take any of that personally. You had a job to do. And I screwed up, so I deserved to get called out." He shrugs philosophically. "Comes with the territory."

That's a relief. I like this man, and deep down, I trust him. "You won't have to deal with any ambiguity this time around," I pronounce. "I saw the tape of the search."

"Yes, we bent over backward to make sure we did everything by the book," he replies with satisfaction. "So in a sense, I owe you."

"You don't owe me anything."

We reach the lobby. The doors open. "I hear you quit," he says. "Going into the civilian world."

"Yep, I did. Elvis is leaving the building."

He offers his hand. Mine is buried in his as we shake. "Have you found out who the anonymous tipster was?" I ask him.

He shakes his head. "We don't know." He looks me in the eye. "Either time."

"Well," I tell him, "good luck."

"And you."

He turns and disappears into the throng. As I watch him go, thinking there is a good chance I will never see him again, I still have that nagging feeling, like a tickle in the back of your throat you can't cough away: who made that first anonymous phone call? The one without which Salazar would never have been arrested.

I have some distance from it all now, so I can examine my feelings more objectively than when I was in the cauldron. Anyway you look at that, it doesn't make sense. Mexican gardeners are a dime a dozen anywhere in Los Angeles. There would have been absolutely no reason for anyone to be suspicious of him.

Unless you wanted to be. Unless you knew there was a cloud hanging over him because of his previous arrest. Unless you knew he had been in the immediate vicinity of one of the earlier murders. Cordova and his fellow detectives had found out about the arrest for the stolen television sets within minutes of calling in Salazar's information, which means any cop, including them, could have known about that not only then, but earlier.

If I were a conspiracy nut and was also paranoid about cops, I could easily put together a case against Cordova and the other members of the task force, for all of the reasons I have been contemplating the past several months. It would be a good case. But I'm not a nut, and I don't want to drive myself crazy. I leave that stuff to the Oliver Stones of the world. I'm out of it now. That is in the past. My future is in my arms.

But still. Who made that first phone call?

FIFTY

THE BABY IS SIX months old today, so her godmother is throwing a party in her garden. Baby shower/half-year birthday. A few of Amanda's friends and some new ones of mine I've met at the gym, who have brought their own babies. Even though my new friends are by any normal standards affluent, they are knocked out by the casual displays of wealth that come with an Amanda Burgess affair. Catered baby food from one of the best and most expensive restaurants in Santa Monica. Catered adult food from the same restaurant. For entertainment there is a juggler, two clowns, an antique merry-go-round, a pony with trainer. An organ grinder with a monkey wearing a fez.

None of these expensive toys mean anything to the babies, although the pony and monkey are objects of intense interest. But the mothers ride the carousel with their babies on their laps, feed the babies the gourmet baby food, nosh on the adult catered food, and swig down glasses of champagne.

Amanda's eyes sparkle with happiness, which is not a common condition for her these days. Salazar's arrest for the second murder has taken all the wind out of her sails. She is still bankrolling his defense, but she has no enthusiasm for it anymore. The tide is running in the prosecution's favor, and is threatening to sweep the defense out to sea. The latest setback was the sudden emergence of Armando Gonzalez, the phantom television thief. He was arrested on a burglary charge in Texas, and extradited to

California. In exchange for immunity on that earlier charge, Gonzalez has sworn that not only was Salazar his willing and knowing accomplice, but that the exchange of the sets from him to Salazar on the night Salazar was caught happened earlier than Salazar swore it did. That means there would have been enough time for Salazar to have had a rendezvous with the victim who was found that night, kill her, and gone on his way.

Joe and I have chatted about this new development over the phone. We are both of the opinion that it's bogus, another jailhouse informant buying his freedom. But unless Abby Lench can completely discredit Gonzalez, he will be another nail in Salazar's coffin. The word on the street is that Abby's main objective now is not winning outright, but trying to avoid the death penalty.

Not my concern anymore. My new job is not as exciting as my old one, but it's very time-consuming. I don't leave at five o'clock on the dot, and I read briefs on the weekends. My clients call me whenever they feel like it. Some of them are on the East Coast, which means my phone can ring at four in the morning. If I'm awake feeding the baby, I'll pick up. Otherwise, I turn it off, and check for messages when I wake up.

Amanda and I have not talked about Salazar since he was arrested, except to acknowledge that it doesn't look good for him. She has had no contact with him, or his family. When he finally goes to trial again, she will not be there. She tries to hide her anguish, but this ordeal has taken its toll. She is aging before my eyes.

One thing I know for sure now. Money can't buy happiness, not always. One child who will never recognize her, another who is probably a mass murderer. How much guilt does she carry around over that? A ton, I'm sure.

But there is a silver lining, which will bring her light for the rest of her life. My daughter and I. The daughter she never had, and the granddaughter she loves as if she were her own. Which little Amanda is, emotionally. The baby is always happy to be with her namesake. Sometimes I have to literally pry them apart, they are so attached to each other. Which is fine with me. I never had a family, either.

Amanda takes the baby from my arms and carries her to the carousel. She takes a seat on one of the rides, a graceful swan, and hoists her namesake onto her lap. The baby whoops with laughter as they rise and dip to the music.

One of the servers, an awkward young woman eager to please who reminds me of myself when I was twenty, asks if I want more champagne. I hold my glass out in answer, and she fills it. I sip—it's delicious. My shoes are off, and I feel the soft grass under my feet. It doesn't get any better than this.

Tonight, my baby and I will take a bath together. Then I will read to her until she falls asleep. I will carry her to her crib and tuck her safely in. Then I will go to bed.

I still sleep with my gun nearby. Just in case.

ACKNOWLEDGMENTS

I am greatly indebted to Kimberly Curran, Deputy Public Defender, Los Angeles County Public Defender's Office, for her help and guidance in writing this book. She has been my eyes, ears, and overall guide in leading me through the great labyrinths that comprise the Los Angeles legal system and community. Any mistakes I have made in legal or other procedural matters are strictly mine, and do not in any way reflect on her.

I also wish to thank Robert Kalunian, Chief Deputy Public Defender, L.A. County, and Laura Green, Assistant Public Defender, L.A. County Public Defender's Office, for their help as well, and for introducing me to Kimberly. I am also grateful for the assistance I received from the Los Angeles Police Department, the Los Angeles County Sheriff's Department, the Los Angeles County District Attorney's Office, and the Los Angeles County Coroner's Office.

Carole Baron and Christine Zika of Madison Park Press, my editors, have done a wonderful job of helping me shape this book, and have been extremely supportive during the entire process of writing it. The same applies to Gail Hochman, my agent. Georgia Freedman, my daughter, herself a fine editor, provided additional editorial help. Susan Lee Johnson's copyediting was superb.

Finally, I want to again thank Markus Wilhelm for initiating this book, and for being my strongest supporter in the publishing business from the beginning of my writing career.